There's a (Slight) Chance
I Might Be Going to HELL

There's a (Slight) Chance I Might Be Going to HELL

A Novel of Sewer Pipes,
Pageant Queens, and Big Trouble

LAURIE NOTARO

VILLARD
New York

A Villard Books Trade Paperback Original

Copyright © 2007 by Laurie Notaro

Published in the United States by Villard Books,
an imprint of The Random House Publishing Group,
a division of Random House, Inc., New York.

VILLARD and "V" CIRCLED Design
are registered trademarks of Random House, Inc.

ISBN 978-0-8129-7572-7

Library of Congress Cataloging-in-Publication Data

Notaro, Laurie.
There's a (slight) chance I might be going to hell: a novel of sewer pipes, pageant
queens, and big trouble / Laurie Notaro.
p. cm.
ISBN: 978-0-8129-7572-7
I. Title.
PS3614.0785T47 2007
814'.6—dc22   2006038730

Printed in the United States of America

www.villard.com

9

Book design by Jo Anne Metsch

To Corbett, who gave me my Burgess Meredith

Prologue

The moment the girl stepped onto the stage, the circle of a spotlight swung toward her, announcing her presence above the audience in a sheer, clean illumination. The crowd before her suddenly quieted, as if expecting something truly spectacular to occur. It would *have* to be spectacular; after all, Mary Lou Winton, the contestant before her, had let loose a greased baby pig onstage, which she managed to lasso, hog-tie, and brand—with a branding iron fashioned to look like a sewer pipe, no less—in a definitive nine seconds flat. It was, in fact, confirmed by the audience, who counted down as Mary Lou whipped that rope and then stomped over to plunge the glowing iron. And it was further rumored that Ruth Watson was planning to bring her rifle out onto the stage and shoot every winged fowl right out of the sky, all in her evening gown attire, for her talent segment.

Farm antics, the girl scoffed to herself, wondering if such a thing really could be considered as a talent or just an episode of unfortunate breeding. She knew she could not let any of that concern her as she looked out over the crowd, searching the faces. She knew almost everyone—everyone who was waiting to hear her sing.

She smiled softly, an expression that seemed gentle.

If only I had ruby slippers, she thought to herself. The light that would have caught them would have been astounding, the sparkle would have bounced off of them like rockets, far more impressive than an oily piglet or dead birds. She looked down at her feet, at her pair of last year's Sunday shoes—now buffed a bright cherry red by her father, who had been so proud when he surprised her with them—and saw that they did not sparkle, but produced a dull, minuscule shine.

Behind her, she heard Mrs. A. Melrose from the church choir begin playing the piano; this was her cue, and the pianist had better keep time. Although she considered herself a devoted Christian woman overflowing with generosity, Mrs. Melrose thought little of donating her time to the endeavor and suggested that instead she exchange her musical services for the girl's scrubbing a week's worth of the accompanist's and her flatulent husband's laundry. Despite the gruesome task that lay ahead in the Melroses' wash bin the next day, the girl continued to smile as she drew a deep, full breath, so full that the replica blue gingham pinafore fashioned from a picnic tablecloth seemed to expand slightly, making the ketchup stains that stubbornly remained on the cloth look like she had encountered Ruth Watson's rifle. She waited: one, two, three.

The next note was hers. She was ready.

"Somewheeeeere over the rainbow . . ."

Her voice glided sweetly over the stage into the audience and twirled in the air above them like magic. She could see it on the faces of the people watching her, listening to her, heads tilted slightly to the side, as they smiled back at her. This was no pig-roping event, and no explosion of feathers was going to trickle down from the clouds.

This was talent.

I have it, she thought giddily to herself as she finished the first verse, as her voice continued on clear, strong, and with the right touch of delicacy. It is mine.

She saw him, standing in the back, far beyond the crowd assembled in the square—the most handsome man she had ever seen in real life, the one who could save her. With a bouquet spilling with flowers in the crook of his arm, he leaned up against his brand-new powder-blue Packard Caribbean convertible with its whitewall tires and gleaming, curvaceous chrome bumpers. It was a glorious machine. It suited him. Cars like that were rare in this town, and so were the men they suited. She saw him smiling at her, and to her he delivered a nod of encouragement.

She felt herself blush a shade. The surge of delight was just the push she needed to soar into the last verse and deliver with earnest, heartfelt yearning, *"Why, oh, why can't I?"*

The moment the last note evaporated into the air, the crowd burst forth with a shower of applause, the hands of the audience clapping heartily, and as she looked toward the back of the crowd, she saw that he was clapping, too, his arms full of tulips, roses, and lilies. Clapping for her.

Excitement raced up her spine like a block shooting up to hit the bell on a Hi Striker carnival game.

It was hers, she had done it, she knew it, she owned it. She could actually feel the weight of the crown being placed on her head, she could foresee the way that it would sparkle. She wanted it to sparkle brightly, feverishly, ferociously. Sparkle so bright it would blind them. Show this town that she was the queen of this scrap heap, this tiny little town with nothing in it but sewer pipes and waste. From this moment, it was all hers, all of it. If she wanted ruby slippers, she would get ruby slippers, not last year's fake, cheap Sunday shoes painted red with a dirty rag. She was more than that.

It was hers, the crown, the town—she had won and she would take it. She knew it like she had never known anything else. As if there was any other choice! The pig tosser, the bird slayer? This was now her town, her kingdom.

To reign as she saw fit.

She smiled sweetly again, then closed her eyes slowly, laid her arm over her chest, holding her hand to her heart the way she had seen it done in the movies, and crossed one leg deeply behind the other in what could only be described as a true queenly and magnificent gesture.

And with that, she took a bow.

There's a (Slight) Chance
I Might Be Going to HELL

1

The Queen Leaves the Hive

Every morning on her daily trip to the Dumpster behind Starbucks, Maye made sure she was wearing lipstick and carrying her lucky stick. Perched on an overturned milk crate, she used the former broom handle to poke at the trash with one hand while batting away the flies with the other.

It was searing hot. Within minutes, Maye could feel the relentless Phoenix sun bearing down on the crown of her head and the flush of sweat trickling down her temples and detouring into her eyes, making them burn with salt. She poked on with her lucky stick, overturning a piece of cardboard to reveal an almost un-eaten enchilada dinner from Starbucks' neighbor, Don Juan's Taco Village, resting perfectly atop an empty Solo cup box.

"Bingo," she sang, smiling like the Cheshire cat as she reached over to snatch the Styrofoam plate from its spot. "Come to Mama." She rose up on tippy-toe as her outstretched arm grazed the blazing metal side of the Dumpster, causing her to flinch slightly.

"I am going to get you," she hissed, determined to reach the objective—from her vantage point, it looked to be a cheese enchilada and a beef taco with rice and beans—as she stretched as far as she could, her fingers now brushing the pearly white dish. With only one foot now balancing on the milk crate, Maye leaned as deeply into the Dumpster as she could and, with one determined push, grabbed the dinner, the cheese on the refried beans still soft in the bubbling summer heat, and pulled herself out of the metal bin without spilling so much as a drop of the red, runny enchilada sauce.

Maye heard the creak of metal hinges as a door opened behind her.

"Hey!" a loud voice shouted.

With the entrée in her hands, she turned around to face a young man wearing a green barista's apron.

"You don't need to dig around in there," the young man said. "I've got something for you here."

"I was wondering where you were," Maye replied. "I was here on time!"

She turned on the milk crate and with a little hop, lobbed the dinner square back into the Dumpster, and with her lucky stick in hand, turned her attention to the perfect, four-sided, undented, untorn, and unstained-with-enchilada-sauce Solo box that was exactly the size she needed to hold her food processor. She beamed as she lifted it from the bin.

"Thanks, Carlos, I'll take whatever you've got," Maye replied as she gazed admiringly at her find. "But this one is perfect. A beauty like this would be seven bucks at U-Haul. But I wish those Don Juan kids would get their recycling and trash bins straight. You don't know how many beautiful boxes have been tragically disfigured and rendered useless by a sinister dollop of nacho-cheese sauce. There should be legislation, I tell you."

"So how many days now?" Carlos asked, shielding his eyes from the sun with his hand.

"Four. Four. I'm moving across the country in *four days*," she replied. "I can't believe it. I'm flipping out. I have so much left to do it's amazing."

"Well, I hope these help, Maye," he said, lifting up a tied bundle of flattened Starbucks cartons.

"Everything helps," Maye said, balancing the lucky stick against the side of the Dumpster. "I would have spent a fortune on cardboard if it wasn't for you and my favorite recycling bin. Thank you. And thanks for not calling strip-mall security on me for the last month."

"Well, these days there's typically more eBayers digging through the boxes than bums, but it never hurts to distinguish yourself with a nice shower and leaving your invisible friend at home."

"And the lipstick," Maye added. "Apparently, sometimes a shower isn't enough for the Dunkin' Donuts people. I learned that one the hard way."

"See you tomorrow?" Carlos said as he opened the back door, the metal hinges groaning.

"Eight o'clock sharp," she chirped. Hugging her perfect box, she stepped off the milk crate and right into a small puddle of hobo throw-up.

♆ ♆ ♆

"I can't, I just can't, Charlie," Maye said as she navigated through the stacks of boxes Carlos had given her, most of which were now half filled with things that once lined the bookshelves in the living room. "I know I said I would go, but I still have so much to pack."

"I'll pack double time," Charlie offered from behind a tower of

Starbucks logos. "I can get it done. You have to go, you promised. This will be the last time you see Kate for a while. You need to go."

Maye looked around the living room. She knew she should go to dinner with her friend Kate as she had promised she would, but it just seemed impossible. She didn't know who her husband thought he was kidding. The movers would arrive in four days, and everywhere Maye looked, there was more to do and it was multiplying by the hour. Their house had become a puzzle of open boxes, packing paper, tape guns, and piles of their belongings. Every time she emptied a bookshelf into a box, more books would appear on it when she turned around. She bought gigantic rolls of bubble wrap more often than she bought food. And there was so much she hadn't even begun to tackle yet. It seemed like she still had three hundred things on her to-do list, including turning the utilities off; doing an Internet search to find out which motels would accommodate Mickey, their three-year-old Australian shepherd, for their drive up to Spaulding, Washington, their soon-to-be home; emptying out the junk drawer; and hoping that if there was a shooting in the neighborhood it wouldn't make the nightly news and cause the lady who bought the house to back out of the sales contract. She had to decide which clothes she might one day fit into again and which were now definitely out of reach—unless a famine and plague hit simultaneously—and thus headed for a Salvation Army donation box. If only Charlie had pushed harder for the moving arrangements when he was negotiating the terms of his new position as an English professor, Maye thought to herself, I wouldn't have to worry so much, but it was his first job and the university was a small one in an even smaller town. As her husband reminded her, he was lucky to even get hired straight out of graduate school by such a prestigious university. Having his new employer arrange and then pay for moving was a little out of the question.

"I know I should go to dinner, but I just don't see how," Maye declared as she picked up one of Carlos's flattened boxes and assembled it. "The dishes still need to be packed. I have to clean out the refrigerator and make it look like humans used it for something other than a scientific testing center for food expiration dates. And I curse the day you learned to read, Charlie. Why do we have so many books? *We have so many books.* There's nothing wrong with illiterate people. I don't know why I stopped dating them."

"*Go to dinner.* I promise I'll pick up the slack," Charlie said, as he took the box from her hands and ripped a tape gun across the bottom of it.

"I had a dream last night that the movers came and the only thing that was packed were all of my shirts," she said. "And I had to pack the last thousand of your books in front of them, topless, while you went out and bought them donuts, after which the movers tried to toss them onto me like I was the ring toss at the carnival."

"Go to dinner," her husband repeated. "I promise I'll finish the next fifteen things on your list if you go. That dream proves you need to relax a little and have some downtime. If you don't go, I'm afraid you'll start sleepwalking and I'll wake up tomorrow wrapped in a giant tape cocoon, wiggling like larvae."

"I just don't know. I don't think I can afford the time," Maye replied.

"You can't afford not to go," he insisted. "Kate is one of your best friends. When do you think you're going to see her again? We're moving fifteen hundred miles away, you know. It's not going to be a walk around the corner anymore."

After thinking for a moment, Maye nodded. "You're right,"

she relented. "I promised I would. I should go. You promise you'll do fifteen things on the list?"

"I promise," Charlie said as he held his hand up. "I swear on the tape gun."

"That doesn't mean you can pack fifteen pairs of socks and call it a night, you know," she told him as she shook her finger. "Because if you pack a box of toothpicks and tell me you've done a hundred and fifty things, Charlie, I'll warn you right now: when the movers show up, they'll be tossing donuts at your shirtless boobs."

ツ　　ツ　　ツ

Within the hour before she was due at Kate's, Maye had finished packing her vase, cleaned out the two top shelves of the fridge, and packed all the books in the bookcase (again). She tore through what remained in her closet and pulled out a light vintage checked cotton shirtdress, perfect for drinking wine on the back patio of her friend's apartment on a hot summer night. In other words, a good sweating dress. For six long months in Phoenix, even after the sun slides behind the mountains, it's a wise move to go straight to wash-and-wear. Anything synthetic will not only cling to your wet, leaking skin like a hickey on the neck of a high school senior on picture day but will cost you more than a reckless cocaine habit in dry cleaning. Maye looked down and realized her stubbly legs could use a little updating, but she was running late and it was far too hot for tights. Well, she figured, it was only she and Kate, anyway, and all they were really going to be doing was losing body fluids and getting tipsy. Unless a hungry cat showed up, no one was going to be touching her prickly legs.

"Charlie," she called grabbing her purse and house keys. "I'm leaving. I'll see you tonight."

"Okay," he shouted from the back of the house. "Have fun!"

Maye started down the three blocks to Kate's apartment. In her own yard, she noticed how the verbena had finally come into its own, reaching and sprawling on the side of the house where she had planted it in the spring. She hoped her neighbor wouldn't mind when it reached the chain-link fence that separated their yards and was the reason Maye had planted the verbena in the first place. By next spring, the plant should have a firm hold on the fence, weaving in and out of the wire diamonds in ribbons of tiny purple flowers.

It was then that Maye realized that she wouldn't be there to see it. In four days, her house, the cute brick 1927 downtown bungalow that she and Charlie had scrimped and saved and struggled to buy when they were barely married, would belong to someone else. The wood floors they had refinished by themselves, the soapstone kitchen counter she had uncovered as she demolished a layer of eroding, mottled tile with a hammer and a flat-head screwdriver one night at 1 A.M. when Charlie was late coming home and she was furious. Those bookcases, and the fireplace they flanked, she had stripped seven layers of lead paint off of, only to discover that the mantel had been devoured by termites decades earlier. It was so far gone she had actually poked her fingers through the wood and decided to rebuild it herself. The jacaranda trees they had planted in the backyard, where a dust storm had threatened to suck them down as she and Charlie struggled, bandannas tied over their mouths, to keep them from toppling over. It was one thing to sell a house, Maye suddenly thought; it was another to understand it wasn't yours any longer.

Once they got the incredible news that Charlie had been chosen to join the faculty at Spaulding University, things had to happen as quickly as the ceremony for a Catholic girl who needs to get married. A city-beat reporter for the local daily newspaper, Maye had highlighted the number of days she had remaining covering meth-lab busts, informed her editor that she'd be leaving by the summer's end, and jumped into action like a superhero. They had two months to sell their house, pack their belongings, and find a new home before the fall term began, which wasn't much time to move an entire life, especially one with a wife whose eBay feedback score was in excess of 550. Both Maye and Charlie had grown up in Phoenix, and they were excited to begin to build a new life in a charming college town in the mountains of Washington. They couldn't wait to enjoy tall pines, cool breezes, and nice people away from the traffic, the heat, the crime, the pollution, and even, Maye now realized, their little house with the burglar alarm and wrought-iron bars over every window and door. They were tired of the grind of a hot, crowded city, and when, during their first trip to Spaulding, they passed a vivacious vegetable garden and smelled an onion that caught the breeze, there wasn't a doubt in their minds. You would never smell an onion in Phoenix under any circumstances unless it was on someone's breath and he was asking for a spare dollar. During that trip, they hadn't heard one gunshot, they'd forgotten to lock the rental-car door on one occasion and *nothing was stolen;* and home invasions simply meant a neighbor drunk on microbrew had outstayed his welcome at a barbecue in the delightful little hamlet. They rushed back home, told their friends and families, and Maye began prowling the Dumpsters with her lucky stick. She had been so immersed in the details of relocating—including flying to Spaulding every other weekend to find a new home—that some things kind of slipped her attention.

Like the fact that she was not just going to Spaulding, but that she was leaving Phoenix.

By the time she got to Kate's, she was sweating more than a chubby man in a backyard cage fight testing out his moves from a $19.98 *Fast 'N Furious Head Bustin' Street Smarts* DVD recently purchased from Wal-Mart and she wanted nothing more than to have a little face time with a glacier. She knocked on the door and heard Kate yell from the back of the apartment. "Come on in, I'm just opening the wine!"

"You are crazy," Maye replied as she opened the door and stepped into the living room. "How do you know I'm not one of the fourteen sex offenders that live within a six-block radius of here?"

"Because your husband just told me it was you," Kate said, laughing.

"What?" she asked, turning the corner into the kitchen.

And there, in fact, was Charlie, smiling. And Kate.

And Sara. And Brian. And Patrick. And Sandra, Curtis, Laura. Chrissy, Krysti, Nikki, Kim, Adrienne, Susan. Mark, Steven, Jeff.

Everybody.

Everybody was there. All of her friends. The friends who had let her crash on their couches when it wasn't wise to drive home in more reckless times, friends who had loaned her money when the electricity was about to be shut off in leaner days, friends who had been there when she broke up with boyfriends, friends who had been her bridesmaids. Friends who had gasped in horror the first time she brought them to the little bungalow she'd just mortgaged, then helped scrape off layers of linoleum on the kitchen floor to get to the honey-colored fir buried below. Friends who had listened to her, friends she had listened to. Friends that she needed. Friends she had spent her life making.

Maye was stunned.

She had never been so glad to see all of them in her life. She gasped with happiness, and although she was grotesquely sweaty and had the legs of a lazy drag queen, she was incredibly happy. And she was also suddenly and horribly ashamed of herself. *These were her friends.* So what if she wasn't at home, packing? These were her friends. How could she even think that it was more important to fill a couple of boxes? This was worth it, she decided—so worth it, even if she had to pack Charlie's books topless in front of the movers. Hands down.

All of these people, she thought as she smiled—they know me. Charlie poured wine into a glass and gave it to her, and she lifted it up with everyone else as Kate made a toast.

"To Maye and Charlie," she said. "May you be happy, prosper, and sweat less in Washington—but you'll never find friends as good as us!"

"Here, here!" they all agreed as they burst out laughing.

"Look at you, skipping town when you still owe me twenty bucks from your bar tab the night you fought tequila and tequila won," Nikki said. "I will continue to hold as collateral the ashtrays you pried out of the back of the cab with a butter knife you pocketed from IHOP when you insisted on having breakfast at four A.M. after the bar closed."

"Oh, Maye, you owe me so much more than that for making me wear burgundy taffeta in public at your wedding," Sara interjected. "And for never sending that picture of you peeing in the woods to that newspaper you worked for. Or . . . the tape."

Maye laughed. "Why did I think we could get through one night without mentioning the tape? Yeah, well, I learned on that road trip that it's never a good idea to get bombed with someone who is more than willing to let a video camera roll for forty minutes on a twenty-four-year-old drunk girl in a tent delivering an impromptu soliloquy on why any man would be lucky to get her," she said.

"My favorite part was the ten minutes you spent proving your case that you had a better rack than any slut with implants," Sara dutifully reminded her. "Complete with a multifaceted demonstration and the pronouncement that you could easily sell your pair to a flat-chested blond girl and pay off your credit card debt."

"Don't forget what she said about her ass," Nikki reminded them.

"No!" Maye protested as she laughed and covered her face with her hands. "Please don't!"

" 'With these pearly globes and a thousand more Marlboro miles, I could get me a triple-wide!' " Kate, Sara, and Nikki recited en chorus.

"I'm filing divorce papers tomorrow," Charlie interjected, smiling.

"That video alone is enough to dissuade anyone from stealing my identity," Maye added as she shuddered and turned a molten shade of red. "A copy of it should be attached to my credit report. Not even a meth addict would want to take on that variety of humiliation to simply assault the credit limit on my Master-Card. No weight-training set is worth that level of cringe, and the fact that you didn't perform a mercy killing that night to spare me from a decade's worth of third-degree embarrassment thus far just speaks to your own selfishness, you revolting hags. The cringe alone was potent enough to kill most ordinary humans."

"Not Super Boob Globe Girl, apparently," Sara added blithely. "She lives on. And on. Even if she is deserting us."

You can move your furniture, you can move your books, you can move your underwear, but you can't move your whole life, Maye really understood as they all laughed at old stories, the humiliating ones, the funny ones, and the ones only one another knew.

Some things, even things that took a lifetime to make, have to stay behind.

2

Decorative Weaponry

Spaulding, Washington, was indeed a charming place.

Nestled at the base of the North Cascade mountain range, the façade and landscape of the town hadn't changed much in almost a century, since Malcolm Spaulding, visionary and ambassador of indoor plumbing, decided to find the prettiest spot in the country to call his home and build himself a sewerpipe factory.

He found his utopia in a rainforest of towering pines, feathery, sweeping ferns, and, as he would repeatedly remark, a soil so rich you could grow love in it. An insufferable romantic despite the fact that his livelihood was shit, Malcolm Spaulding swore that from the base of the mountains, he had a view that stretched almost all the way to the Pacific Ocean on a brilliant day. In the summer it was sunny and warm enough to keep tomatoes ripening until fall; in the winter, a misty rain would swirl in and replenish the forest with the most essential ingredient it required to remain enchanted.

Everything in Spaulding grew, particularly the sewer-pipe factory. Spaulding, Washington, was not only a beautiful place, but its sole export was one of the main reasons that people didn't need to keep poop buckets under their beds anymore. The town spread its beauty every time a toilet gurgled and flushed.

Spaulding had a definite sense of pride in having introduced civilization to the entire, thankful nation.

The town had grown with Spaulding Sewer Pipe's prosperity, and in addition to the general store and streets of little houses came a school. Enamored as he was with the transportation of human waste, Malcolm Spaulding knew a town couldn't survive on that gold mine alone. When he saw just exactly how the school had improved the already lovely town—the spelling bees the whole town attended, the Christmas pageant, and the school dances—he simply couldn't help himself and decided to build a good, solid but small college, which was named, naturally, Spaulding Polytechnic Institute of Sewer Pipe Husbandry.

The residents of Spaulding liked the fact that their town was small enough that they could drive seven minutes to get anywhere and big enough that they could reach outside immediate family for romantic and reproductive purposes. The residents loved their town. To them, the world of Spaulding was perfect. Each street had two lanes, one for coming and one for going. The air stayed fresh and infused with the scent of rising bread dough from numerous bakeries and the hint of growing onions could be carried by a breeze on a warm, but not too hot, summer day.

Spaulding's residents were so enamored with their town and the factory that built it—which had quickly become the biggest sewer-pipe manufacturer in the country, having addressed the country's flushing needs through two world wars and the first moon walk. (It was just a matter of time, Malcolm Spaulding predicted, before Spaulding Sewer Pipe would have the first sewer-pipe outpost in space and would be addressing the issue of sanitation minus gravity.) Every year an elaborate celebration was staged to rejoice in the factory's success. The Spaulding Festival was the favorite and most anticipated event of the year. It was a joyous affair, and to the delight of his employees and their families, Malcolm Spaulding distributed generous prizes to the one who made it through the Sewer Pipe Maze first, the one who stayed afloat the longest in the pipe-rolling contest, and the baker of the best pie baked in a sewer-pipe cap. Children bobbed for apples in an upturned sewer pipe and could dunk their principal in another sewer pipe with a determined, well-planned throw of a ball. Everyone, year after year, had a glorious time.

Nothing of much consequence had happened to change the Spaulding way of life and the speed at which it was lived. The factory went on making pipes; the pipe college went on producing graduates who went on to work at the factory. Things continued in Spaulding just like they always did, except for a brief period during the hot summer months when several buildings— including the sewer-pipe factory—caught fire and burned to the ground. A police investigation later revealed that sewer-pipe rivals had tried to edge in by destroying their main competitor.

The people of Spaulding quietly and solemnly waited until the rubble stopped smoking, then they cleared away the remnants of what was lost and went immediately to the business of building it all right back, exactly as it was before.

Spaulding was Spaulding, and no amount of fire could burn that away.

But the truth was that Spaulding *had* changed. In the time that it took to rebuild, the Spaulding Sewer Pipe factory had lost its place as the largest of its kind. Competitors, particularly the one that was highly suspected of setting the fires, were more than eager to fill the orders the factory could not, and a majority of the business was lost.

And that was how Spaulding, Washington, a sewer-pipe town, became Spaulding, Washington, a university town. The Spaulding Polytechnic Institute of Sewer Pipe Husbandry became Spaulding University, the rebuilt factory building was transformed into dormitories, and new businesses popped up all over town like pimples on the forehead of puberty. The football team won the Rain Bowl, the Fern Bowl, and the Sasquatch Bowl. It became the fastest-growing university in the state.

Spaulding had bloomed again.

And then the hippies came.

In the time of war, the draft was instituted, and a portion of young men from all over the country who couldn't secure a single deferment, let alone four or five, fled to Canada. When the war was over and it was safe to come back, they crossed the border again, drove eighty miles in their VW vans, and then just stopped, unloaded vast quantities of vegetable dyes, yogurt, incense, and bongs, and set up grow lights.

They were friendly enough people, they tended masterful gardens, and although their customer-service skills were somewhat slow, they always had smiles on their faces. Over the years, the hippie folk grew their plants, beat their drums, spun their circles, and simply wove themselves into the community, evident as at least one house on each street became a canvas for a blue sky with clouds or a stretching rainbow. The schools filled up with children named Freedom, Tree, Solstice, and Merlin, with an overabundance of both Jerrys and Garcias. Career orientations changed as well, with resident rosters now including such occupations as birth artist, master composter, unicyclist, and the not-nearly-as-uncommon-as-you-would-think title of wizard.

And Spaulding, unlike many small former factory towns,

stayed clean. Littering was prohibited, recycling was adopted. Fast-food establishments were rare in Spaulding; organic bakeries, bookstores, coffeehouses, lined every street downtown. People rode bikes instead of driving cars when they could, and some of the hippies actually put on shoes and started running. Spaulding was still a charming place, only a little bit more healthy. The university offered degrees in environmentalism, eco-criticism, and folklore studies.

The university football team won the Hemp Bowl.

And today, if on a visit to Spaulding you were to find yourself the only person in the movie theater, and another moviegoer walked in, that person would come and sit next to you without a second thought, and might even lean over and ask to share your popcorn. Your new acquaintance might also mention that you should try it with nutritional yeast sprinkled on top instead of butter and salt. It tastes nutty, your neighbor would say, and it won't clog your arteries or turn them to cement.

Small towns are sometimes like that; familiarity runs high, while regard for personal space is low, if nonexistent.

It was with the fragrance of growing onions floating in the warm summer air that Maye, Charlie, and their dog, Mickey, arrived with an eighteen-wheeler full of boxes and an idea about creating their life in a brand-new place.

It was, however, going to take a little more than that.

ᵞ   ᵞ   ᵞ

Maye held her breath as they pulled into the driveway of the new house for the first time.

They had been on the road for three days, driving through the desert of Arizona, the urban landscape of Los Angeles, the farmland of central California, and the mountains and lush valleys of Oregon. Now they were home.

At least Maye hoped they were.

Charlie didn't say anything as he sat in the car, looking at the new house. Maye didn't know what to make of his silence; in one moment, her stomach dropped to her feet thinking that Charlie hated the cottagelike look of it (it did look rather like a place two Germanic children would happen upon in the woods and nearly become a kiddie potpie), then, in the next moment, she thought the house was so perfect that there was no way he could do anything but love it.

It was Maye's responsibility to find them a place to live, so she flew up to Washington every other weekend. Courtesy of her patient Realtor, Patty, she had seen a wide variety of Spaulding abodes, including a farmhouse painted like a rainbow, which was what the owner's children (Ocean, four, and Wind, six) had chosen, and a 1920s bungalow that was adorned in the colors of an iris—purple siding, chartreuse windows, dark green eaves, lavender door.

"The owner loves color," Patty tried to explain.

"Yes, she does," Maye said, nodding. "Brooke Shields lived in a house that looked like this in *Pretty Baby*."

"The inside is lovely," Patty coaxed. "The seller, Louise, is an old friend of mine."

Taking the cue and not wanting to offend her any more than she already had by essentially calling her friend's home a whorehouse, Maye followed Patty up the sidewalk until they were standing on the Technicolor bungalow's wide, generous porch. Patty rang the doorbell, and a friendly woman in her forties answered it and invited them in.

It was almost the perfect house. The Mission-style built-in oak china cabinet hadn't been slathered with paint, and neither had the columns and the bookcases that flanked the entrance to the dining room. It was in those bookcases that Maye noticed something strange: each shelf held a row of crowns, some elegant and sparkly, some plastic and cheap, and one that rather resembled a Burger King crown found in a kid's meal. What an odd hobby, Maye thought; it puts some of Michael Jackson's to shame. There must have been thirty or forty of them, shimmering and gleaming in the light. What on earth is a grown woman doing with forty crowns that aren't in her mouth? Maye wondered. Not to be cruel, but Louise was no beauty queen, and unless she was living out an unrealized homecoming fantasy à la *Carrie*, the whole thing was a bit puzzling.

The two-bedroom iris house, it turned out, was too small, and Maye bit her tongue as hard as she could and did not ask Patty if they had just visited the home of Spaulding's tooth fairy when they got back to the car. Offending her Realtor and the only person she knew in town would not be a smart maneuver, no matter how funny Maye thought her joke was.

As Patty unlocked the door, Maye just smiled, forced her little comment back down her throat, and got in.

ᛪ ᛪ ᛪ

Three minutes later, Maye gasped when Patty pulled the car to a stop in front of an absolutely perfect house.

It was an adorable English cottage, Cotswold style, with a half-timber and stucco façade and a hipped roof with curves along the peak lines and corners. A massive tapered chimney—complete with a little ash door—sat alongside the rounded front entry. It was as perfect through the front door as it was on the outside. It reminded Maye so much of her house in Phoenix; the layout and proportions were almost exactly the same, the living and dining rooms were painted the same colors, the rug in front of the fireplace was identical to the one Maye had in her own living room fifteen hundred miles away. She had only gotten as far as the kitchen when she turned to Patty and told her that she was so sure Charlie would absolutely love it, she was ready to make an offer.

Patty winced and paused for a moment. "There's something you need to know about this house," she said cautiously, as if she was trying to prepare Maye for something wholly dreadful and nefarious, and put her hand on Maye's arm gently.

"The current owners are . . ." she continued in a whisper, ". . . *Republicans.*"

Maye smiled. "It's okay," she whispered back. "As soon as we move in, we'll make our gay friends get married here."

But minutes after pulling into the driveway of her new house with her husband and dog, Maye's vision for her celebratory housewarming party had taken a downward turn. Her husband was staring at the house expressionless and motionless, almost like he was in shock.

"Charlie!" Maye finally said, desperate for a reaction. "Charlie, please say something!"

"This is our house?" her husband said, looking at her suspiciously.

Maye nodded.

"Are you sure?" he asked her in a very serious tone. "If this is a joke, it's not very funny."

"What's the matter?" Maye said, her heart sinking even further. "You hate it. You hate it. I'm sorry. I thought I was doing the right thing. There just wasn't much to choose from, Charlie, unless you wanted to live in an iris. It seemed right at the time. I'm sorry. You saw the pictures I took, you said you liked it. . . ."

"I *do* like it," he replied. "But what's the catch?"

"I don't understand," she said. "What catch?"

"Everyone on this street mows their lawns," Charlie nearly yelled, pointing to the neighbor's immaculate front yard. "I mean, these people have *lawns*. There are no cars resting on cinder blocks parked on them. I haven't seen a couch on a front porch yet, and a herd of feral cats hasn't descended on our car to pee on it yet. Where's Crack Park? I don't see a crack park! Where will our neighbors get their drugs? Where will our neighbors *sell* their drugs? And where's the halfway house? Every street in our last neighborhood had one!"

Maye smiled broadly and shook her head. "There's no crack park, Charlie," she said, laughing. "There is a park a couple of blocks away, but it has a playground and a soccer field. Our neighbor over there is a psychologist and an artist. The one across the street is a librarian. The neighbor over there was a diplomat in Belgium. We live in a different place now. We don't live in the hood any longer."

"I won't have to pick up needles and bullet casings in the street anymore?" he asked, floored.

"Nope," Maye assured him. "And I'll never have to call the cops on a hooker wearing nothing but a see-through shirt standing on the corner trying to drum up some business while the schoolkids are making their way home in the afternoon."

Charlie paused for a moment and looked at Maye again. "Are you sure this is our house?" he asked.

"Let's go inside, I'm dying for you to see it," she suggested, fumbling for the keys in her purse.

"Come on, Mickey!" Charlie said as he followed, and the dog bounded into the front seat and out of the car.

Maye opened the front door. The house had the eerie quiet of a place that had just been left, the same kind of quiet that floated through the rooms of their house in Phoenix only several days earlier before they left and locked the door for the last time.

"What do you think?" she asked as the sun streamed in, dust particles swirling and suspended in air.

"It's great," Charlie said, smiling. "Just like you said."

"Did you see the French doors to the dining room? And look at the moldings. That's all original. And there's fir in the hallway.

And penny tile in the bathroom. And a dishwasher, Charlie, *there is a dishwasher.*"

"Well, show me around!" he said, laughing as he grabbed her by the shoulders.

"I just want to call somebody!" she said gleefully as she opened the French doors to the dining room. "I want our friends to come over and see it! I'm so happy you like it. Who should we call? We'll call and get a pizza and have some people over."

"Sure. Call everybody. If they leave their houses now, they'll get here by next Wednesday." Charlie looked at her. For a tiny, microscopic second she had forgotten that she now lived in a town where she didn't know anybody except for her Realtor. Her friends were in Phoenix. She was in Spaulding.

"Well," she concluded. "Who says *we* can't have a pizza party, just us? We love pizza and Mickey loves the crust."

"You'll have friends soon," Charlie reassured her. "It takes time in a new place. Please do not get all weird because you've lived in Spaulding for forty-five seconds and you don't have a best friend yet. This is a whole new life. Nothing will be the same, but it will end up just as great and it will be fun getting there. We have this whole town to discover. And if you don't have a friend by your birthday, I'll buy you one."

"Promise?" Maye laughed. "Please get them at the bus station and make sure that they're at least three sizes bigger than me and with awful hair, like a bleach job with a perm on top, even if you have to pay by the pound. For once, I want to be the hot one, even if it means by purely relative terms."

"Whoa," Charlie said as he gravitated toward the backyard-facing windows of the dining room. "It's huge. That lawn is huge. It's bigger than our lawn in Phoenix. You didn't tell me it was so large. It's going to be a big project every week. Every week."

"Nice try, Charlie," Maye replied. "But you can relax, Mr. Big

Project. I can see through you like Paris Hilton's dress. I already got the name of a lawn company from Patty. They'll be here in a couple of days to give us an estimate."

"Oh, thank God," he said, exhaling. "I thought I might have to even go out and buy a lawn mower and then break it for that to happen."

"I learn from my mistakes. Which brings up another point: you are hereby banned from the area under the kitchen sink, any and all inner or outer workings of the potty, and anything in the basement that appears to in any way be even mildly associated with plumbing."

"I can do the under-the-sink thing," he insisted. "I can! I can!"

"The last time you said 'I can! I can!' the toilet wound up sideways on the floor and you were holed up at your computer waiting for Norm from *This Old House* to e-mail you back and tell you what you had done wrong," Maye reminded him. "I left my job at the newspaper to come here, Charlie. I'm freelance now. We're going to be living on an assistant professor's salary until I can get some things going. We don't have the money to pay for plumbing repairs plus the collateral damage that happens when you even think about picking up a screwdriver. And Norm never replied, Charlie. He never e-mailed you back."

"You don't need to remind me. But just so you know, I am still clinging to the thinnest of faith that one day, Norm will appear in my in-box. I haven't given up on him yet," Charlie said reluctantly. "Norm would never let a man and his sideways toilet down. But okay, no under-the-sink thing."

He looked at her and then hung his head in utter disappointment. But if Maye didn't know better, she'd have sworn she thought she saw him smile.

ψ   ψ   ψ

After the movers arrived and unloaded all of their earthly belongings, Maye unpacked, found the grocery store, the dry cleaners, and a pizza place and tried to learn about her new town. So far, she'd learned that the Indian and Thai restaurants were great, the Italian and Mexican horrible. She learned to avoid traveling two streets down when it was sunny, due to the girl who liked to sunbathe or just talk to her neighbors with her banana boobs experiencing as much public viewing as her nose, which, frankly, was much more perky and enjoyable to look at. Running into her was akin to watching the Discovery Channel but with an additional element of lingering horror and the sudden desire to wear a bra at all times.

Maye liked Spaulding; the people were friendly, everyone said hello to her at the grocery store, and Charlie loved his new job. He had been welcomed in the English Department immediately and had been making lunch dates with other professors and occasionally meeting people after work for a beer. He was fitting nicely into the small, tightly knit town, and frankly, Maye was starting to become a little jealous.

With his position at the university, Charlie had a built-in network of potential friends. Maye worked at home; her network consisted of Mickey, the various petition bearers who knocked on her door, and the guy she had hired to mow the lawn, who had little or no best-friend potential. When he arrived, he immediately noticed the Arizona license plates on her car and, after hocking up some rotten lung tissue and shooting it to the gravel of Maye's driveway, mentioned that she ought to go and get new plates. That day.

"Cops drive up and down the street," he explained. "Takin' notes. For you, they'd write down somethin' like, 'Arizona license plates.' Then they'll come back and check on you. If thirty days has passed and you still got Arizona license plates, they'll know you were the Arizona license plates house and write you a ticket. Happened to a friend of mine. Not from Arizona, though. From Arkansas."

Maye nodded politely and promised to take his warning under consideration. As she showed him around the property so he could give her an estimate, he stopped in the middle of the yard and looked her dead in the eye.

"You got yellowjackets in Arizona?" he asked with a grim look.

"I guess," she sputtered. "I don't know. What do they look like?"

"If you don't know what they look like, you ain't got 'em," he said, shifting his weight from one foot to another and pointing a dirty finger at her. "Come July, the yellowjackets get mean and they'll sting you 'cause it's hot. Come August, they'll kill you 'cause it's hotter. You need a trap. A yellowjacket trap to kill 'em afore they get to you. They're killers. Happened to a friend of mine."

"The one from Arkansas?"

"No," he said sternly, and walked toward the fence that separated Maye's backyard from her neighbors'. Something had evidently traveled under that fence a number of times, as the soil was pushed and patted down, making a groove in the dirt deep enough for a small dog to get through.

"Look at that," he said as he pointed to the groove, sucking air and spit between his teeth with a squeak. "You got raccoons somewheres close. They're comin' into this yard. Do you know what to do when you see a raccoon?"

"To be honest, I don't," Maye answered as nicely as possible. "But I'm from Arizona, as you know by my license plates, a land full of scorpions, black widow spiders, tarantulas, rattlesnakes, plague-infected prairie dogs, and hawks that carry golden retriever puppies off into the sky. I'm sure if I see a furry woodland creature in my yard, I'll figure it out."

The lawn man put his hands on his hips, looked away for a second, and then looked back at her. "You gonna figure it out before or after it's got its teeth sunk in your cheekbone and its claws in each of your ears?" he hissed. "Raccoons are nothin' to mess with! You see one in the daytime, *you run.* Raccoons are nocturnal animals, and if you see one when it's light outside, that thing's got the distemper and it's crack-ass crazy. Don't make eye contact. Never look it in the eye, or it will rip your face off with its claws and eat it like it was a Fruit Roll-Up."

After a moment, Maye thought of several things to say.

The first one was, "Am I on *Candid Camera*?"

The second thing was, "Do you live near a lot of power lines?"

And the third thing was, "Take my advice and start buying bottled water, because whatever's coming out of your well should be classified as a biological weapon."

But none of those things were very nice, although, truth be told, Maye would have picked the best one and gone for it if she wanted to mow her own lawn. So instead she looked at the lawn guy, smiled, and said, "So, what about that estimate?"

"Twenty-five a week," he said simply. "And the right to defend myself if a mad coon comes at me."

"Deal," Maye agreed.

Maye's circle of potential friends was smaller than her lawn guy's brain. It was hard to meet people her age—she was a childless woman in her thirties who worked at home. There were few opportunities to encounter someone like herself, unless she were to start stalking candidates in grocery stores. Her days were quiet; she ate lunch alone. When the phone rang, it was a friend from Phoenix calling to check on them, fill them in on the latest gossip, and tell them how much they were missed. Although her friends had the best of intentions, Maye couldn't help feeling even lonelier after each and every call.

Her life, she realized, was going to become very, very dull.

Spaulding, however, had a way of shaking things up.

One afternoon shortly after they moved in, Maye was unpacking books in her office when she heard a loud rustling in the nearby bushes and then quick, heavy footsteps. Mickey raised his head from the corner where he was sleeping and looked at her, his ears pinched back with caution. The footsteps became louder and more urgent and she thought that perhaps a Bigfoot had wandered down from the mountains in search of vittles and maybe a lady friend, two of the only things that could ever make a man leave his cave, because Bigfoots don't use toilet paper (number three in *The Only Things That Could Make a Man Leave His Cave*). The look of alarm on Mickey's face all but confirmed it. Before she had collected enough bravery to investigate, she saw a large, hairy blur dart past the window, and then she heard the thudding footsteps in her front yard. Mickey ran to the front door with a piercing bark, and Maye followed, but when she reached a window that gave her a good enough angle to see what was going on, the figure had vanished. A pot of dahlias lay knocked over on the front porch, much like Charlie's toilet, mulch hurled in a wide, violent spray, with several leaves from the laurel hedge that separated her yard from her neighbor's scattered recklessly about.

Maye was speechless, puzzled, and admittedly a little shaken. She looked at Mickey, who returned her exact expression and quietly whined.

When Maye told Charlie about what had happened, he brushed it off like it was a Mickey hair clinging to his sweater.

"This is a running town, Maye," he said. "People run home from work. The university has a star track team. Maybe someone was training for a marathon or something. No, I don't think it was Bigfoot coming down from the mountains to scavenge an already gnawed-at corncob from our trash, and I don't think it's anything to worry about, just like I don't think your head will be peeled like a boiled tomato by a mad raccoon. Stop focusing on the wacky stuff, and see all the great things this town has to offer. Calm down, and maybe you won't hear an urban legend running through the bushes and the yard; maybe you'll just see a jogger."

The next day, Maye was upstairs organizing the linen closet when she heard Mickey run to the door and begin barking ferociously, his nails scraping the wood floors. From the upstairs window she saw the laurel hedge shake, and she ran downstairs as the dog scratched at the front door and growled. As her hand grasped the doorknob, Mickey dropped to all fours and whined. Maye was too late; the intruder had evaporated. The dahlia pot, again the victim of the unseen, was still rolling slightly on its rim when she opened the door. That night, she said nothing to Charlie.

Maye and Mickey decided that the invisible Bigfoot was not going to make a fool out of them again. The following afternoon, Maye waited by the front door. She wished she had a net. An hour passed, then two. Mickey lay before the fireplace on his side but with his eyes wide open. Maye wished she had a dart gun. They waited.

Suddenly, with almost no warning, Maye heard several thuds, then a loud clattering crash, then more thuds, coming closer, closer, louder, closer, and with a sucking *whoosh* Maye swung open the door with all of her might to catch the intruder in the act.

Click! With a silvery, blinding flash, Maye's camera captured the wide-eyed shock of the hairy creature, evident as it lurched backward and tried to shield its eyes, emitting a tiny, almost inaudible squeal. In a split second, Mickey jumped on the intruder and knocked it off the porch steps. As Maye got her first full view of the suspect, sprawled on the ground with Mickey's paws planted on its chest, she felt a new kind of horror as she saw just who it was that was screeching.

"What are you doing?" screamed the man in navy shorts, a light blue shirt with a blue emblem across the left breast, thick blue socks, and black regulation oxfords. "Call off your dog! Call off your dog!"

"You're the mailman," Maye said quizzically, noticing his long, untrimmed white beard and his silvery hair pulled back in a ponytail that was longer than any girl's hair when Maye was in sixth grade, looking eerily like the dark wizard Saruman in *The Lord of the Rings*. His dark, sunken eyes glared at Maye as she called Mickey to her side; the mailman scrambled to his feet.

"I'm not a mailman," he asserted defensively, nearly hissing. "I am a United States *Letter Carrier*. And that dog of yours is a menace!"

"I'm sorry," Maye replied. "We heard a loud crash and then someone running through the yard. He's just protecting me."

"Garbage pickup isn't until tomorrow," the letter carrier sneered, pointing at the curb. "What was I supposed to do, jump over it?"

And that's when Maye saw her trash bin, which had been full when she placed it by the curb that morning, knocked over, garbage scattered all over the street. She was silent for a moment as she tried to absorb what she had just heard. She even shook her head in case her synapses weren't firing correctly or she had inadvertently stepped into another dimension. "You did that?" she asked. "Why would you do that? Why would you knock over my trash bin?"

"You're a day early!" he shrieked. "And I need exercise! I have a path I follow, you know! And I stick to my path! If you had put your trash out on the right day, I wouldn't have had to push it down!"

Maye was stunned speechless as she looked at the trash that was strewn everywhere. Mickey's dog-food cans, paper plates, the cartons from last night's takeout, packing materials, and old, rock-hard pizza crusts. Scattered in the street like the debris field from the *Titanic*.

"Here is your mail," he said as he handed Maye a stack of envelopes and then unbuckled a square package he had strapped to his body with a long leather belt like a suicide bomber and tossed it at her. "I'm reporting your dog. You're going to get that dog trained or he'll be classified as a dangerous animal and I will no longer deliver the post to you or anybody else on this street!"

"You've got to be kidding me. You're going to report my dog? *You* knocked over my trash! Are you going to pick all of that up?"

The letter carrier scoffed and sneered at her. "You're a *day early!*" he huffed. "Learn your trash schedule!"

Maye fought the urge to bum rush him and knock him down again.

"And I thought I'd never miss the Republicans!" the letter carrier shouted before he leaped across Maye's yard and ran off down the block, his footsteps thudding behind him.

ᚹ   ᚹ   ᚹ

Maye was still shaking her head as she crouched in the street, picking up the remnants of last night's dinner and throwing them back into the bags, when she heard a voice behind her. "Would you like a hand?"

She looked up and saw a tall, lean woman with refined features and a mostly-salt-with-a-few-strands-of-pepper updo smiling down at her.

"I'm beginning to think I need a backhoe," she replied with a little laugh.

"I'm Cynthia," she said, extending her right hand. "I live just across the street."

"I'm Maye. I don't mean to be rude, but I have sweet-and-sour chicken–glazed hands," she explained. "But it is very nice to meet you."

"I've been meaning to come over and introduce myself," Cynthia said. "But I was waiting until you got settled."

"Our mailman doesn't sense such things, does he?" Maye grinned. "I'm a little less settled now than I was six minutes ago."

"He's a stickler for schedules, that's for sure," Cynthia said. "I guess that's how he got to be Letter Carrier of the Year three years running now. And I really mean running!"

"That man, the one who pushed my trash over and who has been trampling my dahlias for days now, is the Letter Carrier of the Year?" Maye said, shaking her head again.

"He has a path," Cynthia said with a shrug. "I guess we've all learned to respect it. I'd move your flowers to the other side of the porch if I were you."

"Duly noted." Maye nodded. "I will do just that."

"I'm having an afternoon tea with some neighborhood ladies next week, and I'd love for you to join us," Cynthia said as she held out a white envelope with a question mark written in broad, swooping script on the front. "I didn't know your name, I'm sorry!"

"Oh, that's all—" Maye was suddenly interrupted by a loud, shrill shriek.

Cynthia was covering her mouth with one hand and pointing frantically with the other. "That . . . that . . . over there . . . what is that? Oh my goodness, oh my goodness!" she said, backing up in fear.

"Oh my God," Maye said, searching the ground with her eyes, looking for something . . . horrible. "What? I don't know—what was it? Where is it? Where did you see it? What am I looking for? A rat? Is it a rat? A mouse? A raccoon? In daylight? What was it?"

"Behind . . ." Cynthia stammered, barely able to get the words out. "Behind . . . the trash . . . behind the trash bin . . . right there! It's right behind it!"

Maye took a deep breath and walked over to the trash bin, still on its side in the street, reached out her sweet-and-sour hand, and prepared herself for a full-on cootie experience, complete with cootie dance to follow. With one quick move, she shoved the trash bin and then immediately jumped back. Cynthia whimpered.

There, behind the trash bin, was a can. A silly old empty dog-food can. Maye sighed heavily, then started to laugh as she leaned over to pick it up. "It's okay, it's fine," she said, trying to comfort Cynthia. "It's just a dog-food can. I'm sure it rolled behind there and the movement made it seem like something else. It's just a can. See?"

The horror on Cynthia's face did not ease, fade, or disappear. Instead, her eyes got wider and her expression took on the proportions of a teenager in a Wes Craven film who had just had dirty sex with her horn-dog boyfriend and was about to get her head ripped off her body like a grapefruit plucked from a tree by a psychopath.

"What," Cynthia asked, her voice just above a whisper, "is it doing in your trash bin? That's *recycling*. That can needs to be recycled. Is it washed out? Did you even wash it out? They can't recycle it unless you wash it!"

Maye decided to do what she was best at: blaming Charlie.

"It must have been my husband," she lied. "I told him that recycling is the blue bin, trash is green. How can I blame him, though? He's completely colorblind. Do you know that the man can't even see a rainbow? It just looks like a giant comma in the sky to him. It's a tragedy. It's the reason we don't have kids. I just can't pass something like that on to a baby! What kind of life is that?"

"Oh my," Cynthia said, regaining her composure. "I'm sorry. I didn't know. I had no idea. Maybe signs taped to each bin would help. He can read, can't he?"

Maye nodded. "As long as the letters aren't in color," she said sadly. "I will try that, Cynthia. Thank you."

"Of course," Cynthia said, then suddenly gasped again. "I have to go. I'm standing on a paper plate! It's a paper plate! Blue bin. *Blue bin!*"

"I'll see you at the tea!" Maye added as she waved, watching her neighbor scurry back across the street to her house, where the trash was washed first, then sorted properly.

She scooped up the remaining debris, returned the bin to an upright position, picked up her package, which was sitting on the curb, and looked through the mail as she walked up to the house.

There, against all odds, was her second invitation of the day. It was from the dean of Charlie's college, Dean Spaulding, inviting Charlie and his Significant Other to a faculty mixer hosted by himself and his wife the following weekend. Maye's appointment book, it seemed, was suddenly filling up.

And of course that, despite the sweet-and-sour fingerprints on the invitation envelope, made her smile.

3

Fair Warning

"I can't believe the bastard really turned Mickey in," Maye said angrily, brandishing the letter she had received that afternoon from the post office. "They're giving us two weeks to comply with the order for obedience training, otherwise Saruman will stop all delivery to our whole street because Mickey is now considered a 'hazardous animal.' Our neighbors are going to hate us!"

"No, they won't," Charlie replied as he turned right down a shaded, elegant street lined with stately old homes. "They won't hate us because we are going to do it and get Mickey into a training class. We can call a couple of places on Monday. There is a simple solution to this. Please don't worry. I think he'll really like training. He loves treats."

"I think the mailman needs to go to obedience training, that's what I think!" Maye cried. "What kind of nut knocks over a trash can because it was in his running route?"

"What kind of nut blinds the first nut with a camera flash because she wants to prove to her husband that an urban legend is sprinting across their front yard? I think it's important that we avoid making enemies, Maye, particularly of anyone on the government payroll." Charlie checked the address on the invitation and pulled into a long, sweeping driveway. "We haven't been here very long, and so far your ratio of friends to enemies isn't looking so good."

"That's not fair," Maye said, pouting. "I might make some friends today."

"I'm sure you will," Charlie said confidently as he drove and drove and drove up the drive. "Everything is going to be fine. Just be yourself. Everyone is going to love you. I bet before the night is over you'll have lunch dates lined up for all of next week."

He parked their sedan at the end of a long line of cars that hugged the circular driveway. Maye looked up at the grand house—really a mansion—with its tall white classical columns on stone piers, arched Palladian windows, a generous, wide stone wrap-around porch, three-story angled turret, and meticulously sculpted topiaries that flanked each side of the glossy black double doors.

"How do you get to own a house like this?" she wondered aloud.

"How do you think, honey?" Charlie said, chuckling. "Your grandfather makes all the sewer pipes for most of the continental United States when indoor plumbing is becoming the rage, builds his Monticello on a hill, then leaves it to your father, who then leaves it to you."

"This is the house that doody built?" Maye laughed as she got out of the car. "Glad I brought matches."

"Maye," Charlie said sternly. "While this may be the house that doody built, we need to keep that as our little joke. It is a very funny little joke, but I would appreciate your not repeating it to any of the other guests. Please don't embarrass me. I beg of you."

"Charlie!" Maye replied, more than a little shocked. "Why would I say that to people I don't know? I would never embarrass you like that in front of your colleagues. I bought new clothes for this thing. I spent next week's grocery money on this expensive pink sweater at the best vintage shop in town, along with the button-down shirt underneath it. The sweater is incredible and I love it, but I'll never wear the shirt again. That's how much I didn't want to embarrass you. I'm telling you, fill up on whatever food they have here tonight, because it's gotta last until your next paycheck. I sacrificed food so I wouldn't embarrass you."

"I know, I know," her husband said, shaking his head. "I'm sorry. I'm just nervous. Making a good impression on Dean Spaulding is important. This could be pivotal for my career at the university."

"If he's such a big shot in this town, why isn't he the president of the university instead of the dean of the English Department?" Maye asked curiously. "Is he the black sheep of the family? Did he do time?"

"He's a very humble man, you'll see," her husband explained. "He could have anything he wants in this place. He decided he loved literature and he loved the English Department. He's very down-to-earth, very unassuming. I like him very much and it's important, I repeat, to make a good impression today. *Capisce?*"

"Everything is going to be fine," Maye said as they walked up to the door and Charlie lifted a big brass lion's-head knocker. "We're going to have a delightful evening. I promise."

ᛘ   ᛘ   ᛘ

Maye was so relieved when the front door opened that she almost squealed like a sorority girl after one beer on an empty stomach.

"Hello and welcome," Mrs. Spaulding said with a big, genuine-looking smile.

"Hi, I'm Charlie Roberts, the new assistant professor in the

English Department, and this is my wife, Maye," Charlie said as they stepped inside.

"Nice to meet you, Charlie," the woman said, shaking Charlie's hand and then moving on to Maye's. "Maye. Please come in."

The dean's wife was not what Maye expected at all. She had short, cropped, low-maintenance hair, full, fresh, ruddy cheeks, and an informality about her that radiated a certain kind of ease.

She was also younger than Maye had thought she'd be by a good twenty to thirty years—Maye pegged her at about her own age, the lines at the corners of her eyes reflecting enough good laughs for early- to mid-thirties—and she seemed so warm and inviting, not stuffy and reserved as Maye had shamefully predicted she would be. She was a naturally pretty girl; she wore not pearls but a modern silver-wire-wrapped chalcedony nugget on a plain silver chain, and no makeup other than a subtle, matte lipstick. Although the woman's nails were short and cleanly scrubbed, Maye knew she was shaking the hand of a gardener. She wouldn't have called Dean Spaulding's bride a trophy wife, not at all; she wasn't plastic-looking and didn't have more pieces of gold and diamonds on her hands than a sunken armada ship. Mrs. Spaulding instead looked more like the award delivered for Best Sportsmanship or Nicest Manners.

Maye liked her instantly.

"What a lovely house," she commented.

"Isn't it?" Mrs. Spaulding smiled unpretentiously as she looked up and around at her own foyer, and Maye could tell that she was earnest in her reply. "It's been in the Spaulding family for generations."

"Is it a Queen Anne?" Maye asked.

"You're right! I believe it's Free Classic Queen Anne. I took a little bit of architecture history when I was at the university—I swear I'm not a know-it-all!"

"Really?" Maye exclaimed. "I did, too! I didn't do much with it after I got a journalism degree, since all it's really good for is mentioning the style of the house when you're reporting the meth-lab bust, and that's easy, slum or trailer."

"Ah, reporter," the woman grinned. "I'd love to hear your stories! Remind me never to tell you my secrets, though."

"Oh no," Charlie abruptly chimed in. "Maye wouldn't tell your secrets, would you, Maye?"

"Oh, it wouldn't do me any good," Maye replied with a smirk. "I've been in reporting retirement for a couple of weeks. I'm writing freelance now that we've moved here."

"I hope you like Spaulding," their hostess said.

"I do," Maye replied. "We're just so happy not to live in a place where my biggest talent was sweating."

The hostess laughed. "Oh, wait," she warned. "You just missed the Sweat Season. Wait until next August when the humidity invades like the Mongols and everyone becomes very shiny. You'll think you've sprung a leak or at least developed adult incontinence. But it's great for the weight-conscious and budget-minded; you can lose fifteen pounds in a weekend just by sitting in a lawn chair, and it's far cheaper than liposuction."

"I'd happily wear a diaper to start a new life as a size twelve," Maye said with a chuckle.

Their hostess turned to Charlie. "How are you finding our university as new faculty?"

"It's wonderful. I couldn't ask for a better position at a better school," Charlie said. "Is the dean around? I'd love to say hello."

"He is." His wife nodded and pointed toward a large formal room where a round of choppy laughter had just erupted. "Can I get either of you a drink? Gin and tonic is the drink of the house."

"That would be perfect, thank you," Maye replied.

"Make that two." Charlie smiled.

"I'll be right back." Mrs. Spaulding smiled. "Please make yourself at home—I believe everyone is hanging out in the library."

As Maye and Charlie crossed the cavernous marble-floored foyer, a distinct sound—*chh chh, chh chh*—floated along with them.

"Is that a cricket?" Charlie whispered, looking around.

"No," Maye whispered back.

"I swear that's a cricket!" he insisted. "Listen—*chh chh. Chh chh.*"

"It's not a cricket, Charlie." Maye insisted. "Can we just drop it?"

"Stop," he said as he pulled Maye's arm. "Listen."

The foyer was quiet, with only the sounds of a happening faculty party drifting in from the next room.

"Listen," he repeated as he cocked his ear and concentrated firmly, as if listening to voices from beyond. "It's stopped."

"Charlie, would you quit it?" Maye asked.

"How do you know it's not a cricket? You're not a cricket expert!" Charlie retorted.

"No, I am not," she said between clenched teeth. "But I do know the sound that chunky inner thighs bound like a hostage in a girdle and then strangled in pantyhose make when they are rubbing against each other causing enough friction to melt a nuclear plant to a bubbling, toxic puddle!"

"Oh," her husband said, then suddenly understood. "That's what fat sounds like?"

"Fat is silent if there's background noise or sounds of nature or something to override it," Maye cried defensively. "But in a mausoleum, yes, that is what fat sounds like!"

"Charlie Roberts!" The intimidating tenor voice boomed through the foyer as Dean Spaulding spotted Charlie approaching the library. "Come in, come in!"

Maye followed Charlie into a room filled with high, dark mahogany bookcases teeming with antique bound editions, long, slim leather couches and chairs, fresh flowers—most of which were not in season—sprouting from crystal vases on side tables and on the broad, sweeping mantel of the imposing, carved-stone fireplace. Maye had never been in a room like this that she didn't have to pay to get into and then gawk at from behind a velvet rope. She felt the sudden urge to curtsy like a Cockney chambermaid but instead tried to follow Charlie's lead, despite the overwhelming feeling that she had quickly shrunk to the size of the phantom cricket that chirped from between her thighs.

Maye was overwhelmed.

"And this is my wife, Maye," Charlie said as Dean Spaulding extended his hand and Maye gave it her heartiest shake.

"It's so nice to meet you," she said as she tried to smile, noticing that the rest of the attendees had suddenly hushed and were all paying attention. "Thank you for having us."

Whether he sensed her unease or it was his regular party protocol, Dean Spaulding gently took Maye by the elbow and introduced her to every person there—Charlie's colleagues and their, as the invitation read, Significant Others. There was Professor Martin Oberling and his wife, Christina; Dr. Maria Albertson and her S.O., Julie; Dr. William Hummel and his charming wife, Meg; Professor This and Dr. That, and this wife, that husband, that life partner, that fiancée. Dean Spaulding went around the room and approximately said, "I'd like you to meet Maye Roberts, Charlie's wife," around thirty times. Maye had always been bad at names, but this was impossible—she tried desperately to match faces with traits but just plain gave up around number eight when she met a perky, tiny blond S.O. named Melissabeth, which was completely unfair, Maye thought to herself. That's a two-trick name. Go with one or the other, but this double duty name is like a Hummer—no need for something that big and that takes up two parking spaces.

When the introduction whirlwind was complete, Dean Spaulding took both of Maye's hands in his.

"I know it's hard being the new person and meeting all of the department at once, but I want to make sure you really love this place," he said to her with a gentle smile. "We value Charlie very highly; he's an incredible asset to us. We'd love to have him stay at Spaulding University for quite some time."

"Thank you for giving Charlie this opportunity," Maye replied. "I can't tell you how much he loves it here."

An older, impeccably dressed woman turned into the library with a pinched, hard face and brushed-back, flipped-curtly-at-the-end Nan Kempner socialite hair in grim reaper black.

"Oh, it's Rowena," Dean Spaulding said as he looked up. "Rowena, I'd like you to meet Maye Roberts, the wife of our newest faculty member."

Rowena looked up, flashed a sudden small smile, and walked several steps toward them.

"It's nice to meet you," Maye said, extending her hand, which Rowena grasped limply.

"Pleasure is all mine," Rowena said politely as she smiled emptily and handed Maye a gin and tonic. "I believe this is for you."

"If you'll excuse me, I hear an argument about Walt Whitman that I feel compelled to settle!" Dean Spaulding said, laughing heartily, then moved to join a group of professors, including Charlie, who were discussing whether the first or deathbed edition of *Leaves of Grass* was more powerful. He looked at Maye and winked, and she smiled back.

Maye looked back at Rowena, whose makeup had settled into the creases of her face like sand in a shipwreck, particularly around the pucker of her tiny, puckered, blood-red mouth. The pencil-thin bridge of her nose was flanked on either side by motionless marble-like eyes, nudged so close together they seemed baboonish. Even the warm pink hue of her genuine pearls looked cold and freezing wrapped around her neck.

Rowena crossed one arm over her tailored, camel-colored wool waist jacket, bent her other arm, and tapped a curry-yellow index finger at her temple twice.

Despite Rowena's tintless and ghoulishly ghost-white skin, Maye thought snidely to herself, that must have been the applicator finger for the self-tanner, in the sense that the skin on her hands had begun to turn to hide.

"How are you finding Spaulding? Is it quite a bit different from your hometown?" she inquired. Honestly, however, Maye knew she didn't care if Maye and Charlie were comfortable and happy in this new place, as it was no matter of concern for her if Maye missed her family and friends in Phoenix and felt a bit awkward at the faculty party. For Rowena, it was simply a matter of standard, obligatory conversation.

"It's great, thank you for asking. I am learning how to recycle," Maye said with a smile, wishing that Mrs. Spaulding would suddenly turn the corner and defuse this conversation bomb like a SWAT team. She longed for something else to say, but having met so many new people at once, she couldn't remember who Rowena was attached to—was it Dr. Castle or Professor Brooks, or was she a faculty member herself? Yes, yes, didn't Dean Spaulding mention something about Professor Brooks's significant other also being a professor of . . . of . . . was it Old English? Medieval lit? Postmodernism? Nineteenth-century American? As hard as Maye tried, she couldn't remember, and she certainly couldn't ask now; horribly embarrassed, she resorted to the obvious. "Have you lived here long?" was the lone, soggy nugget Maye could pull out of her conversation cache. She hoped it might lead to another thread or perhaps even an expression from a woman who seemed to have the emotions of a mineral—that is, if a mineral could hate.

"I was born in Spaulding, and I will die in Spaulding," Rowena informed her matter-of-factly, then pointed her finger at Maye. "By the way, Maye, who is new in Spaulding, that is a lovely sweater. Vintage, yes? The beading is exquisite. However, it is an afternoon sweater for an afternoon event. Which this is not. Perhaps that sweater would be appropriate attire in Phoenix. But this is an evening event, as everyone else understood it to be."

Although Maye knew better, she was still waiting for the punch line about her pretty new sweater when Rowena turned and promptly walked out of the library.

Maye stood there. She looked at Charlie, laughing and joking with a circle of his colleagues. She looked at Dean Spaulding, who was holding open a leather-bound first edition of Whitman. She looked at the other guests, lounging and talking on the sofa, and then she felt her face get hot. Flushed. Burning. Her eyes stung. Her ears buzzed with embarrassment and shock. She felt a little dizzy.

"Oh my God," she mumbled to herself. "That was so unnecessary."

I need to find a bathroom, she thought, and walked out of the library before she even realized she was able to move.

Chh chh. Chh chh. Chhchhchhchh. Maye shot through the foyer in search of a door, any door that could hide her for just a moment.

She didn't know which way the bathroom was; up the stairs, down a long hall, back through the library? *Chh chh.* Was she *that* inappropriately dressed? It wasn't like she was wearing a tube top or exposing her butt cleavage. *Chh chh chh chh.* Did everyone know? Was it apparent to everyone but her? She didn't want to embarrass Charlie; she couldn't embarrass Charlie. How could she find the bathroom? *Chh chh chh.* She darted down the long hall and slid into the thankfully empty dining room, where she stopped and leaned up against a wall.

Stupid, awful sweater, her mind raced; I hate this sweater. I hate pink. Breathe, she told herself; calm down. This is fine. I hate this stupid expensive sweater I spent our grocery money on this hideous pink thing I hate it! Breathe. It's fine. Slow down. Under the pink sweater is a nice polished-cotton white oxford appropriate for any occasion. You can wear an oxford anyplace, to a funeral, to a wedding, a baby shower, a court date. An oxford has no time restraints. You can wear the oxford at your arraignment after wrapping your anger-induced swollen green Hulk hands around Rowena's aging neck, which has more pleats than a Catholic girl's school uniform.

The oxford is fine. The oxford is perfect. See, everything is going to be fine, she thought, and in one motion, Maye crossed her arms, grabbed the hem of the sweater on either side, and pulled up swiftly, as fast as she could, pull, pull, pull, up over her torso, over her boobs, quickly, quickly, hurry, over her head, and just as the sweater released Maye's face and got to her forehead, it stopped there and froze. The sweater was stuck. She pulled harder, but the sweater, now wedged around her skull like a nun's wimple, tugged on either side of her face, which was growing increasingly red and puffy. She pulled again as she grimaced and grunted. And then, for some odd reason, her belly felt cold. Chilly. Somewhat breezy. As if it was exposed. She gasped and looked down, and the oxford was gone. It had vanished. The only thing that was there was Maye's bra, and Maye's belly, and the waistband of Maye's girdle, which from girth pressure had now rolled itself downward into the shape of an enchilada and width of the rings of Saturn.

The oxford, apparently, was now up around her head in conjunction with the pink sweater, as the two articles of clothing acted like a tag team with either static or sudden love gluing them together. It was then that Maye remembered rule one in removing an oxford if you don't want it to become permanently lodged around your head: undo the top button first. She struggled, tried to gather some leverage by twisting from side to side. It stayed put. She rested a few seconds, gathered her strength, gritted her teeth, and pulled up like she was lifting a car off of a baby. The shirt did not budge. She bent over and tried to pull from that angle, hoping that gravity would help, but when she saw shiny, flashing lights floating in front of her, she aborted that attempt, lest she have a stroke as a result and be discovered topless, fat, and drooling on the Spauldings' carpeted dining room floor.

She sighed. Her arms were tired; she was now breaking a sweat. Pretend you're fighting off a crazy, bloodthirsty raccoon during daylight hours and that its pointy sharp distemper teeth are trying to impale your face, her mind told her, and in one last, desperate attempt to get free, she flung herself completely into trying to pretend-save her life and liberating her head from the viselike grip of a polished-cotton collar. *Chhhhh chhhhhh chhhhhh.* It was as she was thrashing about like a chubby, far less attractive Frances Farmer in straitjacket that Maye realized abruptly that unfortunately, due to her hearing being muffled by layers of pink wool and polished cotton and by her cricket thighs but predominately by her very own grunting, she had neglected to hear the call that dinner was about to be served.

Dozens of eyes were now witnessing her earthy dance in the corner of the dean's dining room as she displayed the brand of inhibition typically evinced only after ingesting cactus buttons or licking poisonous toads. Some were filled with disbelief, some with disgust, some with dismay, there was one particularly offended pair that caught Maye's eye and triggered a voice in her head.

"Melissabeth!" it said surprisingly. "I can't believe I remembered your name after all!"

☙ ☙ ☙

"Charlie!" Maye called. "Have you seen the aloe vera ointment?"

"It's in your office," he replied as he came down the stairs and poked his head into the bathroom, where Maye was studying her forehead in the mirror. "It was right next to your keyboard."

Apparently, surviving the disgrace of having thirty academics walk in on you while you're brawling with your apparel as your ta-tas swing vigorously from side to side like you are used to strangers sticking money into your panties was not enough of a challenge for Maye; when she finally got home (after Charlie hastily ushered her to the car) she noticed a dark ring around her face when she passed a mirror—a ring similar to that on an elderly woman who believed that blending the foundation near her hairline was a frivolous waste of however much time her clock had left on it. On Maye, however, it wasn't makeup, and it wasn't a shadow. On her head was an inch-thick rainbow of a self-inflicted road rash from fighting with her shirt while she fantasized it was a homicidal raccoon.

"It looks like a bike ran over your head," Charlie said. "Still hurts, huh?"

Maye closely studied her forehead and decided it looked like a do-it-yourself chemical peel. "Like a ring of fire," she answered. "I thought cotton was supposed to be the fabric of our lives, not the fabric that gives you a third-degree friction burn."

"Um," Charlie began, trying to choose his words carefully. "I saw you, remember? You didn't really look like you were taking a shirt off, you looked like you were fighting off bees. It was a violent act with the exotic spice of vulgarity."

"I'm still really sorry," Maye said, wincing as she poked at the scab that stretched like a scarlet ribbon across her forehead and stretched from ear to ear. "I'll say that every day until I die, Charlie. I'm so sorry."

"It's all right," he said, nodding as he followed Maye into her office and she picked up the aloe vera ointment. "All I had to say was 'hot flash' and everyone understood, plus I reminded them that Sylvia Plath once threw all of her clothes off the roof of the Barbizon Hotel. People are starting to talk to me at work again, sort of, and eventually, they'll be able to look me in the eye. I think you've become the department's Zelda Fitzgerald. Zany, unpredictable, so 'Faculty Significant Others Gone Wild!' Let's count our blessings that I'm not in the film studies department because then the whole thing would be on tape and for sale in the bookstore for $19.99. Really, I just want you to concentrate on having a good time at the tea. And if anyone there tells you they hate what you're wearing, come home, change, and then go back and whip them with your oxford. Remember our new motto."

"I know." Maye sighed. " 'Naked belongs at home.' "

"Say it again," he coaxed. "Just so I can be sure. My mother always warned me this would happen if I married you, but she said you'd be drunk first and sailors would be involved."

"I won't get naked at our neighbor's tea party, Charlie, I swear," Maye promised, dabbing the soothing salve along the line that looked like someone had tried to lasso her like a calf. "What do you think, should I march in like Little Edie Beale with a sweater pinned around my head and holding a baton, go for a simple headband, or proudly wear my scar and use it as an icebreaker?"

"Unless you want to answer repeatedly that no, you are not the French lady who gobbled a fistful of Valium, fell down, had a dog eat her lips off, and then got a face transplant," Charlie exhaled, "I'd wear the headband and leave the baton at home. We don't have enough money for you to be considered eccentric, only enough to be considered a belt that hasn't gone through all of the loops."

Maye tied the silk scarf around her head, put some lipstick on, and fussed with the bronze-beaded collar of the pink sweater. She was actually beginning to like the sweater, the way the beads sparkled, and the intricacy of the beading, and felt the need to exorcize the spicy vulgar act that had been associated with it. Besides, you can't throw an expensive sweater away after one wear, she thought, even if it did peel the skin right off your forehead like a cranial circumcision.

Rowena could go to hell, Maye thought as she opened the front door and stepped outside to cross the street; it's afternoon.

ψ   ψ   ψ

The first thing that Maye noticed when she entered Cynthia's living room was that enormous pieces of plywood were placed erratically all over the floor. The second thing she noticed was that she was the youngest person there.

By about half a century.

In fact, she was one of only a few who didn't bring her own chair, as the room was so crowded with motorized medical equipment that it looked like a Rascal Rodeo, thus the sheets of plywood that were improvising as ramps. There wasn't one model or brand of mobility scooter that wasn't represented, all lined up on the far side of the room: the Zoom 300, the Avenger Series, the Buzzaround, the Legend XL, the Go Go Ultra, the Sonic, one after the other, so that the tea party looked like a Sturgis rally, although one plagued by osteoporosis. Maye resisted the urge to compress her spine and hunch over just to stop feeling guilty about her ability to stand upright without the aid of a torture rack.

Suddenly, the reason for the absence of noisy children on the street became clear. Most of the women in attendance were only there due to the marvels of modern medicine and oxygen tanks, since all of them had most likely felt the tremors of the Great San Francisco Earthquake. And not the one that knocked down the freeway.

Maye sat on a couch between an elderly woman named Agnes, who had skin so thin that it looked like it came off a roll of Saran Wrap, and another lady, who had already fallen asleep.

"That letter carrier of ours is such a dear," one of the ladies in the scooter lineup said, to which Maye scoffed in her head but wisely remained silent. "He told me that a vicious dog just moved into the neighborhood and that if I was going to use the Renegade to go to the store, I needed to use my high speed. He said that dog knocked him over backward and almost ripped his throat out! And the owner just stood there! And they live on this street!"

Every single lady in the room except for Maye and her slumbering neighbor gasped in naked fear.

"How fast does the Renegade go?" a woman with cropped gray hair asked her. "Is it as fast as the Celebrity?"

"The Renegade had speeds up to *six miles an hour*," the first lady boasted.

"Oh, that's fast," another lady said, shaking her head. "That's a little excessive, if you ask me. Where am I going that I need that kind of speed? Space?"

"Not if a crazy hellhound is chasing you!" a lady in a chair leaned over and cried, shaking her crooked, buckled finger.

"Hmmm," the ladies agreed, nodding.

"Where's Alma?" Agnes, the Saran Wrap lady, asked gently as she looked around. "Is Alma here? I haven't seen her in weeks!"

Every member of the scooter gang smiled at her inquiry, but no one said a word.

"That portrait of Cynthia is still so stunning, isn't it?" said one of the women who could still stand, pointing to a black-and-white photograph that hung over the mantel. "I remember that day like it was yesterday. Actually, I remember that day better than I remember yesterday!"

Laughter, sounding like a gaggle of clucking ducks, filled the room.

Maye's gaze followed the finger of the woman to the mantel, and took in the photograph of a very young, coiffed, and elegant Cynthia kneeling, her head bowed forward slightly as an older man with a thick white mustache placed a crown upon her head. To Maye, it looked like a scene from a play.

"Do you remember Cynthia's dress?" the silver-haired matron said dreamily. "The layers of tulle, tier after tier on the strapless bodice. She looked just like Grace Kelly. It was lovely."

"Oh, Maude, I do remember that dress!" Cynthia said as she swept into the living room holding a large tray filled with tiny sandwiches. "I no longer have that dress, but look at all the friends I still have!"

As Maye darted her eyes back and forth between Cynthia and the old photograph, she noted that her neighbor hadn't changed much in all of those years. She was still tall and thin, and clearly stood out in the room as the only one who had drunk the necessary amount of milk during her calcium-needy years. Her complexion hadn't grayed and her skin hadn't dropped like a feed sack; it stayed high and firm on her cheekbones. Age hadn't attacked Cynthia the way it had fought with the other ladies in the room; for a woman who was terrified of a dirty dog-food can, she must have had some pretty quick footing, Maye noted, and ducked each time the sandbag of time came hurtling at her, unlike most of her guests, who had not only gotten socked but stayed down for the count until the geriatric bell rang.

"You know, Elsie, we didn't see you at the last Silver Songbird meeting," Cynthia mentioned, nodding at the woman on the Renegade. "We missed you, but I'm sure we can find a place for you somewhere in the cast. Almost all of the men's roles need filling. My husband can't play every single male role, he's getting a big head! It's hard enough to find a man alive, but to get them to sing—"

"Was Alma there?" Agnes asked. "Has anyone seen Alma?"

"I was getting my colostomy bag replaced," Elsie replied. "It leaked all over my good Sunday dress at the prayer circle! I'm so sorry I missed the auditions. Oh, our last show was so much fun!"

Ah, drama people, Maye thought with a sigh. Being bitten by the drama bug is every bit as dangerous as a nibble from a malaria-ridden mosquito; one person contracts it every thirty seconds, there's always an abundance of excessive gasping and everyone around that person hopes they don't catch it.

" 'Three little maids from school are we,' " sang Maude, in a high, wavery voice, her puckered hands cupped together under her chin. " 'Pert as a school-girl well can be!' "

" 'Filled to the brim with girlish glee,' " Elsie screeched, almost as if on cue.

" 'Three little maids from school!' " the remainder of the women warbled, in a broad variety of pitches.

" 'Everything is a source of fun,' " Cynthia crooned alone as she made her way to the front of the room in a short-stepped sort of shuffle.

" 'Nobody's safe, for we care for none!' " Elsie sang, only over-shadowed by the hum of her Renegade battery pack kicking into action as she parallel parked in the spot next to Cynthia.

" 'Life is a joke that's just begun!' " Maude chirped, finding her way to the front of the room in little hops until she stopped next to her fellow cast members.

" 'Three little maids from school!' " all three sang in the best uni-son they could manage, smiling demurely behind their fan hands, now fully in their roles as Yum-Yum, Peep-Bo, and Pitti-Sing.

Now, if Maye had proven just to be minutely more talented in the area of recreational sports as a prepubescent lass, she would have been completely astounded and perhaps a bit alarmed by the instant production that was suddenly being staged in Cyn-thia's living room, complete with drama faces. But Maye, at the age of twelve, had run a grueling and life-altering fifteen-minute mile in a PE class as her inner ice-white thighs were christened with flagellant red welts, thus beginning her initiation into the plague of Chub Rub. As a result she swore that if sports had this sort of consequence, she would be abstaining from such activity, due to either uterine cramping, common cafeteria corn-dog-induced nausea, a Bubble Yum–blocked esophagus, suspicion of catching an asthma bug from an unhygienic girl in third-period U.S. history, an occasion of sudden and unexpected partial blindness from looking at the sun for far too long, or the most predominant, a headache resulting from drinking an overly hot can of soda. And that is precisely how Maye joined the drama club and came to the acquaintance of Mrs. Gelding, drama instructor, who spoke in a falsetto, rolled her *r*'s, had a belly big enough to house a fifty-pound tumor that truly pushed the miracle stretch of her polyester slacks, and wore her hair in a tight little gray perm reminiscent of a young Roman boy. She was the director, choreographer, costume designer, hairstylist, makeup person, singing coach, and prop master for any and all theatrical productions at the bastion for the arts that was Maye's suburban middle school. Mrs. Gelding, well into her sixties and unwilling to consider any production that she didn't define as among "the classics," ran the Drama Department on a shoestring budget, but given that her entire repertoire consisted of two alternating productions—*H.M.S. Pinafore* in the fall and *The Pirates of Penzance* in the spring—it was a rather easy swing. "The only difference between a sailor and a Keystone Kop," she was fond of saying, "is the hat and a vice or two." It was an easy sell, particularly since neither the students nor their parents ever truly understood the plays and thought they actually were the same production, year after year, as does a good percentage of suburban humanity, being that no one else really cares.

Maye's mother had insisted that all of her children participate in at least one after-school activity for "socialization purposes" and, as Maye suspected, to extend her coffee-drinking-and-talking-on-the-phone-to-her-friends time for an extra hour. So instead of joining the basketball, softball, track, or any other kind of team that required sweating in private places, Maye signed up for drama. She was a sailor in the fall, a cop in the spring, and found out that the difference in the roles really was only a hat. She never had a line in either musical and blended in with all of the other eleven- and twelve-year-old girls who played sailors and cops and pirates with little tiny boobs when all each of them really wanted to do was wear a big frilly hoop skirt and sing a solo.

It was never to be.

Then, in the fall of her eighth-grade year, the drama club met to see which girl would be a pirate and which girl would be a cop, and an odd thing happened. The Drama Department received a windfall when the school budget was increased after the school won a lawsuit against the corn-dog distributor who had poisoned several seventh graders and the vice principal with rancid pre-formed and battered meat sticks. As Mrs. Gelding fought back tears of elation, she announced that instead of buying the sailors white costumes and the cops blackjacks, the money would be used to build a new set, since *Pinafore* and *Penzance* used the same one.

The drama club would embark on *The Mikado,* another musical by Gilbert and Sullivan, based in Japan but really a satire on the "notions and culture of Victorian England," as Wikipedia, the free Internet encyclopedia, will tell you. In other words, another production that seventh and eighth graders and their parents didn't find entertaining, humorous, or in the least bit interesting and dreaded both performing and watching.

"Why can't we do *Grease?*" asked a blond, petite girl with clear skin and a Pepsodent smile, an obvious first-draft pick for the role of Sandy. "Greenway Middle School got to do *Grease!* We want to do *Grease!*"

Mrs. Gelding's tight little-boy perm visibly smoked with fury. "We will not do *Grrrrrrease!*" she said definitively and between clenched teeth. "I will not have that porrrrrnography on *my stage.* The lyrrrrrics to those ballads arrrrre filthy! We will do *The Mikado.* It's a classic!"

And then Mrs. Gelding scanned the crop that lay before her and picked out the lassies with the darkest hair, because although she had a budget for a new set, there was no money for wigs and it was doubtful that any of the truly pretty girls would dye their flowing honey-blond hair Japanese black. "You," she trilled, pointing to Maureen Zemora, a bespeckled chubby girl, the one Maye claimed to have caught asthma from. "Come, come. Up here. And you." Mrs. Gelding pointed to Dawn Lee, who was taller than most boys in the school and had shoulders broader than the principal's. "Come, come. And . . . and . . . and . . . you!" She pointed to Maye's floppy, curly mass of dark brown hair that, in eighth grade, resembled the hind end of a labradoodle. "Come, come."

"Yum-Yum, Peep-Bo, Pitti-Sing," she said respectively, pointing to each girl and declaring her role. "Tonight, each of you must tell your mothers to buy you a shiny, long-sleeved robe that ties in the front, unless you already have one at home. And be warned: if you show up in a robe better suited to a cast member of *Three's Company,* consequences will be dealt accordingly. I will not tolerate the appearance of any triangles below the hemlines of your kimonos. I will give your role to a more respectable blond girl, and the audience will just have to use their imagination by pretending that she's not."

All the dark-haired lassies nodded.

"And make sure you wash the kimono before you bring it in here," Mrs. Gelding said, her eyes boring into Maureen, who then, openmouthed, coughed.

When Maye went home and told her mother she needed a robe that would cover her cookie, her mother momentarily excused herself from her telephone conversation, put down her coffee, and said, "You know, it would be so much easier for this family if you would just run, Mayebelline. I'd only have to watch a two-minute race and shorts are five dollars."

Maye stomped off to her room, where she sulked for nine minutes, wept for three, and then perched her ear dangerously close to her turntable speaker and listened to the *Grease* soundtrack, as did every other drama club member that afternoon. Those who had broader educations in the art of smut or who had siblings in high school indeed gasped, but most, like Maye, were left to conclude in silence that "pushy wagon" was just another term for an aggressively fast car, and as mentioned in the chorus, "Chixel Creme" was probably some sort of fancy 1950s motor oil. Nothing dirty there.

Six weeks later, Maye was sitting in a chair in a barely-below-her-cookie robe after it shrunk in the wash as Mrs. Gelding slathered on white oil-based stage makeup with a makeshift spatula like it was icing out of a can. She had spent half of a semester trying to strike a fragile Pitti-Sing balance between Maureen and Dawn, being that she was the cold cut in the Three Little Maids sandwich, since their musical number required some distressingly close contact. Maye tried painstakingly to (1) remain a minimum of four to six inches away from Maureen's mysterious universe of a head, where undocumented species were rumored to roam and multiply, and (2) muffle her screams of alarm when the choreography called for the maids to turn sideways and lean on one another, in which Dawn would, with her Green Bay Packer body, attempt to surround and entomb Maye in a tomboy cocoon. This was a situation in which Maye once caught her encapsulator sniffing at her hair and eliciting what she hoped was a gas bubble but was most likely, in hindsight, a gurgle of thrill. Maye heard the same sound once more during the first and last performance of the Gelding *Mikado,* as she tried to be a demure maiden while painted up like a Storyville harlot and, as if in confirmation, looked down after she had just sung to the audience that " 'Life is a joke that's just begun,' " to see her robe swinging wide open as if she were Hugh Hefner and learned a hard lesson that cheap, shiny, laundered polyester cannot be counted on to hold a respectable and sturdy bow.

"All I can say," Maye's mother declared that night as she threw Maye's costume into the trunk of the car, "is thank God you wear shorts under everything since you got that running rash."

ϒ   ϒ   ϒ

A couple of decades later, Maye sat in Cynthia's living room calling up her *Mikado* memories as three of her neighbors—who were too old to be simply grandmothers without a multitude of "great"s being placed before that title, let alone schoolgirls— pranced and flounced with what marginal dexterity their Edwardian period limbs could permit without simply snapping off like dead twigs and fluttering to the ground.

"Three little maids who, all unwary, / Come from a ladies' seminary, / Freed from its genius tutelary," the trio squawked, their rice-paper-thin voices wavering frilly and wandering off, on, and beyond key like an elephant on the savannah hit with a tranquilizer dart. The remainder of the party guests looked on with as much merriment as if they had front-row seats at a Broadway show. " 'Three little maids from school!' "

The audience, whom Maye now considered hostages, clapped wildly and cooed at the talents of their hostess and her maiden friends.

"Wasn't that fun?" Cynthia said to her cohorts, slapping her palms against her knees. "That was delightful!"

"Where IS ALMA?" Agnes finally demanded. "I want my bowl! I am tired of waiting for her to return it, and I want my bowl back! That was my favorite bowl!"

"Oh dear," Elsie said quietly, then covered her mouth with her fingers as she shook her head. "No one has told her about Alma's move to the . . . *other side*."

"Listen, Agnes," one of the scooter women hastily offered. "If you're lucky, you can buy it back at the estate sale on Saturday. That is, if her vulture daughter hasn't kept it for herself! I'm going to have to buy my salad spinner back and my favorite half-slip! I'm telling all of you right now if you show up to my house for bunko with static cling and wet lettuce, I cannot help you fight that battle! You are on your own! Fair warning!"

"It starts at seven A.M., so we all have to be there early so we can get first pick," Elsie said. "I'm up at four, so that's no problem for me."

"I'm up at three," another woman boasted. "Did you know they moved *The Rockford Files* to five A.M.? What am I supposed to do for two hours? Oh, I wrote the TV station a nasty letter, I certainly did."

"I noticed that," Maude said, shaking her head in sorrow. "Now *The Rockford Files* and *Matlock* are on at the same time. I can't choose! How can I choose? Thank God they left *Columbo* alone. I have no problem choosing between that and *The View*."

"Oh, I have an idea!" Cynthia sang, shaking her finger as she disappeared into the next room. Within a minute, she was back with a black vinyl disc in her hand.

Oh, please, God, Maye thought desperately as she tightly closed her eyes and crossed her fingers so hard they turned white. If you are a merciful and kind and loving God, the kind of God who invented cotton candy and Oreo O's cereal and S'Mores Pop-Tarts and not the kind of God who invented osteoporosis and colostomy bags and transparent skin, please let it be *Grease*! *Grease* is the word, is the word, is the word!

Instead, in a moment, the sound of an orchestra filled the living room, blanketed by the echoing scratches of an excessively played record. Suddenly, Cynthia was pretending to pull a rope,

Maude jumped to her side and coiled an imaginary line between her hand and elbow, and Maye heard the alarming hum of numerous battery packs thrown into action as all hands assembled on deck until she was the only guest who hadn't boarded a make-believe ship, except for the woman next to her, whom Maye feared had chosen to run into the light as opposed to sitting through the impromptu matinee of *H.M.S. Pinafore* that was unfolding near the divan.

" 'We sail the ocean blue, and our saucy ship's a beauty,' " the sailors sang heartily to the opening tune. " 'We're sober men and true, and attentive to our duty!' "

"Do you know the lyrics, dear?" Cynthia called out to her in between verses as she tugged on her mime rope.

Maye shook her head, adding a small shrug, hoping to secure her release with lies but wanting to add that a small hand mirror might be helpful as she pointed to her couch mate. Things were moving quickly along, however, there is simply no time to check for vital signs when a saucy fantasy ship needs to be polished and swept.

"Then enjoy and clap along!" her host shouted buoyantly before she and her mates attacked the chorus.

So Maye sat in her neighbor's living room and clapped until her hands were as red, chapped, and sore as her forehead, and until both sides of the record had been played. Finally, she managed to escape when the Senior Dial-A-Ride Service bus pulled up in front of Cynthia's house, and she hunched down and scrambled out with a herd of Legend XLs. When she got to the safety of the other side of the street without looking back, she breathed a deep sigh of relief and then realized that she was still completely friendless.

4

It's Just a Thing I Do

How do I do this? Maye wondered.

I have been in this town for over a month, and so far, I have an enemy-combatant mailman, my husband's entire department and his boss have seen my boobs shake like maracas in one of my oldest and least supportive bras, I'm pretty sure I watched an old woman die during an afternoon tea party, and the closest friend I have right now is my lawn guy, who has clearly inhaled more than his share of chemicals and believes that raccoons will pluck my eyeballs out and eat them like olives.

How do I make a friend? How does a childless woman in her mid-thirties who works at home meet people in a new town where she knows no one who actually likes her?

I just want one, Maye repeated over and over again in her head. Just one. One friend to go to lunch with, one friend to call when something funny happens, one friend to go shopping with. Maybe she was asking too much, she reminded herself. She had read once in a magazine that once you moved to a new place, it took three years to build a circle of friends. Still, that hadn't stopped her from gently spying on other women's grocery carts, taking inventory of their contents to see if they had anything in common. A bottle of decent-enough wine, a nice cheese, a baguette, and a pint of Ben & Jerry's were to Maye sinful signals of definite friend potential, someone who wasn't afraid to get tipsy on a Wednesday night, eat a little dairy fat spread on a carbohydrate, and had no fear of chocolate ice cream teamed with Marshmallow Fluff and graham cracker ribbons. Maye's kinda girl. Anyone whose shopping cart contained juice boxes, diapers, yard-long family packs of chicken thighs, incense, and Tofurkys was immediately disqualified, because Maye knew that if you let those sorts of people in, the next thing you know, a dirty, hemp-cloaked two-year-old is throwing up soy milk on you at a patchouli-scented barbecue where you're trying to eat a limp, flaccid, tasteless tofu dog on a spelt bun that weighs as much as an adult human head and is as dense as most, too.

During her spying, Maye had, indeed, found several promising friend candidates, and had softly stalked them in an effort that was not only fruitless but became somewhat awkward when one of them turned and flatly asked if Maye was the one having an affair with her husband. Another woman had sent what Maye interpreted as a signal when they both reached for the same lone bottle of extra-fat caesar dressing. Maye laughed girlishly as she let her potential new friend steal away with the salad dressing, then laughed again several minutes later when they bumped carts in produce, an incident that spawned not a lifelong friendship but nearly a throw-down when Miss I-Am-Nimble-Enough-to-Snatch-the-Last-Bottle-of-Extra-Fat-Caesar-Dressing-yet-Lack-the-Coordination-Skills-Necessary-to-Steer-My-Cart sent her girlfriend over to metaphorically claim her territory as

Maye pretended to be mesmerized by carrots and tried her best to avoid a duel over the woman hiding behind the organic russet potatoes.

To amplify the situation to an eardrum-bursting level, Maye hadn't been getting many freelance jobs, and she realized she had actually spent more time following dessert-loving women around Whole Foods than she had working. While she had ample contacts in Phoenix, it had proved a little harder than she'd thought it would be to secure employment long-distance. So far, she had taken what she could get, which was copyediting a medical-insurance manual, which could tuck any brain in good night more effectively than Ambien and a pint of whiskey in combination. After that, Maye's days were essentially free for her to eat lunch alone, wander the public market by herself, and wait for her lawn man to show up and see if he had lost any teeth to decay and rot since the week before.

It was Charlie that broke Maye out of her fog of thought (not a second before it became a fully blown pity party with hats and horns) when he turned off the car and announced, "We're here!" Maye looked up to see that they had arrived at the pet-food store, where Mickey's obligatory obedience training class was held. Mickey, in the backseat, began to whine and pant with anticipation.

"He must recognize it from last week," Maye said with a laugh as she got out of the car. "He's so excited!"

Indeed, Mickey was. He barreled out of the car the moment Charlie opened the back door, and he charged toward the store with unbridled glee.

"At least someone's excited about this," Charlie spat out as Mickey dragged him along.

Unfortunately, Mickey's community-service requirement was not a friendship well from which Maye wanted to drink. Before their first class began, several unruly dogs and their owners had

sat in a circle of folding chairs in the center of the pet store, separated from shoppers merely by plastic mesh netting—and if
Mickey had not been ordered by the government to attend Bad
Dog School, she would have dragged him out of there as soon as
she saw who their fellow classmates were. Mad Dog, a "lively"
tiger-striped pit bull with yellow eyes, and his Hells Angel owner
were the dog/human pair Maye and Charlie saw as they entered
the mesh corral and sat down. The owner, who never made eye
contact with anyone, either by choice or lack of available coordi-
nation, provided the instructor with a genuine court order from
a judge, not a pansy-ass letter from the post office, due to Mad
Dog's midnight snack of a Domino's delivery guy's shin, which
required not only a skin graft but allegedly a prosthetic. The
Hells Angel now referred to the dog's presence in the class as
"doing time." The realization that the only thing protecting an
unsuspecting public from a dog that had digested a man's leg was
essentially a volleyball net was not only alarming but strangely
exciting when Maye wondered innocently if her mailman ever
shopped there. This clearly knocked Mickey right from the
equivalent of the Charles Manson of dogs to something along
the ranks of Ratso Rizzo, or a shady character out of *Lady and the
Tramp*. Speaking of Lady, the dog class provided two: Lady One,
as the class was required to call her, a Pomeranian terrified of
people who spent the first class hiding underneath her owner's
shirt—which Maye assessed was certainly a more gruesome
place than feeding time in a cell at the pound with Mad Dog—
shaking and crying; and Lady Two, a decaying cocker spaniel
whom the owner communicated with via baby talk and song.
Next up was Grand Duchess Anastasia, a bichon frise show-dog
hopeful who was not allowed near the other dogs per her uptight
and Lincoln Continental–driving and BluBlocker-wearing owner.
Then there was Sammy, Mickey's favorite, a nice but excitable
and wiry greyhound brought to class by his stripper mom, Peb-

bles, and her unfortunate eight-year-old son, who apparently was a product of a skinny dip in the shallow end of the gene pool or one egregiously faulty Friday-night judgment call—the child sported a large head and odd, bulging, Don Knotts eyes.

It was Charlie who had whispered in that first class, "If you slapped some orange paint and some water wings on that kid, he'd be Finding Nemo."

Halfway through that first class—as Lady One quaked under her owner's fat roll, the owner of Grand Duchess Anastasia simply refused to put her on the floor, where she might get dog germs; Lady Two sat once, then lay down and refused to get up; Sammy broke free of Finding Nemo's grip, easily soared over the volleyball net, and ran immediately to the cookie aisle; and Mad Dog was deciding which of their limbs looked fleshy and juiciest— Mickey became the star of the show. He sat on cue, shook paws, lay down, stayed when told. He was a good boy, as good as he was when he tackled Bigfoot to the ground to protect his master. Maye was proud, and now she was happy to see that her dog was eager to return. At least he had made a friend in Sammy.

Now, as Charlie, Maye, and Mickey approached the class corral, Sammy and Mickey came together like magnets, sniffed butts, and then immediately started playing.

"I have a sad announcement to make," said the dog trainer, the pert retirement-aged, Buster Brown–coiffed woman named Gwen. "Lady One has quit and will not be returning to class." She then dropped her arms straight to her side, cocked her head to the left, and contorted an exaggerated frown for two seconds until she perked back up and added, nodding to Lady Two and her owner, "But the good news is that Lady Two—Lady Two? Is she sleeping again? Well, she's alive at least, she just piddled underneath your chair there. Oh, golly. Oh boy. It just spread to your shoes. Well, Lady Two will now be known in class as Lady One!"

There was a smattering of applause, mostly emanating from Gwen herself.

"Couldn't she just be Lady?" asked the owner of the dog formerly known as Lady Two. "Just like she is in real life? She weawy wikes to be called by hew weal name, don't you, Wady? Don't you?"

"Poor First Lady One," Charlie said, shaking his head. "A dog-school dropout. Before you know it, she'll be pregnant with a litter and on federal assistance, just another sad statistic."

Maye burst out laughing, and even Mickey smiled, but everyone else just turned their heads and stared—everyone, that is, but Mad Dog's owner, who was too busy nibbling like a dirty squirrel on the filth from under his fingernails. Then the now-one-and-only Lady's owner bent down to Lady's tear-mucked face and cooed, " 'Wuv child, never meant to be . . .' "

Lady's drippy eyes barely opened as she lifted her head off the ground and responded with a "WooooOOOOOOO-OOHHHHHH!"

" 'Wuv child, always second best,' " Lady's keeper continued as Lady howled, far more on key than any of Maye's neighbors. " 'Wuv child, different from the rest!' "

"WoooooOOOOOOOOHHHHHHHHHHHHHHH!! Hoooo Hoooo!" Lady belted out.

"That's beautiful," Gwen spurted, given that the only accomplishment One and Only Lady had made in class was releasing her bladder.

"You should put that dog on TV!" Pebbles exclaimed (almost jumping up from her chair to find a pole to express her enthusiasm). "You'd make a million dollars! I swear! You'd make a million dollars! You could quit playing Lotto! I would, at least. I'd call David Letterman and put that dog on TV!"

"I wish Sammy could sing," Finding Nemo said woefully as he

moved his huge lips. "All he can do is jump a fence and lick his own nu-nu."

"Lady is singing the blues!" Charlie cried out, and again, only Maye laughed at her husband's joke as the rest of the class sat silently and looked puzzled.

"Woooo-hoooooo," another wayward howl began, and the class turned its collective head again, but this time all eyes were on Mickey. Apparently, not to be outdone except in the bloodlust category, Mickey had begun to howl, or rather, sing.

"Did you teach him that?" Charlie asked Maye, a look of wonderment on his face.

"Why would I teach our dog to howl?" she shot back. "Do you think I just sit at home all day, singing and howling with the dog?"

"I don't know," he replied with a little laugh. "You sat at home all day with the dog for almost a week trying to capture Bigfoot, and as a result, we are HERE."

"It's pack behavior," Gwen said. "Mickey is answering Lady's call. It's like doggie telephone. But Mickey has a beautiful voice, I must say. He's a tenor. There's even a hint of vibrato in there."

It was true, actually. Mickey was a pretty good howler, and he seemed like a natural.

"Sing, Sammy, sing!" Pebbles urged, nudging the greyhound with her knee, though he was otherwise occupied with his nu-nu. "Woooo-hoooooo! Woooo-hooooo, Sammy!"

"Did everyone bring their homework?" Gwen asked. "Last week I asked you to bring the toy your dog loves the most, the thing that is hardest to get away from him. Anyone? Anyone?"

Gwen looked over a sea of blank faces. "Sammy's people?" she asked the stripper, to which Finding Nemo replied sadly, "I forgot."

"Mad Dog's person?" Gwen continued.

"I woulda brought it, but that woulda been considered evidence," the biker answered in a voice laden with a lifetime of bad living and swallowing big bugs. "One thing's for sure, that pizza guy ain't usin' it. Hippity hoppity. Heh heh heh."

Gwen looked horrified, then moved on to Maye and Charlie, whom she stared at wide-eyed without saying anything.

"Um, well," stammered Maye, who had forgotten Mickey's ball. "You know, I put a pair of my dirty underwear in my purse, but Mickey ate his own homework on the way over here when I wasn't looking."

Gwen's lack of response to Maye's attempt at levity was a little less than pitiful, and she moved on to the next dog owner. Charlie donated the sock off his foot to substitute as the favorite toy, and it never really was established if Mickey dropped it because he was given the command or because it tasted like day-old foot cramped in a sneaker with fungicide sprayed all over it.

As soon as they got back to the car, Charlie turned on the radio and the three of them sang the whole way home.

🌱 🌱 🌱

The moment Maye opened the door, she knew something was wrong. The creaking of stairs, the groaning of old beams, the knocking of hot-water pipes, was all standard stuff in the little English cottage, but the hissing was not.

It sounded different. It sounded expensive.

Maye followed the sound directly to the kitchen, Mickey at her side. She carefully knelt down and then slowly opened the cabinet doors under the sink. And there the monster was—a quivering pipe that was spitting and dribbling water, and evidently had been for quite some time, flooding the whole bottom cabinet. Maye suddenly heard footsteps behind her, and Charlie crouched down to take a look at the impending disaster.

"That doesn't look good," he said, and before Maye could even emit the first three syllables of her scream, as in, "Charlie,

NO!" her husband's hand reached out and touched the pipe, which apparently was simply waiting for human contact with a man who knew nothing about plumbing before it actually erupted and began spraying water into the kitchen like a fountain at the Bellagio.

Maye's hair was dripping enough to melt the tissue-thin paper of the Yellow Pages together, and when the plumber arrived, it was still clinging to her skull like a lunch lady's hairnet.

"Hmmmm," the plumber said as he sprawled out in front of the kitchen sink and looked at the pipe. "Hmmmm."

Maye didn't say anything. She was too busy shooting Charlie death rays, although he knew all too well that they couldn't hurt him if he closed his eyes and pretended they weren't there.

"Not good," the plumber informed them gruffly. "You have old galvanized down there; it's coming apart like a celebrity marriage."

"How serious is it?" Maye asked, praying they had enough in the savings account to cover it.

"Well, it's not good, but it's nothing that can't be fixed," the plumber assured them, nodding toward Charlie. "Is he blind?"

"Not yet."

It took the plumber twenty minutes and a hearty check to fix the problem.

"I'm sorry, who should I make this out to?" Maye asked, pen poised in hand.

"Here you go," the plumber said, reaching into his shirt pocket and pulling out a business card. He handed it to Maye just as a burst of loud static shot through the room and made her jump. It even made Charlie open his eyes.

"Dispatch," the plumber informed them, as he reached into another pocket and pulled out what looked like a walkie-talkie. "Smith, 10-2."

"We've got a possible 11-26 over on Elm and Sixth," a garbled, nasally voice replied from the other end. "Can you respond? 10-4."

"Affirmative," the plumber confirmed into the walkie-talkie. "ETA four minutes, depending how fast this lady can write a check. 10-4."

It was then that Maye looked at the business card, which read clearly, "Big House Plumbing, John Smith. Drains, Restraining Orders, and Restaurant Recommendations."

She looked at the plumber and didn't know where to begin.

"I'm a cop during the day, a plumber at night, and I've been in every restaurant kitchen in this town," Officer Smith explained. "You wanna eat somewhere, you call me first. I'll let you know if it's okay. It's just a thing I do."

"Jade Garden?" Charlie asked of his favorite lunch joint near campus.

Officer Smith's face was suddenly awash in disgust as his mouth curled and he shook his head. "Everything you don't eat," he informed Charlie, "goes back in the pot. I wouldn't drink an unopened soda in a can from that place."

Maye didn't need the death rays for her flooded-kitchen revenge after all.

"God, I hope the toilet's working," Charlie said, sprinting toward the bathroom.

"Call me if it's not!" Officer Smith yelled after him as he took Maye's check and headed out to his squad car/plumber's van, where he took off his plaid flannel shirt and replaced it with a blue button-down with a shiny brass badge on it.

ψ   ψ   ψ

Maye and Mickey were learning the words to Nazareth's "Hair of the Dog" when the phone rang.

"So," Kate said into the receiver as soon as Maye picked it up. "Do you feel like having some company?"

"Are you kidding?" Maye absolutely squealed. "Are you serious? You're coming up? When? When can you come?"

Maye hadn't seen Kate since the night of the surprise going-away party. The prospect of having her friend come to visit was such a welcome and happy one that Maye fought hard against jumping up and down.

"How does end of the month sound?" Kate asked. "I have some time off coming and my boss wants me to take it, so I thought I'd head up for a visit. Sara's coming, too. She's got a week or two before she starts setting up her new restaurant. I think it's time for a road trip!"

"I am so excited," Maye's voice spilled with delight into the phone. "I can't believe I'll be seeing you guys in just a couple of weeks! Charlie will be excited, too. I am so happy!"

Having two of her friends to hang out with for several days was just the shot in the arm that Maye needed. She was so joyful that she didn't mind eating lunch alone that day, and she celebrated the good news by eating at a new café green-lighted by Officer Smith.

"I'd drink an open soda there, but stay away from the pork roast. It's a little dry, although a nice condiment like chutney would really fill that gap," he'd advised. "How's that pipe holdin'?"

"Holdin' strong," Maye had replied.

"Gotta go," Officer Smith clipped quickly. "Got a 10-98 happening here in broad daylight in front of the organic bakery!"

"Is that serious?" Maye asked.

"I've got a Prius obstructing a loading zone in front of the Hoo Doo Donuts," he intoned. "Now where am I going to park? After three of their donuts, you go straight to heaven. The rest of the day floats by like you're in a dream, even if you have to bust a meth lab and fight off a three-legged pit bull whose jaws are hanging off your right forearm! *Yes, it's serious.*"

🌱 🌱 🌱

My friends are coming, Maye sang in her head as the hostess at the clean café asked, "Only you?"

"Affirmative," she replied with a broad smile. "Only me."

Following the hostess, Maye passed a rack of free, local arts-and-entertainment periodicals and picked one up to read before her lunch came. The hostess showed her to the smallest table in the place, facing out onto Broadway, the main strip in Spaulding.

My friends are coming, she told herself again, smiling as she saw two older women across the street in front of the flower shop, walking together arm in arm and laughing and admiring a magnificent orchid so full of flowers it looked like it was blooming popcorn.

Table for three, please, Maye thought, and almost giggled at the wonderful phrase. She couldn't wait to show Kate and Sara her new town, with its incredible flower shop, the vast Saturday farmers' market that gobbled up most of downtown with produce stalls and craft booths, and the pine-tree-blanketed vistas from every direction, from every window, of her house. Spaulding was a wonderful place, she finally let herself believe. The streets were almost as perfect as movie sets, pristine and clean, lined with Victorian-era architecture and fronted with generous tree boughs that would transform into green, lush canopies over the pavement in the spring. Now that the leaves were changing into brilliant fall shades, she was eager for her friends to see it. Phoenix didn't have such seasons; when winter came, the blazing sun simply retreated a little, whatever flowers had survived through the brutal summer died, and the grass turned brown. That was it. Here, leaves exploded in bursts of yellow, crimson, and amber, almost as if they were the fireworks of the season, detonating in the last, major finale. The wind kicked up a little, carrying a slight chill like a single ice cube in a drink, and the leaves that had already fallen whipped, fluttered, and twirled down the sidewalks, then huddled together against the curbs. It was fall.

Maye decided that she loved fall.

She smiled again and opened the weekly that she had picked up, eager to see what might be happening in Spaulding in the weeks ahead that she and her friends could do. She must tell them to bring sweaters, she reminded herself as she flipped through the pages of newsprint. And scarves. Scarves were a mythological accessory to Phoenix residents, and in a few weeks, it could be cold enough to use them here. They could spend a day at the coast, she noted, and maybe even go to Mount St. Helens if it wasn't exploding and incinerating people into a poof of dust with a pyroclastic flow.

She came to a page of classifieds for groups and community clubs. Ugh, Maye thought, then continued on to the stripper ads. The picture of Pebbles with her head tilted back and eyes closed was indeed eye-grabbing, but Maye thought the ad would have been a little more tasteful if her classmate had opted to wear even a bra for the shot as opposed to the black rectangle that contained the word INAPPROPRIATE, which had been placed across her chest by the magazine's editors.

It was the last page of the publication, and as Maye hadn't even ordered yet, she flipped the page back again to kill more time. In a desperate attempt to look occupied, she scanned the listings for groups and clubs and was actually entertained by some of them.

"SACRED CREATIVE ART CLASSES," one of the listings read. "Solidify the spiritual passage that was your birth experience. Paints, brushes provided. Bring canvas and placenta."

Maye knew right then and there with a shudder that she'd be ordering a salad.

"MEAN LIBRARIAN," another boldly proclaimed. "Deviant and desperate. I'm allergic to wheat, soy, and strong scents, but intrepid otherwise. Wanna check me out?"

"No, I do not," Maye clipped out loud. "Sorry. Can't take a guilt trip every time I have the craving to eat soy in front of you or light a green tea candle. I can't go for that. No can do."

"DHARMA FRIENDS Irish Eskimo raised by Mexican babysitters has been blessed by the company and cultures of many and seeks friends who practice Buddhist Dharma."

I hated Dharma, Maye thought. I thought that show was canceled.

"ARTISTS COMMUNITY, permaculture project. CLOTH-ING OPTIONAL diverse household seeking like-minded house-mates. NO NEGATIVE ENERGY!"

My God, Maye thought. No wonder I can't find friends in this place. The people here are a bunch of naked, mean Eskimo li-brarians who keep their afterbirth in a Rubbermaid container in their purses. Where are the ladies looking at the orchid? I want to be friends with them, she told herself, just as soon as I check the contents of their handbags.

"Open-minded followers of Gothic literature wanted for book group," another entry read. "Let's discuss theory, study, and most importantly, craft!"

"Hmmm," Maye hummed. Could be interesting. Certainly more interesting than nude permaculturing, whatever that is. Maye loved Gothic lit; in college she'd taken every course she could that pertained to the genre. This could be something, she thought; she'd love to read all of her old favorites again— Mary Shelley, Edgar Allan Poe, Edith Wharton, Bram Stoker. She felt herself getting a little excited, a little hopeful. Some peo-ple don't like the shock and cringe-inducing elements of Gothic lit, she thought; you have to be open-minded to accept and explore some of those themes, although when Maye reread the phrase "open-minded," it suddenly took on another, more Spaulding-like meaning: no conservatives, no Republicans.

Got it, she understood; I fit that. She took out a pen from her purse, which contained no organs or body parts, spiritual or otherwise, and circled the ad in a swish of bright red ink.

5

Bothered and Bewildered

It was a known fact that Maye could not enter a bookstore without reaching the red alert danger level within a mere thirty minutes. Although she chastised Charlie for his boxes upon boxes of books when she was packing, Maye was every bit as guilty of the identical crime; she simply hid her addiction better and was far more talented at being sneaky. In Phoenix, she concealed her overflow books in closets and drawers, by double-parking them in bookcases and hiding them in filing cabinets. In Spaulding, however, it proved more tricky to secure good hiding places, particularly because Maye had to hide her addiction to the printed word by draping her books in camouflage, lest Charlie stumble upon the hidden booty, open them, and out Maye as the book whore she indeed was. As a result, there was an unusually high number of boxes labeled PERIOD SUPPLIES, MAKEUP, and MONISTAT-7, just to throw Charlie off the trail. It was a dicey maneuver, however, and Maye was nearly discovered early one evening when Charlie looked at her after she had been in the house for five days in a row because she said there was no reason to go anywhere.

"You know," he said carefully, "if I had a purple sweat suit, I'd wear it a lot, too, but whaddya say we freshen it up in the washing machine and break into one of the time capsules in your pyramid of makeup boxes in the basement? Because even though I'm not a meal psychic, I can tell that you had teriyaki chicken today for lunch and ham on rye yesterday because a dollop of Dijon mustard is encrusting part of the zipper on your hoodie and a soy-sauce-stained grain of rice is glued to the drawstring. There is a Hometown Buffet on your boobs, Maye. The only thing separating you from the lady who lives under the old oak tree on campus is four dogs, a shopping cart, and the fact that it looked like she washed up yesterday, even if that means sticking her head in the drinking fountain. There has to be a good amount of pretty in any of those boxes—they weigh even more than your tampons."

Maye was thinking precisely of that narrow escape as she hauled around fifteen pounds of books at the bookstore, roaming from section to section as the crook of her arm became red and sweaty with her treasures. She thought of how she had to run to cut Charlie off at the pass, lodging her dirty self in the doorway of the basement to prevent her husband from discovering her nest of deception.

"I wouldn't go down there, Charlie!" Maye warned, preparing to strike at her husband's most tender, vulnerable fear. "I went to get a tampon today, and I saw a spider sitting on the pyramid that was so big that if we caught it and had it taxidermied, we could use it as a Halloween costume. Big as your head, Charlie. It stared at me and I swore it said, 'Hello, little girl. Super or regular-absorbency?' "

"*Spider?*" Charlie barely hissed as he backed away from the door.

"The kind you only see on Discovery Channel, like jumping ones," Maye added in a strike worthy of the devil, since she knew Charlie's most repulsive moment of life came in the seventh grade when he woke up and felt a daddy longlegs about to attempt a little spelunking into the mysterious warm cavern that was Charlie's mouth. "And I think it was laying eggs."

Charlie gasped silently and covered his mouth after emitting a short, tiny yelp. "Spider babies," he wheezed as he stumbled backward until he collapsed onto one of the benches in the breakfast nook. "I can't go down there. I'm sorry, I can't."

"It's okay, Charlie," Maye said. "I'll just have to pretty up with some berries and charcoal sticks I find around the house."

It was a slim getaway, Maye admitted, and looked at the books in her arms as if they were a fifteen-pound bundle of joy that shared half of her DNA and would end up hating her like no other and plucking money from her purse in a little over a decade.

"Oh, books," Maye cooed, caressing them softly. "I have to give you up because of my shame. I can't bring you home. He would never understand." She abandoned them sadly, reshelving each one, and proceeded to the H section of fiction, which was why she was there in the first place.

Still reeling from the happy news that her friends were about to visit, Maye had optimistically taken a chance and answered the ad for the Gothic book club. When the club's leader, Crystal, e-mailed in reply to Maye's inquiry, she seemed kind and nice and was especially welcoming when Maye e-mailed back that she was basically a disciple of all Gothic literature and would spend her life devoted to the craft if she didn't need to earn a living.

"A devoted reader and willingness to explore the text is exactly what we're looking for," Crystal replied. "We want someone who's really going to feel free to examine the possibilities."

"Ooooooooh!" Maye cried upon reading this, delighted that she had found someone in Spaulding she had something in common with. She imagined spending the evening deconstructing Henry James's short story "The Altar of the Dead" or anything by the Brontës. Toss in some brownies and you have heaven, Maye thought, glad she had taken the step to answer the ad. She was therefore a little disappointed when Crystal e-mailed several days later that the next selection the club would embark on was *Practical Magic.* Maye had read the book—a fun one about two sisters who work magic for and against their best interests—years ago and had enjoyed it, although it wasn't exactly what she'd hoped for for the club. She had lent her copy to Sara, who still had it, something Maye was glad about when it was time to move. Maybe I can suggest a more Gothic book for the next reading, Maye thought to herself as she sat in front of her computer screen after reading the e-mail, realizing that Crystal had spelled *magic* wrong, adding a *k* at the end. It's a reader's club, she reminded herself, not a copy editor's club.

"Anyone can make a typo, stop being so damn snotty," she said out loud as she stood up, grabbed her car keys, and headed out to the bookstore. "Maybe Crystal learned to read with Hooked on Phonics."

Now, scanning the "H" section, Maye found *Practical Magic* by Alice Hoffman, pulled it from the shelf, and frowned. There, on the cover, were pictures of Nicole Kidman and Sandra Bullock from the movie version of the book. The copy Sara still had was a hardback and had on its cover a lovely Pre-Raphaelite Dante Gabriel Rossetti portrait of the mythical Proserpine, who was taken to Hades from her home in Sicily by a lovestruck Pluto, and was cursed to spend half the year there because she ate a pomegranate, which in the portrait she holds in her hand. Maye had loved that image—it was why she'd bought the book in the first place—and now she looked with scorn at the cover of this edition. She hesitated for a moment, debating whether she should return the movie cover book to the shelf and head to another bookstore, but she put aside her book cover snottiness and headed to the cashier, passing by three more books that she wanted in the ten steps it took to get there. Maye put the mass-market paperback on the counter and reached into her purse for her wallet.

"*Practical Magic,* huh?" commented the cashier, a woman who looked to be about Maye's age. "This is a quirky little book. I bet you'll like it."

"Oh, I read it already, years ago," Maye replied as she pulled out her credit card. "I joined a Gothic lit book club and this is the first selection, so I figured I should get another copy."

"Gothic lit?" the cashier questioned. "And they picked this? That is a little puzzling."

Maye nodded. "I agree," she said with relief. "I was expecting something different, I guess hoping for something more like Shelley, or even Sir Arthur Conan Doyle. I mean, I liked the book, the movie was okay, but it's not really what I think of when I think classic Gothic literature."

"Are you sure you didn't join the club for books with movie-poster covers?" the cashier joked. "If *Memoirs of a Geisha* or *The Devil Wears Prada* is the next choice, I'd run for the hills if I were you."

Maye laughed. "I know," she said, shaking her head. "I just— I'm new in town, I really don't know anyone, and I thought this would be a good way to meet people. In this town it's a little hard to do that, for some reason."

"Tell me about it," the cashier laughed. "I just moved here, too, and the only people I've met are the people who work here. It is a hard place to make friends."

"I know! I work at home," Maye continued. "So my exposure to civilization is rather limited."

"What do you do that you get to work at home?" the cashier asked.

"Oh," Maye said blithely. "You know. Phone sex, because honestly, desperate men just really want to talk."

"Then you should be meeting plenty of people," the cashier said, laughing.

Maye laughed, too. "None that I want to invite over for a barbecue. I'm a reporter. Well, I *was* a reporter. I *was*. Now I'm freelance, just writing. This and that, whatever I can get my hands on."

"You're kidding me!" the cashier cried. "I'm a writer, too, and I worked at a newspaper. I was the food critic for the *Aspen Sentinel*! I thought I could get something at the paper here when I moved, but no dice. So I'm a bookstore manager slinging books. Could be worse—I could be a phone-sex worker. I'm Bonnie, by the way."

"I'm Maye," she replied, and held out her hand to shake Bonnie's. "It's nice to meet you."

"It's nice to meet anybody," Bonnie added with a chuckle.

"It sure is," Maye said, and signed her credit card receipt.

"Enjoy the book," Bonnie said as she handed Maye a bag. "Again."

Maye nodded and thought for a moment about asking Bonnie if she'd like to grab a coffee sometime, and suddenly felt like an adolescent boy at prom time. Could she ask Bonnie out on a friend date? Would that seem too forward? Was it pushy, was it needy? Should she just play hard to get instead? Would she have to pay for the coffees? Did Bonnie even really like her, or was Maye reading something into the situation that wasn't really there? Was there something between them, or was Maye imagining it? And who asks a cashier out after a fifteen-second conversation, anyway? A pervert, Maye's mother would say, that's who! She'll think I'm a weirdo, Maye concluded, plus, what if she said no? What will I do then? Never be able to come back to the bookstore to feed my degenerate book thirst, Maye decided, and smiled at Bonnie instead.

"Thanks," she said and waved quickly before heading out the door.

ゆ ゆ ゆ

With her copy of *Practical Magic* nestled in her purse, Maye rang Crystal's doorbell and then waited, pulling her coat tight around her. The autumn winds had backed down a little to make room for a quickly approaching winter chill as Spaulding's trademark green landscape succumbed to rusty-colored branches and fallen leaves everywhere. Outside Crystal's house, tall, browning weeds had grown up and through every opening in the front walk; the house matched the ragged, spotty lawn and the front door, which looked like it had been kicked more times than a bad habit. Maye noticed a barrage of stickers covering not only the bumper but also the back window on a beat-up old Volkswagen Jetta with rust gobbling up its wheel wells. BACK OFF, I'M A GODDESS, Maye read quietly, mouthing the words. ANKH IF YOU LOVE ISIS. WHO'S DRIVING: YOU OR YOUR ADDICT? She was still shivering from that last one when the door swung open suddenly and a generously shaped woman in her fifties wearing a shiny black-and-purple corset smiled at Maye, her face covered in glittery sparkles. Maye had had no idea what to expect from the book club, but she did know one thing; she didn't expect to be the only participant not dressed as an eighteenth-century pub wench on her way to a rave. Maye looked down at her own below-the-knee, tan corduroy skirt, her now famous vintage sweater, and her black leather Mary Janes as she took her coat off and felt a little Republican when she saw that the rest of the club was swathed in some sort of flowy gauzy or velvet ensemble, mostly the color of night. Some people, Maye thought as she entered the room and was struck by the parfum de multiple cats, never grow past that *Bella Donna* stage of 1981. It looks like a Stevie Nicks impersonator night at the casino in here. Although, truth be told, a casino, even one on the old strip in Las Vegas with fifty years of cigarette smoke and beer spilled into the carpet, would smell better.

Maye smiled and met the other members: Raven, a tall, pale woman with long, jet-black hair worthy of a part in Mrs. Gelding's production of *The Mikado;* Star, a shorter, very cheery girl in her early twenties who had the figure of a dinner roll and wore a large pot-metal pendant of a dragon around her neck and a bicycle helmet; and Glinda, a middle-aged woman with symbolic celtic tattoos around both wrists and the dryest hair Maye had ever seen that was not sprouted from the head of a Barbie lying naked in a Goodwill bin.

Crystal seemed very pleasant, as did all of the women, really, despite their vampiric taste in apparel. But that's Gothic for you, Maye thought; everyone interprets spooky and creepy in their own way. To one person, it's Catholicism; to another, it's a pierced lip. Crystal kindly offered Maye a seat on her sheet-draped futon couch next to Raven, who smiled politely and passed Maye a tray of Triscuits with an accompanying self-serve can of spray cheese. Maye sat down and made the small talk required when you meet new people with whom you have barely one thing in common, aside from the fact that you're all mammalian, although in this case several of them may have believed themselves to be immortal.

Raven, it turned out, worked at a chain video store; Glinda sustained herself and her body art on disability checks and face painting at street fairs; Star, for whom Maye was still waiting to remove her sparkly silver-and-purple helmet, worked in produce at Fred Meyer; and Crystal made jewelry that she sold over the Internet.

"Oh, that sounds fun," Maye commented. "What kind of jewelry do you make?"

Crystal turned to Star, who picked up the dragon around her neck and jiggled it. The sound-activated chip inside it made a tiny roar that sounded more like a dragon fart and two red dots on the sides of the dragon's head faintly lit up, flickered, then faded away.

"It's interactive," Crystal said, smiling proudly.

"Wow," Maye said as she nodded slowly.

"If you'd like to buy some, I can come to your house and do a show," Crystal offered as she squirted what looked like a star of spray cheese onto her Triscuit. "You can invite all of your friends, and you get the dragon as a hostess gift."

"Well," Maye started, finally glad for her status as loner. "It's a shame I don't have any. When I get some, I'll let you know."

"Great!" Crystal clapped, and then paused. "How about we begin our meeting! As you all know, we have a new member, Maye. Welcome. I hope you all liked the book this month, and if you all want to make a mental list of books you'd like the club to read in the upcoming months, Maye, we can talk about that afterward."

"That would be great," Maye replied excitedly. "I have a couple of ideas."

"Well, let's talk about the book we did read!" Crystal exclaimed, and the five women reached for their books. Maye bent down, grabbed the copy of *Practical Magic* from the side pocket of her purse, and put it on her lap. When she looked up, she scanned the room and did not see Nicole Kidman. Or Sandra Bullock. Or Proserpine holding a pomegranate. She didn't see any of that. In fact, the book cover that the rest of the club had was a deep blue with no illustration aside from a large pentagram. And in the title, *magic* was indeed spelled with a *k*.

And instead of the words on the cover reading "Now a major motion picture!" theirs said, *Complete Book of Witchcraft.*

"Um," Maye said, and she scratched her head, which had suddenly begun to itch as she was engulfed by anxiety and the primal instinct to flee. "I didn't see that one at the store."

"Nicole Kidman is a Wiccan?" Star said from under her helmet as she squinted at the cover of Maye's book. "I thought she was in that weird cult with John Travolta."

"I guess I read a different book," Maye said and tried to laugh. "I read the wrong book. I'm sorry. I think I should go."

"Oh, don't worry about the book," Crystal said as she leaned over and patted Maye on the knee reassuringly. "That's silly. The book is just a portion of what brings us together. We have some fun things planned for the evening. Have you ever danced around a bonfire? There's nothing as spine-tingling as prancing around flames as the shadows lick your bare skin! It's exhilarating. You would look like a fairy goddess if we just brushed a little bit of glitter across your face."

"I'm not very good at dancing or cavorting," Maye stuttered. "Bonfire, Macarena, that cowboy achy-breaky dance, I really can't even skip. It would just end up disrespecting you and your whole . . . um, book coven."

"You get to pick a new craft name," Star, otherwise known as Tiffani in her Fred Meyer life, said.

"And then we get to give you a bath," said Glinda, whose disability checks bore the name Lou Ann. "And then the glitter."

"We will need a lock of your hair," added Raven, who had a Blockbuster employee badge with BETH etched into the plastic settled at the bottom of her purse. "We can take it from the back. You can't even notice mine, and Glinda took a huge chunk."

"You were squirming," Glinda protested.

"I am *ticklish,*" Raven replied sternly.

"I'm not ticklish," Star interrupted in a huff. "And I still have to wear my helmet. What if my mom thought someone at school did it and asked my principal? What would I do then? She thinks I'm unloading an extra truckload of beets right now!"

"Thank you for the Triscuits, Crystal," Maye said as she picked up her purse and stood, her corduroy skirt a virtual trap for six different types of cat hair. "But I really should go. You're not going to try to put me in an oven, are you?"

"Don't be ridiculous," Crystal replied. "You're far too big, and besides, my gas just got shut off."

Then Crystal stood up, too, and for a moment Maye was alarmed that the sparkly woman in her corset was going to cast some sort of spell that either would leave Maye paralyzed and unable to move or scream while four strange minimum-wage workers in velvet gave her an unwanted and unneeded bath or would transform her into a crow and she'd have to fly home and try to communicate to Charlie through caws and pecks that he was now married to someone who had the ability to shit on his head.

But Crystal didn't do that. She didn't wiggle her nose, break out a magic staff, or throw a ball of fire at Maye. Instead, she looked at Maye with her shimmery face that from a distance looked not so much like it was sprinkled with glitter as it did like she had stood over a deep fryer for an entire shift and said softly, "Thank you for coming. I'm sorry for the misunderstanding. I thought we were on the same page."

"Well, I thought so, too, but yours has a . . . pentagram on it. Thank you very much for having me over," Maye replied. "I hope the bonfire is fun. It seems a little cold to be dancing out there . . . with nothing on."

"Oh," Crystal said, laughing slightly. "We stick to the rules. Even though this is coat season, we are in all of nature's glory underneath."

"How about just a little glitter? I have purple and silver . . ." Star called out a second before Maye shut the front door behind her and started walking to her car. As she drove away, she noticed one particularly large bumper sticker on Crystal's car that she hadn't seen before. SORRY I MISSED CHURCH, it proclaimed in red letters, I WAS BUSY PRACTICING WITCHCRAFT AND BECOMING A LESBIAN.

6

Cows Are Pretty

The phone was ringing when Maye got home, and she just managed to unlock the door and get to it before the answering machine picked up.

"Oh, I'm so glad I caught you," her friend Kate said into the other end of the phone. "I didn't want to leave a message."

"What's up?" Maye asked, now completely perked up after spending an unexpected and alarming evening in the company of witches, eating the chief witch's Triscuits. "Are you wondering what to bring? Well, dress warmly, it's getting pretty cold here, but it will be a nice break from Phoenix. I can't believe you'll be here on Friday!"

"Well, that's the thing," Kate said. "I have to go to Wisconsin. My mom is going to have surgery—it's just a gallbladder thing, strictly routine, nothing serious—but I need to be there, she's going to need help. I'm so sorry. Being there will use up all of my vacation time, so I won't be able to come a little later, either. Are you mad? I'm so sorry."

"No, of course I'm not mad," Maye replied, her happiness fading as quickly as it had arrived. "I hope your mom is okay. I'm sure she'll be fine. You completely need to be there, I fully understand. Is Sara still coming?"

"I don't think so; there have been some complications with the restaurant," Kate answered. "Contractors are flaky, everything is behind schedule, she's a nervous wreck. I was going to make her go anyway, but now that I can't go, I doubt she'll take the trip by herself. I really am sorry."

"Please don't be sorry," Maye said. "I'm the one who moved away. You need to be with your mom. That's the most important thing."

Mickey came over and leaned against Maye's leg as she hung up the phone. He nudged her hand, looked up at her, and whined, his speckled face offering up as much consolation as he could.

" 'Did you ever know that you're my hero?' " Maye sang melodramatically to him.

"WOOOOOOOOOOOOOOOOOOOOOOO," Mickey responded.

"You're the wooooooooo beneath my wings, Mickey," she said, laughing as he panted.

ᚼ ᚼ ᚼ

Outside the bookstore, Maye parked her car, put the money in the meter, and with the movie-cover version of *Practical Magic* in one hand and her receipt in the other, headed inside to return the book, thankful that she hadn't taken the time to reread it.

And ask Bonnie out on a coffee date. Her friends weren't coming to visit, her book cult meeting had almost read like an Edgar Allan Poe short story, with Maye as the victim, and she had nothing to lose. Maye was absolutely friendless, with no prospects and fewer options for finding any. She was determined not to spend her life in Spaulding watching from across the street as two old friends, arm in arm, admired an orchid. She wanted to *be* one of those friends.

She pushed open the door, and with a whoosh the cold air swirled in around her and the covers of the magazines nearest the door fluttered. Immediately she saw Bonnie, who was behind the register writing something down, so she put the book on the counter and said, "I'd like to exchange this book for *The Idiot's Guide to the Phone Sex Worker Industry*, please."

"Excuse me?" Bonnie said as her head shot up. She saw Maye and laughed.

"If you don't have a copy of that, I'll take *The Jackass's Guide to Making Friends Without Having to Join a Book Club Coven*," Maye joked.

"No!" Bonnie said incredulously. "You're kidding. That's crazy! The book club was a coven?"

"I wish I was kidding," Maye said. "They wanted to give me a bath and then cut off chunks of my hair. They were a bunch of witches. I mean, they were nice little witches, but they didn't look as fun to hang out with as the ones on *Charmed*. There was also talk of dancing naked under their North Face coats around a bonfire. I guess it's hard being a naked bonfire cavorter this far above the equator. Excessive body hair can only keep you so warm. Thank goodness I escaped with the minor casualty of my skirt being swallowed by cat fur, but my soul is still mine."

"Oh, you're lucky," Bonnie commented. "I once went to a block party but first had to watch an hour-long demonstration on how to compost responsibly by my hippie neighbors. A fight broke out about whether a bin or a tumbler was the most effective way, and the bin advocate threw a brick of soy cheese at the tumbler enthusiast, who then tried to stab the bin advocate with a stick of burning incense, but no one got hurt because it was all ash. Then someone claimed that the hamburgers really were hamburgers and not bean burgers, tears were shed, someone else got banished from the drum circle, I ended up with hummus in my hair, and my head smelled like a sphere of garlic for days."

"Wow, that sounds amazing," Maye commented. "Which one of the dueling composters lived in a rainbow house?"

"They both did, one on either side of the street, which I think caused the competition in the first place," Bonnie said as she picked up the receipt and typed the item number into the cash register. "Well, let's get this copy of *Practical Magic* off your hands. I guess they were reading *Practical Magick: The Complete Book of Witchcraft*, huh?"

"Blue book, giant pentagram on the cover?" Maye asked.

"That's the one," Bonnie laughed. "Bibbity bobbity boo."

"We should have lunch sometime," Maye blurted out.

"I would love to, but I don't eat lunch," Bonnie explained, and Maye instantly felt stupid for asking for a friend date, for even entertaining the thought of forging a possible Mary/Rhoda connection. Maye smiled and nodded, pretending that she understood, but she was embarrassed and hurt and she wanted to leave. "We don't have enough staff to cover lunches, and I'm the only full-time person," Bonnie continued. "But . . . there's always dinner. Whaddya say? There's a new Spanish-style place I'd like to try out, very chichi. Which is not exactly my style, but I'd like to see what Spaulding chichi is. It may just mean cloth napkins and soap in the bathroom."

"I'd love to, that sounds great," Maye said, grateful to be redeemed. "I'll call my plumber and get the okay." Bonnie looked puzzled. "Trust me on this one, I know you were a food critic, but he's never wrong," Maye told her.

"How about Friday?" Bonnie asked. "Depending on what the plumber and his crystal plunger say."

"Perfect," Maye agreed. Charlie had a faculty dinner to entertain a visiting professor on Friday, and dinner with Bonnie would kind of take the sting out of not seeing Kate and Sara that day. "That would be great."

It couldn't have worked out better if Maye had cast a spell herself.

⚡ ⚡ ⚡

Maye had just walked out of the bookstore with a dinner date and three new books hidden in her purse when she ran into a crowd of people chattering and laughing on the sidewalk between her car and the vegetarian salad-only restaurant, Let Us, next door. She got out her keys and wove between as many people as she could to get to her car, but it was like trying to fight your way through the crowd on a day that free rain barrels were being given out. "Excuse me, excuse me, excuse me," she chanted repeatedly, and she'd gotten as far as the driver's side door when a round of cheers suddenly erupted and the people in front of her began to move and the people behind her began to push. She tried not to panic as she was moved along with the herd, holding on to her purse and reassuring herself that she was not going to get trampled to death outside of a bookstore and a salad-only restaurant. She might get a Teva imprint on her forehead, or tire tracks on her torso, but she told herself that she refused to die in a spontaneous lettuce stampede at the feet of Spaulding's vegetarians.

"You look startled," the graying older man next to her said as he took her elbow and gave her a cheery, full smile. "They did open the doors rather quickly. I'll help you in!"

"Why are there so many people?" Maye asked him as she was jousted about and tried to follow his lead.

"Oh, it's gonna be a big night," he replied, and helped her through the door.

Once inside, Maye found an empty spot near a back wall and hovered there for a bit, curious as to what the commotion was all

about. The crowd settled into the chairs around the dining tables, and the friendly man who had helped her in stood at the
front of the room and called for everyone's attention.

"Here," a woman at a table not far from Maye whispered.
"There's a chair over here! Come sit with us!"

That's awfully nice, Maye thought to herself as she smiled
back and took the seat.

"Welcome, everyone, welcome," the friendly man said. "I
heard we have some new members among us tonight, so I will introduce myself; I'm Bob, your Vegging Out facilitator. I'd like to
open tonight's meeting with a joke. How many vegans does it
take to change a lightbulb?"

"Two," the audience responded en chorus. "One to change it
and one to check for animal ingredients!"

They all laughed.

"Okay," Bob conceded, laughing heartily. "How 'bout this
one: How many vegetarians does it take to screw in a lightbulb?"

The crowd was quiet except for some murmuring. The man
looked pleased.

"I don't know!" he shouted. "But where do you get your protein?"

The audience bubbled over with hearty laughter. Even Maye
cracked a smile.

Vegetarians, she thought. Hmmmm. They seem nice and welcoming, pretty normal except for the sandal-sock combo in the
winter. Vegetarians would be kind and gentle. No one here
wants to bathe me. So far. They have a sense of humor about
themselves—that's always a very good sign. You don't have to
pick a vegetarian name, like Patty Pea or Tommy Tomato. This
could be good. This is good. This could work.

Aside from the fact that Maye was not a vegetarian. Not that
she didn't want to be, not that she didn't find it admirable, she
just found the menu rather . . . limiting. For Maye, cabbage

parmesan really couldn't take the place of chicken parmesan. A zucchini strip couldn't really compare to a New York strip. Mashed potatoes and gravy just wouldn't team up with buttermilk-fried tomatoes as it would with buttermilk-fried chicken. On Thanksgiving, she didn't want a slice of preformed soybean loaf snuggled up next to her cranberry sauce. And tofu balls would never be the same as meatballs, no matter what anybody said. Maye had attempted to eat a vegetarian hot dog once, and it was akin to biting into a rolled-out tube of Play-Doh. She frankly did not care that it was intestine casing that gave real hot dogs a little *pop!* on the bite; the limp, flaccid tofu dog seemed much more deceased that any Nathan's dog she had ever gobbled up.

Could she give up meat? she asked herself silently. Could she, if it meant gaining friends? She didn't eat meat every day anyway, maybe only every other day. She loved macaroni and cheese. Could she do it? Plus, cows are pretty, she reminded herself.

"Let me remind you all that the potluck dinner is next weekend, so please sign up for the vegetable that you are going to honor in your dish so that all of our vegetable friends may be represented," Bob continued.

Maye tried very hard to ignore that.

Then someone read a poem about a cucumber (Maye tried to ignore that, too), people discussed how they were going to celebrate National Soup Month, which was in January (ignore), the treasurer announced that the Vegging Out cookbooks were at the printers and would be delivered by the next meeting.

"And now," Bob announced, "is the moment we've all been waiting for! Thank you all for being so patient. After a count and recount, it is officially announced that the . . . drumroll, please . . ." Someone at one of the front tables, most likely one of Bonnie's dueling drum-circling neighbors, strummed his hands on the table to accelerate the excitement. "The vegetable of the month IS . . ."—he smiled as he tore open the envelope—"a BEET! It's a BEET!"

Half of the club clapped and cheered, while the other half scowled and grumbled.

"Why does the beet get it?" a woman with waist-length gray hair said as she stubbornly crossed her arms. "Beets are the unsexiest vegetable you can find! They're hairy, bumpy, and dirty, like my ex-husband!"

"Beets are beautiful," a woman in a poncho said. "They come in purple, pink, and white. How can anything purple and pink be ugly?"

"Well, there was Boris Yeltsin's nose . . ." a man from the back tossed in. He received a collective chuckle.

"And the inside of a sweet potato is the color of a tequila sunrise," the first woman bickered. "I was really campaigning for the sweet potato. I just don't feel like it's gotten its due respect. You can bake it, mash it, fry it, it's the chameleon of the winter, and it gets confused with its evil twin, the yam. It's versatile, it's fresh; the sweet potato is the new asparagus. I'm telling you. I read it in *Herbivore Today.* I just want to be ahead of the curve before everyone starts doing the sweet potato. We need to jump on this NOW."

"Maybe the sweet potato's time will come next month," Bob offered. "I see some new faces here. If we have potential new members, I'll leave the Vegging Out info sheets on this table right here. And now, the meeting is closed."

Maye sat back in her chair as the rest of the group stood up and milled about, socializing. She watched as they laughed, chatted, and exchanged earnest pleasantries like they were all old war buddies or school friends. I want that, Maye said to herself. Although there are benefits to having no one in town who knows you, like being able to go to the grocery store in the purple sweat suit with old rice clinging to the zipper, I want friends. I want to invite people over for dinner, even if it is only for a bunch of side dishes. I want to bump into people I know at the store instead of stalking them. I just want to be a part of something.

I want to know people. And these people seem so nice, except for the sweet potato advocate, who is apparently one beet away from staging her own sweet potato coup.

And just like that, Maye stood up, walked to the front of the room, and picked up a Vegging Out info sheet.

"Hmmmm," she heard a voice say from behind her. "Do we have another convert, or are you a beet hater, too?"

"Oh, no, I love beets," Maye said, laughing, as she turned around and faced Bob. "Roasted with goat cheese, olive oil, and a pinch of sea salt. Now *that* is sexy food."

"Whaddya think?" Bob said, flashing a bright, white smile. "Are you ready to join up?"

"I don't see why not," she decided, and nodded once.

"Okay then!" Bob cheered. "We have a short questionnaire to fill out. Ready?"

"Sure," Maye said.

"Why are you a vegetarian?" Bob asked.

"I think it's something I need to do right now," she answered, then suddenly added, "and cows are pretty."

"They *are* pretty," Bob agreed, still smiling. "Now, what kind of vegetarian are you?"

Maye was stumped. There were different kinds? Did he mean a sweet potato person or a beet lover? Did she have to profess an allegiance to a fruit and a vegetable? Or maybe there was a Greenpeace kind or a PETA kind? She was lost. She had no idea what kind of vegetarian she should lie to be. Vegetarians would know what kind they were. She had to answer—the danger of exposure was so close it was dancing on her fingertips. "Um," she stumbled. "The nice kind?"

"Well, it needs to be more specific than that," Bob said, laughing. "Are you demi/semi, pesco, lacto-ovo, ovo, lacto, vegan, macrobiotic, fruitarian, or not sure?"

Maye was stunned. She knew what vegan was, but everything else was a meatless mystery. *Ovo* made Maye think of ovaries, and although she wanted friends, that terrain was a little too personal. She knew *lacto* had something to do with milk, and if breast-feeding was involved here, especially on a community level, she was going to run faster than she did from the witch's house. *Lacto-ovo* sounded like it bordered on pornography, and *macrobiotic* seemed like it had something to do with a combination of economics and science, an emphasis Maye found even more distressing than the community breast-feeding.

"Not sure," Maye replied, figuring that being noncommittal was the best option. No one likes to be pigeonholed. Or beetholed, in a vegetarian's case.

"Does it bother you to watch others eat meat?" Bob asked, and Maye was thankful he'd moved on to the next question.

She bit her lip. She really wanted to say, "Oh, certainly, if the person can't close their mouth when they chew like my Uncle Ray since the accident," but instead she replied, "Absolutely. Like I said, cows are pretty."

"I feel that way, too," Bob said softly. "Last one. How long have you been a vegetarian?"

Maye thought for a moment. What was today? Tuesday? She hadn't had dinner yet, had a peanut-butter-and-jelly sandwich for lunch, and couldn't for the life of her remember what she'd eaten the day before.

"Seems like quite a while," she lied honestly.

"Well, congratulations, you're now a Vegging Outer," Bob said as he handed her a schedule of the month's club events and looked over her sheet of personal contact information. "We are happy to have you . . . Maye, is it?"

"Maye Roberts," she answered.

"Welcome, Maye Roberts," Bob said. "There's nothing in the world that makes me happier than finding another vegetarian."

"Thanks, Bob." Maye smiled and nodded, wondering if this was the sort of thing that a person might wind up going to hell for.

𝔶   𝔶   𝔶

Cucumber, cucumber,
Green, long and round,
Emerald of my garden,
Sleeping gemstone on the ground.

Cucumber, cucumber,
A versatile fruit is thee;
Brave and rugged in a salad
Or dainty sandwiches fit for tea.

Cucumber, cucumber,
Far too fine for the likes of smut
As any doctor will tell you
It doesn't belong in a butt.

Maye giggled as she recited the poem for Bonnie over a glass of wine.

"You are kidding," Bonnie replied with a grin on her face, then took the last sip from her wineglass. "Someone stood up and actually read that?"

"I couldn't make that up," Maye replied. "There was almost a fistfight over whether a beet or a sweet potato was more worthy of Vegetable of the Month!"

"Oh, sweet potato, definitely," Bonnie said as she falsely furrowed her brow. "Everyone knows it's the new asparagus!"

"Most of them were very nice, though," Maye added. "You should come with me to the next meeting. I think it's going to be a great way to meet people."

So far, on Maye and Bonnie's friend date, everything was going swimmingly at La Vaca Bonita, the Spanish restaurant Bonnie had heard about. Maye had gotten the A-OK from her plumber, who not only said he'd drink an open soda from the place but also strongly suggested the *filete poblano*, what he considered the strongest dish on the menu. "The layering of flavors is impeccable," he declared. "You'll dream about it for three days afterward."

So Maye followed his advice and ordered it, as did Bonnie. Over their second glass of wine, they talked about their former careers at newspapers, and Bonnie told Maye how she'd followed her TV-reporter boyfriend to town when he was offered an anchor position, only to have the relationship disintegrate within months.

"Wow, that must have been really hard for you," Maye said. "You didn't know anyone else in town?"

"Not a soul," Bonnie replied. "And not only do I have to see him on the news every night, but also the *whore* he left me for!"

Maye winced slightly. "Oh, I'm so sorry," she offered.

"Yeah." Bonnie nodded, taking another swig from her glass. "Doesn't get any more predictable than that. I was dumped for the weather girl. Fake boobs, bleached hair, nose job, you name it. The only original thing on that girl is her belly button, and I'm sure she has something shiny and cute dangling from *it*."

That would be horrible, Maye thought, if Charlie brought me up here and then dumped me for another professor, or worse, a grad student. What would she do then? Drink all the wine I could get my hands on and use the word *whore* as much as possible, she concluded.

Suddenly, Maye smelled something wonderful, and she looked

up to see their server set before each of them a dish of a steaming poblano-wrapped filet with roasted garlic mashed potatoes and last season's "it" vegetable, asparagus.

"I need another glass of wine," Bonnie said, with a somewhat curt flip of her hand toward the waiter. "This looks so good. I haven't eaten a thing all day. I'm starving!"

"Well, let's dig in," Maye said, her fork and knife poised to cut into the filet, which indeed looked incredible.

"Aw, I'm going to wait for my winc," Bonnie said. "I can't stand to eat without a drink."

Maye smiled, noticing that Bonnie seemed to have a nice little buzz going. Well, two glasses of wine on an empty stomach will do that to a hungry girl, she realized. She also realized it would be rude to begin eating without Bonnie, so Maye put down her fork and knife and waited.

And waited.

And waited.

After ten minutes had passed, Bonnie flagged down the server with a rather exaggerated wave and got his attention. "Wine?" she asked loudly, with a furrow of her brow and a shrug that was so overdone it belonged in a silent film.

"So sorry," the waiter apologized profusely. "You'll have it in two seconds!"

"ONE MISSISSIPPI," Bonnie replied in a tone that rather resembled shouting as he scurried away. "TWO MISSISSIPPI!"

Maye noticed that the diners at the next table stole a glance at them and then looked back with something of a smirk on their faces.

"THREE MISSISSIPPI!" Bonnie proclaimed even louder.

Other diners were looking at them, too, and if Bonnie noticed, she didn't care. She kept counting, louder and louder, until at "EIGHTEEN MISSISSIPPI," a full wineglass was delivered to their table and Bonnie smiled and then remained quiet. Until she cut into her very expensive, once delicious but now faded-into-a-lukewarm *filete poblano* and took her first bite.

"Ugh," Bonnie protested, and she slapped her fork and knife on the table. "Cold. It's cold. Is yours cold?"

"Mine's fine," Maye said, trying to bring her dinner partner down a notch, although her filet had become cold and coagulated. "It's great. I'm okay."

"Lie," Bonnie said disgustedly and began waving her hand again as she gulped down the new glass of wine. When the waiter heeded her call again, Bonnie pushed the rim of the plate toward him and declared, "This steak is cold. I would like it reheated. And hers, too."

"Nope," Maye said as she shook her head and cut her steak up as fast as she could. "I'm cool. Steak is good. I'm fine here."

"Are you sure?" the waiter asked as Maye began to chew vigorously. "I can take it back into the kitchen."

Sure, Maye thought to herself, so you can throw it on the floor, spit on it, stick your hands down your pants, and then fondle it? *No thank you.* I worked in a restaurant in high school, I know what happens to food that gets sent back, and it's not pretty and it's not nice, and it's not something I want to stick into my mouth. A cold steak is better than ass steak any day of the week, and if Little Miss Food Critic hasn't figured that out yet, let her think that after her food gets reheated, the curly black hair on her meat just fell out of her own head.

The waiter tried to grab Maye's plate, but Maye was quicker and stuck another huge bite into her mouth. "Please don't do that," she said, smiling and still chewing. "I'm armed."

"What can I do here?" a new voice said, and Maye looked up to find a nicely coiffed woman standing at their table with her hands cupped together. "I am the owner of La Vaca Bonita, and I sense that we may have a problem here?"

"Everything's great," Maye said, now mortified beyond belief because at this precise moment, her nice dinner experience at the new chichi restaurant in town had become the show. She was the entertainment for all of the other diners, who were scoffing and rolling their eyes at her because they weren't dining with a lightweight who had become positively lit after three glasses of wine on an empty stomach. Maye didn't want this, she hadn't asked for this, but now the owner of the restaurant was insisting that Maye send her steak back, and she was trying desperately to diffuse the situation.

"Really," she replied quietly and calmly to the owner, her face red with embarrassment. "I have no problems with my meal. It's wonderful. Thank you for offering, but I am very happy with what I have."

"Then please let me comp your dinner," the owner insisted.

As tempting as it sounded, Maye couldn't agree to that, either. It wasn't the restaurant's fault that Bonnie's blood alcohol had turned her into Zsa Zsa Gabor, that at any moment she could begin slapping people. Bonnie's behavior on a first friend date was so unacceptable that Maye was not only embarrassed but disappointed as well. All Maye really wanted to do was pay the check and flee. "No, thank you," Maye answered. "I can't let you do that."

And when Bonnie realized that she was alone in her hissy fit, the lone marcher in her anger parade, her face dropped and she began to stammer. "I'm okay, too," she said quickly. "My thteak is fine. I'm thorry."

"Please don't apologize," the owner said. "I want to make sure you have a good experience in my restaurant."

"I'm thorry," Bonnie said again. "I didn't mean to make it thuch a big deal."

"I understand," the owner responded. "I want everyone to be happy."

"I'm happy, I'm happy," Bonnie insisted. "I am. I'm very

happy. I'M THORRY, I. . . . I JUST THTARTED MY PE-
RIOD TODAY."

The restaurant became so quiet that Maye heard herself stop
chewing.

Maye didn't know what to do, if she should just throw a wad
of cash on the table and run like an anchorman who spent
too many nights apologizing to restaurant owners on behalf of
his blasted lady friend only to hook up with the weather girl instead, or if she should go to Bonnie's aid and pretend to be her
nurse.

But instead, she sat there, in complete silence, along with the
whole restaurant, including people from the kitchen who didn't
speak English, and watched the show's denouement. The audience was indeed, captive.

Several moments after the owner and waiter had silently and
carefully left the table and chatter was beginning to fill the restaurant, Bonnie looked at Maye and apologized.

"I'm thorry," she whispered. "I'm puffy and I have crampth.
Not even the wine helped. I'm ready for another glath."

You know, Maye thought, as desperate as I am, I just don't
have any openings on my friends list for a shit-faced woman with
hormone rages that should be measured on a Richter scale.
Thorry about that. She tried to smile, and that was when Maye
heard someone call her name, which was impossible since she essentially knew no one in this town. She thought she was certainly
imagining it until she heard it again.

"Maye?" a man's voice said. "Maye Roberts?"

Then she gasped.

She could not have been more alarmed if Satan himself had
traced his burning finger right up her spine.

And as she slightly crooked her neck in the direction of the
voice, she saw that it was not, thankfully, Dean Spaulding, who
had seen Maye do her Charo impersonation in the place where

he takes his meals when she was neither under the mind control of her menses cycle or had even had so much as one drink. No, it was not Dean Spaulding, and she felt a tremendous rush of relief until she realized that the man coming toward her with the wide white smile and the gray hair was Bob.

Vegging Out Bob.

"Hi, Bob," Maye said, suddenly slapping a fake smile on her face. "It's so nice to see you."

"Well, I was a couple of tables away when I heard about your friend's cramping issues," he said, and turned to Bonnie. "When you go home, nibble on some rose petals and place some warm, but not hot, banana leaves over your lower uterine area in a fan-like sequence. You should be right as rain by tomorrow! I just had the best chile relleno I've ever had in my life! The menu here for veggies is outstanding, isn't it? It's the most extensive one in town, which doesn't quite make up for the meatery that abounds, but I'm good at eating with my eyes closed—"

Bob suddenly stopped and stared at the chunk of meat impaled on the glistening spires of Maye's fork.

"Oh my," Bob said, as if all of the air had been sucked out of his lungs like a Seal-a-Meal bag. "Oh my God. How could you? How could you do that? How pretty was that cow, Maye Roberts? How pretty was that cow when you were chewing on her flesh like a zombie?"

For the second time within a matter of minutes, Maye didn't know what to say. The gig was up. The news was out. They've finally found me, she thought.

"You said you were VEGGIE-CURIOUS," Bob shrieked even louder than Bonnie had about her period. "But you neglected to mention that you were a KILLER!"

"I'm sorry, Bob," Maye began. "Everyone was so nice to me, and I . . . I just wanted to be a part of your group. I'm sorry I lied to you."

"Thee?" Bonnie slurred. "The's thorry. Hey, are you the guy with the big cucumber?"

"Liars are not welcome at the Beet Bonanza dinner," Bob shot back angrily. "And neither are the candied beets that they signed up to bring! We don't want your dirty food made by meat hands! You are excommunicated from Vegging Out, and I am hereby banning you forever!"

"I imagined you would," Maye replied. "I'm still really sorry."

"Your colon will pay for this, Maye Roberts," he warned. *"It will."*

"Actually, I've decided I'm making Bonnie do that," Maye said.

"I bet your cucumber ithn't that big," Bonnie declared as she swayed in the chair like a swami's cobra.

"CARNIVORE!" Bob yelled before stomping away.

"Check, please," Maye said calmly as she raised her hand, one step closer to securing a seat in a fiery hereafter. "I'd like to pay for my *meat*."

ϒ ϒ ϒ

After Bob stormed off to his own table and Maye had delivered Bonnie into the safety of a taxi, she got her car keys out and headed into the parking lot to make a not-very-clean getaway.

She was fifteen steps away from the driver's side door of her car when she heard her name being called again. Afraid that it was a mad mob of vegetarians come to tie her up with leeks and thrash her with carrots, Maye ignored the call and picked up her step.

"Maye!" she heard louder, this time determining it was a woman's voice, and almost broke into a run when she realized that she was probably being stalked by a bunch of glittering chubby women with frizzy hair straddling broomsticks, armed with Softsoap and an organic sea sponge.

"Please, leave me alone," Maye called, not turning around, decidedly focused on getting into her car. "Again, I've already bathed. Next time, catch me in the morning when I might be more receptive to your advances!"

"Maye!" the voice called out again. "Maye! I showed you thirty different houses before you finally bought one, the least you could do is stop running from me!"

"Patty?" Maye said as she stopped and turned around to see her Realtor almost jogging toward her with another woman Maye vaguely recognized. "Oh, thank goodness it's you!"

"Why are you running?" Patty asked, panting. "Is it because of Bob's little fit? He has those all the time! At the Spaulding Festival last year he saw a little girl eating a real hot dog, burst into tears, and then curled up into a fetal ball. People expect it from him."

"Oh, you saw that?" Maye said wincing. "Is the whole town eating at this one restaurant tonight?"

Patty laughed. "It's new, it's in, and no one's sick of it yet," she said, and then turned to her friend. "You remember Louise? We looked at her house before you moved here."

"Of course," Maye said, shaking Louise's hand. "The iris house! I loved your house! It's nice to see you again."

"Sorry to hear that your friend is under the weather," Louise commented.

"You heard that, too, huh?" Maye asked.

"Well, let's just say it was a little hard to ignore," Patty said diplomatically.

"She's not really my friend," Maye explained. "I was hoping things would work out, but tonight was our first little 'friend date,' and as you saw and heard, it didn't turn out so well. I simply cannot make a friend in this town. I have never had to actually go out and make friends before. Apparently, I'm not very good at it. It was easier for me to lasso a man, throw away all of his crappy furniture, and get him to marry me than it is to find someone just to have coffee with!"

"Ah, but there's a magic way to make friends in Spaulding," Louise said. "Plus you get to keep the crowns."

"I remember your crowns in the bookcases!" Maye cried.

"You should run for Sewer Pipe Queen," Louise and Patty said together.

"What?" she asked. "Why would I want to get into a sewer?"

"No, no, no," Patty explained. "You don't understand. The Spaulding Sewer Pipe Factory used to be the biggest one in the country. It built this town. A Sewer Pipe Queen is chosen every year and has been for almost a century to pay tribute to that accomplishment. Once you're a Sewer Pipe Queen, you're one for life. Those crowns are badges of honor. And Louise was one of Spaulding's favorites. She joggled for her talent segment!"

"Joggled?" Maye asked.

"Juggling and jogging simultaneously," Louise explained. "They don't have joggling in Phoenix?"

"Not that I was aware of, no," Maye replied carefully. "So the Sewer Pipe Queen is kind of like a 'Miss Spaulding'?"

"In a way," Patty answered. "But the rules have become pretty flexible. It's not like it was when I was a kid. Nowadays anyone can enter the pageant. The City Council thought it was sexist to discriminate against men and ageist to discriminate against kids or the elderly. You just wait and see this spring. The Sewer Pipe Queen coronation kicks off the Spaulding Festival. The whole town comes. It's a huge party for the entire weekend."

"You win that thing and you'll have friends for life. Everyone wants to know you. You're the queen! I was the queen twenty years ago, and I still can't shake Patty!" Louise laughed. "There are a couple of exceptions of course, but for the most part, a queen is the pride of the community. She'll attract more friends than a barbecue does homeless people in a park."

Maye's mind suddenly rewound to Cynthia's tea party, stocked heavily with friends, gathered in front of a fireplace with a portrait above it of the hostess being crowned, decades before.

"But I couldn't do that," Maye protested. "I couldn't enter a beauty pageant."

"It hasn't been a beauty pageant for decades," Louise informed her. "It's more about being vibrant and eclectic, it's about having a queen who's as fun and endearing as Spaulding is. The queen reflects the town. It's open to anybody willing to get on a stage and put on a good show in the name of amusement."

"So it's that easy? I just march up and join this pageant?" Maye asked skeptically.

"Well, not exactly," Louise explained. "You need to have a coach, or what they call a sponsor. A sponsor has the rank of Old Queen, a former queen who knows the ins and outs of the competition and can tell you what to work on, guide you through your training."

"Training?" Maye asked hesitantly.

"A person isn't born a joggler," Louise noted. "A good coach will bring out your natural talents and help you develop them."

"Who are you coaching this year?" Maye asked slyly.

"I'm not coaching anyone this year," Louise replied. "In the next pageant, I'm a celebrity judge!"

"Don't you know any Old Queens?" Patty asked. "They're all over the place."

"I'm not saying that I'm doing this, but I do know someone who might have been a Sewer Pipe Queen who lives across the street from me," Maye said. "Her name is Cynthia, but I don't know her last name."

Louise gasped. "Could it be Cynthia McMahon?" she asked.

Maye shrugged. "I don't know," Maye replied. "I just know her as Cynthia, my singing neighbor."

"I bet it's Cynthia McMahon," Patty snapped. "She was in the Silver Songbirds' production of *The Mikado* last year. That woman refuses to age!"

"That's her!" Maye said excitedly. "That's Cynthia! She was Pitti-Sing!"

"If I were you," Louise advised, "I'd walk across the street to-morrow morning and talk to her—that is, if she hasn't already taken someone on. Cynthia McMahon was one of the most ele-gant queens Spaulding has ever had. You'd be lucky to get her. She was very popular."

"I gathered that." Maye nodded and smiled.

"I think you should do it!" Patty exclaimed. "You're a shoo-in! You said no to thirty houses and I still liked you!"

"I don't know," Maye said. "I'll think about it."

She said good night to Patty and Louise, and gave the parking lot a quick glance to make sure no one else she had met, stalked, or exposed her cans to was hiding in the shadows before she drove home.

7

Suddenly, She Found
Herself There

As soon as Maye heard the backyard gate close and knew that Charlie had bicycled off to work, she opened the front door and headed across the street.

She had been thinking all night about the pageant and decided it wouldn't hurt to talk to Cynthia about it; besides, Maye was sure that she had probably taken on another contestant by now. She hadn't really decided if it was something she was ready to commit to, anyway. Had she honestly reached the point where she needed to make friends by becoming the town queen and forcing people to befriend her? Like royalty? She reasoned that maybe she should just take a pottery class at the recreation center but then realized her established margin of error was far too high. Her companion quest required vast quantities of people—with any group of fewer than twenty, her chances of finding someone friendship-worthy was cut significantly, almost to a guaranteed zero. Look at what had happened so far, she thought. No, she needed to reach a large population; she needed to send her message far and wide. Spread it to the masses. There *has* to be someone in this town who is like me, she told herself; there has to be a Spaulding version of Kate or Sara, and if I have to comb through this entire town I will do it to find her—if only I knew my own mating call. On Maye's own, it would take years, possibly decades; but if she presented herself to the whole town at once, her chances of remaining friendless and eating lunch alone would drop dramatically.

It wouldn't hurt just to talk to Cynthia, Maye thought to herself as she stepped off the curb into the street. Just to see what would be required, what it was like, what it involved. She hoped there was no swimsuit competition; that would nix the whole idea right there, unless she could show up wearing a swimsuit with a T-shirt and bike shorts over it. Maybe she could be convinced if she found a long-sleeved swimsuit. And if she had to dance and sing in a group opening number, she was definitely out. She could imagine herself dressed up like a flowing roll of toilet paper, a sequined toilet brush as scepter, and frankly, she would rather repeat her Charo dance in public than strut around onstage like a Ziegfeld Follies girl dressed as a glittery poop pipe.

Maye opened the gate of the cream-colored picket fence that fronted Cynthia's yard and heard the hinges groan with age. Charlie, Maye knew, would be a hard sell, and truly, who could blame him? She had already mortified him in front of his entire department, and now she might do the same thing in front of the whole town (although at the competition, she'd have a sniper in the audience to pick her off immediately and put her out of her misery in case one of her bare-naked fat rolls exposed itself to strangers). But Charlie had friends, Maye argued to herself; he had built-in friends at the university, and he had gotten close to several of them, going fishing on the weekends and catching a beer or two after the workday was over. Charlie didn't see an empty Spaulding the way she did. His days were filled with students, conferences, and university business. He had become one of the most popular professors on campus—not only with students but with faculty, too. Everywhere they went, they ran into people who knew him and liked him. Maye didn't have that. She only had the hope of one day finding a pal who had the good sense to eat a little bread before downing a bottle of wine and discussing her flow with waitstaff and diners at every table of the "in" restaurants in town.

Maye walked up the front steps to Cynthia's wide, wraparound, tongue-and-groove porch. At the front door, she reached up and knocked, knowing if she hesitated, she would never make the move. Within moments, Cynthia swung open the front door, presented her perfectly coiffed self, and invited Maye in as the scent of pageant-strength hair spray swirled in the air. "It's so good to see you!" she said warmly. "How did you know I was just about to take a trip over to your house?"

"Were you really?" Maye asked, surprised. "Were there dog-food cans in my trash again?"

"No, no, no," Cynthia said, wagging an almost wrinkleless finger crowned with pale pink nail polish. "But close! You had Styrofoam! I saw some peeking out of the container lid on the last trash day."

Maye didn't know how to blame this on Charlie, but she quickly tried to come up with something—"Due to the lack of sensory neurons in his hands, all solid white things feel like potatoes to him" or "Perhaps his absence of depth perception led him to believe it was a brick of solidified cottage cheese that teetered on biohazard status and needed to be discarded immediately or risk quarantine"—but truly, she had lied to Cynthia enough. So she told the truth. "I thought I read that Styrofoam couldn't be recycled," Maye said, wincing. "I thought it wasn't on the list of acceptable recyclable materials for our bins."

"Oh, it's not!" Cynthia said, nearly delightfully. "That's why we have Styrofoam Day. Everyone saves it and on one special day of the year, you're allowed to take it to the recycling center and they send it to a special Styrofoam-reuse plant!"

"You save your Styrofoam for a year?" Maye asked. "Packing materials, peanuts, the sheets of it you get in brand-new frames? All of it? You save it for a year?"

"Absolutely," Cynthia confirmed. "I have a whole room upstairs devoted to it. But you have to get a good spot on Styrofoam Day. People line up early."

"Like for Madonna tickets?" Maye asked. "Or a *Star Wars* movie?"

"Oh, no! You don't have to sleep on the sidewalk for this!" Cynthia laughed. "Goodness, could you imagine sleeping outside in the winter with all of these bags of ghost poop around you? No, no, no. Everyone lines up in their cars. That's where you sleep!"

"Wow," Maye said, somewhat startled. "I had no idea."

"Apparently," Cynthia declared. "Otherwise you wouldn't be throwing chunks of it away as you poison the earth. Now, Styrofoam Day is next Saturday, so make sure to mark your calendar and cancel any plans. Last year it took me seven hours to get to the front of the line! Would you like some organic donuts? I just came back from Hoo Doo Donuts, and they are truly outstanding. They only stay fresh for a day, and I have a whole dozen. After your first three, you literally buzz with delight."

"That's what I've heard. Thank you for asking, but I need to watch what I eat," Maye replied. "Because I actually came over to ask you about the Sewer Pipe Queen Pageant."

"It was a glorious time, glorious time," Cynthia chanted. "What was it that you wanted to know?"

"Well," Maye started, "I'm not exactly sure. Since we moved to Spaulding, I've had a hard time making friends, so my Realtor thinks it would be a good idea for me to compete so I can meet people and get more involved in the community."

"That's the perfect way to do it," Cynthia agreed, then confirmed what Maye had suspected. "This is a hard town to break. People have lived here for generations and generations. Cliques get formed, and people are very happy with what they've already got. People in the earthworm-tea composting club socialize with other earthworm-tea people. People in the unicyclists group tend to be attracted to other unicyclists—they wouldn't dare dream of becoming bi. The folks who are protesting field-burning pollution are consumed with that; you won't see them cavorting with the greenhouse-gas people who look for Expeditions, Hummers, and Yukons so they can slap an I DRIVE AN OVERSIZED CAR BECAUSE MY IGNORANCE HAS TO FIT IN, TOO bumper sticker on them. Most aren't looking to make new friends. Spaulding is a nice place, but it's a tight little town with plenty of causes, plights, and principles. Have you tried joining any groups or clubs?"

Maye nodded. "I was banned from Vegging Out because I was exposed as a carnivore while chewing a filet mignon, and my book club wanted to dance around a fire with only coats on," she said as simply as possible.

"Then, honestly speaking, my dear lonely neighbor, I think this may be your only shot," Cynthia informed her. "At the very least, if you don't win, you'll probably meet some nice people."

"But do you think I have a chance?" Maye asked. "I'm new, no one knows me here. I would think they'd want to pick a queen who has lived here for a while."

"I thought that, too," Cynthia said. "I was a very gawky girl growing up, didn't have many friends at all. My father moved us here when he got a job rebuilding the pipe factory. I was a senior in high school. Didn't know a soul. My mother saw how lonely I was, so she concocted a marvelous scheme. She said to me one day, 'You're going to enter that pageant, and you're going to win!' She was determined and sewed that dress you see right there in that picture by hand. Night after night with the needle and thread. After seeing her work so hard, there was no way I couldn't compete, so I did, and I won. And the day after I was crowned, I knew everyone in town and everyone knew me. Like I said, it was a glorious time."

"If I did enter, I would need a coach," Maye said gingerly. "I would need a former queen as a sponsor, and I was wondering if . . . if you might be willing to take me on. Should I decide to do this. And if you haven't already sponsored someone this year."

"As luck would have it," Cynthia said, smiling widely, "I was indeed supposed to sponsor Elsie's granddaughter for this year's competition after she returned from the Peace Corps. Between you and me, she would have been a shoo-in. She's just returned from Cameroon, and was planning to do this wonderful native dance for her talent segment, and it's performed almost in the nude! Apparently, it's typically danced by a man and a woman and the woman spends most of the time nearly doubled in half as the man holds her waist from behind. It was banned from being performed in that country because it's so provocative! She had to learn it in back alleys under the cover of night! Unfortunately, while she was there, she also drank some dirty water or ate a dirty animal and they found a tapeworm in her the size of a sea serpent. I won't tell you how they found it, either, except that you could see it at nighttime with a flashlight when it thought it was safe to come out by the back door."

Maye cringed.

"As you might guess, her condition isn't very conducive to dancing in the almost nude and bending over like that, lest her parasite should wiggle its head out. That could cause a stampede. So she decided to skip this competition until she can evict her visitor," Cynthia continued. "So that means I am available!"

"That's wonderful," Maye blurted. "Thank you so much."

"Ah, ah, ah," Cynthia warned, wagging her perfect pink-frosted finger again. "On one condition. I will need something from you."

"You need a ride to Styrofoam Day?" Maye asked.

The former queen laughed. "No," she said. "Elsie's grand-daughter also dropped out of our production of *H.M.S. Pinafore* because a rumor started that giant tapeworms are contagious, and you know how rumors go. Can't put them out with a fire extinguisher! So I have an opening for the role of Dick Deadeye. It's not a big part, only sings one song, but what do you say? Fair trade?"

Maye hadn't bargained for this, and she desperately, desperately, didn't want to do it. *Desperately.* But if Cynthia was willing to help her, she needed to be willing to help Cynthia. Plus, it was a step up from a chorus cop role. Fair was fair.

"I guess we have a deal." Maye smiled, and they shook on it in front of the fireplace, trading an Old Queen for a Dick.

ψ   ψ   ψ

"I have something to tell you," Maye said to Charlie that night when he came home from the university.

"I bet I have something worse to tell you," Charlie lobbed back, and he looked grim. This was assuredly bad news.

Ooooh, Maye thought. *Leverage.* What has Charlie done? Had he been touching the pipes in the basement, willy-nilly, causing them to explode, flooding all of it, and affording them only enough time to grab Mickey and a light snack and flee? Was Charlie a CIA agent about to be outed by the vice president? Maye looked at Charlie, and still he didn't say anything. This was worse than busted pipes. This was serious. "Charlie?" Maye began. "What is it?"

"I don't know how to say this," her husband said, shaking his head. "I've held off telling you for as long as possible, hoping I could get out of it. But I can't. I can't. It's important that you know I tried. Because I did. But I can't get out of it. I'm sorry."

What could it possibly be? she thought. Are there people buried in our backyard? The appearance of a love child from Charlie's forgotten past with an Eastern European maidservant? How bad could it be? "Well, what is it?" Maye asked. "I'm sure it can't be that big of a deal."

"We have to go to Dean Spaulding's for a holiday party," he blurted out so quickly it sounded like Morse code.

If Maye had an eighth of an ounce more of Lifetime Television for Women tendencies mixed into her DNA, she would have crumpled into a heap on the floor and immediately lapsed into a bad habit, like a cocaine addiction, become a high-class but self-loathing call girl, started a baby-stealing ring involving the Russian mob, or had a love child of her own, preferably not with an Eastern European maidservant.

But she didn't. However, a thought flickered across her mind, that she should claim that at the last faculty party, the woman they saw grunting and nearly nude doing a Cameroonian fertility dance in the Spauldings' dining room had been her evil and exhibitionist twin, Faye, while Maye was trying to escape from a PODS storage unit where Faye had imprisoned her after the surprising, yet if you really think about it, expected, kidnapping.

"Charlie," Maye said slowly. "I will let you touch every pipe in the house if I don't have to go. And then I'll let you tinker with the sprinkler system."

"I'm sorry, Maye," he replied woefully. "Dean Spaulding mentioned you specifically."

"Of course he did!" Maye shouted. "I'm cheap entertainment! I was the party stripper and I only cost him a gin and tonic! I didn't even get to eat after my show! You can't hire a homeless clown or one with felonies for as cheap as he got me. Please, Charlie. Please don't make me go."

"I told you I tried to get out of it," Charlie replied. "I even told him you were going to be in Phoenix, and he said he wanted to see the plane ticket!"

"Then I'll buy one," Maye said defiantly as she marched from the kitchen into her office and sat down at her Mac. "When is this party?" Charlie stood silently as Maye typed in the address of a travel website. "Well?" Maye asked, ready to punch in the date. "When is it?"

"Tomorrow," Charlie said, wincing.

"Charlie Roberts, I should have killed you when I had the chance!" Maye shrieked. "If I even got a flight out, it would be a thousand dollars, at least!"

He looked puzzled. "When did you have the chance to kill me?" he asked.

"Every time you have a screwdriver in your hands and I make you put on rubber-soled shoes, that's when!" Maye cried. "It's just a matter of time before you fall into a toaster or an electrical outlet! Tomorrow! Oh, Charlie, why didn't you tell me?"

"Maybe I was afraid you wouldn't take it well," he offered. "But I want you to be positive about this, okay? Think of this party as a second chance. Think of it as an opportunity to show them that Maye Roberts can keep her clothes on at a party and still have a good time. I'm sorry. But I really, really, *really* need you to go."

Then Maye, wicked, wicked Maye, in a move that was more characteristic of evil twin Faye, had a brilliant, exquisite, radiant, and surprising (but when you really thought about it, unsurprising) idea. And she borrowed a tip from her new mentor, Cynthia.

"I'll tell you what, Charlie," Maye said, pretending she had jet-black hair, brushed back and flipped at the ends, wore sunglasses and a leather jacket, and spoke in an English accent. "I'll trade you for it. Fair is fair, isn't it, darling?"

"What?" he asked. "How much salt did you eat today?"

"Let's trade. I'll go to your party," Maye clarified, "if you let me do one thing."

And that was how Charlie—well, he didn't really agree, but he didn't have as much veto power as he would have liked in a situation in which his wife had just told him she was planning to overthrow the town by staging a coup to its throne and making her royal subjects befriend her in the spirit of Queen Elizabeth I.

And it wasn't even her evil twin talking.

$$\text{🦌 🦌 🦌}$$

Maye was wearing the ugliest sweater she could possibly find at the mall, and that included scouring both of the shopping center's medieval stores. What she found was pure gold; it was kelly green and boasted not one badly knitted reindeer pulling Santa's sleigh but a pair of them, complete with real live bells on what was probably meant to be their harness but resembled more of a rope, suggesting the reindeer had escaped from their own lynching amid snowflakes the size of hubcaps, proportionately speaking. Reindeer number one particularly was in grave danger, as a boulder-sized chunk of hail was virtually an inch from crushing his little holiday skull. It was a wretched, horrible thing, fit a bit too tightly, the sort of sweater a mother-in-law gives to her son's wife when she thinks he has married poorly.

Initially, Maye had pulled out her best dress and planned on wearing that, but she'd changed her mind when she realized that anything she wore would be nothing but ammunition to the awful woman who fancied herself a sweater expert. Maye didn't know if that woman would be at the party, but one thing was for sure: if she was going to be mocked for her apparel, it was going to be apparel worth mocking.

Despite the fact that she had little warning about the get-together, Maye was determined to make the best of it, and she realized Charlie was right. If she shied away from faculty gatherings from now on, Maye's Nearly Nude Fat Dance was all they would ever remember her for. She had a chance to set the record straight and to show Charlie's peers that she was more than the party stripper, although the sweater sort of reinforced the lack-of-decorum aspect. And she was looking forward to getting to know the dean's wife a little better—if there was any upside in going to the party, that was it. Maye thought they most likely had a lot in common, and she thanked the universe that Mrs. Spaulding had not witnessed the spectacle with the rest of the guests. Still, if Maye could have wiggled out of the occasion, she would have taken the chance in a heartbeat, although she also knew that if she didn't show the faculty set that she had a good sense of humor about herself, then no one else would see it in that light, either. And last but not least, she had a mission—a score to settle with one amazingly rude woman.

Maye held tight to that determination to go in with her head held high and her sweater staying down. She held tight when she pulled the jolly holiday sweater over her head, and it clung to her torso like moss on a log. She held tight when she got into the car for the drive over to the Spauldings' and she was still holding tight as they drove up the curvy driveway to the dean's estate, the gift of a poinsettia on her lap.

And Maye kept that sense of humor strong, healthy, and dominant until the shiny black front door opened and there she stood, the Wicked Witch of Spaulding herself, fresh from dodging a falling house. Maye had not expected to see her nemesis on the other side of the door; she had expected to see a cheery, delightful Mrs. Spaulding who would immediately put her insecurities and fears at ease like the good hostess that she was. Maye also thought it typical of Rowena's rude behavior to take it upon herself to answer someone else's front door. If she had that much nerve, she was starting out strong, which meant it was going to be a long, tedious night.

"Hello," Rowena said with scowling, judging eyes.

"Hello, happy holidays," Charlie said diplomatically.

"Hi," Maye said, her blood pressure shooting up so high she nearly crushed the poinsettia she held in her arm. She put her other hand on her hip and swiveled from side to side, giving Rowena a grand, full view of her disgusting sweater.

Rowena said nothing as Charlie grabbed Maye's arm and pulled her inside, walking past the old wreck, who was dressed impeccably in a crimson, well-fit matching jacket and skirt.

Chh chh chh.

"Uh!" Maye whispered. "I hate this entryway!"

Again, Dean Spaulding was the first one to spot them as they entered the library, and he came over immediately to greet them.

"How are you, how are you?" he said, taking Maye's free hand. "Thank you so much for coming. Maye, I'm so glad you pushed back your trip after all so you could attend our celebration!"

Then he winked.

"I am, too," Maye said, smiling, and winked back. "This is for you and Mrs. Spaulding. I didn't see her when I came in, so—"

"Oh, she's right there," Dean Spaulding said, pointing behind Maye, but as she turned around to greet the pleasant young woman, she saw only the craggy face that belonged to Professor Brooks's significant other, and thought jokingly to herself that Rowena had probably just eaten her, but no one could tell because Rowena, the professor of Old English, Middle English, or Old Hags, take your pick, was already awash in the color of blood.

"I'm sorry, where?" Maye asked.

"Oh, right there." Dean Spaulding pointed again, and before Maye could take another look in that direction, he laughed and called, "Look, Charlie and Maye have brought us a lovely poinsettia, Rowena. Wasn't that nice?"

Maye thought for a moment that perhaps she had misunderstood or hadn't made herself clear, realized perhaps Rowena was indeed Mrs. Spaulding, but in the form of Dean Spaulding's mother. Why would he call her Rowena instead of Mother? An old, wrinkled stepmother? That would certainly fit the bill.

"I'm sorry. I meant the other Mrs. Spaulding, the one I met at the last party," Maye said, suddenly feeling ridiculous that she had to explain to the dean which wife she meant, trying hard to push down the words "You know, your young, pretty wife!"

"She answered the door," Charlie added, trying to clarify the puzzle.

Even Dean Spaulding looked confused, and then after a moment or two, he began to laugh. "Oh, I see," he said, nodding. "I understand now."

Maye felt a wave of relief and was about to fake-wipe her brow with the back of her hand and sigh "Whew!" when her left side suddenly went cold and she turned to see Rowena standing next to her.

"That was my assistant," Rowena said dryly, sucking every ounce of heat out of the room like a demon. "She was at the party to answer the door and take drink orders. I am Rowena Spaulding, the dean's wife. Our next anniversary will be our golden one. And your sweater tonight is every bit as lovely as the last one you wore here, my dear."

Maye felt as if she had just stuck her head into a beehive. Her face stung, grew flushed, her ears rang, and she felt dizzy. No, no, no. How could it be true? she thought to herself. How could that nice, charming, friendly man be married to such a gorgon? How could that have even happened? He must drink a lot, Maye decided; that man must sleep at night curled up at the bottom of a bottle of Night Train.

The buzz in Maye's head only stopped when she felt a sharp pain on her thigh. Her first thought was that Rowena had speared her with an arsenic-laden dart that she probably had hidden behind a jowl for such an occasion, but then she quickly realized it was Charlie pinching her to tell her to get the horrified look off her face. Stat.

"I hope you like the poinsettia," Maye quickly offered with her best smile.

"There's nothing like some pretty poison during the holidays," Rowena said, smiling, and then swept into the hallway with the plant in her hands.

Before Maye could make a break for the door and spend the next six days running and screaming down the long, winding driveway, the only person she still remembered both the name and the face of walked over and began a conversation with her as her husband talked with Charlie.

"That's a great sweater," Melissabeth said. "Rabbits pulling sleighs are so cute, and it's unique how the Santa has no eyes. Was it knit by a special-needs person?"

"Oh, I think he does have eyes," Maye replied. "They're just behind the gargantuan snowflake that has suctioned itself to his face like a giant squid."

"Do you play cards, by any chance?" Melissabeth said without breaking so much as a smile. "My husband, Stuart, and I are always looking for another couple to play cards with."

"Oh, I'm not much of a card player, but I do love to play hearts," Maye offered. "Charlie's really the card shark. He loves rummy and poker. He even had a standing poker night with his friends in Phoenix."

"I love hearts!" cried Melissabeth, narrowly missing squealing by a note. "I haven't played hearts in years! We should get together and play! Stuart knows how to play. Does Charlie?"

"It's easy enough to pick up. He has a knack for things as long as they don't involve tools or moving parts," Maye replied.

"All righty then!" Melissabeth responded. "What are you doing on Wednesday night?"

"Oh," Maye said, a little surprised at the nearness of the date. "Wednesday is bad; we have dog school on Wednesdays. In fact, our dog is graduating from obedience school that night."

"How about Thursday?" Melissabeth offered. "Will that work?"

"Charlie has a late seminar on Thursday," Maye explained. "But we're free Friday or Saturday."

"Oooooooh," Melissabeth said in a pitying tone as she cocked her head to the side. "We should really start out on a weeknight and work our way up, don't you think? We like to reserve our weekend nights for real friends."

Maye's jaw dropped as if she had just injected an Orange County–sized dose of Botox into her face and was no longer able to control the physical workings of it.

She really had no comeback for Melissabeth, and realized that if the woman didn't understand that she had the manners of Joseph Goebbels, then it probably wouldn't bother her if Maye flatly turned and walked away.

At what point did I step into another dimension? Maye wondered as she did just that and headed straight for the bar. Is the *chh chh chh* hallway a portal to the David Lynch version of a work party? Is there a bottle that someone is passing around labeled "Drink me?" Where are the midgets? If she had passed into an alternate universe, there ought to be midgets, goddamn it, dressed as cops, pirates, and little maids. The Spaulding living room is a Salvador Dalí painting, she decided, and I must be a melting clock wearing a sweater depicting a Santa with no eyes in a sleigh pulled by rabbits. One thing was for sure—should any rabbit materialize before her eyes, she would sure as shit follow it down any hole to get out of there, she told herself.

Maye tossed down a vodka gimlet and found Charlie just as dinner was announced and the party moved into the dining room.

"Whatever you do, Charlie," Maye whispered, "don't leave me."

"Oh, I won't," he assured her. "Your shirt is tucked in, right?"

"My shirt?" Maye asked. "What shirt? I've got a unitard underneath this."

To Maye's great dismay, she arrived at the table to discover that dining room democracy had been quashed and name cards rested above each place setting. She let out a small groan, then was heartened when she saw that Charlie was seated across from her. Two seconds later, that was an aspirin's worth of comfort when she saw who flanked her: Rowena to her right, who sat at one of the heads, and Melissabeth to her left.

She suddenly had the urge to yell out, "I JUST STARTED MY PERIOD TODAY!"

Maye and Charlie took their seats and waited for the Most Torturous Event Involving Food to begin. When Melissabeth appeared, she looked disappointed to see that she wasn't sitting next to a real friend but did ask Maye politely to scoot her chair in so she could pass to get to her seat. Maye pushed the chair in as far as it would go, not only to make room for her neighbor but mainly because as she moved her own seat in, she noticed how her snug-fitting sweater was now contoured around the pair of jelly rolls that rented space around her abdomen. The sweater stretched tightly around her middle, as tight as a balloon that's been pushed beyond kind limits, although it wasn't so much uncomfortable as it was unpleasant to look at. On a baby, it would have been darling and cute, but protruding from the undercarriage of a malformed reindeer on an adult woman, it some-how lost its touchability appeal.

Rowena was too busy ordering her waitstaff around to be nasty before the first course, and when the wine was poured, Maye couldn't have been more grateful. On her first gulp, Charlie gave her a stern look; on her second gulp he kicked her under the table. Suddenly someone was behind her and a salad was being passed over her shoulder. Oooooh, she thought as she looked at the dish, sprinkled with Gorgonzola, dried cranberries, and her all-time favorite salad accessory, candied pecans. Yummy, yummy, yummy, Maye thought as she took her first bite.

"I'd like to make an announcement," said Rowena with a smug little grin, from the head of the table; then she turned and looked Maye square in the eye. "I'll have all of you know that we have the front runner for the Sewer Pipe Queen title sitting among us."

Maye was shocked. She hadn't even filled out the entry paperwork. How did Rowena know this? How could she have possibly known? Did she know Cynthia? Had Cynthia mentioned it? She'd only talked to Cynthia yesterday? My God, this Old Queen network operated at the speed of sound!

Maye didn't know what to say, so she smiled gently, vastly suspicious of Rowena's kindness, which she recognized as bait, and tried delicately not to get the hook plunged too far into her lip. "Well, that's kind, Rowena, but I wouldn't exactly say that," Maye replied. "I don't even have my talent segment coordinated yet."

"Excuse me?" Rowena said, clearly shocked. "You? I wasn't speaking about you! I was referring to Melissabeth, whom I happen to be sponsoring. And who will happen to win. So tell us, Maye, when was it that you entered? And who on earth is your sponsor?"

Maye's ears sizzled with embarrassment, although they would have burst into flames if it hadn't been for the vodka gimlet and the two glugs of wine. The entire table had grown silent, as if waiting for Mother Superior to release her brimstone on a particularly disobedient student.

"I haven't entered yet," Maye said, slowly and cautiously, "but my sponsor is Cynthia McMahon."

Rowena raised her eyebrows and put her waxy index finger on her chin. She paused for a moment.

"Is that right?" she said. "Cynthia McMahon? And how did you stumble upon Cynthia McMahon?"

"Cynthia," Maye began, "is my neighbor. And she has agreed to sponsor me. Do you know her?"

Rowena nodded. "Yes, I do," she said through her pinched mouth. "She held the title several years after I did. I had heard she was sponsoring a UNICEF girl from Africa who was going to dance in native costume, which was, by the way, nonexistent."

"No," Maye corrected her. "She was sponsoring a Peace Corps volunteer who had worked in Cameroon and caught a parasite."

"Well, that's a relief," she said with an exaggerated, full-blown smile and a cackle. "With no naked, native disease-ridden girl, there is a chance for first place after all! Melissabeth is a trained opera singer, isn't that right, dear?"

"Absolutely," Rowena's protégée chirped. "I got into Juilliard but went to the University of Virginia instead to be near Stuart. I did get a five-minute standing ovation for my Queen of the Night aria when I sang with the Virginia Opera. I can't wait to sing it again."

"She was amazing," her ruddy-faced potato of a husband said.

"Now, now," Rowena cautioned. "Let's be a little careful with our cards, shall we? We don't want to give our whole hand away."

Maye realized that unless she had been a former prima ballerina with the Bolshoi Ballet, she couldn't touch Melissabeth's talent segment, and Rowena knew it. But Rowena apparently also knew what Maye had heard—that Cynthia had been one of the most regal Sewer Pipe Queens in Spaulding history, and that made Rowena nervous. Maye could tell by the way she pursed her lips tighter than usual and picked at her salad, just moving the pieces around. She was thinking. Her hooked finger was tapping against her fork.

Maye was about to whisper to Charlie to ask if she could have his pecans when one of her molars bit into something much harder than a pecan. Much harder than any nut, even if it was entombed in a glorious hard-shell candy coating. It was so hard Maye thought it might be a penny.

Suddenly, she gasped, and sucked a gulp of air into her mouth, immediately sending knives of pain into her jaw. Within a fraction of an instant, she knew what it was, covered her mouth with her hand, and hoped Charlie had good dental insurance.

Charlie looked at her, perplexed, but Maye could say nothing. She just waved her right hand discreetly but quickly to signify, "Holy shit, Charlie, that woman planted a candied concrete pecan in my salad that has now wrenched the massive filling out of my molar that was the only thing keeping it whole and in my jaw!"

She couldn't spit it out, and she certainly couldn't swallow it. Maye took the only avenue she saw open to her—either finding the elusive restroom or at least holing up in the hallway where she could find the filling privately. She quickly pushed her chair back, but as she did, in slow motion, her wineglass, salad dish, and silverware moved oddly toward her as if being pulled by a magic force, like she was a magician. The wineglass teetered from side to side, sloshing its contents, as the china crawled closer and closer to the table's edge. Maye was entirely perplexed by the unexplained parlor trick as the dishes and glasses kept moving and moving as if they were on a conveyor belt until Charlie jumped up and in one sudden, heroic swoop yanked the tablecloth trapped between Maye's two holiday belly sausages away with the precision of a bullfighter and without sacrificing a single drop of wine.

While Charlie got a mild round of applause for his magnificent efforts in releasing the hostage tablecloth from Maye's fat rolls—whose size was clearly exaggerated and magnified, by the way, by the cheap acrylic and ill-fitting sweater—Maye stood up, the fat rolls vanished into the girth of her belly, and she tried not to choke on her filling.

"I'm so sorry," Maye said as the chunk of silver swam around her mouth. "But we have to go. I need to find a dentist on call, apparently. Thank you for a wonderful evening."

And as Charlie and Maye left the room, they both heard Rowena chuckle and then announce, "Well, I think we all know what her talent segment should be, now don't we? I bet there's enough suction there to pull a tractor!"

8

Blood on the Street

Mickey's best friend in dog school, Sammy, looked at Maye with sad, longing eyes. "Please take me home and raise me as your own," they said. "I live with a stripper and her son, Fish Face. He's a decent kid, but they feed me generic Lucky Charms for dinner and the only clean dish in the house is the one I wash myself. I drink out of a toilet bowl, and I would give my left nu-nu for a patch of green grass. I often pee in her stripper shoes for well-deserved revenge. She never notices."

"Sit, Sammy, sit!" Finding Nemo instructed, but the greyhound was not a bit interested in performing a command for which the reward was a dirty chunk of a Milk-Bone the mother had fished out of the bottom of her purse.

"Please sit, Sammy, please!" the child cried again, and clearly out of pity, the dog finally obeyed, although he refused to gobble the lint-covered reward that Finding Nemo held out so proudly for him.

"Yeah, Sammy, whoop, whoop, whoop, whoop!" Gwen, the

dog trainer, called, winding her arm in the air as the crinkled flesh beneath it swung wildly, grazing her face several times. "Now, can Sammy lie down?"

The dog collapsed to the floor without any further encouragement, almost as if to get the show over with. "Yeah, Sammy!" Gwen ballyhooed again, and this time Maye knew what was coming and averted her eyes.

"Eat the cookie, Sammy!" Finding Nemo insisted. "Don't you like it, boy? Don't you like it?"

"Shh! Give me that," Mama Nemo whispered as she grabbed her son's arm, plucked the rotten purse turd out of his fingers with her glittery, pterodactyl nails, and placed it on the floor in front of the dog. "There, Sammy! Leave it! Don't eat the cookie, Sammy. Don't eat it!"

The dog wasn't remotely attracted to the cookie, which on closer inspection didn't look so much like a cookie as it did a mummified rabbit's foot or a chunk of hashish or Dick Cheney's dehydrated, rock-hard, and coal-like soul. Luckily for Sammy, dogs have sharper senses, and he probably knew that digesting the mystery lump would have most likely led him down a truly dark path, like an encounter with a tube shoved down his esophagus and a stomach pump.

"Okay, I am happy to say that Sammy has now graduated from obedience school! Congratulations, Sammy!" Gwen cheered as she handed the stripper a diploma at the same time that Sammy launched his body over the volleyball net that surrounded the class and tried to find another family on the adoption aisle to take him home. "Who's next? Grand Duchess Anastasia?"

Lady, the one and the only, had already had her turn and successfully responded to every command with a nice little spray from her bladder, and Mad Dog had been expelled from class several weeks before when he showed up with blood on his face that had not yet dried.

Maye was not really even sure if Grand Duchess Anastasia, the bichon frise show dog, even had a heartbeat. She had never seen it so much as blink, and it never once in the course of the class left its treelike perch in its owner's arms. Maye and Charlie had speculated that the dog was not so much a stuffy dog as it was a stuffed toy made in an Asian sweatshop by child workers, and that there were some deep-rooted loss and abandonment issues taking place behind those BluBlockers.

"Okay," Gwen started. "Can Grand Duchess Anastasia sit?"

"Yes," the owner said in a rusty, deep voice.

"Oh, good, that's good," Gwen agreed. "Can we see it?"

"You'll have to take my word for it," she said from behind her windshield of sunglasses. "She can sit."

"Can she lie down?" Gwen asked, getting frustrated.

"Of course," the owner said, completely unflinching, as was her dog, both of them staring at Gwen like prey.

"All right, we'll come back to you," Gwen said, moving on to Mickey, who sat, lay down, stayed, shook, rolled over, and left his cookie (a real cookie, not some leftover narcotic residue Maye found at the bottom of her purse) when he was supposed to, and ate it when he was given a reward.

"Congratulations, Mickey!" Gwen announced when Mickey finished his last test. "You're the valedictorian of your class!"

"There's a valedictorian?" Maye asked incredulously. "Wow, Mickey! That's amazing! What a good boy!"

"I will even write a letter to the post office to let them know how well he did," Gwen said. "Mickey was a joy to have in class. I wish I had more like him."

"We had fun," Charlie agreed. "I know we arrived by dubious means, but it turned out to be a good thing for all of us, even though Mickey still goes ballistic when the mailman—I mean *letter carrier*—comes. There's something about him that does not agree with Mickey."

"That's so odd, Mickey is such an agreeable dog. Actually, I think Mickey should continue his training," Gwen added. "He's very bright, loves a challenge, and is quite responsive. And he can sing! I would like to see Mickey go on to our agility-training course, in which he will not only jump hurdles but learn how to drive a doggie car and play a piano!"

"I don't know if Mickey needs to know how to play a piano," Charlie began.

"Are you kidding? Yes he does!" Maye interrupted. "What if he's a canine Mozart or Elton John? We can't just stop his education now, when it's going so well! Consider him in."

"Class starts next week," Gwen informed them.

"We'll be there," Maye said, smiling.

♯ ♯ ♯

"Mickey does not need to learn how to play a doggie piano," Charlie said as they drove home. "We fulfilled the post office's demands. Let's just leave it at that."

"Charlie," Maye said sternly. "Are you insane? There is only one way I'm going to beat Beverly Sills singing one of the most difficult arias in all of opera, and that's singing a song accompanied by my dog, at the piano."

"Ahhhhh," Charlie said, nodding and grinning wide as he pulled to a four-way stop sign. "I see your dastardly plan now! That's true. If you could incorporate the element of fire as well, you've got it hands down, baby."

"I have to beat them," Maye replied as the driver of a VW bus at the south stop sign, whose turn it really was to go, motioned for the Honda at the west stop sign to go ahead. "It's become a whole thing for me now, it's taken on a completely new meaning. I went in and filed my pageant paperwork today and paid the five-dollar entry fee. It's official now. I have to beat Rowena Spaulding."

"You *have* to beat Rowena Spaulding at her own game," Charlie agreed as the Honda waved to the bicyclist at the east stop sign to go ahead. "Dean Spaulding has always been nothing but kind and generous to me, but that crone of a wife of his is so awful she comes complete with her own opera-singing henchman. You have to beat her, Maye, there's no two ways about it."

"Well, certainly, the name of Cynthia McMahon sent a shock through her system," Maye said as the bicyclist waved to the VW bus to go first. "Did you see her? I thought I heard a train whistle blow as steam came shooting out her ears. She has the kind of self-esteem you only see in people like Genghis Khan or a housewife in Orange County."

" 'I'm Dean Spaulding's wife and I have been for fifty years,' " Charlie mocked her, scrunching up his nose and squealing in a high-pitched voice as the VW bus made a run for it, then stopped when the Honda did the same. "She thinks she runs this town. You need to show her she can't have everything."

"I just don't know why she hates me so much," Maye added as the Honda started to go a second before the VW bus got a hit of gas, too, then both stopped short, just inches from the center of the intersection. "Does the woman really hate me because of a sweater? How can you hate someone because of a sweater? You can hate the sweater, but hating the person inside of it is ridiculous!"

"There's something about you she can't stand," Charlie agreed as the Honda waved at the VW bus to go, the VW bus waved back, and in the meantime, the bicyclist shot through the intersection clear to the other side. "That is very clear. Maybe you remind her of someone she knows or used to know. I've met people like that before, haven't you?"

"Sure," she complied as the Honda waved to Charlie and the driver of the VW bus threw up his hands. "But I wouldn't aggressively pick on them at a dinner party in front of their husbands' colleagues!"

"Well, that's true, but you didn't help your cause much with the sweater of cows pulling a blind Santa," Charlie chuckled as the VW bus, the Honda, and a new arrival, a Subaru, all turned and waved Charlie on at the exact same moment. "That stab was a bit obvious, if you ask me."

"It was obvious, but I was trying to make a point," she replied. "But I am worried that she hates me so much that she'll make it difficult for you at the university."

"Listen," he said, turning toward her. "As long as you play fair and square, which I know you will, I don't think there's anything to worry about. I respect Dean Spaulding, and I really doubt that anything will happen to my position because of his meddling wife. When it comes to the department, I would be surprised if he let the workings of it become disrupted because of a beauty contest. That hardly seems professional."

Charlie gunned through the intersection, and Mickey began to make a forlorn groaning sound.

"Why are you singing, Mickey?" Maye asked. "We don't have the radio on."

"That's not singing," Charlie said. "He's not singing. I've never heard him make that noise before."

Mickey continued to moan, and when they were four blocks from their house, the groan became a full somber howl.

"What's the matter?" Maye said as she turned and tried to comfort her dog, but Mickey was inconsolable, his howls taking on a higher pitch.

"Oh God!" Charlie cried. "You don't think he ate that hashish brick from Pebbles's purse, do you?"

"He was the valedictorian of his class, Charlie," Maye shot back. "If Sammy wasn't going to eat a stale chunk of hallucinogens, Mickey wouldn't either."

"What's wrong, boy?" Charlie asked Mickey. "What's the matter?"

Charlie and Maye simply needed to look up to answer that question. What looked like a flashing parade lined and blanketed both sides of the street in front of their small, English-style cottage. Revolving red lights of fire engines whipped quickly across their front windows, alternating with flickering blue lights from the squad cars that silhouetted the towering pine trees and created a strobe-light effect. The bright, white lights of the ambulance lit up the usually darkened street like it was a movie set. There were so many emergency vehicles clogging the street that Maye and Charlie couldn't even get close to their house.

"Oh my God," Maye said as she looked at Charlie. "What is it? Can you see the house? Is it still there? Is it on fire?"

"I don't know, I can't get a good look from here," Charlie replied, trying very hard to stay calm. "It looks like it's standing; I can't smell smoke. Do you smell smoke?"

Maye shook her head and got out of the car. They left Mickey in the backseat, now oddly and mournfully quiet, and started up the street. Even as they got closer it became hard to tell what was going on, and although there were dozens of people milling about, the street held an eerie silence, broken only by the static and garbled conversations of emergency radio broadcasts.

Now, in front of their house, which was indeed standing, Maye and Charlie stood and watched the scene for several moments, still unsure of what had happened, until Maye saw John Smith, the plumber cop, getting out of his police car.

"John!" Maye called into the stillness of the night, waving her hand, and walked over to him with Charlie by her side.

"Hey, Maye, Charlie," John replied, nodding. "Sad thing. Sad, sad thing."

"What happened?" Maye asked anxiously. "We just got home, we don't know—what happened?"

John dropped his head and shook it again, this time more slowly, as if trying to collect himself. "I've never seen anything like it," he finally said, looking up at them. "There was an attack. It was murder, you could say."

Maye and Charlie were too stunned to say anything. A murder. On their street. Dead. Someone was dead, possibly someone they knew.

"Someone's dead?" Maye finally squeaked out. "Who? What happened? Someone on the street, one of our neighbors? Who was it? What happened, John?"

"We think it happened a couple of hours ago when it was still daylight," the plumber cop explained. "She must have looked at him funny, is all we can figure, but when the husband came home, she was lying out in the backyard and there was that masked bandit, clawing at her face like it was trying to eat a Fruit Roll-Up. Doesn't look like there was much of a struggle, maybe she was caught by surprise, but her neck is broken. In any case, she was dead by the time we got here. Nothing we could do. Not a thing. Like I said, never seen anything like it."

Maye gasped and covered her mouth.

"A masked bandit? Did you catch him? Is he still out there?" she whispered.

"Probably up in one of these trees," John said, pointing above them. "They can climb pretty fast once they get spooked."

"What? Um, I'm sorry, if there's a murderer in these trees, I think you guys should try to catch him *now*," Maye said sternly. "What if he strikes again? What if there are more killings?"

"Naw," John said, almost pooh-poohing her. "I'll bet he's sleeping up there. Just be careful in the daytime, if this one's got distemper like we think."

Maye was struck dumb for a second when she finally realized what the cop was saying. "You think the murderer is a raccoon?"

Plumber John pointed at her. "That's what we're thinking," he concurred. "But the perp is still on the loose, we haven't appre-hended it yet, so I'd be careful in the daylight if I were you."

Finally, Maye brought herself to ask again who it was that had been attacked. Was it one of the scooter women at Cynthia's tea party who wouldn't upgrade to the faster and more stylish Rene-gade model because it was too flashy when an extra two-mile-per-hour push might have saved her life from flying claws? Could it have been Agnes, with the Saran Wrap skin, who failed to fight off a mammal the size of a basset hound because of her tooth-pick bones and transparency? Who could it have been that was not strong enough to fight off a raccoon?

"It was the lady across the street," John answered, and pointed at the cream-colored picket fence. "Nice lady. Real nice lady. Never so much as got a parking ticket, and kept her drains so clean they would sparkle, that Cynthia McMahon."

ৡ   ৡ   ৡ

Maye still couldn't believe what had happened when she saw the headline on the front page of the paper the next day: MAD COON EATS OLD QUEEN.

It was incredible. It was simply inconceivable to Maye that Cynthia was not only dead but that she'd had her life light snuffed out by an adorable woodland creature, a friend of Bambi's, no less, armed with alleged claws of death. It was akin to being mugged by Goofy or carjacked by Piglet, Maye thought. She walked around in a daze for the entire morning, hoping that Cynthia hadn't suffered and that it was over quickly. Maye felt horrible—if she had been home, perhaps she would have heard the attack and been able to help in some way. And Cynthia's poor husband, to come home and find his wife being nibbled on by a stuffed animal with bloodlust.

Although she admittedly didn't know Cynthia all that well, the woman had never been anything but nice to her, except that part about accusing Maye of poisoning the earth, but then again, Maye had had no way of knowing about Styrofoam Day. It was a comment most easily forgiven, especially now.

It was just so unreal. She had just seen Cynthia several days earlier, and it seemed completely impossible that she was dead. And honestly, the more Maye thought about it, the more implausible the entire Killer Raccoon scenario became: Cynthia, a woman a little past her prime, sure, but otherwise in excellent physical shape, being ambushed by a scheming, plotting Rocky Raccoon, and mauled to death? How exactly would that happen? Why wouldn't Cynthia have run back inside if the animal was acting odd? She hardly seemed the type to engage in feral-beast wrangling, even with one that had a high Disney snugglability factor. The more she thought about it, the more she didn't believe it. Maye decided there had to be more to the story than a crazy raccoon with murder on its mind.

And then there was the pageant. Maye tried very, very, very hard not to be selfish in this time that required not thinking about yourself but being concerned only with others, but she couldn't help it. There you go, Maye thought to herself as she slipped into Sewer Pipe Queen mode for the nth time that morning; there you go. And there was the equally bothersome thought about Maye's playing Dick Deadeye and the question of whether she was still obligated to be in the play now that Cynthia was no longer alive. She didn't want to be Dick Deadeye. She'd only agreed because fair was fair, and right now the scales of justice were a little tipped out of Maye's favor. There's a slight chance I may be going to hell now, she told herself when the selfish thought popped back into her head for the seventeenth time that day, but then she almost laughed when she asked herself who she thought she was kidding. It was simply another level of the underworld conquered and accomplished. By sneaking out of Cynthia's house crouched behind the less mobile on scooters, Maye had already qualified for the basic level of hell that consisted of trudging along on a treadmill with nothing on television but *The View* for all eternity.

She had earned the intermediate level of hell by lying to Vegging Out Bob, which meant that she would spend the hereafter in a Wal-Mart store at 6 A.M. the day after Thanksgiving as shoppers jostled, pushed, and rubbed against her to secure the cheapest things hellishly possible, while their children, also known as demi-demons, cried, screamed, and begged for hell's cuisine, corn dogs and Mountain Dew. She had graduated to the advanced level of hell shortly thereafter when she was caught by Vegging Out Bob whilst gnawing on a piece of pretty cow, which entitled her to experience the forever after in Miami in August, sitting in a filthy deli across from an old woman who smells of cat pee eating a pastrami sandwich with her mouth open.

Now, with her new sins propelling her to the doctoral level of hell, Maye was assured a spot back in seventh grade, where she would be forced to run that Chub Rub mile and then take a shower with girls much thinner, and prettier, and who had not reached the ranks of puberty that Maye had, until the end of time.

So to combat her guilty, selfish concern about losing her royal flush in the game of Sewer Pipe Queen, Maye decided to do the only nice thing she could do, and got her car keys to go and order flowers for Cynthia's service. She was almost to her car when she saw a man who looked to be in his mid thirties crossing the street in her direction, carrying a video camera and a tripod.

"Hey!" he yelled, running faster as Maye opened the door to her car. "Hey! Excuse me! Excuse me!"

"Yes?" Maye replied. "How can I help you?"

"Well, I'm the reporter, anchor, producer, and photographer

from WDRK, Spaulding's Number One and Only News Choice, We Are News to You!" he called out as he slowed his moderately hefty body to a jog and then stopped, breathing heavily.

"Okay," Maye said, shrugging.

"Um, did you know the victim across the street? The woman who was eaten?" he stumbled as he flipped over the cover of a small notebook he pulled from his shirt pocket. "Cynthia, Mrs. Cynthia McMahon? Did you know her?"

Maye nodded. "Yes, I did."

"Oh, fantastic!" the man said as he set up his tripod in Maye's driveway. "Do you mind if I ask you some questions about what happened last night?"

Maye hesitated but couldn't really see the harm in it. She had been a reporter, she knew how important sources were when working on a story. "I guess that would be all right," she answered. "What was your name?"

"Richard Titball," the reporter/producer/photographer said. "Call me Rick."

"Rick Titball," Maye repeated, marveling that he'd physically survived a childhood surely overflowing with enough school-yard torture to qualify him for a serial killer's profile or enrollment in clown college.

"Now, if you could just stand there . . . perfect," Rick said. "That's great. Just stand still, I need to set the shot up."

He ran back behind the camera, adjusted the angle, apparently pushed "play," and then ran around in front of the camera, next to Maye. He took several deep breaths, closed his eyes tightly, and counted to three, and at the same moment his eyes flew open, he shouted, "ACTION!"

"I'm here at the scene where . . . where . . . oh, shit! Cut!" he yelled angrily, hitting his leg with his microphone, then ran around to the back of the tripod and pushed "stop." He flipped open his notebook again and Maye saw him mouth the words "Cynthia McMahon" several times until he was convinced he got it right. He pushed "play" again, ran in front of the camera, counted to three, and again shouted, "ACTION!"

"I'm here at the scene where Cynthia McMahon was tragically murdered last night," Richard Titball reported. "And I'm with her neighbor—"

He flipped his wrist and pointed the microphone at Maye, who was taken by surprise for a moment and finally said, "Maye Roberts."

He flipped the microphone back to himself. "That's okay," he whispered into the microphone. "We can edit the pause."

Maye sort of shrugged and nodded.

"Now, Miss Roberts, you were a friend of Cynthia McMahon?" Richard Titball asked her.

"I was," Maye answered. "She was a lovely woman."

"Were you surprised by what happened?" he asked.

"Of course I was," Maye replied. "You never expect anything like that to happen to people you know, or on the street where you live. I can't believe it."

"Can you tell us what you saw here last night?" the reporter dug. "Was there blood on the street?"

"Excuse me?" she replied, shocked. "No, there was no blood on the street."

"Are you afraid the raccoon will come back for more?" Richard Titball asked dramatically.

"I'm not sure if it's been established that that is what happened," Maye commented. "You'd have to confirm that with the police."

"So you doubt the police report?" Richard Titball probed.

"No," Maye said, shaking her head. "I just think that it needs further investigation for some definitive answers."

"Do you think we should round them all up and exact justice for what's been done to one of our own?" Richard Titball asked.

"Well, you can't blame the whole raccoon population for the alleged actions of just one," Maye said, then remembered her earlier thought from that morning, "I'm sure most raccoons won't attack unless they're being attacked first. It's unbelievable. It's like being mugged by Goofy or carjacked by Piglet."

"That's great, thank you," Richard Titball said, then looked into the camera and screamed "CUT!" before he ran behind the tripod and pushed the "stop" button.

ᛘ ᛘ ᛘ

At the florist, Maye chose a bouquet of white roses, calla lilies, and tulips to be sent to Cynthia's husband, whom she had waved to on the street now and then but had never met. She returned home and was making dinner when she switched on the television to see if there had been any update in the investigation of Cynthia's death. Naturally, it was the lead story that night, and she hoped desperately that her interview had been forgotten on the editing-room floor as she watched Rick Titball introduce his own story, "A Killer in the Backyard: When Raccoons Murder."

"I'm here at the scene where Cynthia McMahon was tragically murdered last night," Titball reported. "And I'm with her neighbor—"

Suddenly, Rick Titball's face appeared in a close-up as he said, "MAYE ROBERTS."

"Now, Miss Roberts, you were a friend of Cynthia McMahon?"

"I was," Maye said.

"Can you tell us what you saw here last night?"

"— blood on the street," Maye suddenly said.

"Is it true that a raccoon went crazy and killed your neighbor?"

"Raccoons won't attack unless they're being attacked first," Maye told the reporter.

"So you doubt the police report?" Rick Titball inquired.

"It's unbelievable. It's like being mugged by Goofy or carjacked by Piglet," Maye interjected.

"I'm Rick Titball, WDRK, reporting," Rick Titball said. "Back to you, Rick."

Titball then followed his own story with tips on how to survive a small-mammal attack and a tip line to call for anyone sighting a suspicious raccoon that fits the description, although the only description given was "a raccoon." He went on to explain that the suspect was still believed to be in the vicinity, probably because of family ties.

Maye couldn't believe what she had seen.

"Oh, Titball," she said between clenched teeth. "I'd like to squeeze you until you're blue!"

She immediately called the tip line, hoping to set the record straight and get her interview pulled from the later broadcast. After five rings, the station finally picked up.

"Rick Titball," the voice said.

"This is Maye Roberts, and I just saw your report," she said angrily. "And I have something to say to you!"

"Yes! Have you seen the killer? Quickly, give me the info. I'm on commercial," Titball replied.

"I want to speak to the station manager!" Maye said sternly.

"Um, he's at lunch," Titball stammered. "Try the community-service line."

"Do you answer that phone, too?" Maye asked.

There was a pause that couldn't be edited out. "Sometimes," Rick Titball said quietly. "Gotta go. It's time for the weather, and the weather girl ran off to Miami with her body piercer."

Maye slammed down the phone and fumed silently as Rick

Titball appeared on the screen in front of a map of the country with a laser pointer in his hand.

That Rick Titball, she thought to herself. He was a Dick after all.

※ ※ ※

That Saturday, Maye and Charlie arrived at the Spaulding Memorial Chapel to attend the service for Cynthia. To their amazement, the parking lot was empty save for a few cars.

"Are you sure we're here at the right time?" Charlie asked. "Is this even the right place? There's nobody here."

Maye pulled out the notice of Cynthia's service that she had clipped from the paper. "Spaulding Memorial Chapel," she read aloud. "Two P.M. Right time, right place, Charlie. Then again, all of Cynthia's friends will either be taking the senior shuttle or riding their scooters down here. If you want an aisle seat, we'd better get in there now."

As they entered the chapel, they saw that the seating area was just as empty as the parking lot. Not a soul in sight except for an older man sitting in the front row, whom Maye recognized as Cynthia's husband.

"Hello, Mr. McMahon," Maye said as she and Charlie walked to the front row. "I'm Maye, and this is my husband, Charlie. We live across the street."

"Oh, yes," the older man said, standing up and shaking both their hands. "Thank you for coming. Please call me Pat."

"We're so sorry about Cynthia," Maye said. "She was such a nice person. She was always very kind to me."

"Oh, you were the girl she was going to work with for the next pageant," Pat said, nodding in recollection. "I know she was really looking forward to it. Didn't I see you on the news the other night?"

"Yes, that was me," Maye replied hesitantly. "But I was horribly misquoted; everything I said was taken out of context. I even called the station to complain, but the only person to talk to was the reporter who did the story. I'm so sorry you had to see that. I really am, I'm quite angry about it."

"Oh, that Rick Titball," Pat scoffed. "Rick Screwball, if you ask me. He's misquoted just about every person in town! Plus, it turns out that a raccoon didn't kill Cynthia after all, just like you thought, Maye. Medical examiner found a three-inch long beetle stuck in her hair, and the best he could figure is that she was trying to get it out when she fell down the stairs and broke her neck taking some old donuts out to the trash. That woman loved her hair spray, and in the end, it trapped that beetle like it was in a cell. I guess during the fall, some of the jelly from those donuts smeared on her face, and that's what the raccoon was trying to eat. I tell you, it was a sight, though."

"I can't imagine," Charlie said.

"I guess it's better this way than being a murder," Pat said, shaking his head. "I love nature, but I didn't want it to make a meal out of my wife, you know."

Maye wasn't sure how to reply to a comment like that, so instead, she chose door number one, trivia.

"I'm sorry if we came too early," she said, motioning to the empty chapel. "We didn't mean to interrupt your alone time, but the newspaper said the service was starting at two."

"No, no," Pat replied. "That's right, it was two o'clock. Unfortunately, you can't really book a funeral in advance, unless it's an execution or something, and well, it just so happens that today, of all days, is Styrofoam Day. Everyone's out at the plant."

"Oh," Maye said, again not really knowing what to say. She tried to be optimistic. "I'm sure more people will come to the funeral."

"Nah," Pat said, waving his hand. "There won't be one. Cynthia had decided to donate her body to the Automobile Institute for Crash Testing. She loved the aspect of reuse. It only makes sense that she got recycled herself. In fact, I'd better wrap this thing up. Elsie is out there, holding my place in line. Nice of you to come, though. Are you heading out there yourself? It will be one hell of a line by now."

"Got a bag of peanuts in my car," Maye answered, nodding.

Already knowing that they had done their fair share of poisoning the earth with what the Styrofoam gods had bestowed on them, Maye and Charlie lied to the new old widower. There were no peanuts. The last piece of Styrofoam from their house had entered the trash and Cynthia had secretly plucked it from their bin and added it to her own collection days before a loud and large black horned beetle had become entombed in her lacquered hair and she tumbled down eleven of the twelve back stairs.

9

The Ghost of Ruby Spicer

The Sewer Pipe Queen Pageant had been going strong for as long as Spaulding had been a town, Maye realized. Considering the average life span, that meant that there had to be at least several dozen Old Queens walking around—after all, Maye hardly knew anyone in that town, and she had already bumped into three of them. There had to be someone she could dig up who wasn't already sponsoring a contestant, and the odds were finally in her favor.

After she read the morning paper, which had been consumed by Cynthia's death—the headline read RACCOON CLEARED: BEETLE SUSPECT IN QUEEN MAULING while the one below it read, "*H.M.S. Pinafore* Sunk After Lead Runs into White Light"—she decided to put her rusty reporter's skills to work and find out just how many Old Queens were rattling around the streets of Spaulding.

On her way to the library to start on some research, Maye felt guilty about her joy over being released from her obligation as

Dick Deadeye, but it was a feeling that she simply could not deny. Still, she felt bad for Agnes, Elsie, and the Rascal Rodeo, who all but lived for those performances, although, as the paper had reported, the production would simply be impossible to execute since Cynthia herself was playing four of the eight roles that were of any substantial merit.

At the traffic light in front of the library, Maye stopped as pedestrians tumbled into the crosswalk, including one dark, hooded figure complete with face obscured and staff in hand. Was there a new *Star Wars* movie opening that she didn't know about? Maye wondered. Then she realized that she wasn't sure what was more bizarre—that a Grim Reaper was in the crosswalk or that no one else in the vicinity seemed to take any notice. Maye parked, making sure to pay special attention to any flying beetles coming her way. Another Spaulding Moment, as she and Charlie had begun to call their encounters with something unusual, like a girl walking around downtown topless, or a mailman attempting to hurdle your trash can. This town was full of them.

Maye made her way to the Spaulding Room, where the old directories and newspaper clippings were collected. Although the room wasn't huge, its oak-paneled bookcases were filled from floor to ceiling with binders, books, and volumes of documents and ledgers; beyond the bookcases sat several rows of old wooden filing cabinets. Maye hadn't the faintest idea where to start looking for old Sewer Pipe Queens.

"Can I help you?" a woman at the front desk asked, obviously sensing Maye's confusion.

"I hope so," Maye said, laughing. "I'm doing some research on the Sewer Pipe Queen Pageant. And I was hoping to find some old newspaper stories or some kind of list of women who held the title."

"Hmmm," the librarian hummed as she quickly typed and hit "enter."

"Welllll," she said as she studied the computer screen and winced slightly, which made Maye wince slightly. "It doesn't look like there's a whole lot in the file, but it should be a good start. Let me pull it for you, and while you take a look at it, I can check some other places."

"That would be great, thank you," Maye said as the librarian walked to one of the old oak filing cabinets, yanked heartily on a stubborn drawer, and pulled out an ample manila folder with newspaper clippings sprouting out of it.

"Here you go," she said as she handed it to Maye. "I'll be right back. I have a hunch I'm going to follow up on. We might be able to find additional archives under the Spaulding Festival."

Maye brought the file over to a small table with an accountant's lamp on it. She turned the light on, illuminating the green shade, sat down, and opened the file.

Looking up at Maye from inside the folder were pretty, young, smiling faces now yellowed and aged on fragile newspaper that had become antiqued with time. In clipping after clipping, their crowns glistened and shone, as each winner embarked on a year as the town's queen. Paulette Newsome, for example, won her title in 1927 by exhibiting her Charleston dancing skills; Marion Perkins captured her crown by her demonstration of sewer-pipe construction with a jelly roll 1943; in 1962, Peggy Notham took the throne with her interpretive dance to "Puff, the Magic Dragon"; and in 1973, Sharla Sunflower took the throne by reprising her community-college theater role of Mary Magdalene in *Jesus Christ Superstar* by singing "I Don't Know How to Love Him," using a holographic portrait of Jesus with eyes that alternated between open and closed, which, it was reported, made the Christian savior look rather narcoleptic.

There were dozens and then more dozens of Sewer Pipe Queens in Spaulding's past, making Maye feel a little overwhelmed. How could she find out who was alive, who had moved, who lived here still? Many of the last names must have changed through marriages and divorces, and the hunt for each individual queen could become an investigation on its own and could take weeks, maybe even months. She even found photographs of the male Sewer Pipe Queens, and although she knew it was a bit sexist, she passed them by. Maye decided to eliminate anything that dated so far back that it was most likely the Old Queen wasn't available being that she was embalmed or was so old that springing her from the assisted living facility might be a little difficult. Still, faced with a file full of clippings and more than fifty possible leads, Maye couldn't help but feel a little bit defeated.

And if that wasn't enough, she looked up to see the librarian walking toward her with yet another file in her hands.

Maye took a deep breath and waved her hands. "I have so much here already that I'm not sure if I even want to open that folder," she said to the librarian, motioning to the one she held in her hands. "All of these queens. There were so many of them!"

"I think you'll want to see this," the librarian said with a knowing smile. "Now, I don't know exactly what it is you're looking for, but if you're interested in the queen history, you can't ignore the Queen of Queens. I remember hearing about her when I was a kid. She was incredibly beautiful, she was very nice, everyone loved her, and then one day, she simply vanished. She was just gone. Ruby Spicer. I guess she was something else."

The last thing Maye needed was one more queen to track down, but she took and opened the smudged, bent file, which looked like it had been hastily crammed in the back of a deep, dark drawer a decade ago. The minute she opened it, she knew that this queen was different.

Ruby Spicer was not pretty.

Ruby Spicer was not beautiful.

Ruby Spicer was absolutely remarkable.

Maye couldn't help but stare at the weathered coronation

photo from the fifty-year-old *Spaulding Herald*. Wow, she said to herself; I thought faces like that only happened in paintings. Ruby's head was turned slightly toward the camera as she looked slightly past it, her straight, classic nose centered by high, regal cheekbones, her full, heart-shaped mouth smiling, radiating genuine joy, and her soft, almost deep-set eyes shining brilliantly despite the fact that even many decades later, they were still only thousands of dots on aged paper that together comprised a face. She did not seem like a tall woman, in fact, she looked somewhat petite next to the graying man who placed the tiara upon her head. She held not a bouquet of roses, but more like a bushel, and her wavy hair fell to her shoulders with a slight curl under at the ends. Ruby Spicer was, as the librarian said, the Queen of Queens. Even Cynthia paled in comparison.

And she had vanished. How does a woman like that vanish? Maye wondered. Does a prince from Monaco land his plane in her front yard and offer her a ride to a magic kingdom? Someone like that doesn't vanish; there are too many people who want to be them. Maye dug deeper into the file and found more pictures of Ruby, one at the opening day of the state fair, another at a barn dance, and one of her on a throne, riding atop a lavishly decorated float. The caption read, "Our Darling and Reigning Queen, Ruby Spicer, welcoming her beloved crowds at the Spaulding Festival Parade. What a gal! We'll say it again: What a gal!" Ruby waved to the camera, flashing what Maye now recognized as her trademark smile. Oddly, however, Maye noticed that in almost every photo in the file, Ruby held a pencil in her right hand, in between her index and middle fingers. Ah, Maye noted, a girl after my own heart. Always ready to take notes. Could it be that Ruby was an aspiring journalist?

Ruby was it, Maye could feel it. Ruby was the one she needed. If there was anyone who could help her beat Rowena and her protégée, it was Ruby Spicer.

Maye took the file back up to the counter and rang the service bell. As soon as the librarian saw the look on Maye's face, she smiled. "What did I tell you?" She laughed. "I thought you might want to see that."

Maye held the file in both hands. "I need to copy this," she said urgently. "How can I copy this?"

"Well," the librarian hesitated. "It's in Special Collections. I don't think anyone has seen that for years—it was misfiled, in the locked cabinet."

"What do you know about her?" Maye asked. "Is she alive, is she dead? Do you remember hearing anything else about this woman?"

"Hmm-mmm," she said. "Just what I mentioned before. Then again, I was a little girl, but I haven't heard anyone talk about her since."

"How can I get a copy of this?" Maye asked.

"I'm not supposed to let you take it out of this room, but I will let you take it across the hall to copy, on one condition."

"What's that?" Maye asked, curious.

"Whatever you find out about her, I want to know," she said. "You have to promise to come back and tell me what happened to Ruby Spicer."

"Let's shake on it," Maye said as she extended her hand and smiled.

𝇇 𝇇 𝇇

With Ruby Spicer's file copied and in her hand, Maye did the first thing any reporter would do—she went straight to the city directory and looked her up, but to no avail, which was no surprise. Then she searched all the directories going back fifty years, to when Ruby was crowned, but still nothing was listed. It was entirely possible Ruby had just gotten married and moved away, and if that was the case, she was determined to find that, too.

Then she did the first thing any obituary writer would do and headed over to City Hall, where the vital records—including death and marriage certificates, land deeds, house titles—were kept. Just as she was about to cross the street, Maye heard a strange noise coming up from behind her.

WHOOOO! WHOOO! WHOOO! She turned as a voice suddenly rang out, "ON YOUR RIGHT!," and a unicyclist ripped by her and knocked the photocopies out of her hand, sending the pages fluttering all over the sidewalk.

"ASSHOLE!" Maye automatically yelled out as the other pedestrians turned to stare at her rather than the rogue one-wheeled biker, as if pointing out his assholian nature was a far bigger crime than accosting someone with a recreational vehicle. And that made her even angrier.

"What? When's the last time you were hit by a piece of circus equipment?" she bellowed at the gawkers as she started attempting to collect the pages that were fluttering and also skipping down the street.

As she was bent over trying to catch the copies, she felt a tap on her shoulder and turned around to see her plumber and cop, John Smith.

"Looks like you dropped this," he said, handing her several sheets of paper.

"Yeah, I think I was just the victim of a hit-and-pedal," Maye said as she took the copies from John, who was clearly on law-enforcing duty.

"If I see the one-wheeled bandit again today, I'll make sure to give him a ticket," John said, laughing. "So, what's this you have here? Stuff about Ruby Spicer, I see."

Maye nodded, hesitant to say too much. "Yeah, it sounds like a fascinating story, I was thinking about checking it out," she replied.

"It's a story, all right. She's a little legendary in these parts, but stories are sometimes just stories," he told her. "They grow and

get bigger when sometimes there wasn't anything there to begin
with. Pretty lady, though. I remember that parade, even though I
couldn't even hold a wrench or a gun back then."

"Yeah, she was beautiful," Maye agreed, getting a little bit of a
feeling that there was something John wasn't saying. "Striking.
Odd how she just one day vanished. Because I was thinking, she
was this lovely girl, it seemed like the town adored her, and one
day she's just gone? It doesn't really make sense. Not to me. Does
it make sense to you?"

"Well, you know," John started, then looked past Maye.
"Sometimes there are people who just don't want to be found.
One day they *are* just gone, for whatever reason. There's no
telling for what—their reasons are their own. Maybe Ruby Spicer
went off to a big city and had herself a nice modeling career,
maybe she got married to a nice farmer out near Bellingham and
had a bunch of kids, or maybe she moved to Paris and became a
singer in a nightclub and was kinda famous. Or maybe she's just
a lady named Ruby Spicer and she doesn't want to be found."

Maye found that last statement a little more than curious.
"What do you know about Ruby Spicer, John Smith? Because
I'm thinking you might know something," she said, trying to read
his face.

"I know she was a pretty lady in a crown that I saw when I was
a little kid," he said simply with a sigh. "And that's about it. What
do you want with her, anyway? She must be a million years old
by now."

Maye thought for a moment. "I need her help," she finally
concluded. "I need her to help me drop a house on a wicked
witch."

John smiled. "Good luck with that," he said. "Houses are
heavy."

Then he blew his whistle at a jaywalker and strolled away.

🜨 🜨 🜨

Maye felt hopeful as she climbed the steps of City Hall; if there was one place where there would be a record of Ruby Spicer, this would be it. She opened the large, creaky, century-old door next to the historic plaque that listed the date the edifice was constructed and finished, more than a hundred years before. She walked into the cavernous entryway, where the floors of white-and-black marble shone in a checkerboard pattern, and a grand carved central staircase led to a rotunda on the second floor. The building was simply exquisite, and Maye marveled over its elaborate architecture and the detail. It must have been quite a point of pride, she thought.

She followed the arrow that pointed to the Records Office. It was smaller than she expected, and resembled an old bank with its carved oak counter and what looked like separate teller windows. She seemed to be the only one there who wasn't on the payroll.

She walked up to one of the windows and smiled at the woman sitting behind it, her large, round glasses resting on the tops of her full, ruddy cheeks. She looked back at Maye and asked in a dry, deep, lifeless voice if she could help her.

"Yes," Maye said, trying to smile even harder. "I'm looking for the records of an individual, anything you might have on this person—birth, death, marriage, titles, anything at all, really."

"Fill out this form, please," the woman said as she slid a piece of blue paper under her window toward Maye, then watched as Maye tried to find a pencil in her purse and then as she filled out the form. Maye slid the blue paper back under the window toward the woman, who then stamped it "Received."

"Relative?" she asked without expression.

"I'm sorry?" Maye asked, not really understanding what she meant.

"Are you a relative?" she asked louder. "Are you related to this person? You didn't check the 'relations' box."

"That's because I'm not related," Maye replied.

"Then what do you want with this Spicer woman?" the clerk asked, boring her eyes into Maye's as if it was an interrogation.

"It's personal," Maye finally said, and left it at that.

The clerk studied the form, then looked back up at Maye from behind her oversized lenses. "What personal year are we looking at here, then?" she asked.

"I'm not sure," Maye said. "I guess a death certificate could be at any time, but everything else—I don't know, maybe fifty, sixty years ago?"

The woman pressed her lips together and shook her head. "Nope, sorry," she said without remorse. "Can't do it."

"Excuse me?" Maye replied. "Why? Did I do something wrong? Did I fill something out incorrectly? Those documents aren't sealed; they're public records."

"That may be, but I can't show you what I haven't got," the woman answered. "Everything over fifty years ago is gone. We don't have them. A fire destroyed City Hall and everything in it. If you need anything more recent than that, we can help, but anything back there just doesn't exist anymore."

Maye was sure she looked as confused as she felt.

"City Hall burned down?" she repeated. "Fifty years ago? But what about the plaque by the door and the historic marker? This is an old building. It's a Victorian building. It was built one hundred years ago."

The clerk shrugged as she turned on her revolving stool, got up, and began to waddle away. "They built it back," the clerk said simply. "Just the way it was. Don't ask me."

Maye stood there for a moment, not sure what to do or say.

"There weren't any copies?" she asked the clerk, who returned her query with a deadpan expression.

Maye sighed. "Okay," she continued. "How about anything, then? Any record you've got from the time of lost records until now?"

"You want me to do a search of all public records until now?" the woman repeated. Maye nodded. The waddler waddled back to her stool.

"For Spicer?" she asked. "Ruby?"

She typed in the name and looked truly bothered and put out as she waited for the results, which took several long, imposing seconds.

"Nope," she informed Maye quickly. "Got nothing. Not a thing. That's odd, usually something pops up. But no birth, no death, no marriage records. And you wanted a search in this county?"

"Yep," Maye nodded again, feeling defeated.

"Maybe you got the spelling wrong," she suggested as she hoisted herself off the stool and began to walk away. "It's almost like this person was never here at all."

"I know for a fact she was," Maye replied stoutly as she called out to the woman, who had disappeared into a back room where Maye saw the hulking shadow of a soda machine, but there was no response.

Maye shook her head, furrowed her brow, and retraced her steps through the marble-floored entry hall with the grand staircase that did not hold any possibility of being only fifty years old.

That is ridiculous, she said to herself. That woman doesn't know what she's talking about. Idiot! What a jackass to even say something like that, just because she's too lazy to look up some records. Making up a lie like that! That woman was as useless as a room full of Styrofoam!

And just like that, Maye had a brilliant idea.

♀   ♀   ♀

As Maye climbed up the steps to the cream-colored tongue-and-groove porch, she wondered if this was something she really needed to be doing. Mr. McMahon had just lost his wife. Did she really need to be bothering him with such a matter as trying to find what apparently was the ghost of Ruby Spicer?

If I had any other choice, Maye told herself, I would take it. If I knew of anyone else around here who has lived in Spaulding as long as Cynthia's husband, I'd knock on that front door instead. I need to get this story and there is no other way, she said to herself again, and maybe Mr. McMahon would be happy to have some company. If it looks like I'm bothering him, I'll just give him the gift and leave.

Maye reached up and knocked on the door, and after several seconds she heard some shuffling from behind it. As the door opened, the notes of Artie Shaw's "Moonglow" drifted into the hallway from a back room.

"Hiya, Maye," Pat McMahon said with a smile. "How have you been? Did you get your peanuts recycled all right?"

"Oh, fine, thank you," she said as her neighbor motioned for her to come in. "And you? I hope you didn't have to wait too long on line."

"Oh, no, Elsie just piled that Renegade of hers up with bags and boxes and even attached a little trailer to the back of it that she usually uses to pull her dogs, grandkids, or oxygen tanks in," Pat said. "By the time I got there, she was at the front of the line."

"This is for you," Maye said holding up the orchid with pure white blossoms on a long, elegant stem. "If there is a flower that personifies Cynthia, it would have to be exquisite. I saw this one yesterday, and it reminded me of her."

"That's so nice," he said, taking it from Maye and admiring its flawless, snow-colored blooms. "She would have loved it."

Maye smiled. "At Cynthia's memorial service, you mentioned that you met her in high school," she began. "And I was wondering if I could ask you some questions about Spaulding's history. You know Cynthia agreed to sponsor me for this year's Sewer Pipe Queen Pageant, and now, with her passing, I'm not sure if I'll go on to compete without her."

"Oh, she'd want you to," Pat said, nodding vigorously. "She loved that celebration and the contest. She would want you to go on. She may have only held the title for a year, but Cynthia was a Sewer Pipe Queen for her whole life. Have you found another sponsor yet?"

"No," Maye said. "That's what I wanted to talk to you about. I went to the library to do some research, but I have no way of knowing what their names are now, if they're still in Spaulding, or if they've—"

"Run into the white light," Pat finished.

Maye nodded. "There was one in particular that I was hoping you'd know something about," she added carefully. "From the newspaper clippings, it looked like she was a Spaulding favorite and would be the perfect sponsor. But I can't seem to find anything about her at all, and the clerk at the Records Office gave me some odd story about City Hall burning down, if you can believe that!"

"Oh, but it did," Pat confirmed. "City Hall went up, the movie theater went up, the hardware store was gone, and even Spaulding Sewer Pipe got a match to it. That was a bad summer. You won't get too many people ready to talk about that. Besides, it's all back to the way it was, can't even tell—even I forget most of the time. That summer is all over with. No need to think about it again."

"Oh," Maye said. "I thought the clerk was lying to get out of trying to help me."

"Nope," he said, taking a seat on the couch exactly where Maye had sat during the afternoon tea. "She was right. Now, who's this lady you're trying to find?"

"Her name was Ruby Spicer," Maye started. "She was the Sewer Pipe Queen decades ago. And except for those clippings, I can't find anything on her. She was never listed in the phone book, and now the records really are all gone."

Pat looked at Maye and nodded slowly, then reached for his pipe on the side table next to the couch.

"She was young, I don't know how old, but she had dark, wavy hair, shoulder-length. She seemed short, even tiny, almost," Maye continued, hoping her description would trigger something in Pat's memory. "Her eyes were very big, but also quite soft-looking, and she was just incredibly—"

"Beautiful," Pat finished for Maye as he lit the pipe and sucked on the tip several times to get it going. "Marvelously beautiful."

"You know who I'm talking about?" Maye asked, seeing the first spark of hope in her search. "You knew Ruby Spicer?"

"Of course," he said, exhaling a ring of smoke. "This was a small town then, even smaller than it is now. Everybody knew everybody. Ruby was a nice girl, very kind, very sweet. And she was a looker, I tell you. Looked just like Rita Hayworth *but prettier*. But she had a mind of her own, that gal. She was a firecracker, I tell you. A redhead."

"What happened to her?" Maye asked, trying to tone down her excitement. "Do you know where she is? Is she still in Spaulding? According to anyone I've talked to about her, she just vanished."

"Yep," Pat agreed. "That's about what happened. I don't know where she went. One day she was just gone, right in the middle of her year as queen. What about some of the other Old Queens? There are plenty of them rattling around here."

"But," Maye began, hoping that wasn't all he knew, "did she get married, did she move away? I mean, all of a sudden, she was just gone? A girl that everyone knew? A girl that everyone liked? And no one knows what happened to her?"

"Aw, Maye," Pat said with a small chuckle. "This was a small town back then, a really small town. A pretty girl like that saw a way out to a bigger life and took it, that's all. I don't know why she left, but it's not something a bunch of people in Spaulding back then wish they hadn't done themselves."

"And she never came back to visit? No one kept in touch with her? She had no ties back here at all?" Maye asked.

Pat shook his head. "Even if she did come back to town, her folks lived miles outside of town by Crawford Lake—not much reason to go by there. Bad fishing, hard to get to, the road still hasn't been paved out there. People come, people go. Do you know what happened to the people you went to high school with, except for good friends?"

"No," Maye said, seeing his point.

"Well, there you go," Pat concluded. "Now go on out there and find yourself another Old Queen."

"And you don't remember anything else about her disappearance?" Maye asked in one final effort.

"I wouldn't call it a disappearance as much as I'd call it leaving," he said with a smile. "Now, I just bought some donuts from the organic bakery, that Hoo Doo Donuts place. Would you like one?"

Maye smiled back. She couldn't bear another tragedy on her hands.

"I'd love one," she said.

ᚦ   ᚦ   ᚦ

Maye heard the car pull into the driveway and got up quickly to unlock the front door. As she turned the bolt, she looked out to see him getting the toolbox out of the back of his car.

He had fallen for the bait.

Well, that's a bit dramatic, Maye thought. The bathroom sink was really broken, sort of. In a way.

She had been standing in front of it washing her face the night before, rubbing at particularly stubborn jelly donut spots on her chin, neck, and cheek, when she had the most magnificent revelation after eating several of the best donuts she had ever had at Pat's. So good and happy she felt almost light-headed, quite possibly teetering on the verge of a sugar-induced coma. She was not ready to abandon the mystery of Ruby Spicer. Not just yet. And now she had a plan.

"Charlie!" Maye yelled for her husband, who was apparently too busy being a victim of Selective Man Deafness to answer.

She decided to try a more direct approach.

"Charlie!" she screamed this time. "Charlie, oh my God! The sink is backing up! It's filling up with water! It won't drain! Help, Charlie, help!"

Within a second, Maye heard his size-thirteen feet flopping against the pine stairs. It sounded like buffalo pounding down the prairie.

"Charlie, hurry!" she called as she let the water flow over the basin rim and dribble onto the floor. "Help me, Charlie, help! It's overflowing!"

Charlie burst into the bathroom with a wrench in his hand, ready to save his family from certain danger.

"Do something!" Maye egged him on as the water began to puddle at her feet. "Charlie, it's flooding!"

He pushed Maye out of the way and immediately went to work on the bathroom main with his wrench instead of simply turning off the faucet, which Maye gingerly did when he wasn't looking.

Her husband studied the pipe, looked down the drain, and stuck his finger into it as far as it would go, undoubtedly pushing the little wad of toilet paper Maye had stuffed in there down even farther. After he waited for the sink basin to drain, he attacked the pipes with vigor, and within six minutes and after breaking a sweat worthy of a woman giving birth, he had a chrome pipe puzzle on his hands that rivaled the difficulty of getting Pakistan to have lunch with India.

"It's okay, honey," she said after he had spent a good hour trying to fit the pieces together again. "But we have two choices here: you could e-mail Norm or I could help you fix it."

"Fine," Charlie said, throwing down his wrench. "Call your cop. And remember to ask him about Bueno Gusto. I found a questionable hair and what looked like a tooth in my fajita wrap the other day."

So, armed with an ulterior motive, Maye opened the door as John Smith trudged through it, his toolbox in his right hand and the answers that Maye needed locked away somewhere in that brain of his.

He nearly gasped when he saw the mess on the bathroom floor.

"It's a massacre in here," he said, scooping up the pipes gently. "And I certainly recognize the signature of the lunatic who did this. I believe he also bludgeoned your kitchen pipes into a coma, did he not?"

"He did," Maye affirmed. "But he thought he ate a fajita tooth at Bueno Gusto yesterday, so he was a little unnerved. What's the prognosis on this?"

"Hundred and fifty bucks," he answered. "And tell him he's lucky if a tooth is all he ate at that place. I once saw them serve something that looked like it was blinking."

"Speaking of husbands," she added, "my next one is going to be an orphan *and* a plumber."

Maye went into the kitchen, got a plate and a napkin, and returned to the bathroom to witness a yeastier, doughier version of plumber's crack, this one more potent because the plumber was also a cop with a Hoo Doo hankering.

"Boston crème," she said before she took a bite, "is my favorite."

John Smith slowly turned around. "Whatcha got there?" he asked.

"Just a little donut," she said. "Have you ever had the Boston crème from the organic bakery?"

"Ooooh, you mean Hoo Doo Donuts?" John asked, tackling the pipes. "No, I've never had that one. Those run out early! It looks good."

"Well, they use this French vanilla custard made from scratch with fresh cream," Maye explained slowly. "And then they drizzle a Belgian chocolate glaze on top. They're incredible. I've never had a donut like it. I don't even mind the fourth chin I just sprouted because of it, it's that good. "

"It sounds pretty yummy," John said, fitting the plumbing pieces together expertly. "And the kitchen in the Hoo Doo is so clean you could do DNA testing in there."

"Very good to know!" Maye said, taking another bite. "What's your favorite kind of donut?"

John grinned. "Jelly," he said.

"Strawberry or raspberry?"

"Both." He laughed. "But I shouldn't. I'm watching my weight. It's getting hard to bend over, and I got a strange rash the last time I had to chase a perp."

"Pffft!" Maye pooh-poohed him. "They're organic! And besides, your luck is incredible. You should buy a lottery ticket on the way home, because have I got something for you! And about the rash—bike shorts are God's secret little miracle for donut lovers like us."

Maye disappeared, and after a moment she popped back into the bathroom—now perfectly reassembled with the wad of toilet paper resting on the soap dish—with a plate holding two jelly donuts, one strawberry, one raspberry.

"Thank you!" he said with wide, Hoo Doo eyes, then dug into one.

"How about some coffee?" Maye asked, and John, his mouth occupied with the donut, nodded vigorously. "Come on, come into the kitchen."

John followed Maye into the kitchen, where she put a hot cup of coffee and a box of donuts on the table of the breakfast nook.

"Hoo Doo donuts make me . . . happy," he said as Maye slid into the bench across from him.

"Have another one," Maye said as she placed another circle of love, a custard-filled, on his plate before he could protest. "So, John, tell me, why are you a cop and a plumber?"

"Well," he managed to get out in between mouthfuls. "I'm a plumber because I can charge you a hundred fifty bucks to put some pipes back together and I can't charge you a hundred fifty when I find out who stole your bike. I solve problems in both of my jobs, but one bought me a small fishing boat and the other one makes me feel like I'm doing something. My dad was a policeman in Spaulding, so far back that there weren't any radios then, you know. There was just a tall, red light in the center of town, right in the town square, and when that thing flashed, all the officers knew to get to a phone ASAP and call in to find out what was going on. He loved helping people and keeping them safe, so I kind of wanted to carry on the tradition, you know?"

"Was there really a red light in the town square?" Maye asked, intrigued. "I've never seen it. Is it still there?"

"Nah," John said, finishing off another donut as Maye slid yet another onto his plate. "The light was on top of a tall pine pole. It burned the same night City Hall did, but no one knew it because it burned before it could even be turned on."

He took another bite as powder grazed his nose, making him look like he just stepped out of the restroom at Bungalow 8.

"The department got radio communication equipment after that night, you bet," he continued. "Whole town changed after that night. Well, not really, I mean, it looks the same now as it did then, but you know, when your town burns down, things are bound to turn."

Maye nodded. "I found out about City Hall when I was trying to do research for a project," Maye replied. "Before that, I had no idea. The building looked old, it smelled old, it certainly fooled me. How did it catch fire?"

John took another bite and shrugged. "I was a kid," he said, chewing. "But it just did. Everything here is built of wood, we're in the middle of the forest. Doesn't take much to get a spark going, especially in the summer."

"Didn't a lot of things burn down that year, though?" Maye questioned. "That seems kind of odd. The movie theater, the hardware store, the pipe factory?"

"Could have been a dry year," John said as he plucked a cruller out of the box. "A cigarette butt and some dry weeds is all it takes sometimes. Rumor had it that a rival pipe company took a match to everything to drive our factory out of business. Is it hot in here?"

"I don't feel warm," Maye commented. "Probably all of this fire talk. But that sounds like quite a story. For such a small town, Spaulding is full of stories."

"Yeah," the plumber cop said, finally beginning to slow down after eating more than half the box—approximately 2,170 calories, 260 grams of carbs, including 125 grams of sugar, 119 grams of fat, and absolutely no protein value. In a moment or two, he would be riding the best sugar high money could buy, because even though Hoo Doo donuts were organic, a Hoo Doo donut without a substantial amount of sugar, albeit pesticide-free, would be a lonely, out-of-business, chapter 11 donut.

"Oh," John professed, "I feel a little dizzy, but these donuts are so good. They are the best donuts. THE BEST DONUTS! Dude, like, you don't even know! No WAY, they're so good! So, now—wait, what did you say? Hee hee hee."

"I said 'Spaulding is full of stories,' " Maye repeated.

"It is," John said, giggling, his face flushing a little as the charging wall of sugar entered his bloodstream. "I feel like I'm flying! Do you feel that? Hee hee hee. If I was a bird, I'd be a . . . scrub jay. So pretty. Pretty little scrub jay! No! *No!* I'd be a heron! I'd be a heron so this way I could still fish. How would I drive my boat, though, if I was a heron? Could wings drive? Oh, that's funny. A heron driving a boat! Hee hee hee. *Dude.* Have you been there the whole time?"

Maye nodded. "Tell me some stories, John," she coaxed. "Tell me some Spaulding stories."

"In fourth grade I ate a Sloppy Joe too fast and threw it up all over my desk and it got all over my teacher's shoes. We never ate Sloppy Joes again in school after that."

"That's funny." She smiled. "How about another one? What about the story of Ruby Spicer?"

"She was pretty," John slurred as he chewed. "Ruby Spicer was prettier than a scrub jay, but she was a spitfire. She left town, though. She had to, she didn't have a choice. My dad, he gave me a dog he got from her. He liked her, said we needed to be nice to her. I love that dog, Rocky. He's a good ole dog."

"Rocky was the dog you had as a little boy?" Maye asked.

"No, no, no, nooooo," John said, shaking his head somewhat sloppily. "He's the dog I have now, a boxer. She breeds them out on that old farm she lives on. All alone. Not a friend in the world."

"Really?" Maye said as she took the chocolate-glazed donut with rainbow sprinkles out of John's limp, intoxicated fingers. "Really. Now drink your coffee, John. Drink it all up."

10

No Promises, No Demands

"Okay, Mickey," Maye coaxed as Gwen looked on. "Are you ready?"

Mickey looked at Maye with his soft brown eyes and thought, I don't need to be playing a piano. I'm a dog. I should be messing with my nu-nu.

"Now, when the music comes on, put Mickey's paws on the keys, say 'Tinkle,' and then give him a cookie," the trainer instructed.

" 'Tinkle'?" Maye asked.

"Unless you use that command at home for Mickey's personal business, this word is new to him," Gwen explained. "It could mean anything."

Maye figured she was right, and waited for Gwen's cue.

The trainer nodded as she pushed the "play" button on her boom box, which was as big as something out of a Run-D.M.C. video, and they heard a roll of electronic drums, then the notes of what sounded like a Moog synthesizer. For some reason, Maye suddenly got the image of a dance-hall girl shimmying in a skirt of rags. "Tinkle!" Gwen shouted. "Tinkle!"

Maye placed Mickey's paws on the keyboard, said, "Tinkle!" and then gave him a cookie, although now, for some unknown reason, she had in her mind the picture of a white-vested grinning pimp with a gold tooth.

" 'We are young!' " she heard an echoing voice sing. " 'Heartache to heartache we stand!' "

"Um, Gwen? Gwen?" Maye called loud enough to be heard over the blasting music, giving her the time-out sign. "Gwen, could we possibly teach Mickey to play piano to something other than 'Love Is a Battlefield'?"

The trainer looked utterly defeated. "You don't like that song?"

"Well, um," Maye stuttered, "it's, um, not that I don't like it, but when I hear it, I'm transported back to 1983 and a red-headed mongrel of an adolescent with a whitehead the size of a nickel on the tip of his nose is attempting to shove his slug of a tongue down my throat as I am sitting in a swiveling bucket seat in the front of his dad's Chevy van on the bad losing end of a double date while my best friend has basically completed a conjugal visit with her companion, who just got out of juvenile detention the week before for setting fire to an apartment building. Not the makings of a yearbook memory."

"Oh," Gwen said sadly. "Well, this is the only record I have."

"Okay," Maye said, trying to smile. "Maybe we can try another one next week."

"No," Gwen said, emphatically shaking her head. "I mean I only have this one. This is my only CD. I don't have another one."

Maye stopped for a moment. "You mean, *ever*?" she asked. "You don't own another CD?"

"Well, I like this one," Gwen said defensively. "There was no reason to get another one. I know all the words."

Maye didn't know what to say to a middle-aged woman whose entire musical universe revolved around Pat Benatar, but it was clear that Gwen probably hadn't done too much dating in the eighties, otherwise her scars would have run as deep as Maye's. Deep as a river, thick as an eager tongue.

"This is Pat Benatar's *Greatest Hits*," Gwen offered hopefully. "What about 'Hell Is for Children'?"

Maye cringed inwardly and waved her hand. " 'Love Is a Battlefield' will be fine," she said, stretching her lips across her teeth in what was supposed to be a smile but looked more like she was getting a rabies shot. It couldn't be helped—she remembered Pat Benatar having a dance-off with a pimp as she's backed by a clan of fellow whores and hussies as they snap their fingers and shimmy their way out of a sex dungeon and arrive underneath a bridge near the docks, where they find freedom.

"We are strong!" Benatar insisted as Maye placed Mickey's paws on the keyboard, told him to tinkle, and gave him a cookie. They did this for the remainder of the hour, while Gwen mouthed the words and shuffled her anvil-like weight from one leg to the other in what Maye presumed was an unnatural attempt at dance.

Mickey caught on quickly, as he always did when liver-flavored cookies were involved, and when Maye cued him with a howl, he would sing back as he "tinkled" on the keyboard, making him a four-legged and slightly hairier version of Barry Manilow getting down with a song about sex workers.

When the class was over, Maye waited as the rest of the dogs cleared out.

"Gwen, I was wondering if you might be able to help me with something," she said as the trainer packed up her mammoth, circus-sized boom box.

"Sure," the trainer said as she carefully removed the CD like it was evidence at a crime scene, laid it to rest in its little case, then snapped the case closed. "What do you need?"

"I was hoping that you might be familiar with dog breeders in the area. Do you happen to know anyone who breeds boxers?"

Gwen sucked in a torrent of air, clasped both hands to her mouth, and clearly squealed.

"Oh my goodness!" she gushed, appearing to be fighting back tears. "Really? Oh, that's wonderful! A puppy! A baby puppy for Mickey! How wonderful! What great news! Look at you, you're glowing already! Can I throw you a shower? We can have it right here in the store and get a puppy-shaped cake!"

"No, no," Maye replied, waving her hand slightly. "It's not for us, it's . . . for a friend of Charlie's at work. He was thinking about getting a boxer, and I thought you might know of someone in the area."

"Oh," the trainer replied as disappointment deflated her spine and she resumed her Charlie Brown posture. "Well, I do know of a fellow out by New River who has boxers."

"Mmmm." Maye squinted and shook her head. "Anyone else? I heard there might be a breeder out by Crawford Lake."

"Oh, yes." Gwen nodded, thinking. "Yes, I do remember a boxer lady out that way. From what I heard, she was a bit of a pistol. The fellow by New River is a much nicer man. And he has beautiful dogs."

Maye had struck gold.

"Do you know how Charlie's friend could get in touch with the Crawford Lake lady?" Maye asked. "A phone number, an address?"

"Oh, sure," Gwen said as she wrapped her boom box cord in a precise pattern of tight, bundled eights. "We keep a list of certified breeders up at the Pet Station info desk. Let's go and take a look."

Maye and Mickey followed Gwen to the front of the store. Gwen flipped open the binder holding the list of breeders, and her eyes followed her finger as she scanned the names. "Ah! Here we go," she said with a snap of her fingers. "This must be her: 'Royal Loyal Boxers, the only friend you'll ever need.' Seventeen Crawford Lake Road, and here's a phone number."

Maye copied the information down feverishly, almost as if she was afraid it would evaporate suddenly.

I know where Ruby Spicer is! I have found her! Maye's mind shot back and forth like a Ping Pong ball. I'm pretty sure I've found her. I think I've found her. I might have found her.

"Thank you so much Gwen," Maye said as she stuffed the piece of paper into her purse. "You've been a tremendous help. Charlie's friend will be so happy."

"Well, I'm glad." Gwen shrugged. "I'll see you both next week!"

"No promises, no demands," Maye said, and she winked.

ᛣ ᛣ ᛣ

Pat was right. Crawford Lake Road was not paved, and not only was it a bumpy dirt road, it was full of potholes that looked more like spots where meteors had bounced off the face of the earth the way a basketball inevitably rebounds off the head of the fat girl in freshman gym class. Maye's forehead still stung with the slap of orange rubber every time she thought about it.

As Maye drove along, topping speeds of seven to ten miles an hour, the car rocked, dipped, and fell every couple of feet. She was grateful to have eaten more than an hour earlier, otherwise, she was sure, she would have succumbed to seasickness. Vomiting was not on her schedule today. Hopefully, unless she drove straight into a sinkhole—a real possibility—she was going to be face-to-face with Ruby Spicer in about ten gut-churning minutes.

If she could find her.

Once Maye had the phone number in her hand, she had grown gradually and strangely anxious. She'd surprised herself by letting the scribbled-on piece of paper soak in her purse for the rest of the day.

When Charlie came home that night, she had finally dug it out and handed it to him without a word. He'd looked at it, rolled his eyes, and shaken his head.

"No," he'd commanded. "Absolutely not. We don't need another dog, Maye. I agree that a dog band would be funny and they could perform at weddings and bar mitzvahs and we could retire, but no. Especially if this one played the drums, because I'm calling dibs on the drummer spot in Dog Band. I am the stick man."

"Charlie, sometimes even the mere fact that you found your way home at night seems like a miracle to me," Maye had said, shaking her head back. "You are an idiot. I don't want another dog. This is the phone number of Ruby Spicer. She raises boxers."

"The Queen of all Sewer Pipe Queens?" Charlie had asked. "The one you read about in the library? Wow. How did you get that?"

"I got the plumber high on donuts and exposed Mickey to repeated, three-minute shock treatments of Pat Benatar," she had explained. "All skills taught in Journalism 101. Worked like magic. Imagine what I could have done had I let three women with bad perms give me a bath in a backyard. I could have ruled the world."

"Wow," Charlie had said. "I can't believe you found her. That's some detective work you did there, Columbo."

"Well," Maye had said, then paused. "I'm not exactly sure it is her—I mean, all of the pieces fit, but I don't have one hundred percent confirmation that it's Ruby Spicer. And after the fifth donut, the plumber was pretty wasted. He could have been making the whole thing up for all I know, or having sugar-related hallucinations."

"So, did you call her?" Charlie had asked.

Maye had shaken her head. "I want it to be her. I wanted you to be here in case I was disappointed and it wasn't her and I'd have to hand the pageant over to Rowena and Melissabeth after all on one of my tablecloth-eating fat rolls."

Charlie had walked over to the phone, picked it up, and handed it to her. "I'll stay right here," he had promised.

So Maye had dialed the number with shaky, hesitant fingers, and on the fourth ring, the sleepy voice of a woman answered. Maye hadn't asked for Ruby—since there was no name listed in the breeder's directory, she hadn't wanted to tip her off to anything other than being interested in a dog—and had simply inquired if Royal Loyal had any available boxers.

"Sure," the woman had replied, yawning. "I have some available from the last litter." She'd given Maye directions to "the farm," told her to come out the following afternoon, and promptly hung up the phone.

Now, twenty miles out of town, with the directions in hand, Maye was closer to meeting the vanished Sewer Pipe Queen of Spaulding. Deep in the rain forest of the Cascade foothills, the western hemlock, cedar, and fir trees loomed high above the floor carpeted with ferns and huckleberry bushes and spotted with patches of sunlight that had pushed its way through the dense branches of the canopy. Moss clung to trunks and tree branches, and the farther Maye drove, the darker it seemed to get. She followed the curvy road that had begun to resemble more of a path as it wound deeper still into the woods until it finally opened onto a meadow, bright and clear and flooded with sun, fronted by an old gray farmhouse. As she got closer, Maye realized the house wasn't actually gray but was weathered by the elements after most of the paint had flaked off of it and fluttered away, pulled by the wind.

She turned in to the driveway in front of the house and stopped the car. Ramshackle (and that was being kind), it was the sort of place you'd typically only see in documentaries about the Unabomber or people who refuse to pay taxes but then decide that shooting at government agents with rifles from their kitchen window is an appropriate avenue of recourse. It was definitely not a place you'd expect to find a former Sewer Pipe Queen holed up unless she had stopped paying taxes and was planning a hoedown with the ATF through a scope.

Maye left the safety of her car and headed for the front door, which featured a giant carved relief of the face of a boxer. Wow, she thought, you really have to make sure your devotion to a breed isn't a flight of fancy to chip away at your front door until the head of one pops out. Maye couldn't find a doorbell, so she rapped her knuckles on the boxer's forehead. For quite a while she heard only the barking of what sounded like numerous dogs, but as she was getting ready to rap on the door again, she detected a fair amount of shuffling from behind the door and finally heard a thin, nasally, crackly voice call out, a little slowly, "Hold your horses, would ya? I'm coming, I'm coming."

Maye immediately thought she had gotten the time of their appointment wrong; the person behind the door sounded like she'd just awoken. She felt foolish, ashamed of herself for disturbing an old woman napping, even if it was in the middle of the afternoon.

But as the door with the head of the boxer swung back, an old woman was not standing behind it.

A wrinkled old crone was.

Maye was so stunned, surprised, shocked, that she was speechless and couldn't find a thing to say or, for that matter, a tongue to say it with.

Now, to be fair, Maye hadn't known what to expect when Ruby Spicer answered the door—she'd thought perhaps she would resemble Cynthia in her impeccable appearance, her perfect posture, and unmistakable grace, but this wasn't exactly the case behind the boxer door number one. In the pictures Maye had seen, Ruby looked to be in her late teens to early twenties, vibrant, beautiful, and with a sparkle in her eye that suggested she was the kind of girl who wasn't afraid to make a little bit of mischief if it meant a good story and a laugh later on. True, five decades had passed, but Maye couldn't find any trace of that young woman in the old woman who stood before her.

That beauty queen plus fifty years had equaled a tiny, skinny, wilted, wrinkly, red-lipstick-encrusted old woman with fiery red hair and only one eyebrow—the remnant of a previous eyebrow had been singed as if in a brush fire, and she was sucking on a Viceroy cigarette, looking a lot like Bette Davis in *Burnt Offerings* but apparently way more drunk and not nearly as well kept.

"You called about the puppy?" the woman asked in a raspy voice, and after a moment, Maye nodded in the only form of communication available to her in that moment.

"Come on in," the old bag said, stepping back so Maye could enter.

Maye tried to smile as she passed the biddy, but the combination of decades' worth of cigarette smoke and the eau de doggie from the numerous boxers that were standing guard—even several who had come into the room since Maye's arrival to evaluate the visitor—made smiling a challenging task indeed.

The crone, dressed in a yellow terrycloth sweat suit with several burn holes directly below the neckline, closed the door and motioned for Maye to sit on the couch. As she did, Maye looked up at the grungy yellow-stained walls, the stinky brown barkcloth curtains, and the mud-colored bald carpeting, all shellacked with a grimy, dull film of exhaled nicotine and exuding its coordinating smell. Christ, she thought, it's like this woman is living inside of a diseased, shabby lung.

"So," the woman said, lowering herself nearly to the ground and taking a seat on the floppy, disintegrating sofa that even Maye could feel the springs through despite her well-endowed derrière. "Have you ever had a boxer before?"

Maye shook her head.

"Well," the woman said, taking a deep drag on her cigarette before continuing, "they're very loyal, very strong, very smart, very tolerant around children. You can count on them. Excellent companions. Would you like to see the puppy now?"

Maye suddenly realized that she didn't really know if this was Ruby—this woman could have been anyone, really—she hadn't introduced herself, making it possible that there really was a beautiful, elegant Ruby Spicer somewhere locked in an upstairs bedroom who spoke in a flawless Brahmin accent and was on the verge of being fed her pet canary by her jealous, decrepit evil sister.

"I'm Maye," she said suddenly, and stuck out her hand.

The old woman seemed to be taken off guard and looked at Maye out of the corner of her eye.

She paused for a moment, switched her cigarette from her right hand to her left, then begrudgingly held out her nicotine hand in a gesture that made her seem even smaller than she really was. "I'm," she said quietly, "Ruby."

"Nice to meet you," Maye said as she shook the tiny skeleton hand with fingers that resembled twigs freshly snapped off a branch.

"Do you wanna see that puppy or not?" the old woman snapped suddenly, pulling back her hand.

Maye thought this would be a good time to come clean, but

before she could muster up the courage, Ruby, with a rattle and a wheeze from her lungs, called out as loud as she could manage, "PUPPY! PUPPY, COME!"

Within seconds, a gangly, large, and quite robust dog emmerged from the dog crowd, took a bounding leap, and flew onto the couch beside Maye, where it proceeded to dance and bounce on the beaten, weary cushions.

"This is the . . . puppy?" Maye asked as she tried to pet the clearly very adult dog, so adult that the fringes of his snout were turning gray.

"He's the last of the litter," Ruby replied with her raspy voice. "Is he what you were looking for?"

"He looks a little big to me," Maye said as Puppy took a swipe at the side of her head with his welcome mat of a tongue. "I'd put him at sixty or sixty-five pounds already."

"Achh, he's fifty if he's ten," Ruby hedged. "He's big for his age."

"Actually, I was looking for something a little different," Maye started, the courage bubbling up from her stomach and finally reaching her throat as Puppy's tongue climbed up her face again in a full-throttle slurp. "I'm looking for Ruby Spicer, the Sewer Pipe Queen."

Within the moment that it took Maye to finish that sentence Ruby had sprung to her feet and immediately brandished her cigarette at Maye as if it were a shiv.

"Get out!" the old shrew roared as loud as her craggy voice would permit, her breath soaked in alcohol. "GET OUT or I'll torch you!"

Maye hadn't expected that—in fact, she realized then that she'd never really anticipated any specific sort of response, let alone a violent, angry one by a loaded woman waving a lit cigarette at her. She was entirely shocked, as was Puppy, who had stopped in midlick to stand at attention before his wailing master.

"I'm sorry," Maye said immediately. "I'm so sorry. I didn't mean any harm. I didn't mean to upset you. I'm sorry that I've upset you, but if I could just explain why I'm here—"

"You'll be amazed at how fast an eyebrow can go up!" Ruby screeched, her jaw protruding, her eyes wide and angry. "All of that queen business is behind me. Haven't you people had enough?"

Apparently, Maye hadn't been the only one who had sought out the once-mighty queen for her sponsorship. Maye had overstepped her bounds, invaded the guarded privacy of an old woman, and she felt ashamed of herself. She was shrouded in embarrassment.

"I'm very sorry," she said, grabbing the handle of her purse and trying to launch herself off the depths of the rotting couch. "I am so sorry to have bothered you."

"And I won't talk to you either, no matter what channel or newspaper you're from."

"I'm sorry, I didn't mean to start any trouble," Maye tried to explain.

"The only trouble we have here is what you brought in," Ruby shot, jabbing her tiny torch at Maye again. Slowly she moved aside as Maye walked past her and made her way to the door. The old woman seethed silently as Maye reached for the doorknob, turned it, pulled the door open, and walked out of the house.

Maye was horrified at herself. What was she doing, driving out to the middle of the woods only to wake an old woman up and bother her under false pretenses? What was she doing? Did she really just ambush an old lady who hadn't even been seen in town for so many years that it was thought that she had run away? Just so Maye could enter a contest?

What had she been thinking? Had she ever even once stopped to think how Ruby Spicer might react to the fact that Maye had dug her up out of the library archives and snooped around until she was eventually standing on the woman's front porch? She probably scared that drunk old woman half to death, having a stranger bring up a past that had by now been obviously forgotten and buried until Maye, like a wild animal, had dragged it out of its grave. What kind of careless, selfish person does that, Maye asked herself, especially to an elderly, wrinkled old shut-in?

"An asshole does that," Maye answered herself out loud as she walked to her car, hot tears of embarrassment flushing her eyes. "A Rick Titball variety of asshole. This is what I get. This is what I deserve. Now I have no sponsor for the pageant, and I deserve it. I deserve nothing. Pouncing on an old woman like that! Now Melissabeth and Rowena Spaulding will walk away with the title and I will just have to suck it up. Right into the fat roll. That's what I deserve. Every Christmas and faculty party from now on I will have to look at their gloating, hateful faces. I hate Rowena Spaulding!"

Maye had just opened the door to the car and had gotten behind the wheel when she heard a craggy, thin voice behind her croak, "What did you just say?"

Maye turned around, and there, through her blurry eyes, was a corncob with a crop of fire for a head. It was Ruby. Maye brushed away the tears with the back of her hand and tried to catch her breath.

"I said I was sorry for ambushing you, it was a horrible thing to do," she called from her car. "I had no right to bother you. I was so determined to find you that I didn't think that you might not want to be bothered or found or whatever it is that I did. I'm just very sorry."

"I heard that part!" Ruby creaked with an impatient wave of her hand. "I was standing right there! What was that name you said? What was that name?"

"Rick Titball?" Maye replied. "The one-man news team, 'We Are News to You'?"

"That jerk? No," Ruby shot back, shaking her head quickly. "The other name."

"Melissabeth?" Maye said, her nose still running. "She's an opera singer and she's awful. I mean, she's a great singer, but an awful person. She won't be weekend friends with me, and her husband is a root vegetable."

"No!" Ruby screeched with a stamp of her foot, which was barely clinging to a shoddy, filthy slipper. "The one after that! You said you hated somebody! Who do you hate?"

"Oh," Maye said, shaking her head. "Rowena Spaulding. She's the wife of my husband's boss, so to speak. She hates me, and I have no idea why. She was a Sewer Pipe Queen once, too. She's Melissabeth's sponsor."

"The hell she was," Ruby said, furrowing her one eyebrow and pointing her cigarette at Maye. "Blow that nose. You have shiny snot on your face. Come back into the house, I'll get you something to wipe it with."

Maye sat in the car for a moment, honestly not sure if she should follow a relatively unstable drunk woman who had minutes ago threatened to put a cigarette out on her forehead back into a claptrap of a house or turn the ignition and leave a trail of billowing dust behind her as she drove the hell out of there. Her survival instinct told her to flee, and just as Maye put the key into the ignition, she heard something hit her windshield with a small *tap!*, which was followed by another a second later and then another. *Tap! Tap!* She looked up just in time to see Ruby, in midthrow, lob a pebble into the air, which then sailed nonchalantly in a perfect arc to hit Maye's windshield with a *tap!* and then bounce off it.

Ruby Spicer was throwing rocks at her car, her left hand holding the cigarette as well as a handful of gravel. If I sit here long enough, Maye thought, that deranged old bat is going to stone me to death like I was in a Shirley Jackson short story.

"Girl! *Come on!*" the crone called impatiently. "What are you waiting for? If you're waiting for an engraved invitation, I ran out of 'em in 1957."

So Maye, devoutly ignoring her gut and subscribing to her reporter's instincts, got out of the car, picked up the frayed, soiled slipper that remained in the driveway after it had tumbled from the old woman's foot without notice, and followed a pebble-throwing drunk back into her weathered, peeling gray shack.

11

No Rest for the Wicked

Boxers circled Maye like sharks as she entered the house again, and Ruby handed her a wrinkled and mostly stained paper towel that she had pulled from her sweatpants pocket. In return, Maye handed her back the dirty, matted slipper that had been orphaned in the driveway despite the indications that it had been the favored and likely only footwear of Miss Ruby Spicer for quite some time. The old woman motioned for her to sit on the couch. Reluctantly, Maye gave a decent honk into the thin paper towel, trying diligently to avoid the stained portions, wiped her nose, and then sat down.

"I'm sorry for not being honest with you when I called," Maye said. "I wasn't looking to stir up any trouble."

"Yeah, well," Ruby replied, glaring harshly at Maye. *"The only trouble we have here is what you brought in."*

Maye paused for a moment, puzzled by Ruby's returning hostility. "Well, that's exactly what I meant. I'm still sorry, then—?"

"Eh," Ruby said. "It's from *Johnny Guitar.* Joan Crawford says that to Mercedes McCambridge, a big trouble-making woman who comes into her bar with a lynch mob, ready to throw a rope around her neck. You've never seen it? It's on all the time. It's on more than *Matlock* is."

Maye shook her head.

"You should see it sometime, then," Ruby said, taking a seat in a plaid burlap-covered rocker with maple arms that had been chewed like chum by litters upon litters of boxers dating back to the beginning of time. "Now, what's your business with Rowena Spaulding?"

"She's a horrible woman," Maye declared. "Even the first time I met her, she was insulting and condescending and she made me feel so awful and for no reason. I didn't know her, I had never met her before. It was my first bad experience in Spaulding. Do you know her?"

Ruby nodded. "I used to."

"My husband and I just moved to Spaulding, after he got a job teaching at the university in Dean Spaulding's department," Maye continued. "I don't know anyone, and it's been hard to make friends. I know it takes time, but I tried all kinds of things. I met these witches, I stalked people, I even lied, I mean, I was really trying. I had so many friends back home, and here it's so lonely. So I thought that if I entered the Sewer Pipe Queen Pageant, I could meet people that way, especially if I won the title. But then I found out that Rowena's sponsoring the opera singer, my sponsor got eaten by a raccoon, and now I have no one. Everything has fallen apart, and I am so afraid that I'm going to spend the rest of my life in this town where I don't know a single person. I just wanted a friend to go to lunch with, or someone who knew me well enough to notice I was wearing a new sweater. That's all. That's all I wanted."

Ruby said nothing and just stared at Maye for a long time, her red, smeared mouth puckered tightly. "So you're not a reporter," she finally said. "And you don't work at the TV station."

"Well," Maye replied, shaking her head, "I used to be a reporter, but I'm not anymore. I came out here to talk to you because I want to be the Sewer Pipe Queen."

"But I could swear," Ruby rattled, "that I've seen you on TV."

Maye nodded. "I was on the news once," she admitted. "When my sponsor was supposedly killed by a woodland creature."

"That's where I saw you!" the old woman declared, snapping her bony fingers. "I thought you looked familiar! You were awfully nice to the rapscallion who snacked on your neighbor. I knew that girl in high school, although she was a couple of years behind me. Pretty thing."

"No, no, no. That was Rick Titball's handiwork," Maye protested. "I never said those things, well, not exactly in those terms. That whole segment was pasted together like a ransom note."

"That one-man news team is always coming out here, trying to get me to talk to him," Ruby continued. "Doing his own makeup, setting up the camera, yelling 'Cut!' to himself. I won't have anything to do with it. I usually just send a couple of the dogs out after him. That does the trick."

"I don't know how he found you," Maye replied. "You were pretty hard to track down."

"Mmmm," Ruby said, grinding out her cigarette before lighting a new one. "They find you. Not very often, but once in a while, some nosy body comes snooping along. I guess it's not okay with some people to leave well enough alone. It's none of their damn business anyway!"

"I feel badly that I am one of those nosy bodies," Maye said. "I understand why you would be so upset, but it truly wasn't my intention."

"What exactly is your intention?" Ruby crackled, then burped without pause. "Why would you go through the trouble of driving all the way out here just to see an old Sewer Pipe Queen? There are plenty of them left in that shithole town, I'm sure. Why did you want to see me? Everyone else has forgotten everything about me except for Dick Titball."

Maye laughed. "I'm entering that Sewer Pipe Queen contest and I want to win," she explained. "That's why I'm here. I need your help. I need a coach, a sponsor to show me how to win. When I found your file in the library, it had more newspaper clippings in it than all of the other queens put together. Photographers took pictures of you everywhere you went. Every time you did something, there was a clipping of it with a photograph of you. People were fascinated by you, they had to be, otherwise why would you be in the paper so often? All those headlines— RUBY SPICER OPENS GROCERY STORE, RUBY SPICER TO ATTEND WEEKEND PARTY, RUBY SPICER KICKS UP HER HEELS AT BARN DANCE. You really were the queen of that town. No other title holder seemed to have the effect on Spaulding that you did. You were the best. You were the Queen of Queens. They *loved* you."

Ruby looked into Maye's eyes for a moment, then looked away.

"Yeah? Did you see one that said RUBY SPICER VANISHES?" the old woman finally asked quietly.

Maye didn't know what to say. It was true, the old woman was right. She didn't see a single clipping about Ruby's sudden disappearance or even speculation about what might have happened to her. It was as if Ruby Spicer got sucked into a black hole one day, and no one noticed or said a word about it. It was as if Spaulding just kept on going.

"Well, I do know that in all of my asking around about you," she said to the town's former favorite daughter, "some people thought you moved to a big city because you were so young and pretty that you'd have more opportunities there. Or that you met some fellow, ran off, and lived happily ever after."

"Heh," the old woman scoffed. "I guess it never crossed anyone's mind that I was living twenty miles out of town off a stinking dirt road in a farmhouse that my father built. No one ever thought that. Or why it might be."

A long moment passed before Maye was able to assemble enough courage to open her mouth and say, "And why was that?"

Ruby turned her head sharply and glared at Maye. "I don't need to tell you anything," she hissed as smoke billowed out of her mouth. "I don't even know you. Who are you to ask me questions? You're in my house! A stranger in my house, asking me questions!"

"I'm sorry," Maye said, standing up, not willing to be threatened again with the nearest item that Ruby could get her knotted hands around. "I think I should go. Again, I'm sorry that I disturbed you."

"I'm such a fool, such an old fool," Ruby said, suddenly weeping into her hands. "These are only tears of gratitude—an old maid's gratitude for the crumbs offered. . . . You see, no one ever called me darling before."

Again, Maye was stumped. Maybe the old woman was senile, she thought—perhaps she was hearing voices? Being stuck out in an old farmhouse for fifty years couldn't have provided too much stimulation for mind clarity or preserving whatever was there to begin with. Oh boy, Maye thought as she looked at the sobbing woman, not knowing what to do.

"Well," Maye said gently, touching Ruby on the shoulder as the woman sobbed. "Despite the fact that you tried to burn my face with your flaming cigarette, I can see that you may have some inner potential for a primitive form of kindness, but I'm sorry, I didn't call you darling. I think maybe you have misunderstood something I said?"

"Oh, goddamn it!" Ruby suddenly shouted, looking up with a somewhat disgusted dry face and throwing her hands down with a fast, hard slap on her legs, followed by a sudden, rumbling shot sounding similar to *pppppppppppppptt* that was entirely unaccounted for. "Don'tcha ever watch TV? It's Bette Davis. *Now, Voyager.* Old crazy fat lady goes on a diet and becomes beautiful, then takes a cruise and falls in love with a doctor? Have you ever seen that one? Do you even *have* a TV?"

Maye was still trying to figure out exactly what had just happened when she became engulfed in a smell that called to mind the essence of a stagnant swamp.

"Mmm," she said, trying to keep her mouth closed as tight as possible to avoid inhaling the foul odor. "I have a TV. Seen *Now, Voyager,* but it was years ago. I don't remember that line."

"How could you not remember that line?" Ruby asked, incredulous. "It's the best line in the whole damn movie! The spinster, that was Bette Davis's part, she was once in love when she was young, to a nice fellow, too, and just like that, it gets taken away from her. Snap! Just like that because of her evil mother. She spends the rest of her miserable life cooped up in an old house going insane and getting fat because of what she lost until her psychiatrist makes her lose the weight and puts her on a cruise where she meets the doctor. You might as well not ever have seen the movie if you don't remember that line. I remember that line. For years, I have remembered that line."

"I'll make a note to keep my eye out for it," Maye said quickly as her breath ran out.

"Agh!" Ruby screeched, waving her hand vigorously. "Puppy! Christ, that was a stinker!"

Puppy, knowing all too well that he had been falsely accused and convicted, no less in front of a stranger, lowered his graying snout, climbed off the ratty sofa, and slinked down the hall.

"I really should go," Maye said. "I've taken up enough of your time. I'm sure you have a lot of . . . things to do. Thank you for inviting me back in. I really enjoyed meeting you."

"Oh," Ruby said, looking surprised. "So soon? You're gonna go so soon? Well, all right then, I suppose. Don'tcha want help with the pageant? Did you change your mind?"

"No," Maye said, smiling and shaking her head. "I'm going to do it. I'll just keep looking for a sponsor if you're not available."

"I never said I wouldn't do it," the shriveled woman said. "Never said that. It's just that—well, how 'bout I think about it? I'll think about it. I'll know by tomorrow."

"Okay," Maye agreed. "Should I call you in the afternoon?"

"No, no, no," Ruby protested, seeming affronted. "Just come by. Around this time. That's a good idea, I think."

The thought of driving another forty-mile round trip to the middle of nowhere just so Ruby could refuse to help her didn't sit very nicely with Maye, but she had already realized that you didn't compromise with Miss Ruby Spicer. There was barely room to stand, let alone wiggle.

"That would be fine," she agreed.

"Good," Ruby replied victoriously. "Right around this time would be good."

"Sure," Maye complied as she headed out the door toward her car. "I'll see you then."

🍐 🍐 🍐

"Wow," Charlie said that night at dinner, his face consumed by astonishment. "I can't believe you met her. The Old Sewer Pipe Queen herself. I'm a little worried that you went out there alone, though—I don't know how I feel about that, it makes me a bit uneasy. Next time you go, make sure you take my cell phone. And bring some hobbits with you, too."

"Well, you'll have to help me travel to the Shire and trap a couple, because I'm going back to Ruby's tomorrow," Maye said.

"That's fast. Are you starting your . . . training?" he asked with a smirk, scooping a second helping of mashed potatoes onto his plate.

"Nope," she replied. "She hasn't taken me on yet. Said she needed to think it over and she'd know by tomorrow. That's why I have to go out there again."

"You can't just call her?" Charlie said, a little annoyed. "Why do you have to go all the way out to the woods to find out if she'll say yes?"

"It's Ruby, and it's a whole different world out there," Maye tried to explain. She almost added that if you pushed Ruby a fraction of an inch the wrong way, you'd wind up needing a skin graft somewhere on your body, but decided against it. "She's been out there by herself for a long time. I think it's been quite a while since that old woman has had any kind of human interaction aside from that jackass Rick Titball knocking on her door. She's even sort of—feral. It's like she's a one-person tribe who's been living deep in the forest for years and years without seeing anyone else, just her and her pack of dogs."

"So what you're telling me is that you're trying to get the Blair Witch to be your coach in a beauty pageant," Charlie commented.

"Not exactly the Blair Witch," Maye said, sort of laughing. She took a sip of wine. "More like a hybrid of Ruth Gordon and Witchiepoo from *H.R. Pufnstuf.*"

"Great," he jeered. "If you vanish in those woods and all they find of you is some videotape and a couple of teeth, I'm making them into earrings and giving them to my next wife."

"Listen," she said. "If there's even a drop of that Ruby Spicer charm buried deep in the layers of crust that she's now become, I'm never going to find that anywhere else. She had something about her the other queens simply couldn't touch, not even Cynthia. She's the Obi-Wan Kenobi of Sewer Pipe Queens, I'm telling you. She has the power. I know it's in her somewhere—a quality like that just doesn't vanish, even if *she* did. I need her as my coach, because whatever it is that Ruby Spicer has, Rowena Spaulding certainly doesn't."

"Rowena Spaulding has pickle juice in her veins," Charlie agreed. "She's nothing but brine and vinegar and a tiny raisin heart. Dean Spaulding is such a nice, gregarious man. I can't figure that pairing out for the life of me. He must see something in her we can't."

"Or maybe he can't see what we do," Maye suggested. "All I know is that I want to beat her for the title. I have to win this thing. I'd rather have liposuction in a dirty basement than see Rowena Spaulding win the right to gloat over me for the rest of my life."

"Well," Charlie said as he stood up and started to clear the dishes. "I guess tomorrow you'll find out if you have a sponsor. Save these dinner rolls, Maye; bread crumbs are cheaper than GPS and far less trouble than Frodo and friends."

ᛘ ᛘ ᛘ

The next afternoon as she was driving toward Ruby's shack, Maye found the woods far less foreboding than she had the day before. Maybe there was more sunlight illuminating the badly worn road, or perhaps the morning rain had freshened the woods up a bit, making them look more green than dark, but when she finally got to Ruby's house, even that didn't seem nearly as ruinous as it initially had. On a fresh approach, it might have only needed a coat of paint and the minor talents of a handyman. And a gardener. And maybe a roofer. Still, it was clearly not what the home of a celebrated town queen should have been.

Maye knocked on the boxer head and stood there for quite some time without hearing any signs of life inside. She knocked again, this time much louder, concerned that she didn't even hear the herd of dogs stirring. Cupping her hands around her eyes, she peered into the window next to the front door and saw two black-bottomed slippers hanging off the edge of a recliner, attached to two skinny, wrinkly legs poking out of a ragged old blue robe. Boxers lay scattered around her feet, encircling her as each breath rumbled in and out of her tar-filled lungs like a train chugging through the mountains. Maye knocked as hard as she could on the dog's head and finally heard some shuffling from behind the door. After a couple of agitated grunts, a raspy voice shouted, "Whaddya want?"

"Ruby, it's Maye!" she called. "It's Maye from yesterday."

"Who? I don't know any Maye."

"I'm the girl from yesterday."

"Oh, yeah," the gruff voice yelled back. "Whaddya want?"

Maye took a deep breath and shook her head. "You told me to come back today," she replied firmly. "So here I am."

"All right, all right," the old woman conceded as the lock clicked loudly and the door swung open on dry, creaky hinges, revealing Ruby standing behind it, exhaling a cloud of smoke through her red-lipstick-smudged mouth as the light hit her. Wearing a robe that was more threadbare than the slipper she'd left in the driveway, she stared at Maye so intently that Maye was able to tell that the brittle, stubbly eyelashes the old woman had once had on her left eyelid were now gone, leaving nothing but whiskerlike stumps of charred hair.

"Did I wake you?" Maye asked. "You said afternoon, remember?"

"Of course I remember," she snapped. "I was just resting. I had a party here last night."

"You did?" Maye asked, looking around at the tattered couch, the overflowing ashtrays on any available flat surface, and the empty plastic tumblers that left a sticky, dark circle of residue at their bases. The place looked exactly as it had the afternoon before, only a day dirtier.

"Oh, sure," Ruby said as she walked over to the couch and lowered herself into it. "Susan Hayward was here. We had ourselves a nice time, we did. Watched *I'll Cry Tomorrow, Valley of the Dolls, I Want to Live!,* and my favorite, *Smash-Up: The Story of a Woman.* They had a whole marathon on last night. I thought I'd never get to bed."

"I've seen her movies. Doesn't she play a rambling alcoholic in all of them?" Maye asked, knowing full well that Ruby had passed out in the chair.

"*No!*" Ruby scoffed. "No! In *I Want to Live!* she plays a convicted murderer sentenced to the gas chamber!"

"And during which movie did you and fire have a fight?" Maye said, pointing to her eyelashes.

"What?" the old woman replied, then felt for each of her sets of eyelashes with her nicotine-stained fingers, stopping when she touched the singed, burnt remains of her left one. "Oh. Oh, that. I lost my matches. Burner on the stove must have blown me a kiss."

With the amount of alcohol fumes currently evaporating through Ruby's skin, Maye thought, it's amazing that she didn't go up like an oil tanker.

"So," Maye started, "I was hoping that you would agree to be my sponsor for the pageant. Did you have a chance to think about it?"

"Oh," Ruby stalled. "That. I'm pretty busy, you know. I have so much to do around here. I don't know if I'd have the time. But, if I had another set of hands to help me with some things, that might make the decision making a little easier for me. You know. I might be able to decide faster, clear my head."

Maye nodded, fully getting the drift of the old woman's message. After all, she had come to this house asking for help; what was Ruby going to get in return? What was in it for her? Did Maye really expect Ruby to help her, a complete stranger, out of the goodness of her little heart when she could be watching TV and nursing her drink instead? The left hand washes the right even if one of them is a little more stained than the other—fair is fair. And the truth of the matter was that the house, despite the fresh perspective of a new day, was still a hovel in the process of tumbling down.

"What would we need to do to make your head clearer?" Maye prodded.

"Hmmm, let me think," Ruby said without pause. "Hmmmm. Oh! I think I know. Yes. Yes, this will help me make my decision so much easier."

She walked over to the small side table beside the recliner, picked up the garden spade and a plastic bag, and handed them to Maye, then pointed toward the back door.

"I have trouble bending over," Ruby explained, suddenly grabbing her back and hunching her shoulders. "And my eyesight isn't what it used to be. Sometimes, I come in and find out that all I have is a bag full of brown rocks. I can't make decisions when I have a bag full of rocks."

Half of Maye said defiantly that this was ridiculous; she was not going to pick up dog turds in the old lady's yard, especially because Ruby had more dogs than most Eskimo villages. She could be out there mining poops for the rest of the week. The other half insisted that it was no big deal; that there was really nothing wrong with helping an old woman, even if it was with an unsavory chore. Didn't she pick up Mickey's by-products? Besides, it wouldn't exactly kill Maye to do something nice for someone. She had some good karma to make up, not only for her vegetarian lies, ditching a drunk and obnoxious dinner date, and frightening innocent shoppers by stalking them, but now she needed to add to her Evil Deeds list drugging a cop, which Maye was pretty sure was a felony with mandatory prison time. Thus, she could consider this her community service if Officer Smith's sugar blackout never permitted him to recover the incident in his memory and thus press charges. There's no rest for the wicked, the good side of Maye reminded herself. Now, pick up that spade and start shoveling some shit, sister.

"Okay," Maye said as she took the bag and the shovel from Ruby, put a smile on her face, and headed outside.

A couple of hours and ten poop bags later, the backyard was finally clean—until Puppy wandered out and promptly made a fresh deposit. Maye scooped it up, added it to the last bag, and then placed the whole load in what she hoped was the garbage can and not a laundry basket.

In the living room, Ruby was back in the recliner, her eyes closed, breath shallow in a wheezy whistle. The flickering light from the black-and-white television was the only brightness in the otherwise darkened room, despite the fact that the sun had barely begun to set.

As she passed Ruby asleep on the recliner, Maye saw that she'd been watching *Hush . . . Hush, Sweet Charlotte,* in which Bette Davis, a lonely spinster shunned by the townspeople, lives in a rambling mansion and goes more and more insane by the day. The scene showing was the one in which Davis goes completely ape-shit and begins hurling objects and verbal epithets alike.

"You're a vile, sorry little bitch!" she roars at her quietly evil cousin, played by Olivia de Havilland.

Maye giggled a little. It was one of her favorite movies.

She lifted the still-burning cigarette from between Ruby's waxen, saffron-tinted fingers and ground it out in the overflowing ashtray. She shook Ruby's hand, careful not to startle her, lest the geriatric woman have the tendency to wake up swinging or trying to claw some eyeballs out.

"Ruby," she called quietly. "Ruby, the backyard is clear of brown rocks. Is your head clear enough to make a decision now?"

The old woman's head rolled from left to right. "I have always depended on the kindness of strangers," she mumbled in a ragged southern accent, her eyes still closed, her hand still hanging limp and loose.

"It's Maye, Ruby," she called to the sleeping woman again.

"Come back tomorrow," the old lady barely murmured, still not rousing.

Maye stood up, exhaled, then stepped over the pack of dogs that surrounded Ruby as she slept. As she picked up her purse and found her keys, the old woman waited in the chair, her eyes closed tight, and it wasn't until she heard the door close that she opened one of them.

ᛈ ᛈ ᛈ

"You did not spend the entire afternoon culling poop from that crazy woman's backyard," Charlie said, astounded, when Maye arrived home and told him of her afternoon.

"If she helps me, that's the least I can do for her," Maye responded as she walked through the front door and set her car keys on the entry-hall table.

"What do you mean 'if' she helps you?" he asked. "I thought she was going to tell you today if you two were a team or not."

Maye shook her head. "By the time I got done scooping up the debris field of Ruby's dog collection," she explained, "she'd fallen asleep again. When I left, she was muttering dialogue from *A Streetcar Named Desire*, then told me to come back tomorrow."

"I'm sorry to say it, but it's time for you to rethink this whole thing," Charlie cautioned. "Someone isn't playing fair."

"If I had another option, I would," Maye replied. "But I'm a little stuck where I am. Plus, I really do believe that once we get down to the training, she'll come through, I know it. She's just taking advantage of the situation, and if I was a shut-in who didn't want to pick up dog shit, I'd certainly push that on someone else, given the chance."

"I don't know. Maybe you should drop out and enter the pageant next year," Charlie offered. "This way you'd have a whole year to find another coach who wouldn't try to force you into indentured servitude."

"No," Maye said resolutely. "It's going to be this year. It has to be this year. I don't want to spend another twelve months stalking people at the grocery store, friend-dating people who down bottles of wine that have adverse reactions with their behavior-modifying medication, running away from covens, and lying to vegetarians. I won't do it, Charlie. I am starving for friends. I have no one. I am a stranger in this place. Do you know what I want? I don't want a bigger house or a fancier car. I want to run into people I know at the grocery store, I want to warn someone that I saw a rat scurry under the cheese case at Pioneer Market, I want someone to gross out over that rat with me. I want someone to tell the people in this town that I was not rooting for the raccoon that tried to eat Cynthia's face. I want someone in my corner. I want friends, Charlie. And I am determined that this is how I'm going to get them, because I can't figure out another way. And if I wait one more year, that's one more year that I sit in this house by myself and order take-out food for lunch and eat in front of the TV. It's one more year the phone doesn't ring. It's one more year of people I could eventually know eating cheese that literally came from a rat's nest. And it will be a whole year that Rowena Spaulding will know that she was right about me, that I'm an outsider who doesn't deserve to be let in."

Charlie nodded. "I know," he said. "I'm sorry. I wish I could help you. I would love to help you."

"You can help me," Maye replied. "By letting me do things my way with this pageant, with Ruby, with picking up dog shit or just hanging out with a lonely old lady, someone who's even, believe it or not, lonelier than I am. I have to follow my gut, Charlie, and my gut says that Ruby is the key to my winning the Sewer Pipe Queen title. It has to be true."

"Okay," he said, walking over to Maye and enveloping her in a long hug. "Okay. Pick up dog shit. Empty her ashtrays, scrub her toilet bowl, whatever it takes if this is the way you think it's going to work. I believe in you, Maye, and I want you to be happy in Spaulding. And I will support almost anything you have to do to achieve that."

"Almost anything?" Maye asked, returning the hug.

"I know how desperate lonely women get, so no matter what she asks," he said with a straight face, "just don't pimp me out."

12

A Very Lucky Thing

Ruby Spicer opened the boxer-head door with a hammer in one hand and a box of nails in the other.

"Did you ever notice," she commented as she stepped outside, her pack of dogs following her, "that the front step there on the porch is a little loose?"

A little loose? Maye wanted to laugh—it was the most stable architectural element on the whole house. It was the only thing not leaning over at a forty-five-degree angle.

"See?" the withered woman said as she put all the weight of her ninety-pound body on the step and tried to make it creak as she bounced on it. "Do you hear that?"

"Sure," Maye lied, thinking that the creaking Ruby heard was really the sound of her own lungs exhaling.

"Here you go," the old woman said, handing over the hardware and hammer before she disappeared back inside the house, the pack of dogs following her.

"And then I thought," she started up again as she came back

out to the porch, this time with a large set of rusty hedge clippers in her hands along with a lit Viceroy, "well, as long as that girl is out there, she ought to take a swipe at some of those bushes."

Maye shook her head and smiled. She had done well in speculating that she was going to be put to work and had worn her old house-renovation clothes—paint-splattered overalls and faithful work boots.

"That sounds good," Maye said as she took a couple of steps back to the car and pulled out two small paper bags. "As long as you have lunch with me while I'm working on the step and the bushes."

Ruby was taken aback. "You brought lunch? What did you do that for?" she asked.

"I like lunch," Maye answered. "Everybody likes lunch. It's just some sandwiches from Hopkins Market and a couple of sodas."

"Hopkins Market? Well, well. I used to eat there all the time at the lunch counter," the old woman said as she inhaled deeply on her cigarette. "They had the best malteds. My favorite was chocolate, and they'd put a cherry right on top with a mountain of whipped cream, and the real stuff, too, not the stuff in the tub. I sure do miss that place."

"Well, I didn't bring any malteds, but I do have a ham-and-cheese sandwich and a chicken salad sandwich," Maye offered up. "I like both, so you pick."

Ruby thought for a moment. "Chicken salad," she said, taking a seat on the porch. "I haven't had a chicken salad sandwich in years and years. We used to have chickens on this farm, up until my folks died. Got to be too much to take care of after that, so I just let them go."

"I heard chickens were messy, but I always liked the idea of going and getting an egg whenever you needed one," Maye said, positioning a nail where the step had the most wobble. "And fresh ones taste so much better."

"Naw, they're not too messy if there's more than one person runnin' things. We had Americanas," Ruby said, smiling to herself as she unwrapped her sandwich and her dogs settled in around her. "Big, beautiful blue eggs, almost turquoise, they were, such a pretty blue-green. Twice the size of those silly little eggs you get at the store. Pfft. Takes four of those damn things to make a decent omelette."

"So, how long ago was that?" Maye asked, careful to practice restraint. She had already seen what happened when Ruby was pushed too far, and she didn't want a repeat performance. "How long has it been that you've had to use silly little eggs?"

"Ah, it's been a long time," the old woman said as she brushed some crumbs off her lap, then took another drag. "Twenty-some years, I bet."

Maye tapped in the rest of the nail and then put the hammer down. "That's a long time to be running things on your own," she said.

Ruby nodded, not releasing any expression at all. She exhaled and took another bite of her sandwich. "I've got the dogs. My Royal Loyals. What else do I need? I've got Papa," she said patting the biggest boxer on the head as he reached up and softly licked her hand. "I've got Mama there, and Lula—she's the one with the pretty eyes. That's Captain over there, the stocky one, and Junior, who has the one floppy ear. Next to him is Minty, the most handsome of all the Royals, I think. And then there's Puppy, who just never got a name because I was always so sure someone was gonna come along and take him home, just like the rest of the puppies. I've got all I need and they're always with me. Nobody is as loyal as a dog. Nobody. Do you have a dog?"

"I do," Maye said as she positioned another nail on the step.

"His name is Mickey, the singing Australian shepherd. We never knew Mickey could sing before he went to reform school for attacking the mailman, who he mistook for a menacing mythical beast. He's a good dog. I know what you mean about being loyal—Mickey is my best friend. I would be lost without him, too."

"That's good, a dog is good," Ruby said, taking a drag and positioning her sandwich for another bite. "So, who is 'we'?"

"I'm sorry?" Maye said after she finished pounding in another nail. She leaned all of her weight onto the step and pushed as hard as she could. The step was now completely creakless and no longer had the characteristics of a teeter-totter.

"You said 'WE,' " Ruby croaked louder, as if Maye was deaf or possibly foreign. "WHO IS 'WE'?"

"Oh, I see. *We*. My husband, Charlie. I told you about him. He's the one who works at the university. He teaches in Dean Spaulding's department." Maye finally took a seat on the porch and grabbed the bag that held the ham-and-cheese sandwich.

"Been married long?" Ruby asked as she inhaled.

"I don't know," Maye said with a laugh as she unwrapped her lunch. "Is ten years long?"

"Depends if they were good or bad," the old woman answered. "It's like being at a dance: if you're on the floor, hopping to every song, it's over before you know it; if you're stuck by the punch bowl waiting for someone to notice, the punch can't dry up fast enough."

Maye nodded. "We're lucky then, it's gone by like that," she said, snapping her fingers. "On the subject of dances, I know your dance card must have been always full. Did you ever—?"

"What? Get married?" Ruby cackled as she fed the remnants of her sandwich to Papa, Lula, and the other dogs. "To who? I've been holed up in this house for most of my life."

"You must have had beaus, admirers, boyfriends," Maye continued. "I saw the newspaper clippings—you were the prettiest girl in town."

"And it did me so much good, didn't it?" Ruby snapped. "Yes. I had a beau once. A nice fellow, very handsome, very kind. He was a good man, I was lucky. Everyone said so."

The old woman scrambled to her feet and all of the dogs followed her lead, except for Puppy, who was too busy trying to catch a bothersome fly with his mouth.

"You'd better start on the bushes soon, Girl," she said as she marched into the house. "You want to be done with that by sundown."

Maye couldn't say anything; Ruby had retreated inside and had slammed the door before she even realized what had happened. She sat there for a moment, then gave the remainder of her sandwich to Puppy, who followed Maye as she picked up the loppers and they both headed over to the bushes in the front of the house, side by side.

ᚹ ᚹ ᚹ

She had trimmed the laurel bush outside the living room window in a perfectly even line to the center when she looked up and gasped. There, she could barely make out through the nicotine-veneered windows, was Ruby in her recliner, pushed all the way back, her dirty, slippered feet twitching and a cigarette barely dangling from her lips that was millimeters and a dollop of drool away from singeing her chin.

Maye dropped the shears and ran up the now sturdy steps to the porch, threw open the front door, and ran to Ruby just as the still-lit butt tumbled from her mouth, slid off her chin like an Olympic skier, and dropped straight to the bib of her yellow sweat suit, where it began to create a dark-ringed hole in the synthetic, flammable material.

Before she could pluck the cinder from Ruby's wheezing chest,

Papa, in a heroic giant leap, hoisted his broad chest and positioned his two muscular legs on the arm of the chair, bent his head forward, and picked up the filter end with his teeth. He then promptly jumped back down and released the smoldering remnant into the almost empty cocktail tumbler that sat on the floor next to the chair and already had several bloated butts floating in it.

"Holy shit," Maye said, astounded, thinking that Gwen at dog-training school was sort of wasting her time teaching dogs to sing when she could be training service dogs for alcoholics and other substance abusers. It was a gold mine waiting to be tapped. Dogs could not only extinguish fires, but they could bring buckets and pails over when their owners had the inclination to barf, and bring them the phone to call the liquor store that delivers.

"Good Papa," Ruby croaked, rousing from her nap and haphazardly patting the dog on his gargantuan head. "That's a good boy."

"That's incredible," Maye said. "I've never seen any such thing before! Did you teach him that?"

"You could say it was a joint venture," she answered. "He saves me from having a Viceroy burn a tunnel through to my rib cage, and he gets to live and eat breakfast in the morning. It's an even trade."

"By the looks of it, he's done that trick a number of times," Maye commented, pointing to a collection of blackened circles that dotted Ruby's yellow collar like charred pearls.

"He's a smart dog," Ruby offered as she shrugged. "He's easy to train. He wants to live."

"I'm sorry to bother you about this again, but what do you think about the pageant training?" Maye asked carefully. "I'd like to get started with whatever we'll need to do if you'll agree to be my sponsor."

"I'll tell you what," Ruby said as she tapped the newest ringed hole in her sweat suit top to extinguish any lingering embers. "I'm a little busy around here, but I think I could fit you into my schedule. We'll talk about that tomorrow, after you've finished painting the fence. I was taking a nice nap before that cigarette tried to ignite me, so I'm going back to sleep."

"Ruby, thank you so much," Maye said gratefully. "This means so much to me, and I know I couldn't do this without you. This is wonderful. This is really wonderful."

"Yeah, yeah. One more thing," Ruby said as she stretched out in her recliner, causing another *pppppppppt!* to shoot into the air. "I want a chicken salad sandwich for lunch tomorrow, too."

ψ ψ ψ

The last thing Maye wanted to see the next morning was the thinning bald spot on the back of Rowena Spaulding's jet-black head, but as she walked into Hopkins Market to fetch Ruby's chicken salad sandwich, that's exactly what she saw.

Crowded together at the deli counter in the typical lunch-hour crunch, the store patrons patiently waited for the numbers they pulled on their way in to be called. Maye migrated to the back of the crowd, hoping that Rowena would get her stuff and be gone before she had to move up to the counter.

"Twenty-two!" the deli man bellowed, scanning the crowd for the look of hope on the chosen number's face, but no one stepped forward to claim the number.

"Twenty-two!" he yelled again, to no avail.

"If twenty-two is missing, you can take me instead." As Maye heard the familiar, nasaly voice that sent chills up her spine, she looked up to see Rowena stiffly waving her arm at the counterman as she brazenly stepped forward.

"What number are you, Mrs. Spaulding?" he asked with a

sudden, convenient smile that only people in the service industry know how to produce without thinking.

"Uh," Rowena scoffed with disgust. "What does it matter? If twenty-two is delinquent, then I'll fill the spot."

"Well, I just want to make sure that everyone has a fair turn," the deli man explained. "That's why we have numbers, to make sure that fair is fair."

"I'm number twenty-nine," Rowena snipped in a huff. "But that hardly matters. If twenty-two has abandoned the number, then I step forward to claim it. There. I am claiming it. I am now twenty-two."

Sure you are, Maye thought. In dog years.

"Uh—I suppose," the deli man stammered, clearly uncomfortable. "That is, if everyone else is all right with that."

The deli suddenly turned into a feudal society as almost every customer waiting in line nodded and mumbled something to the effect of "Of course, Mrs. Spaulding," "Naturally, Mrs. Spaulding," and "Be my guest, Mrs. Spaulding."

Maye's mouth dropped. She was horrified. What is this, she wanted to scream, a scene from *The Remains of the Day*?

"Very well, then," Rowena said as she stepped closer to the counter. "I need a pastrami sandwich. It's my husband's birthday, and it is the only thing he requests. So. Just one sandwich."

"All right," the counter guy said, nodding and smiling. "What kind of bread would you like that on?"

"Oh," Rowena said, looking puzzled that there was more than one pastrami-compatible bread. "I have no idea. What kind do you usually put it on?"

"Rye?" he asked. "Does he like rye?"

"Certainly," she said quickly. "Rye would be good."

"And," the counterman dared ask again, "mustard?"

"Of course," Rowena shot back. "If that's what you do."

"Okay," the man replied. "Sauerkraut?"

Rowena opened her mouth, though amazingly, nothing came out.

"Swiss?" the man continued. "Onions?"

"I—I don't know," she stumbled. "The housekeeper always does this, but she's ill and I really have no idea. I don't know. I don't know."

"How about I give you pastrami on rye with mustard, I'll put everything else on the side, and your husband can pick what he likes?" he suggested.

"Yes," Rowena said. "That would be fine."

The rest of the customers stood while the pastrami sandwich was being made, the entire deli shrouded in silence, exaggerating the whooshing sound of the slicer cutting the meat. It wasn't until the deli man handed Rowena a paper bag and she paid for it that anyone dared make a sound.

As number twenty-three was being called, Rowena headed toward the back of the store for the door, and that was when Maye found herself in a very odd position—walking toward the door as well, pushing her way through the crowd and quickening her step to make sure that Rowena could absolutely not miss her. She was one step closer to the door than Rowena when the puckery shrew saw her.

"Why, Maye Roberts," she said with a look of honest surprise on her face. "What a stunning pair of dirty overalls. What are you doing here?"

"Just getting lunch," Maye said simply as she smiled. "For my sponsor."

"Oh, that's marvelous," Rowena responded, forcing a smile. "I'm so glad you've come to terms with your affliction and have joined Alcoholics Anonymous. But I'm sure we'll all miss the entertainment value you so dutifully provided. Honestly, I don't see how you could have topped yourself, however—well, that's a poor choice of words now, isn't it?"

"My sponsor isn't an alcoholic, Rowena," Maye lied with a jolly little chuckle. "She's my sponsor for the Sewer Pipe Queen Pageant."

"Maye, Maye," she replied, pressing her lips tightly together as she paused, revealing more furrows around her mouth than an earthquake fault. "That's impossible. Release yourself from your reverie, my dear. No one in this town is sponsoring you."

"That is true," she replied, raising her eyebrows. "No Old Queen in this town *is* sponsoring me. But one Old Queen right outside of town is."

Rowena scoffed and chuckled. "So you're flying someone in? Oh, Maye, your desperation works against you. So, who exactly would that be?"

"That Old Queen," Maye said directly, "would be Ruby Spicer."

Rowena's face dropped faster than an elevator with a cut cable. Then her eyes narrowed, boring straight into Maye.

"Is that so?" Rowena said. Her puckered mouth now stretched with fury, her jowls tense along her jaw. Maye was acutely aware that she hadn't just hit a nerve, she'd hit a bone.

"It is so," she replied without flinching, still retaining the smile on her face.

"You won't win," Rowena insisted through her yellow, stained teeth. "You won't. She's been sitting out on that farm for fifty years, drying up each year more brittle and bitter than the year before. What's left of her soaks herself in whatever liquor is within arm's reach. Her and those filthy dogs. It's a wonder they haven't eaten her yet. That wretch can't even help herself, let alone help you win that pageant. Ruby Spicer! How does she plan to be able to step one foot in this place after what she did? That woman will be lucky if she doesn't get lynched when she rolls back into town."

And with that, Rowena Spaulding gave Maye one last dirty

glare, turned, and stormed out of Hopkins Market like a rhino. Maye was dumbfounded as she vaguely heard her number being called in the background, because against all odds, she had done the impossible.

She had found the one person in the world that Rowena Spaulding hated more than she hated Maye.

ᚦ   ᚦ   ᚦ

The moment Maye set foot on the newly fixed step of Ruby's dilapidated front porch, which was half draped in an old sheet, the boxer head swung back and there she was, in what might have been a freshly laundered green terrycloth tracksuit, with a fresh slather of red lipstick on that hadn't yet run into the crevices that burrowed around her lips but had already veneered her teeth. Her dogs gathered around her knees.

"Have you seen the sun today?" she exclaimed excitedly as she looked upward at the sky. "Did ya see it? Look at that sun, so bright and warm! It's just glorious!"

"It is," Maye agreed, surprised—she had never seen the old woman this gregarious.

Ruby stepped forward, directly into the sun, and the light exposed her face. Maye almost gasped. The woman's face was covered with bruises, especially around her eyes. The hues of hematomas surrounded them, and her skin reflected shades of green, fading into blue, then purple, drifting into black, and each side of her face had either been scraped raw or had suffered a sudden inflamed rash of some sort.

"Oh my God, Ruby!" Maye said as she gasped, covered her mouth, and stepped forward to see the extent of her injuries. Upon closer look, she saw that the damage was so severe she didn't think Ruby should even be standing and was about to insist on an ice pack when she noticed a twinkle in the sun that bounced off Ruby's cheek, almost like a minuscule shard of glass.

Had she broken a window, Maye wondered, but with her head? Did she get that drunk last night that she put her face through glass—without getting cut? Then there was another glimmer, up higher on the same cheek, and as Ruby turned slightly to look at Maye quizzically, both of her eyelids began to glimmer and gleam.

"What?" Ruby finally asked, looking a bit annoyed.

"Your face!" Maye shrieked, taking another step closer only to comprehend that the glass dust on Ruby's skin was not from a window or a door at all—it was eye shadow. And blush. It was makeup. Ruby had dolled herself up, only her rendition was much like what a four-year-old would do if presented with the bounty of Mommy's cosmetics drawer and an unsupervised hour.

Maye stumbled, aware that she had been a bit too dramatic for her own good, and now had to cover for the fact that she had mistakenly interpreted the results of Ruby's Beauty Day for a face that had been jumped in a back alley by guys carrying pipes.

"What about my face?" Ruby said carefully, her eyes, or what Maye could see of them, narrowing.

"It's so pretty!" Maye responded with an extra dose of enthusiasm, at which the old woman's face relaxed.

"So what'd ya bring me, Girl?" Ruby asked with a wide smile, exposing all of her lipstick-streaked teeth. "Is it chicken salad?"

"Absolutely," Maye said, then from behind her pulled out one of Charlie's old lunch coolers. "And a chocolate malted."

Ruby stopped in midreach for the bag and looked at her with soft, sinking eyes that Maye had never noticed before. "You brought me a malted?" she asked slowly, just about as shocked as Maye was to see her smiling. "I haven't had one of those in years. In about fifty years. Do you think they'll taste the same?"

"Give it a shot," Maye said, handing over the cooler that had kept the malted from melting. "I bet it will be delicious. Straw is in the bag."

"I thought we could eat outside like we did yesterday," Ruby said, pointing to the sheet that covered the old, graying wood. "Kind of like a picnic. It's such a nice day. Whaddya say we take the blanket and spread it out under that old redwood?"

Maye nodded and helped Ruby bring the sheet down the steps and under the only tree left alive in front of the house.

"There," Ruby said, smoothing out the sheet. "This is such a good idea."

She opened Charlie's little cooler, lifted the lid off the tall Styrofoam cup, and sucked in her breath with delight. After unwrapping the straw and sticking it slowly into the center of the cup, which still, remarkably, had some whipped cream sitting on top, Ruby wrapped her wrinkly crimson lips around it and sucked in her first malted in fifty years.

"Oh, that's good," she said, dragging her finger through the whipped cream and tasting it. "I don't know how I managed to live without that for so long."

"I don't want to be one of those nosy bodies, and you tell me straight off if I am," Maye started, taking the opportunity of Ruby's good mood to settle some things that had been bothering her. "But how do you manage? I mean, it's just you out here, and I know that you breed the dogs on occasion, but by the looks of Puppy, it's been a while since you had a litter. How do you manage, Ruby? How do you live out here on your own?"

"Oh," the old woman said as she unwrapped her coveted sandwich. "There's always a way. Papa built this house, I've never had to make a payment on it, and he owned some property in town that he rented out, like Hopkins Market, for instance. It's Hopkins's place, but it's my father's property. Property was always better than stocks, he'd say. It's not much, but it's enough for me to get by. And then, when I need to, I'll just sell something I don't need anymore to get a little extra. Things like old thirty-three records, or an antique lamp, or even—old clothes. Can you believe it? People actually buying your old clothes! And then those people sell them again to other people! I was never going to fit into any of that stuff again, anyway, even though some of it was real nice. So you do what you gotta do, that's all."

Maye attempted to visualize Ruby trying to sell her inciner-ated sweat suits to resale shops, and she grinned. And then she realized that it meant Ruby had been in town—Ruby had been in Spaulding—without consequence. Without anyone noticing her, much less lynching her. She thought then that perhaps she should tell Ruby of her run-in with Rowena, but decided not to ruin the old woman's good mood. Maye had learned firsthand that Miss Ruby had a temper like Mount St. Helens—one mo-ment, it seemed she was resting peacefully, and the next thing you knew, a red, glowing cinder was flying toward your head with the speed of a comet. With things going so well during their pic-nic, Maye certainly didn't want to push her luck.

"So you've been to Spaulding to sell records and lamps and clothes," Maye asked, smiling at Ruby wryly. "How did you man-age that?"

"Eh." Ruby laughed slightly. "It's easier than you think. People are too wrapped up in themselves to pay attention to anything else these days. Everyone is invisible to everybody else. You just gotta know how to dress to blend in."

Maye knew that all too well herself. Unless she was disrobing or performing magic tricks with her protruding abdomen at par-ties, hardly anyone in Spaulding had ever noticed her at all.

"Now, you think you're the one with all the questions," Ruby continued as she ate her lunch. "I have some for you."

"Okay," Maye shrugged, unable to imagine what Ruby wanted to know of her.

"How did you find me?" she asked. "How did you know I was out here?"

Maye paused for a moment, trying to decide how honest she should be, then realized quickly there was no decision to be made at all. If she and Ruby were going to be a team, she needed to be up-front and lay everything out on the table. You have to respect the other half of your team, she understood, and if she respected Ruby, then she needed to tell her the truth.

"I drugged a cop," she finally said. "I drugged a cop with his favorite organic donuts and got him to talk during a sugar rush. I bumped into him at the library when I first found your file in the archives, and I had a feeling he knew more than he was telling. I already knew he was addicted to those donuts, so . . . I just performed the necessary evil and asked him questions until he spilled it. I know it wasn't right, but I didn't know what else to do. I didn't know how else I could find you. I tried the courthouse, I looked in every old phone book back half a century, and I asked around. It wasn't easy; he ate almost a dozen before I broke him. He was even hallucinating by that point. He slept off the rest of the afternoon on my couch before he was okay to drive again, and he almost threw up."

Ruby was quiet for a long time. She stopped eating her sandwich, stopped slurping her malted, and looked off into the distance.

"This cop," she said slowly after she finally took another sip from her malted, gurgling it. "He wouldn't happen to also be a plumber, would he?"

Maye nodded and winced. "I know that you know John Smith," she confessed. "He said he got his dog Rocky from you. Please don't blame him. I knew his weakness and I pounced. He never knew what hit him."

"Some excuse for giving me up," she said as she shook her head, her voice brittle. "He sang like a bird for a donut. What a stoolie."

"He put up a fight for quite a while," Maye relayed. "He fought like a swordfish, but he sadly underestimated the power of a jelly."

"If those things are so powerful, I hope you bring some for the judges," Ruby commented, and by her tone, Maye couldn't exactly tell if she was irritated or not. "If it could make John Smith spill a secret he was sworn to keep, something that to my knowledge he has never told another living person, well then, you have a royal flush in a baker's dozen."

"I'm sorry, Ruby," Maye said honestly. "If there was another way to find you, I would have taken it. I looked all over the place, but you hid your tracks pretty well. I have to give it to you. You wiped yourself off the map of Spaulding."

Ruby laughed choppily. "I had some help there," was her reply. "But I'm in the phone book—under Royal Loyals."

He must have been one hell of a man, Maye thought to herself as she finished her lunch; he must have been something else to make Ruby turn and run all the way out here with a broken heart and nowhere else to turn, spending the rest of her life alone on this old, barren farm. And then there were Rowena's harsh words from this morning. Maye didn't trust anything Rowena said, and knew all too well that she loved to invoke fear in anyone she couldn't outwardly control. That was Mrs. Spaulding's strength and great talent—she was a marvelous distributor of alarm and trepidation; she spread it like peanut butter. If there was anything Rowena loved, it was that people feared her, and if they didn't, she was certain to come up with a reason indeed. Before Maye could give the threat any more thought, Ruby had smacked her on the arm.

"Hey, Girl!" she yelled. "Did you hear what I said?"

"What?" Maye replied, rubbing the sting with her other hand. "No, I didn't hear you."

"I said, can you do the splits?" Ruby shouted. "Because if you can do the splits, you can win this thing. Everybody loves the splits! Let me see you try."

"No, I can't do the splits," Maye yelled back. "And I'm not going to try, either. I like my lady parts right where they are, thank you. There's no need to relocate them by choice or foolishness."

"Come on, just try," the old woman croaked, in an attempt to coax.

"You have got to be kidding," Maye replied stoutly. "I can barely cross my legs. No way. Let's see you do the splits if you think it's so easy."

"Oh," Ruby said, looking straight at Maye. "Sure." The old woman put her malted aside, stood up, and with her soiled slippers heading in opposite directions, she slowly slid down to the ground like a Barbie doll in the hands of a four-year-old.

Maye tried to scream but nothing came out, and as she looked at the wrinkled, skinny old lady with a huge red mouth and fiery red corn-husk hair with her legs apart like the Godfather of Soul, James Brown, her stomach did a flip. She knew that experienced drinkers could fly in the face of quantum physics with their unexpected and zombielike physical flexibility at times—such as, say, getting flattened by a bus and managing to make it to the next bar before last call despite the fact that their knee is bent around their neck—but Ruby's splits were incredible and revolting at the same time.

"Please tell me one, and hopefully both, of those legs can come off with an Allen wrench," Maye whispered.

"Ta-da!" Ruby garbled as she lifted one arm above her in an act of showmanship and smiled wildly, exposing a whole set of canary-colored teeth. Papa sauntered over and drew his big juicy tongue up the side of her old face, and she laughed.

"Let me guess," Maye began. "You did the splits for your talent segment in the pageant. And I'm going to have to carry you back to the house."

"Psshh!" Ruby replied as she bent her back leg in and brought it around until she was back in a sitting position. "I didn't just do the splits, Girl! I *tumbled*. I did cartwheels, I did flips, backward and forward; I had a whole routine. Of course, dropping the splits was the grand finale. I had a lit slow-burning sparkler in each hand, and I slowly went down, and I tell you, the crowd went mad. Right when I got down to the floor, Lula—who was hiding in the back—threw a handful of lit poppers that shot off red sparks and big, rising plumes of red smoke. I brought the house down, I tell you. Got a standing ovation. But really, how can you top the splits?"

Maye laughed. "Was Lula your sponsor?" she asked, thinking it sweet that Ruby had named a dog after her.

"No!" Ruby screeched. "Lula, my *sister*. She was in charge of what we would call nowadays 'special effects.' Her timing was impeccable. She threw those poppers right at the perfect moment—it really put the fire in the routine, so to speak. Now, what big plans do we have for your talent segment? What are you good at?"

"I write a mean hard-news story," Maye confessed. "And I'm a decent detective. But that can hardly be translated to the stage."

"Well, then," Ruby continued, thinking. "What can you do that nobody else can? What do you have that no one else has?"

"I have a singing dog," Maye offered. "And he also happens to play the piano."

"You don't say," Ruby said slowly with a sly look on her face. "That could be as good as a flip. It's not the splits, I'll be honest with you, but it could be a flip. Is he afraid of flame? Because I could really see a flaming hula hoop in here somewhere. Fire is always the cherry on top. It's a nice touch."

"I'm not so sure about the fire part," Maye said, trying to extinguish Ruby's penchant for pyromania. "I'm not so sure Mickey would do that well with an uncontrollable element of nature that could envelop the outdoor, dry wooden stage with a wall of red death if the wind was blowing the wrong way. I was thinking more along the lines of a duet, like 'I Got You, Babe,' or 'Let's Call the Whole Thing Off.' Something like that."

"Hmmm, I like it," the old woman said, scratching her chin and nodding. "We could certainly do something like that. It's traditional, yet different. It has a nice twist. I've got some old records. I'll dig through them and see what we can come up with."

"That's would be wonderful, Ruby, thank you," Maye said. "Now I have a question for you. What puts you in such a good mood today? I've never seen you quite like this."

Ruby laughed heartily. "Are you kidding? Why wouldn't I be in a good mood this afternoon?" she replied as she stood up and gathered the ends of the picnic sheet. "I'm getting my fence painted today! And for free! Who wouldn't be happy about that? And you'd better get hoppin'. That fence is longer than it looks. The paint and brushes are right over there on the side of the porch. Chop, chop, Girl!"

𝍖 𝍖 𝍖

Ruby was right.

The fence was far longer than it looked. As Maye finished up her best Tom Sawyer impersonation, the sun was sinking quickly into the tree line. She was covered in white—from her shoe, which the paint can had tipped over on, to the speckled spray that dotted every inch of her arms and hands—and resembled a giant marshmallow. She had been painting for hours. Her arms were sore, and she was tired of standing, crouching, and standing again, and all she wanted to do was wash off as much of the latex color as she could and head home.

She knocked on the front door, and when no one answered, she glanced in the living room window and saw the two grimy, matted feet twitching on the kicked-up footrest of Ruby's recliner. She went back to the front door and tried the knob; the door was unlocked. She could either wake the old woman up from her afternoon slip into unconsciousness, she realized, or go quietly into the house, wash up, and be on her way.

Maye chose the easier option, and with the cleaner of her two hands, turned the doorknob slowly so as to not make too much noise and startle the dogs, who were lying like a herd of sea lions all around their snoring, drooling master. Papa was the first to lift his head to see who was breaking into the house, and Maye smiled, then whispered, "Good boy!" to put him at ease. He dropped his head back down.

She tiptoed through the living room and into the kitchen and headed directly for the sink. Quietly, quietly, she turned the "cold" handle on and waited for a moment, but the faucet was dry. Maye tried the "hot" handle as well, but it, too, released no water. She turned both handles off and sighed, leaning up against the counter. Her hands and arms were covered in paint—there was no way she was going to get in the car like this, she'd get smudges of white all over the interior.

Suddenly, she heard the clicky toes of a dog behind her on the old, cracked linoleum floor, and she turned to see Papa in the doorway, nudging his empty water bowl. He licked the last droplets of water from the bottom and turned to climb the stairs.

Ah, Maye thought to herself, a thirsty dog will always know where to find water if there's any around, but at the same time she prayed she wouldn't have to dip any part of her body into Ruby's toilet. She followed Papa up the creaky, spongy stairs, completely fearful that she had could drop through them at any minute. These stairs were used to supporting an old, skinny woman who weighed as much as a fifth grader, not a girl who could create a rhythm section when she walks, complete with castanets, with her plentiful thighs strangled in the prison of a spandex girdle.

Against the laws of gravity, Maye made it up to the dark landing where she could see only the outlines of two doors on her left and two doors on her right. One of them had to be a bathroom, she said to herself, hoping that Papa would show her to the right one. He just stood directly at her side. She remained on the landing for a minute or two, waiting for her eyes to adjust to the shadows and the absence of light, because this was Ruby's house after all, and if the stairs were any indication, there might be floorboards missing or a trapdoor left open or any number of unimaginable horrors just panting with anticipation to break her leg. When she was confident that she had a straight shot to the door closest to her right and that the floor before her seemed intact, she took the necessary number of steps to reach it, turned the doorknob, and pushed.

Maye knew immediately she was not in the bathroom.

She was not in the bathroom.

This was not the bathroom.

Because, Maye reasoned to herself, when you go to the bathroom, there shouldn't be two people in there already. The outline of two people, standing and looking at you.

Christ Almighty, Maye thought to herself in a split second, that old bat has been killing people and mummifying their bodies, and posing them like they're at a party! In the next second, her mind flashed to an alternate scenario—Holy shit, these are crazy relatives she's hidden in the attic, but if she's the sane one out of the bunch, I'm in real trouble here. Then, in the following moment, she reasoned, they're dead, they're dead victims, and she's going to keep me as her prisoner and I'll spend the rest of my days picking up dog shit and my nights chained up in this room with dead bodies looking forward to picking up dog shit.

Thankfully, Papa whined precisely then and more or less broke Maye from her Janet Leigh moment. She took a deep breath, calmed down, and berated her irrational side for thinking that there were mummies of crazy relatives having a party in a dark, spooky, rotting old house. She felt along the wall until she came to a lightswitch and flipped it on. As the room was illuminated, it took Maye just as long to comprehend what she was seeing in the light as it did to try to figure out what it was in the dark.

In the room were two figures in what looked to be a neat, tidy, and undisturbed bedroom; dressmaker's dummies, each adorned with an exquisite gown. One was a striking sky blue, a cap-sleeved satin dress with tiny beads and rhinestones dotting the neckline. It was cinched tightly at the waist, from which the blue material spilled over into a wide, generous, sweeping skirt that barely reached the floor. There would be only two purposes for a dress of its stature: a ball gown fit for a debutante, or a pageant gown, fit for a hopeful queen.

The second dress was a soft, light ochre color. It still held the shimmer of a good-quality silk, reflected in the light that shone brightly from the fixture directly above it. Its skirt was not nearly as broad; it was more subtle, more fluid in its lines, with the silk flowing instead of billowing to the floor; the entire bodice was gently shirred. Abundant cream-colored pearls were meticulously sewn to the rim of the sweetheart neckline. Maye thought there must have been thousands of them. They also gathered on the cuff of the wrist-length sleeve, making nearly a bracelet. Maye stepped closer to the dress, admiring the hours and hours of work it must have taken to attach all of those tiny little pearls. It was then that she noticed that only half of the neckline had been embellished; the other half was naked silk, looking plain and simple. The other sleeve, too, was not yet completed; pieces of it were pinned to the side of the dress, as if not to lose them. As Maye brought a piece of the sleeve between her two cleanest fingers and felt the texture of the silk, a whiter, fresher color showed itself beneath it. She lifted more of the unfinished sleeve up and realized the dress was not ochre at all; it had been white, and had aged into a deeper hue with time.

There was only one purpose for a dress like this, Maye thought as she returned the folds of the sleeve softly, putting it back exactly as it had been and smoothing it with her fingers.

It was a wedding dress.

13

There's a Fire Inside of
Every One of Us

"What are you doing in here?"

Maye turned around quickly. She hadn't heard Ruby come up the stairs, hadn't heard her standing in the doorway behind her.

"Who said you could come in here?" Ruby demanded angrily, her voice growing louder as she came closer to Maye. "What are you doing? Why are you in here?"

"I . . . I needed to wash up," Maye stuttered. "And Papa needed water—the sink in the kitchen—I couldn't get it on, so I followed Papa up the stairs and I thought this was the bathroom. I didn't know, Ruby, it was the first door, I thought it was the bathroom."

"Well, it's not the bathroom!" Ruby roared. "Do you see a sink? Do you see a toilet? This is not the bathroom! This is Mama's room!"

"I didn't mean any harm, Ruby, it was an accident," Maye said calmly. "I didn't mean to upset you. I came in here by mistake, and the dresses were so beautiful I had to look at them. They're exquisite."

Ruby looked at the floor, shaking her head, and didn't say anything until she looked back up at Maye with glassy, tear-filled eyes. "Those dresses," she said in the smallest little voice. "My mother made them. It was a long, long time ago."

"They're beautiful," Maye said. "Are they yours?"

"Can we go back downstairs?" Ruby didn't ask, but demanded. "I don't come in here. No one should be in here."

"Sure," Maye replied, stepping closer to Ruby but keeping an arm's distance just in case she had a basket of rocks or a blowtorch behind her back. Since Ruby hadn't tried to stone or sear anyone since the day she first knocked on the boxer head door Maye figured the time was ripe.

Ruby turned the lights out, returning the dresses to darkness, and shut the room back up.

"*That*'s the bathroom," the old woman said as she pointed to the second door on the right and started down the stairs. "You can clean up in there."

Maye washed her hands off, wiped them on the back of her overalls, and climbed back down the shaky stairs. In the living room, Ruby sat on the edge of the couch, smoking a cigarette and sipping out of a plastic tumbler.

Maye wasn't sure what to say—she had never seen Ruby so upset, and in the short time that she'd known her, she had mistakenly thought she'd experienced the old woman's range of emotions. Bitterness to rage to extra bitterness. She decided on the inane, not because she didn't want to know what was up there in that room, and not because she didn't care, but because a tough old battle-ax had been pushed into terrain they were both unfamiliar with, and that was just about enough for anybody.

"That fence sure was long," Maye relayed to Ruby, who didn't turn around. "It's ten times longer than it looks."

Ruby didn't turn around. She said nothing, She simply sat on the edge of the sofa, sucking on her cigarette and sipping from her cup.

"When I won that pageant fifty years ago," she finally said after a tense, long pause, still not looking at Maye, not looking at anything really, "it was the most exciting thing that had ever happened to me. Sure, I had done the splits, but I was the *queen*. Me. Ruby Spicer. I had never been the queen of anything, the first place in anything, not even in my imagination. Not even in any wild thought I mighta had. That day—it was like I had passed through some kind of magic door. After I tumbled and Lula set off the fireworks, I put on that fancy blue dress up there and I stood on that stage in the town square and they put a crown on my head. They put a crown on this mess of red hair! I just laughed and laughed, but inside I was waiting for them to announce that they had made a mistake. But it was real. Nobody counted wrong, none of the judges took back their vote. It was true, I was the queen. I had won."

Maye walked around the couch and sat down next to the old woman, who still did not turn to look at her, keeping her eyes fixed straight ahead.

"Everything was good, everything was perfect, just the way it should be for a young girl," Ruby continued. "I was going to be a queen for a year. I went to all the dances, and everywhere I went, people took pictures of me doing this, doing that. It almost got to be silly. The opening of a grocery store, even! Who would have believed it! I got to sit on a throne during the Spaulding Festival, waving to all the people on either side of the street, watching them waving back. Waving back at me! People were so nice. My folks were real proud, and I was proud to have made them proud, see? They were always proud of Lula—she was a good student and a thoughtful daughter and did all that was expected of her. She married the Captain, settled down, whereas I was a little bit more of a troublemaker. Skipping school, staying out late, smoking."

Ruby cracked a bit of a smile. "I started young," she added. "I had a nice beau. He was so handsome and polite, and so kind to me. He was the smartest man I had ever met, and once he finished up his studies at the Polytechnic Institute in a couple of years, we were to be married. And my mother started sewing that dress upstairs, with that beautiful silk she went all the way to Seattle to get.

"He was a lovely man. Brought me flowers all the time, and the day I was crowned, you should have seen the ones he had made up for me. It wasn't a bouquet—they were so heavy I could barely lift them. All of my favorite flowers—roses, tulips, peonies. Some of them weren't even in season, that's what a nice fellow he was. He went to some trouble there. I knew I was going to have a very happy life with him.

"But things don't always happen the way you plan them, or even the way they are supposed to. Things sometimes get a mind of their own and follow a path you never imagined. All of a sudden, you are where you are. And there's not much you can do about it."

"Is that why you're out here?" Maye asked gently. "Because of that fellow? Did he break it off?"

"Of course he broke it off!" Ruby cried as she turned and looked at Maye harshly. "What kind of man wouldn't? Of course he did. There was nothing else he could do! There was no choice. He had no choice. I know that. Don't think I don't know that!"

"I'm not sure I understand, Ruby," Maye said slowly.

"Wendy Dulden had been my best friend since I was four years old," the old woman began again, almost impatiently. "We did everything together—wore the same clothes, took all the same classes, had malteds every day after school at Hopkins. The kind of friend you make once in a lifetime. I had known her since I was a bitty girl. Her folks lived out on the next farm over. Oh, we liked all of the same things, we flirted with the same boys, cheated off each other during tests, shared our homework. We skipped class when the days got hot and went for a dip in New River. We could be a little smarty-pants at times, but we had so much fun together. I could just say one word and Wendy would know exactly what I was thinking. It was wonderful having a friend like that. Almost like a twin.

"But between going to events and doing all the engagement things you're supposed to do, I couldn't spend as much time with her as I used to. I was busy, day and night, planning, sewing, making appearances. I barely had time to sleep! And then one day, at an event, something bad happened. Hopkins Market got a big, new beautiful sign and I was supposed to be there to cut the ribbon on it before they hoisted it up. And as soon as I got to the market, there was a little girl who asked to wear my crown. So I took it off and gave it to her to try on, but then the photographers showed up, and I needed it back. Well, she started to cry, and I tried to explain that I needed it for the pictures, and that it was my job to stand and smile with the crown on my head so the photographers could do their job, but that little girl did not care. She wanted the crown and that was it. She kept jumping up at me trying to snatch the crown from my head, and her mother stood there and did absolutely nothing! After the little girl kicked me in the leg for ignoring her, I lit a cigarette. Well, I had just cut the ribbon, the cameras were flashing away, and as I stepped back so they could get a better shot, I heard a little girl cry."

"So that's what you had in your hand in all of those pictures!" Maye exclaimed. "It wasn't a pencil, it was a cigarette?"

"Well, of course it was!" Ruby rattled. "You've got everybody looking at you, staring at you, taking pictures, 'Look this way, look that way, over here,' and if I had a cigarette, I was smooth as glass. If I didn't, I'd be shaking all over!" And to that, the old woman wrapped her wrinkled accordion lips around the filter of her Viceroy cigarette and drew on it deeply.

"Then the little girl started to scream, and as I turned around, I saw that a bit of her hair—just a little bit, mind you, a little tiny bit, not even a fistful—had been singed as she was jumping up to get my crown again, and maybe there was a small, minuscule flame, barely visible to the naked eye. So little it wasn't even a match's worth. So I took the only thing I had with me, my little blue satin purse, and swatted her head and beat that fire out. I tell you, I felt awful, and I did everything I could to help her. But then she pointed at me, screaming, 'She did it! She did it!' I had no idea what she was talking about until one of the photographers said I had burned her with the tip of my cigarette when I backed up. Well, it was just a tiny bit of hair—in a month, no one would have known any better—and I put the fire out myself! But then an anonymous letter to the editor popped up in the newspaper, demanding that I stop smoking at events because now 'all of Spaulding's children were in danger.' And then there was another unsigned letter, and another. Pretty soon, the whole town was up in arms and before I knew it, people were demanding that I not smoke at all during events. Well, I was furious! It was only one little girl I burned, and it never would have happened if she wasn't trying to steal my tiara! I would have given her some of my own hair if I coulda, but to take away smoking? Everybody smoked then, it wasn't just me! People even smoked in restaurants; it was very acceptable back then. I couldn't fulfill my duties. It was hard, I got so nervous, kind of like stage fright, and the more I thought about it, the more nervous I became, until it took everything I had just to get to the event, let alone get in front of people! Smoking was a part of my image, a part of my glamour."

Ruby put down the cigarette long enough to cough deeply in

what sounded like a lungquake, shaking and tumbling those lungs until she got up what she needed and then hocked it into a previously hidden—and stained—crumpled paper towel she drew from under her sleeve.

Maye shuddered and wished she had a paper towel herself, but one from her own sleeve.

"I was so afraid I was going to lose the crown. I was so afraid I was going to get impeached, or revoked, or whatever it is they do to queens when they don't do what they're supposed to. What is that called? "

"Beheading," Maye offered, "but I don't think you were in any danger of that here."

"Well, they didn't take away my crown," Ruby went on. "But they did have a City Council meeting about it, and who should stand up and speak out against me? My best friend, Wendy Dulden. My best friend! How do you like that? She said I was a danger to everyone within an arm's distance of me and that the innocent, harmless hair of all little children would be in jeopardy if I wasn't stopped. I couldn't believe it. The council agreed to let me keep the crown as long as I just went to an event once a month or so. But I tell you, I was so angry. I was the queen! I deserved to serve out all of my duties, not just one a month! What harm was one little cigarette going to do as long as a rotten little kid wasn't lurking behind me? And I let it be known, too, that their decision was not fair. And I let Wendy know that best friends don't do that to best friends. They stick together, and she was just mad because I was getting married! And I let the City Council know it wasn't right what they did, and that I was going to put up a stink and speak my mind until they changed theirs. And I meant it. They had no right to take away my cigarettes; they had no right. It made me furious!

"So I decided I just wasn't going to pay attention to their silly rules, and at my next event, which was the spelling bee, I lit up a cigarette and I smoked it. And Wendy saw me, and told a police-man, and he gave me a ticket! I was fined ten dollars! So, at the next event, I was giving an award to the Employee of the Year at the factory, and I lit up another cigarette and smoked that one, too. And I got another fine. And another and another. And soon I ended up owing the town a hundred dollars!"

"What did your fiancé say?" Maye asked.

"He offered to pay it!" Ruby screeched. "He said he should just pay it and forget the whole thing, just be nice and quiet, he said. Lula said the same thing; so did Mama and Papa. Do my one event a month and keep my crown. Go back to living our lives the way they were. But my life wasn't going to be the way it was, whether I kept quiet or not. And then, things started burn-ing down."

"Fire?" Maye questioned. "You mean when the courthouse caught fire?"

"Oh, more than the courthouse," Ruby explained. "More than the courthouse. Half this town burned right to the ground. The movie theater, the bakery, the market, the bank, and even City Hall went up, right when the City Council was having a meeting. Almost every corner of town had something lit up. Places just went up, no rhyme or reason. It was just gone."

Maye gasped. "What happened? Was it during a drought? Was it like the Chicago fire? How did the fire start?"

"Not just one fire," the old woman said. "There was almost a fire every night for weeks. It seemed like it would never end. Peo-ple were scared, they were frightened, they wanted to find out who was doing it, who was setting the buildings on fire, but all the police knew was that the fires were started by cigarettes. Every single one of the fires was started by a lit cigarette. They found butts at several of them. It was a mystery, who was setting these

fires. Until someone on the City Council decided to point a finger at me, because I had said that I would do whatever I had to
do to make Spaulding let me smoke at events again.

"But I'll tell you, Girl, every time one of those damn fires was
set, I was here, right here in this house, right here in this room,
listening to the radio, playing cards with my folks, or adding
more beads to that white dress. But they didn't believe me. No
one believed me, except for Mama and Papa because they knew
I was telling the truth. So they put a policemen outside the house
to watch me and where I went, and don't you know, those fires
stopped. They stopped. Then everyone was convinced I was the
one. The town decided to take back the crown, and I lost my
Sewer Pipe Queen title.

"Then I got the letter calling off the wedding, as I figured he
would. I was heartbroken, everything had crumbled so quickly, I
was so confused. How could all of these people think I did it? My
whole life was gone one day, just as if someone had set a fire to it.
It just came undone. I thought it couldn't get any worse, and
then, in a couple of days, the Captain secretly came out to the
house and told me I needed to leave."

"Was he going to help you to escape by boat?" Maye asked.

"A boat?" Ruby scoffed. "He wasn't a *ship*'s captain, he was a
police captain. He said I needed to get out of town because the
chief was sure I had done it and it was looking like they were
going to charge me. They all told me to go; my folks and Lula
said I should leave Spaulding and start over somewhere else
where no one knew me while it was all sorted out. I thought they
were crazy; I knew I hadn't done anything, and I thought I could
just wait it out here until the whole thing blew over. And besides,
where would I go? I'd never known any place but Spaulding. I
couldn't just leave; this was the place I wanted to be. It was the
place I loved to be. The Captain told the chief I had skipped
town and was gone, so they just let it be. And that was that."

"For fifty years," Maye thought, and realized she had said it out loud.

"For a long time," Ruby said, nodding. "A long time. After my folks passed on years later, I'm sure a few people figured I was out here at the farm, but by that time, no one said anything. Lula covered up pretty well and took care of basic things for me, but then she went over, too, about ten years ago, after she got sick with cancer. So I started breeding the dogs for something to do, and for the company, and that turned out to be a fine thing. I finally got a phone, but no one much comes by, except for the nosy TV reporter, and then you. So I've just been out here, ever since. I stayed in this house, and waited and waited."

Maye looked at the old woman as a slice of light illuminated her face, her deeply set wrinkles, her thin, lipstick-smudged lips, and her soft, folded eyes that Maye just noticed were a forlorn shade of gray.

"What were you waiting for?" she asked quietly.

Ruby finally turned, her gray eyes looking into Maye's.

"I kept hoping they would change their minds about me," the old, weathered woman said simply.

But it never happened. The town that Ruby Spicer loved so much went on and rebuilt itself exactly as it had been, exactly how it needed to be, while a once-pretty girl sat just outside of town, waiting for the town to forgive her when instead it just forgot her.

ψ   ψ   ψ

Mickey smelled the dogs before Maye even turned the corner into Ruby's driveway.

Puppy was the first one out of the house, racing up to the car and springing on his hind feet into the air, as if he wanted to be the one to officially greet the new visitor.

"Careful, Puppy, careful," Maye said as she tried to keep the dog from jumping on her sweater amid his trampoline-style hops, some of which brought them nose to nose. "This is vintage and it needs to be dry-cleaned."

Papa and Mama followed close behind, with Captain and Junior bringing up the rear. Other dogs might have been hesitant to enter such an established pack, but Mickey jumped right into the fray and immediately threw himself on his back as if to say gleefully, "Smell me—I'm new!" and the boxers greeted him as if they were old friends. Once everyone was satisfied they'd had a good-enough whiff, Mickey leaped back up and happily returned Puppy's playful nudges and bites.

So far, so good, Maye thought as she lifted Mickey's Fisher-Price toy piano out of the trunk. She was hoping that by getting the dogs invigorated, a little energy might rub off on Ruby, too, who had been less than her usual irritable self since Maye had stumbled upon the dresses earlier in the week. She had tried to be patient with the old lady, but all Ruby wanted to do was sit in her recliner, gulp from her tumbler as she lit cigarette after cigarette, and watch old movies. She even refused Maye's offer to pick up the latest crop of dog shit, and that troubled Maye. The old woman insisted that Maye do nothing but sit and watch movies with her, both of them saying nothing. On this afternoon, Maye entered the living room with the swarm of dogs to find Ruby on the recliner again, watching the black-and-white images of *Smash-Up: The Story of a Woman.*

"We watched this one yesterday," Maye said, to which Ruby grunted.

"I told you this was my favorite movie," Ruby growled, not even turning her eyes to Maye.

"Ruby, I don't know how many times you can stand watching a drunk Susan Hayward almost setting her baby on fire," Maye commented.

"Shhh!" the old woman demanded. "It's almost to the part where she beats up her husband's secretary in the ladies' toilet."

"I brought Mickey and his piano," Maye stated. "I thought we could start our training today."

"Pfffff," Ruby jeered, her eyes still locked on the TV. "Start training? Start it? What do you think we've been doing all this time? Have you seen what's dangling under your arms? It's like a tire swing! You can't wave to an unsuspecting public with fat flaps like that! You could play Ping-Pong between those two! I should have had you paint every fence in Spaulding to tighten those things up! I should make you go out there right now and lift your car!"

Maye tried to ignore the comment. "And I have a CD of Sonny and Cher's two greatest hits," Maye started.

"SHHHHH!" the old woman demanded. "This is it! This is it!"

On the television, Susan Hayward was in a fancy ladies' lounge, where, with numerous women looking on, she had cornered her husband's diligent secretary. Loony with booze, she struck the match to ignite a ferocious cat fight.

"So self-contained, aren't you?" she asks the secretary, then steps closer to the woman, getting ready to strike. *"So poised. Look at you, not a hair out of place. I'd love to see you all messed up. I can't think of anything that would give me a bigger kick. I bet you're like this when you get up in the morning, aren't you, Martha? Or should I ask my husband?"*

Ruby chuckled as Hayward launched herself onto Martha, clawing at her dress, yanking chunks of her hair, and gloriously open-hand slapping her.

"Oh, I could watch that all day!" Ruby exclaimed, turning to Maye with an ample grin. Then she suddenly stopped, as if she was flash frozen.

Maye had seen that look once before, in Hopkins Market, almost a week ago.

Ruby's face had lost all expression except shock as her jaw dropped.

"What," she said as she pointed at Maye with a twisted finger, "what are you wearing? Where did you get that?"

"The sweater?" Maye asked. "A clothes store in town, why? Can you see the makeup smudges on the collar from there? I got it stuck on my head and in the struggle to get it off, my makeup just got ground into it. Is it that obvious?"

"Which store?" Ruby asked, standing up slowly.

"I don't know the name of it. It was a vintage clothing store downtown," Maye explained. "Is it really that ugly? I think it's so pretty. Cost me a fortune, with all of this beading. This is the sweater Rowena Spaulding made fun of the first time I met her, at the first faculty mixer."

"Well, she shouldn't have," the old woman said as she walked over to Maye, then picked up the hem of the sweater and touched it. "It's her sweater."

Maye stared at Ruby. "What?" she replied. "How could this possibly be Rowena Spaulding's sweater?"

"I sold this a while ago, found it in a box upstairs with some other old things," Ruby explained. "Had no need for it. I need something that can breathe, something I can move in. I like to move. Gotta be able to move. Plus, I like zippers better. Buttons are such a pain in the ass."

"Okay," Maye said impatiently. "Back up. Rewind. I will speak slowly. How is this Rowena Spaulding's sweater?"

"Well, I borrowed it, we wore the same clothes, I told you, we were like twins," Ruby said. "Me and Wendy, who you know now as—"

"Rowena Spaulding," Maye surmised, feeling that all the air

had just been punched out of her like a Seal-a-Meal bag, which was quickly replaced by the urgent, uncontrollable need to get the repugnant sweater—plus any remaining skin cells from its previous, hideous owner—off her. Away from her. "Oh God. No wonder it got stuck on my head, it's got her evil all over it!" She squirmed as she struggled to take it off, neglecting to undo the buttons, which were a pain in the ass, first.

"Get it off me!" she screamed as she tugged at the sweater. "Get it off! It has mean cooties all over it! Please tell me you got this dry-cleaned."

"I sold a lamp to buy cigarettes and dog food last week," Ruby informed her. "No, I did not have it dry-cleaned."

Maye continued to struggle, now with the neckline of the sweater lodged all the way around her flushed and sweating head.

"God," Ruby sighed, and with a cigarette lodged between her lips, she tried to help Maye, who was flopping about irritably like a big, fat-armed fish. "Hang on, I'll help you. We have a ways to go before Susan Hayward burns her house down. Stay still and I'll get it off your head. *Stay still.* Aw, Christ. You really should be wearing a shirt underneath that. I can see your boobies, we're gonna have to work on those, too."

Only after Maye relaxed somewhat was Ruby able to yank the sweater all the way off her head, and as the brilliant red color dissolved from Maye's face, Ruby looked at her and shook her head.

"Now look at what you and your hissy fit went and did," she said, pointing at Maye's scalp line, the thickest part of her skull. "You went and got yourself a rash there, a little burn, all around your head, like the rings around Saturn. I hope you're happy, because that was stupid. Now you have to be in the pageant with a face scab."

Maye's head did sting, a sting she had felt once before.

"Um," she said self-consciously, "can I borrow a shirt?"

"Sure," Ruby replied. She waved disgustedly and trudged upstairs, her filthy slippers making a muffled thud on each step.

"I was just beginning to like that sweater," Maye called as the old woman rooted around upstairs. "And I can't believe Rowena Spaulding was your best friend. I just can't see it. What was she like when she was young?"

"She wasn't Rowena then, she was Wendy." Maye could barely hear Ruby answer. "She liked to have fun, she laughed a lot, we always had a great time together. She was just like any other girl, nothing special, just nice."

The old woman came back downstairs carrying something green with a zipper up the front. When she got to the living room, she handed it to Maye, who put it on without so much as a glance.

"Here you go," Maye said, handing Ruby a used tissue she found stuffed in the sleeve of the terrycloth tracksuit jacket Ruby had worn the day before. Ruby promptly stuffed it up the sleeve of the tracksuit jacket she was wearing today.

"So that's why she hates me?" Maye asked. "Because of that sweater?"

"Well, if you ask me, I bet it's like when you get the flu or something and you throw up green-bean casserole through your nose," she concluded. "I bet it's something like that."

"I think I follow you," Maye replied. "Like when you throw up something that wasn't what made you sick, but you can't ever eat that food again and just the thought of it makes you queasy."

"Exactly," Ruby said. "I can't eat tuna casserole anymore because of that. Fish shot out of my nose like it was a cannon. That ever happen to you?"

As her stomach was doing a tumbling act of its own, Maye resisted opening her mouth for fear of what might come shooting out of it. She just shook her head.

"Happened with corn once, too. Those were like bullets. One even bounced back and hit me," Ruby added, then quickly turned toward the television. "Hup, look at that, there goes the house, up in flames. Grab your baby, ya stupid drunk! Run! Run!"

"So because I wore this sweater, Rowena is going to forever hate me," Maye said.

"My guess is yes," Ruby answered. "She may be the high and mighty Mrs. Spaulding now, but she's still the girl I knew, and that girl can hold a grudge. She's got everything she ever wanted—a big-shot husband, a grand, fancy house on a hill, and a crown that she didn't earn, but she can stay pissed for a long time."

"A crown she didn't earn?" Maye repeated. "Wha—how— you mean that she . . ."

"Rode to glory on my coattails?" Ruby sniped. "That's exactly what she did! What, you think she could do the splits? She could only do it if she bent her knee behind her, *and that's cheating!* No, she didn't earn it! She slid right onto my throne after I got kicked off because she was the first runner-up! Rowena Spaulding is no queen, she's a lady-in-waiting!"

"You mean to tell me that woman forced you out of your crown and then took it?" Maye said, feeling the anger in her rise up as quickly as the volume of her voice. "She stole your crown. She stole it, the thief! How have you not killed her yet? Oh my God! I hate her! I hate Rowena Spaulding! She is such a revolting hag!"

"I like to think of her as a fury," Ruby said more calmly than Maye thought she could be. "I've been living with this for fifty years. Fifty years I've been waiting to take back what's mine. And that's why we are going to beat her. Once and for all, we'll settle this. Once and for all, we'll see who ends up with the crown."

"We'd better," Maye said. "I think Melissabeth is going to be hard to beat. She's some champion opera singer with lungs of gold and the voice of a thousand angels."

"Opera singers, those broads are a dime a damn dozen," Ruby pooh-poohed. "A singing dog that plays piano? Once in a lifetime, sugar. What you've got there isn't a talent segment; it's *an act*. Where is he? Where's your star? Show me what he can do!"

"Really?" Maye said. "Are we really going to start training? This is wonderful! I brought his piano, and I have a CD player that I just need to plug in. Mickey! Mickey, come!"

The white, tan, black, and gray speckled dog bounded into the living room accompanied by Puppy, who was apparently loath to leave his new friend's side.

Maye popped the CD into the player and positioned Mickey's piano just as it had always been in class, with the dog sitting behind it. She cued up the song and pushed "play." The first notes of "I Got You, Babe" floated through the room.

"Tinkle, Mickey!" Maye called. "Tinkle!"

Mickey just looked at her.

"Tinkle, Mickey!" Maye called again. "Tinkle, tinkle!"

Mickey did not lift his paws up onto the keys, and he did not begin. He looked at Puppy, who was sitting pensively on the couch, then at Maye and back at Puppy, and did nothing.

Maye stopped the music.

"Mickey, what's the matter?" Maye asked. "You love to do this in class!"

"Maybe he's embarrassed in front of the other dogs," Ruby suggested. "Are you sure he can really play piano?"

"I'm positive!" Maye insisted. "And he does this in front of other dogs every week in his class! He's used to it. What's the matter, Mickey? Let's try again, okay?"

She pushed "play" again, the first note of "I Got You, Babe" sounded, and Maye gave the command, but still Mickey simply sat there with no response. He didn't make a sound, didn't lift a paw.

"Oh, hell," Ruby said, throwing her arms up. "This isn't working. I'll go get you the matching pants to your jacket, and when I come back down we're going to make you do the splits."

"He did this the night before last in class," she told Ruby. "He was fine. In every single class, she plays the song, he hears the notes, 'dum dum dum, de dum dum,' and he starts!"

"You mean like that?" Ruby asked, pointing to Mickey, who now had one paw on the keys and was looking at Maye in anticipation.

Maye looked at Ruby, who nodded just once. "Keep going," she whispered. "Keep humming."

"Dum dum dum, de dum dum," Maye continued, to which Mickey lifted up his second paw and placed it on the keys, much to Maye's surprise.

" 'We are young,' " Maye said softly. " 'Heartache to heartache, we stand.' "

"Woooo, wooooo," Mickey began to sing along.

" 'No promises, no demands,' " she went on. " 'Love is a battlefield.' "

"Woo woo woo woo woo woo woo woo wooooooo!!" Mickey sang.

"Holy shit," Maye said after a short pause as she rubbed her temples. "I'm going to kill Gwen."

"Let's try another song," Ruby suggested, sensing Maye's distress.

"That's a great idea," she agreed, and eagerly cued the CD player to another track.

The light, plucky notes of a keyboard sounded, followed by a deep, rich voice.

"I was born in the wagon of a travelin' show," Cher lamented.

Mickey simply sat there, looking at Maye.

"Come on, Mickey!" Maye cried. "Please! It's 'Gypsies, Tramps and Thieves'! This is a great song! Think of all the fun we could have with it!"

The dog wasn't buying it and didn't make another move, even though the music kept playing. Maye shut it off.

"Dum dum dum, de dum dum," Ruby whistled, and Mickey put his paws back up on the piano keys.

"Well, Mickey," Maye said, slapping her hands on her thighs in resignation. "Looks like we've got ourselves a song."

14

Two Women in the House—and One of Them a Redhead

Maye arrived at Ruby's in the morning armed with Mickey, a copy of Pat Benatar's *Greatest Hits*, and a padded mailer that UPS had delivered the night before.

It was clear to Maye on that disappointing afternoon that Mickey had been trained to play piano to one and only one song, thanks to Gwen's resistance, where music was concerned, to spread her wings and fly beyond the eighth grade. Maye decided she truly hated her for that.

But the moment she inserted the CD and pressed "play," Mickey hopped right behind that piano and began wailing like he was a hairier Billy Joel. And that was how it was decided that Maye's talent segment would be a song that reminded her of being tongue-mugged during a bad double date in the back of a van with bar stools as seats. Even Puppy had come over to give Mickey a lick of approval.

Maye shuddered as she handed the package over to Ruby, who smiled broadly with anticipation as she inserted the bootleg tape, which Maye had used her honed and sharpened eBay skills to win, into her dusty VHS player.

Ruby clapped her hands together and stepped back, eager to see if the "Love Is a Battlefield" video was as repugnant as Maye had recounted. A minute into it, the old woman clearly saw how it could bring down the house.

"Look at all of those shimmies!" she exclaimed with glee. "All you gotta do is shimmy here and shimmy there—don't worry, we'll get you a good support bra for your water balloons—snap your fingers a couple of times, and you can pull off that dance number. That elfin-looking girl in the video is even wearing a headband, so we can hide that scab around your head."

Maye did not look happy. "I'm sorry," she said. "I just never had visions of myself onstage in front of my new town trying to win a pageant by wearing a skirt of rags and having a dance-off with my dog, who is dressed as a pimp."

"Mickey's a perfect pimp!" Ruby argued. "We'll get him a little white polyester suit and paint his front fang gold. You wait and see. You will shimmy to glory, and put Rowena Spaulding in her place."

"I hope you're right," Maye added. "I'm still worried about Melissabeth."

"Psh!" the old woman spit. "Anyone can go up there and sing a little opera! Opera shmopera. Fa la la la la! You're going to go up there and *entertain* them! You're going to get up there and give 'em a *show*! That is gold! *That* is what counts!"

"All right, if you can show me how to do it, I'm game," Maye asked. "Just out of curiosity, I want to know what Rowena did for her talent segment?"

"Please," Ruby began to laugh wholeheartedly, a rumble that came from deep within what was left of her lungs and sounded like a diesel engine missing a cylinder. "Whaddya think? She braided her hair, put on a gingham dress, and sang 'Over the

Rainbow.' Can you believe it? Predictable. Milk toast. Bo-ring. Christ, all I had to do was show up and they basically handed me the crown. Now, let's practice shaking your totties."

"What?" Maye laughed.

"Your bazongas," Ruby replied, stretching her arms out sideways and shaking what a medical examiner would call her bazongas, but with that sudden movement, they didn't so much shake as they did almost completely orbit her body.

"Rowena Spaulding is a revolting hag!" she screeched as she shimmied from side to side, swinging her totties out like seats on a YoYo carnival ride.

"You're good at that!" Maye commented.

"I come alive in front of an audience," Ruby shouted, her bazongas in full velocity.

Maye tried to avert her eyes from the whipping carnage and stretched her arms out to her sides, too, mimicking Ruby's grinding and shaking.

"Rowena Spaulding," she shrieked, "is a vile, sorry little bitch!"

Ruby abruptly stopped her shimmying, doubled over, and burst out laughing. *"Hush . . . Hush, Sweet Charlotte!"* she cried, holding her sides. "That's good! That's good!"

"Well, look at this," a male voice said from behind them. "Two women in the house—and one of them a redhead!"

Maye spun around immediately and was shocked to see John Smith, the plumber and cop, standing in the doorway in his officer's uniform.

Oh shit, she thought to herself in a panic that clearly bore itself in her expression. He's finally come for me. He's finally come to bring me in. I'm going to the Big House for getting a cop all hopped up on organic cane sugar. "Hi there, John," she said, trying to sound cheery.

"Hello, Maye," he said flatly, in no way returning her attempt at cheeriness. "Been a while. How's the bathroom drain?"

"Good," Maye said, nodding, trying to act as nonchalant as anyone would when an officer of the law you've drugged walks into the room in the middle of your nasty-lady dance. "Good. You know. Draining. "

"What did you bring me?" Ruby croaked at her guest. "Did you bring me eggs? I needed eggs! And I'm outta coffee and I'm getting close to wiping with leaves."

"It's all in the car, Aunt Roo," John said, finally breaking a smile. "I brought everything on your list, and I've got my tools so I can work on the kitchen sink."

Maye looked at John, then Ruby, then John again. "He's"—she pointed at one of them, then the other—"What? You're related? I'm—why didn't you tell me?"

Ruby and John looked at each other.

" 'Cause it wasn't none of your business," Ruby quickly quipped.

"You're Lula's son?" Maye asked. "Lula and the Captain's?"

"I'm John junior," the cop explained. "The Captain was John senior."

"He's plain old Junior to me. And he's also the reason you couldn't find me in the public records. After Papa died, this house passed over to John, thank heavens," Ruby said. "Now I'm going out to the car, and there better be some toilet paper in there, 'cause I gotta go."

"No, I'll get it," he said, stopping her at the door. "I just wanted to make sure you were up and around before I started making a racket bringing stuff in. I had no idea you were running a stripping school."

Ruby hit John on the shoulder and cackled. "The Girl here is working on her act for the Sewer Pipe Queen Pageant," she said. "We've just got a little bit of spice in our show, that's all. Her dog sings, too. It's gonna bring down the house, I tell you."

"Mmmm," John mumbled, nodding. "I'll bring your groceries in."

Maye waited until she saw John out next to his car before she said anything.

"Why didn't you tell me he was your nephew?" she whispered to Ruby.

"Why?" she whispered back. "What difference does it make?"

Maye thought about it for a moment, and other than the fact that she had roofied up an officer of the law to rat out his old, alcoholic, allegedly arsonist aunt, she supposed it didn't really make a difference if they were related or not.

"Well, I guess it doesn't," Maye whispered back. "It's just a surprise, that's all."

"Not as much of a surprise as waking up in the passenger seat of your patrol car on the wrong side of town as the sun is setting with jelly on your face," John said as he crossed the doorway with a full grocery bag in each arm. "There's more out there, Maye, if you'd like to help."

"Of course," Maye said, feeling instantly foolish, and she trudged out to the patrol car, where the backseat contained a forty-pound dog-food bag and a jug of milk. With the dog food hoisted over her shoulder and compressing her spine like an accordion, Maye made her way back into the house and to the kitchen, where John was unloading the groceries. She lifted the dog food off of her shoulder and onto the floor and placed the milk in the fridge. He kept unloading the bags onto the counter and didn't say a word.

"I really owe you an apology, John," Maye said with his back turned toward her. "I know what I did was really wrong. It was a horrible thing to do. I knew your weakness for Hoo Doo donuts, and I took advantage of it. I'm really, really sorry. I can't say it enough."

John spun around quickly and put his hands on his hips. "You didn't just drug me and make me spill secrets I had kept for my whole life," he said sternly. "You put that old woman in danger. Do you know what would happen if some people knew she was out here? Do you? Sure, most everyone's forgotten about it, but some people lost their livelihoods, they lost their homes and businesses. Even if they've gone on to rebuild, that's an anger that doesn't die away. There are people out there who, I dare say it, maybe wouldn't like to see her dead, but they'll like to see her in prison."

"I didn't know any of that when I force-fed you donuts, John," Maye tried to explain. "I would never have done anything to hurt her, or you for that matter. I thought you were keeping a silly little secret and that she was some sort of Greta Garbo figure, hiding all the way out in the woods because she wanted it that way. I had no idea about the fires. I had no idea until she told me. When I was looking for her, the idea of Ruby Spicer was romantic and so mysterious. I didn't know it would turn out to be . . ."

Maye stopped. She didn't want to say it.

"Tragic, sad, and drunk," John said it for her. "Drunk, tragic, and sad. Thank God no one takes that idiot Titball seriously, otherwise they would have swarmed her already. He's been out here all sorts of times, trying to get her story out of her, trying to expose her, and I have warned him. Unofficially, of course, but he's another one who never takes into account what would happen if they found out the woman who burned the town down was still living less than twenty miles away, and she'd never gone anywhere."

"You . . . you think she did it?" Maye asked incredulously. "You can't think she did it?"

"I would love to believe that she didn't do it, Maye, that she was wrongly accused," he said. "But she's . . . she's got a temper, and imagine that temper when something that she loved so dearly was threatened. Now, I love that old bag, she's the only family I've got left. But I'll tell you, I wouldn't want to cross her. The pieces fit, you know? Now, sure, the town made up some bullshit story about pipe-manufacturing competitors coming down here to set the fires to drive the factory out of business, but the truth is, she did it. Ruby Spicer burned down the pipe factory, City Hall, the movie theater, the bakery. Was it right? Hell, no. But is she to blame? I don't know. You can't tell me that you think she rows with both oars in the water. It's not her fault, really, but that doesn't take away from the fact that she did it, and that my father, despite the risk to his career in law enforcement and what it could have done to the rest of his life, protected her all of those years because he made a promise to my mother."

Maye didn't know what to say; her head was spinning. But she couldn't believe it, she did not believe that Ruby had set those fires and had actually deserved to pay the penance that she had without so much as a fight.

"I don't know, John," she finally said, shaking her head. "I just, I don't think I can believe that. Did your father believe she was guilty? She said she was here with her parents every time one of those fires broke out."

"Maye," he said, shaking his head. "That's what *she* told you. That's what she believes. He had proof it was her. She dropped a scarf at one of the fire scenes. My father found it. He never entered it as evidence, but he knew it was hers. And it was, my mother even said so. He covered it up. That wasn't right, but for Ruby to do that, there was something else there, something not right. They tried to make her leave town, maybe even get some help. They knew that if it came out, the people would go berserk on her and that would make everything worse. This is a small town, Maye. They would have eaten her alive if she was a suspect. They would have gone after the family, too. But she wouldn't listen, she was that crazy. Too crazy to even save what she had left

of her life. In the end, she served her sentence anyway, sitting out
here, watching old movies, setting herself on fire, and drinking
enough to embalm herself. You didn't tell anybody that you knew
she was out here, did you?"

"I don't know anyone, John," Maye said, wanting to laugh.
"Up until I drugged you and left you on the bad side of town
with jelly on your face, you were my closest friend. Wait—no—I
did tell someone. I told Rowena Spaulding that Ruby was coaching me for the pageant."

John shook his head slightly. "Oh, Rowena knew she was out
here," he replied. "Her folks used to live on the next farm over.
They were good friends of the family, nice people, watched out
for Ruby after my grandparents died, for a while. They were
nice, not like Rowena."

"Yes," Maye agreed. "I've had my run-ins with Mrs. Spaulding myself. She's a piece of work. "

"Well, concerning pieces of work, I gotta be honest with you,
Maye," John said, taking a deep breath. "I was not too happy
with what you did and how you did it. That's kidnapping, you
know, and I also gained six pounds overnight. I had to buy new
police pants. I was really going to let you have it the next time I
ran into you, and when I saw your car out front when I pulled up,
I thought for sure the showdown was on. And then, when I
walked up to that door and heard that old girl laughing, well, I
thought it was probably the right thing to do to put my anger
aside and just let it be."

"Well, we were just having fun, " Maye answered. "We do that
sometimes when she's not threatening to ram a lit cigarette into
my face. I like her. She's grown on me."

"You don't understand," John interrupted. "She was laughing.
I'm a middle-aged man, Maye, and I have never heard that
woman laugh."

Maye suddenly felt very heavy, like something had suddenly pressed down on her.

"Ever?" was all she said.

"Ever," her plumber replied.

ϒ ϒ ϒ

"Sure, she's a little loopy," Maye said to Charlie that night as she was making dinner. "But I just don't think she did it. Even if John does."

"He knows her better than you do, Maye," her husband reminded her as he lifted his briefcase onto the counter and rustled through it. "Just the thought of you out there alone with her makes me nervous. What if her nephew's right? What if she's capable of suddenly snapping and just going off the deep end?"

"Charlie, please," Maye said with a chuckle as she pulled a pot from the bottom cabinet. "If you ever saw her, you'd know there's nothing to worry about. She weighs about as much as a toddler, and I can see all of her vital organs decomposing through her skin. She can do the splits, I'll give her that, she's as limber as a lemur, and I wouldn't necessarily categorize her as harmless, but unless she's packing a stun gun, even I could outrun her."

"Well, according to her nephew, she's a full-fledged arsonist with one oar in the water and a wooden house that's a thundercloud away from collapsing," he said. "Doesn't sound so safe to me."

"Charlie, you're going to have to trust me on this one," Maye tried to reassure him. "You're worrying about nothing."

"And what kind of cop was this Captain person, anyway?" he asked as he pulled a stack of mail from the front pocket of his briefcase. "I mean, if you have the criminal, you have the evidence—what kind of person just lets them go, even if they are a bit wacky—and your sister-in-law? Isn't that a cop's duty? To follow the law no matter what? Don't they take a cop oath where they promise to serve and protect and obey and patrol or something like that? 'Cause I could have sworn I saw them do that on *CSI*. I mean, the Sopranos have an oath, don't cops?"

"Who knows what was going through his mind," she replied, filling the pot with water. "If you think this is a small town now—and there's a hundred thousand people here, Charlie—can you imagine what it was like then? I mean, I see the same people at the grocery store, the bank, at restaurants—people I don't know but just recognize from around. That never once happened to me in Phoenix, but here, I am always seeing people who made my checking deposit, people who served me pizza, people who are begging for a dollar on the street holding up a sign that says 'Hungry Mom and Kids,' and half an hour later, they're sitting next to us eating a New York strip and there's nary a child in sight. It's easy to get found out in this town as it is—imagine it back fifty years ago when everyone knew everyone else. Even insinuating something would probably be enough to get a person and their family condemned to a life of shame and completely ostracized forever. You'd be convicted merely on suggestion and instantly become a pariah. All on one little red scarf? Anyone could have set those fires—Ruby was all over town at different events. She could have dropped it then."

"Surrounded by photographers wherever she went?" Charlie scoffed. "I really doubt it. I think you're just trying to believe something that you want to believe, Maye. That old lady set the fires. And I think you know it."

"Well, for an insatiable firebug, she's pretty lazy," Maye said, taking the pot to the stove. "There hasn't been a fire since."

"That we know of," Charlie reminded her. "We've been here less than a year. Who knows when she'll get bitten by the pyromaniac bug again? If I start noticing a lot of spent matchbooks around here, or see that you have an unnatural attraction to

Duraflame logs, I'm calling this whole thing off. I have the feeling she's a bad influence!"

Maye laughed. "Charlie, you're ridiculous."

"Well, she's teaching you how to shimmy," he said dryly. "Are you going to sing to this song, or just lip-synch?"

"I am an entertainer now, I will remind you," she said. "The shimmies are mine, and so is the voice, no matter how deplorable it is."

"And you're dressing up exactly like Pat Benatar?" he queried. "Wasn't she a sex-trade worker in that video?"

"Yes. I shredded your old T-shirts to make my slut skirt," she answered.

"Isn't that what every man hopes his wife will do with them?" he asked wistfully, shuffling through envelopes. "Look, here's your best friend, right on the cover of the English Department newsletter. Boy, what a smile on Rowena, huh? Even the Grinch is more photogenic. She looks like she was just impaled with something. What a smile."

"What is *she* on the newsletter for?" Maye asked. "Is she having people burned at the stake for using the passive voice?"

"No, there was some sort of dinner for Dean Spaulding's birthday," Charlie mumbled as he read the accompanying story. "Dinner and a golf tournament—for two hundred dollars a head. Glad we weren't invited."

"Who has a birthday party and charges people two hundred dollars to come?" Maye asked, clucking her tongue.

"No, I think . . ." Charlie said as he continued to read, then reached out his arm to hand it to Maye. "Here, read it."

"No, I have my hands full," she said as she tasted the spaghetti sauce with a wooden spoon. "Read it to me."

"Hmmm," Charlie replied, mildly protesting. " 'It would be fair to say that the birthday of everyone's favorite Dean went straight to the dogs. On Friday, a four-course meal catered by La

Vaca Bonita was followed by an afternoon golf tournament hosted by Dean and Mrs. Minturn Spaulding, the proceeds of which are to benefit the Spaulding Humane Society, Dean Spaulding's favorite charity. Although the Dean did not walk away with a trophy, he did successfully blow out all the candles on his birthday cake, which was shaped like a giant golf ball. The tournament winner, Ms. Heather Megyesi, clobbered the competition by—' "

"Wait—wait—what did you say?" Maye said suddenly as a bubble of sauce popped and shot a red streak onto her T-shirt. "Read that again."

" 'Although the Dean did not walk away with a trophy, he did successfully blow out all—' " he repeated.

"No, Charlie, the name," she said irritably. "What's his name?"

"Dean Spaulding?" he asked, furrowing his brow. "It's Minturn, but I've never called him that. That is a fancy man's name. I've always just called him Dean. No one calls him by his real name."

Maye stood in silence as the water on the stove began to boil.

Papa. Mama, Lula. Captain, Junior.

She named them after people she cared about, people she missed, Maye realized. She named them after people she loved.

Minty.

In the pot on the stove, the popping water spilled over the silver rim and hit the burner, sizzling away to nothing with a hiss.

ᛋ ᛋ ᛋ

"And one, two, three, four!" Ruby yelled, calling out each number with a snap of her fingers. "Shimmy left, shimmy right!"

Ruby, missing the chunk of hair in front of her ear due to an overly exuberant butane lighter, had been snapping her fingers for weeks, Maye had been shimmying her heart and fat flaps out, and Mickey had been busy playing his toy piano and wailing in the background. The three of them had put together quite a little number, complete with a dance sequence in which Mickey got to roll over and play dead, courtesy of the bribe of a beef chewy stick Maye held secretly in her palm.

Ruby had even helped Maye construct her costume; the raggedy slut skirt, the pinned-together top, little rag wristbands, and torn fishnet stockings. Maye felt ridiculous in it, but that, honestly was the point—she was going to entertain, put on a show, and hopefully make some people laugh.

"Come on, give me a shimmy!" Ruby screeched from the couch as she ground out one cigarette and then lit another. "You're fighting a battle of good and evil with your dog pimp! Your only weapon is the shimmy! There is power in the shimmy! Make him fear your shimmy! Now, goddamnit, *show me your war shimmy!*"

"I'm trying," Maye wailed pathetically as a drop of sweat the size of a nickel flew from her forehead. "My back hurts, my arms hurt, my shoulders hurt, and if I shimmy any more, I'm going to need a boob lift. I think I've shaken the joy out of them."

"Go ahead, then, stop," the old woman said, taking a gulp out of her tumbler and ashing her cigarette. "Give up, surrender. What do you think Melissabeth is doing right now, huh? She's singing, is what. Doing her scales, drinking tea with lemon, holding her breath, whatever those opera people do. If you wanna let her win, go ahead and stop, be my guest, I could use the rest."

"I don't want to stop," Maye gasped in midshimmy. "I just want a break!"

The music abruptly halted after Ruby quickly hit "stop" with her warped, barnacled finger.

"There," she said as an exhaust pipe's worth of smoke shot from her mouth. "There's your break."

"Release, Mickey," Maye said, breathing heavily, and stopped as her dog ran off to tackle Puppy, who had been watching the rehearsal from Ruby's recliner.

"Now, I'll let you have a short break, but hard work will pay off when you're up there on that stage," Ruby reminded her as she pulled a paper towel from her sleeve and handed it to Maye to wipe her sweaty and, thankfully, healing scab brow. "When I'm down there looking at you doing this number for real, don't make me wish I hadn't given you this break, Girl."

"Ha-ha," Maye said. "If you want, though, I will have Charlie videotape it so you can see it later."

"What do you mean, see it later?" Ruby asked, duly offended. "What kind of coach would I be if I didn't show up? I'll be there, all right. I wanna take the credit when you win! I wanna rub it in!"

Maye sat down on the couch next to the old lady. "Ruby, I don't think it's a good idea for you to come into town," she said as gently as possible. "I'll come out here as soon as the pageant is over, I swear, whether it's good or bad news. But I—I just think it's better if you don't go. I would love to have you there, but I'm sorry."

"You can't tell me what I can and can't do," Ruby warned harshly. "I have just as much right to go into that town as anyone does."

"I think you do, too," Maye said, trying to comfort her. "And I wasn't going to tell you this, but one of the times I went to Hopkins to get you a malted, I saw Rowena. She was being her typical nasty self, and she got me into a huff. I mentioned that you were my coach, and she replied that if you tried to step foot into town, you'd be lucky if you didn't get lynched. I'm afraid she'll start something there and that you might get hurt."

"That's what she thinks!" the old woman cried. "She thinks she runs it all! I go into town whenever I please, and no one says anything!"

"I know," Maye said. "But this time is different. This time she'll be looking for you. This time she'll know you're there."

Ruby looked lost and defeated. She shook her head, which caused little singed bits of hair to tumble from the ends.

"But I want to go," she said weakly, almost sounding like a child. "I was the queen, remember?"

"You're still the queen," Maye replied, patting Ruby's gnarled hand. "And that's why Rowena is so horrible. She knows that's not her crown, she knows she didn't win. But look at what she did to get it, and that woman still has that in her. She'll do anything to get—or take—what she wants. Particularly from you."

"My crown is not all she got," the old woman mumbled quietly.

Maye took a deep breath. "I know, Ruby," she said, finally forcing it out. "I know about what Rowena did."

Ruby shook her head again. "No, you don't," she said tiredly. "No, you don't."

"I know about Dean Spaulding," Maye reiterated. "I know about Minty."

Although Ruby took a deep breath, it seemed like she had suddenly deflated. The old woman's shoulders dropped and fell, as if she had just tossed off a load she never wanted to be carrying.

"You shouldn't think poorly of him. He was only doing what he thought was right," she said, not so much to Maye but in a mantra that she had ingrained in herself for the last fifty years. "Anybody would have done what he did. He thought I burned down his family's factory. They lost everything, everything his family had built up. The town lost jobs, they weren't even sure if that place would survive. Any man would have done what he did. He had no choice. He had to . . . he had to send me that note. I understood. I did. I thought he did the right thing, too, if I had to make that choice."

Suddenly, Maye realized what she hadn't been able to connect since the first day she pulled up into the dirt driveway of Ruby's tumbledown gray shack. How a vibrant, fiery, beautiful young woman had drifted away, away, away, until a weathered, acidic, and turbulent recluse finally took her place.

Ruby Spicer blamed herself.

She blamed herself for nearly ruining a town she never touched with a badly intentioned hand, she blamed herself for losing the opportunities that had been stolen from her. She blamed herself for getting a note that said the kindest man she ever met could not spread that kindness to her. Even if Ruby Spicer didn't set that fire, she might as well have; she had even convicted herself.

"Have you seen him?" the old woman asked, not looking at Maye. "Can you tell me what he's like now?"

Maye nodded. "He was very nice to me," she said. "He came over and talked to me at the faculty mixer when no one else would. He remembered my name. And he insisted that I come to the holiday party because I think he knew I was too embarrassed to go. And they always have the most beautiful flowers at the house; they're usually out of season."

"That's Minty," Ruby said, nodding slightly. "Did he seem happy to you?"

Maye winced, then shook her head. "I don't know, Ruby," she answered honestly. "He always seemed happy when I saw him, but he is an excellent host, he made sure everyone always had what they needed, and that they felt welcomed. I do know, though, that Rowena attempted to order his favorite pastrami sandwich from Hopkins but had no idea what he liked on it."

"Oh," Ruby replied.

"Are you all right?" Maye asked, to which Ruby nodded.

"You know, I'm a little tired," the old woman said, finally looking at Maye. "I think I'm going to pop in a good movie and relax in the chair. You can go on home. The act is as good as gold."

"Well, I have some more strips to sew to my skirt, anyway," Maye said. "The backside is a little bare. Are you going to be okay?"

"I'll be fine, I'm fine," Ruby replied, waving her away. "I'm in the mood for a little *Johnny Guitar*. The idea of Joan Crawford playing piano in a flowing white gown as everything burns down and a lynch mob is coming at her sounds very appealing."

"I can stick around, Ruby," she said. "I can call Charlie and tell him I'll be a little late."

"Nope," the old woman said adamantly, with a cigarette dangling from between her teeth. "Go on and work on your costume. You'll look adorable. Now go out there and be so swell that you'll make me hate you."

Maye looked at her quizzically.

"*42nd Street,*" she offered, smiling.

"Okay then," Maye said hesitantly as she got Mickey's leash and hooked it to his collar. "I'll go."

She turned off the CD player, picked up her purse, then headed for the door. She had her hand on the doorknob and was about to pull it open when she stopped.

"It's very simple, really," Ruby called out to her. "On rye with lots of mustard."

15

Trouble Jumps Off

When Maye arrived at the Sewer Pipe Queen Pageant
check-in table at the back steps of the town square
stage in her Pat Benatar slutty rag outfit and her dog dressed like
a Huggy Bear, no one even came close to asking where her sponsor was, despite the fact that it was listed on the entrance application that she'd filled out months ago. The pageant director,
a nervous-looking fifty-ish woman, gave her a badge with her
name on it for backstage access, told her to be ready at 7 P.M.
sharp for the contestant introductions, where to find the music
coordinator, who needed her musical selection if she had one,
and what place she had. Then she plucked the thirty-five-dollar
entry fee, in cash only, from Maye's hand without so much as a
"Thank you very much."

And Maye was in. She and her pimp dog walked up the whin-
ing wooden stairs to the backstage area, which was hidden from
view by a large, heavy canvas curtain. Backstage was a buzzing
little community of its own, with sponsors rushing back and forth

and contestants siphoning the last minutes of practice in before the pageant started.

Maye was amazed at how many contestants there were shoved together between the canvas curtain and the stage itself. She wasn't exactly sure what to expect, since in Ruby's day, the competition had been more formal and traditional. Over the years, it had lost all traces of conventionality, and in turn, it had become a free-form contest. In order to compete, the competitors needed to meet only three qualifications: they had to be a citizen of Spaulding, they needed a sponsor, and they needed a talent routine. That was it. Gone were the pageant gowns, the swimsuit segment, the host in a tuxedo. Instead, Spaulding's modern-day Sewer Pipe Queen Pageant was open to anyone who had a spare thirty-five bucks and a hankering to get onstage.

With Mickey by her side, Maye set off to find the music coordinator and hand over her CD. She passed by a five-year-old dressed in exquisitely frilly pageant wear, dutifully practicing dance steps; she skirted by a man mumbling out of the side of his mouth while operating a dangling marionette dressed in what looked like a baby unitard; she stood behind someone dressed like a scarecrow holding a staff with jangly bells attached who was blocking the hallway, shaking her stick at no one; and just as she reached the man who looked harried enough to be the music coordinator, she saw the back of a young, slim woman dressed in an elegant, floor-length silver evening gown. She was speaking quietly and calmly to the harried, sweat-drenched man.

It was Melissabeth.

Maye took a deep breath, attempted to smile, and waited. She couldn't make out exactly what it was that Rowena's flying monkey was saying, but she did see the music coordinator pat his brow several times with a hankie from his pocket as he compulsively nodded in agreement. It took less than a minute for Maye to feel a chill against her back, but she already knew it was coming by the sound of determined, furious pumps rushing toward her as they clipped the worn wooden floors.

"HA!" Rowena bellowed, bending her arms and throwing her palms up when she saw Maye. "I did not think you would really do this. I have to give you credit, Maye Roberts. Do you have a thirst for public humiliation? Well, I feel a little sorry for you, about to get beaten into the ground by a perfect rendition of Mozart's Queen of the Night aria, one of the most difficult any-one can perform. My girl is going beat you."

Her coal eyes flicked down to Mickey, who was panting pa-tiently in his little white suit and gold lamé vest.

"She'll beat you and your little dog, too," Rowena threatened with a smirk. "And just where is your sponsor?"

It took everything Maye had to contain her hatred for Rowena and not let it leak out all over her. She wanted to punch her. She had never in her life wanted to sock anyone before, but she could feel her fingers curling up into her palm just from want. Her rage had become that solid and real, not because of what Rowena had done to Maye, but because of what she had ground Ruby into. Maye knew just where she would hit her—slightly above the cheekbone so she'd be sure to provide a nice, fleshy black eye with all the trimmings. More than anybody, Rowena deserved it. For all she had stolen from Ruby, for all that she had assumed, it was only proper that Maye hit her and hit her hard.

"She'll be here," Maye lied, retracting her fingers up tighter in her hand, not wanting Rowena to know that she had indeed struck fear into Maye about what might happen to Ruby if she did come.

"She's not curled up underneath the stage swigging from the cheapest bottle of gin she could find, is she?" Rowena shot, the grin still pinned across her yellow teeth.

Maye leaned in closer to Rowena and put a sweet smile on her face.

"That's not very nice talk," she whispered loud enough for Rowena to hear her clearly, "from a runner-up."

Rowena pulled back slightly, the smile sucking back into the folds of her face. "We'll see you out there on that stage," Rowena hissed. "We'll see what you're made of *then*. I'm afraid we're going to clean you up with your own little mop skirt by the end of the evening. Melissabeth! Come, dear, you have a hair out of place."

Melissabeth turned toward Maye and, without a word, was whisked away.

The music coordinator, who wore a laminated badge with the name Merlin on it, pulled out a white cloth that almost looked like a surrender flag and pressed it against his forehead.

"It must have taken acid to get the green color out of her skin," Maye remarked. "But then again, for her that only entails spitting into a napkin."

"Well," Merlin fudged, "she's taken a lot of her protégées to the top. She's got more wins under her belt than anyone else can claim. You must be Maye Roberts. You're the last one to check in. You're also the last one going on. Where's your music?"

"Right here," Maye said, handing over the CD that held the version of the song one of Charlie's computer-guy friends at the university had managed to wipe the vocal tracks from. "It's the only song on there."

"Any special instructions?" he asked quickly.

"Do you have a clip-on mike?" Maye asked.

"You're singing?" Merlin asked.

"If you can call it that," she replied. "I'll be dancing, too, so I'll be moving around a lot."

"I'll track down a clip-on for you, but in the meantime, you'd better get over to the side stage," the sweaty bald man advised. "The show is going to start any minute, and you'll need to walk out when they call your name."

Maye and Mickey walked over to the holding area, where

Maye was able to size up her competition. There was Melissa-beth, looking like the real winner right out of the gate; the tiny pageant girl with so much makeup on it was entirely possible that she'd been held by the ankles and dipped into a vat of Cover Girl, accompanied by her equally cosmetic-laden, hair-spray-cocooned mother; the scarecrow, whose jingly staff produced a constant, slight hum of tiny chimes; the marionette and his equally creepy master who whispered to each other in low mumbles; and a young man wrapped in a red-sequined dress sitting in a wheelchair that was manned by a middle-aged lady who looked nervous.

Standing there, with all of the contestants and their sponsors hidden off to the side, Maye second-guessed her decision that Ruby shouldn't come. She wished she was there, standing off to the side with the other sponsors, farting, belching, coughing, and setting herself on fire, especially if she was standing next to Rowena. It would have made Maye feel a little protected, in a sense, and definitely not so all alone. In the days before the pageant, the two of them had spent long hours together, putting the finishing touches on the act, figuring out where to hide a spe-cial treat pouch inside of Maye's slut skirt to lure Mickey to come, walk backward, and stay in their dance-off, and working the routine into a perfect symphony of shaking totties, finger snaps, and dramatic looks that were sure to get a laugh.

Sure, she realized, Ruby had her rough spots—on an average day, she was like a case of eczema: red, swollen, bumpy, and irri-tated. On other days, though, she could be eczema with salve applied—a little smoother, not so inflamed, and not quite as crusty. In fact, a day spent without trudging out to Ruby's or try-ing to walk through a herd of dogs or coming home with the aroma of Ruby's cigarettes lingering on her clothes would seem a little strange, somehow lacking. She would still see the old woman, she was sure of it, but they had spent so much time together, par-ticularly within the last couple of weeks, that it now seemed like habit. Not a particularly good or fun habit, but one that Maye had grown fond of nonetheless.

The more she thought about it, the more she knew she was wrong; she should have let Ruby come. Like Rowena was going to start anything, especially in front of the whole town where someone might see her acting like the real Rowena and not in the socially pristine role of Mrs. Spaulding. Maye began to fill herself with regret, and with guilt for even stepping foot on that stage without Ruby there to see it. It was, after all, her work, too.

She remembered the words the old, wrinkled woman had said to her before she'd left the night before with finished costumes for herself and Mickey and the assurance that the act was as polished as it was going to get. Ruby had handed her the rag skirt and shirt, smiled, and said with a Viceroy hanging from her lips, "You'll look adorable. Now go out there and be so swell that you'll make me hate you."

A burst of loud, recorded pageant music suddenly blared from the speakers on either side of the stage, making Maye jump. Through a sliver in the curtain Maye got a glimpse of the stage, and she saw something she hadn't expected. A vast, buzzing audience. The crowd there to witness the pageant swelled all the way into the town square, past the grassy park that surrounded it, and almost onto the street. It was amazing. Maye knew that a good number of spectators turned out for the event, but to her, it seemed like the whole town was there. It had to be, unless they were bussing people in from outlying areas that were desperate for entertainment. And somewhere out there, she knew, was Charlie, probably getting ready to cringe at his wife's behavior as he had never cringed before.

The crowd suddenly erupted in a sea of applause, and then Maye heard a loud, booming voice bellow from onstage.

"Welcome, welcome to Spaulding's annual Sewer Pipe Queen Pageant!" the announcer boomed to even more applause.

Backstage, the level of charged electricity in the air quickly spiked as the contestants were gathered by a handler to walk on-stage for their introductions. Maye and Mickey took their place at the back of the line.

"Our first contestant is Melissabeth Nipkin," the emcee nearly sang.

As the line began to move out into the bright lights of the stage, another blinding white one forced Maye to squint and cover her eyes with her hand.

"And one, two, three! Action! What are your thoughts about getting ready to compete for the Sewer Pipe Queen title?" a familiar voice buzzed into Maye's ear like a big, bothersome, bloodthirsty bug.

Titball.

"And next we have Kaytlynne Brytanni Syznowski, also known as the reigning regional Miss Teeny Royalty Universe!" the emcee announced.

"Dick Titball is a liar," Maye said into the camera despite the retinal damage incurred in her eyes by its light. "Dick Titball makes up stories."

"Our next hopeful contestant is . . . Pinky Tuscadero? Is that right? Yes? Pinky Tuscadero, ladies and gentlemen!"

"One comment, come on!" the reporter insisted, still walking next to Maye as her turn to be introduced approached.

"The next contestant for the Sewer Pipe Queen Pageant is Frankette, it says here. Is that a last name? No, no? That's the whole thing? Okay, then, welcome, Frankette!"

"Leave me alone, Titball," Maye warned, taking another step forward. "I've already been your victim once."

"And next, the marionette team of Lord Karl and Little George!"

"One comment!" the reporter insisted. "Can't you give me one thought?"

"I think Dick Titball has a fleshy, fat ass that flops around in his pants when he runs and everyone on TV can see it," she said just as her name was called and she walked out into the glare as the sun, although still burning brightly, was beginning to slide into the horizon.

Maye smiled brightly and waved to the audience as Mickey walked beside her perfectly and they took their spot on the far side of the stage.

"And here they are, people of Spaulding!" the emcee announced. "One of these contestants will be your new Sewer Pipe Queen!"

All six and a half contestants stood there, beaming on cue, waving to the audience, hoping that when the sun rose the next day, the townspeople of Spaulding would have become their loyal subjects.

"Now that we've met the contestants, let's meet our panel of celebrity judges!" the emcee called, making a wide, sweeping motion with his arm to the opposite side of the stage.

"You know her as Sequoia," he said with a grin. "But you can also call her Mayor! Ladies and gentlemen, Mayor Sequoia Montoya!"

The audience whooped it up as the mayor stepped onstage, her waist-long jet-black hair clipped neatly into a ponytail by a silver-and-turquoise barrette. The fringe on her leather vest swung vigorously like the fringe on a flapper's dress as she walked over to the judge's table, smiling broadly, then took a seat.

"Please welcome our next judge with a warm round of applause, Spaulding's own State Champion Hot Dog Eater, Kenny Hicks!"

Chowing down like the incarcerated at feeding time, overall-wearing Kenny Hicks sauntered onstage with his trademark food in his hand, his choppers voraciously feeding off it as chunks of bun and wiener tumbled from his mouth. On the seesaw of judgment, this tipped heavily in the favor of obscenity.

"Now may I introduce one of Spaulding's Old Queens, Her Royal Highness Sewer Pipe Queen Louise Taylor!"

It was the friend of Maye's Realtor, Patty, whom she had met the fateful night of the I Have My Period but She's Eating Meat Incident with Bonnie and Vegging Out Bob. It had been Louise who had encouraged her to enter the pageant to begin with.

Maye smiled as they made eye contact, and Louise winked at her kindly, putting Maye at ease. Somewhat.

"And our last but far from least celebrity judge, may I introduce Balthazar Leopold, Spaulding's Letter Carrier of the Year!"

With a flash, the silver fox jumped onstage, ran to the judge's table, and without hesitation leaped over it and took his seat. Maye hardly recognized him without numerous packages strapped to his torso like ammunition à la Pancho Villa.

Mickey, however, smelled him immediately, and although he had been sitting patiently next to Maye as she fed him his favorite liver treats as a bribe to stay put, the dog's eyes abruptly widened when the mailman, the very mailman who had sent him to doggie reform school, began his gallop across the stage.

Maye lightly tugged on the leash to get Mickey's attention, and he stayed. As she and Mickey left the stage with the rest of the contestants, Maye looked over at the judges' table, where Balthazar Leopold was not merely staring at the two of them, he was glaring.

ψ ψ ψ

Melissabeth herself was ready to put on a show.

Not only did she arrive in a tailored, perfectly fitting evening gown worthy of Gwyneth Paltrow at the Oscars, she brought friends with her. Four of them to be exact, all musicians in tuxedos and black dresses, with their own seating as well, all arranged behind her.

Melissabeth had not brought a CD; the singer had brought her own orchestra.

The girl who had rejected Maye as a weekend friend politely and elegantly stepped out onstage and clasped her hands in front of her; after the orchestra played a few notes, she opened her mouth, and heaven came out. On hearing the first notes of the Queen of the Night aria, Maye thought, well, opera shmopera, she's trained to sing that way; I bet there are a couple of opera tricks you need to learn and anybody with an untrained ear wouldn't know the difference between a novice and a pro. Kind of like ice skating. You see someone at the rink do a jump or a forward spin really fast and you are blown away, you think, Wow, that is talent! And then you watch the Winter Olympics and realize the goddess of the skating rink is really a hack in leg warmers and what's probably just a swimsuit.

And then, in the next moment, Melissabeth ditched her forward spins and went straight into opera's version of the Death Drop, the portion of the aria known for its extreme difficulty, and the generator of its fame.

Each peck of a note that rocketed from her lungs was like a perfectly tuned bullet that exploded as it hit the air, filling the entire town square with her booming, crystalline voice and eventually landing—whether Mozart intended it or not—where it was to do the most damage: in the center of Maye's self-confidence. When Melissabeth hit the F6 note, a note that always makes people gasp when they hear Mariah Carey reach it in "Emotions," even Maye, with her bread-crumb knowledge of opera, knew was a pretty accomplished feat. She prayed from where she stood backstage that the singer was pulling a Milli Vanilli and that the tape would slur, then snap, leaving the flying monkey with a gaping, mute mouth.

But Melissabeth's talent was no rumor, and the voice that

pierced the evening air was no tape. She hit every note with precision and astounding clarity and in such speedy succession it
seemed inhuman.

The audience was amazingly quiet, as if speaking or producing any noise during the performance was akin to engaging in a
round of farting, as if any sound emanated could never come
close to being as worthy as what had just punctured the air
around them. To speak or make a noise would soil the trail of a
perfectly achieved note, and even as Melissabeth clearly and dramatically charged to the close of the aria, Maye herself couldn't
predict the scale of the reaction. Indeed, when the orchestra's
last note was sounded, several seconds passed as people in the audience weren't sure how to respond, their efforts at gratitude
falling so short with mere applause that it seemed a paltry way to
show thanks for such a lovely gift. The audience simply clapped
politely, as if the aria demanded accolades containing the same
refinement as the performance itself.

If Melissabeth was shocked that the audience didn't figura-
tively set off fireworks at the conclusion of her segment, she
didn't show it. She smiled politely, kindly even, took a slight bow,
and then glided backstage with her orchestra trailing behind her.

ϒ ϒ ϒ

When Miss Teeny Royalty Universe stepped onto that stage, she
had some pretty big lungs to fill. Backstage, her mother had
quickly stripped off her pink, puffy, layered show dress right in
the main hallway and slipped her into a tiny gray mechanic's
jumpsuit with two name patches on it; one for Kaytlynne and the
other, naturally, for Brytanni.

To complete the look, the Miss Teeny Royalty Mommy
yanked her daughter's perfectly coiffed, curled, and poofed hair
right off her head and threw the set of golden ringlets onto a
nearby chair like a dirty pair of underwear. Maye gasped for a

moment, thinking she could never win against a child with cancer, until she saw the hairnet snapped to the skull of the little girl, and that, too, landed on the bed of Barbie hair on the chair. Maye sighed with relief as the Miss Teeny Royalty Mommy combed out the child's unfortunate and genetically dictated locks, which were straight as a toothpick and the color of a rotting banana. The mother pulled a jar of Vaseline out of her purse and combed it through the child's bob, thus completing her look as the oil-change guy at Lube 'N Go.

"Are you ready?" the Miss Teeny Royalty Mommy said, holding the kid's chin up with her finger as she spat onto her other hand and wiped a red lip-gloss smudge off the child's cheek with it.

"Yes," Kaytlynne Brytanni said, nodding.

"Then *smile*," the mother hissed between gritted teeth. "I want you to think of how good this will look on your beauty résumé. Queen of all of Spaulding! Now *smile!*"

"I have to pee-pee," the little girl, who could not have been older than eight, complained.

"Did you drink something today?" the mother asked, her eyes widened. "Who told you you could drink something today? You're not allowed to drink on event days! Who gave it to you? Was it her? Was it her?"

Miss Teeny Royalty Mommy began pointing at the other contestants.

"Was it the pervert man with the puppet? Who was it? WHO WAS IT, THEN? Who gave you water? *Who's trying to throw this show?*"

"I was just thirsty," the little girl cried. "I just have to pee!"

"No you don't. There's no time to undo that jumpsuit! Right now it's time to sparkle. It's time to shine. You're going to go out there and be the beauty that my genes made!" the mean mommy said. "You'd better hold it! And let this be a lesson to you why you're not allowed to drink on event days!"

"Lord Karl is not a pervert," Little George said, lifting his stringed arm up, pointing at his partner. "He's a dreamer."

". . . Kaytlynne Brytanni!" the announcer called from the stage.

The mean mommy took Miss Teeny Royalty's jaw in her claws. "You'd better hold it!" she hissed and then pushed the little girl toward the stage as the lights went down.

Maye and Mickey scrambled through the backstage hall to the other side of the stage, where the wing wasn't nearly as crowded—since the sound booth took up most of it—and she had a perfect view.

Miss Teeny Royalty's choice for the talent segment became all too clear when from the darkness of the stage John Travolta's voice boomed the opening lines of "Greased Lightnin'."

Oh, I get it, Maye thought to herself; the jumpsuit oil-monkey outfit made perfect sense now.

Suddenly, the stage lit up and there was Kaytlynne, performing her excessively rehearsed rendition of the song as she pranced, danced, cartwheeled, and lip-synched to it. She had the routine down pat; there was no doubt that she had performed it numerous times—in fact, it seemed to come to her almost naturally. There she was, moving her mouth perfectly to the words, almost so perfectly you could nearly believe they were hers until at the end of the first verse, it was highly unlikely, ultimately impossible, that an eight-year-old lassie wearing lipstick and false eyelashes would blurt, "You know that ain't no shit, we'll be getting lots of tit, Greased Lightnin'!"

Kaytlynne spun twice, did a couple of kicks, then bent her knees, outstretched her right arm and dittoed the choreography of Danny Zuko, pointing, shooting her arm up and out, and no one seemed to notice that anything was even remotely out of place, that it was completely preposterous for a second-grade girl who had moments earlier been wearing a pink party dress and a baby Dolly Parton wig to throw out in a male's baritone voice, "You are supreme . . . the Chixel cream . . . for Greased Lightnin'!"

At least that's what Maye's ears, which were at the moment still in eighth grade, heard, understood, and comprehended, until her mid-thirties brain finally realized that there was no such thing, and never had been any such thing, as Chixel cream. "Holy shit," she whispered to herself in astonishment as she gasped and watched Miss Teeny Royalty Universe run around the stage while mouths were dropping in the audience. The song still held all the magic for the little girl, who delivered all of her drama faces, pretended to comb her hair like a greaser, shook her fanny, somersaulted, and snapped her fingers.

And then Kaytlynne, a little girl who collected My Little Ponies and loved anything with a fairy on it, a little girl who several months earlier had gotten her TV privileges revoked for a week for saying *turd*, took a defiant stance on the stage with her feet firmly planted, pointed directly at the audience, and declared, in the way-past-puberty male voice of Vinnie Barbarino: "You know that I ain't bragging she's a real—"

Hmm, Maye thought to herself. I thought "pushy wagon" was odd, but take out the *h* and add an *s*, and you've got yourself some real misogynistic filth for a musical. You'd never hear that in *H.M.S. Pinafore*!

As Miss Teeny Royalty took off skipping around the stage and waving her hands in Greased Lightnin' jubilation, heads began to shake in the audience, people covered their mouths in shock, and several people made their way through the crowd to leave. Maye saw one woman in the front row mouth the words "That better be a midget."

The tiny dancer was oblivious and did the monkey, then the

swim. In the moments that Kaytlynne was getting ready for her big hand-jive segment of the routine, Maye heard a shrill banshee scream backstage and a ruckus that sounded as if a gorilla had just escaped its pen.

"What the hell are you doing?" the mean mommy roared, charging at Merlin, the sound coordinator. "You played the wrong version! I told you the singles version, not the movie version! Do you hear me? You have to stop it! You have to stop it NOW!"

Merlin was so stunned by the sudden commotion that he couldn't say a word and backed up with his hands raised like either he was about to be taken hostage or a hungry bear had invaded his campsite.

"I said NOW!" Miss Teeny Royalty Mommy roared, and she meant it. She pushed her way into the sound booth, which was basically nothing more than a boom box and a lot of wires, and stopped the music herself before her daughter had an opportunity to tell the audience about Chixel cream again.

With the music stopped, the mean mommy stomped onstage, which was honestly really where she wanted to be, and pulled Kaytlynne Brytanni off by the arm as some members of the audience shook their heads in disgust. The mother dragged Her Teeny Highness backstage, where she chastised her for not realizing she was dancing to the Jenna Jameson version of the song, and at the same time her mean-mommy shoes were being splashed with droplets.

She glanced toward the ceiling to see where the leak was coming from, then as she looked back down at her wet shoes, she could only growl one thing: "Who gave her water?"

"Look on the bright side," Maye said to the little girl, who looked tired and, frankly, quite relieved. "I bet the hot dog guy will vote for you."

ɣ   ɣ   ɣ

Shaking her jingly-jangly staff, Pinky Tuscadero took her position in the center of the stage and slammed the stick into the floor, almost as if she was trying to stake it. She stared out into the audience in a full, determined glare some people would take as a challenge.

She stabbed the staff into the stage again, the chimes of the bells fading quickly into silence. Her shabby scarecrow clothes rippled slightly in a breeze that swept over the stage. Her straw cowboy hat bore dry, deteriorated patches that exposed her head, and the blond-streaked shoulder-length hair underneath looked stringy and perfect for the part. Maye noticed she wasn't wearing shoes, but then again, she hadn't met many scarecrows that did. This one was fortunate even to have feet.

Maye glanced over at Merlin, who didn't appear to be getting any music ready, even though she was certain that any moment now, *any moment*, a dirty little somebody onstage was going to break into a bumbling shuffle and begin crooning the opening lines to "If I Only Had a Brain."

But Pinky Tuscadero did not. Instead, she took a deep breath, opened her mouth, and screamed, "It's going to rain on you! It's going to rain on everybody!"

Immediately, every face in the crowd looked up toward the clear, bright sky. There wasn't a rain cloud in sight.

"I am Pinky Tuscadero," she continued. "I am Arthur Fonzarelli's girlfriend."

And then she shook her stick.

"Do you know how to get to Sesame Street? Ask Mr. Hooper, but not Big Bird. Big Bird drops acid. Does anybody have a burrito I could eat?"

Oh goody, a shitty spoken-word artist, Maye whined to herself. I hate spoken-word people. It's all fun and games until a poet shows up and sucks the life out of everything in six seconds flat.

It seemed like the audience collectively shifted its weight from its right foot to its left.

"I'm tired of the cops hassling me!" the scarecrow informed the crowd. "I'm sick of people sticking their nosy noses into my life, taking away my kids because I won't take my medication! My butt itches!"

More stick shaking.

"I don't need pills, I don't want your poison! I want Section Eight housing! Give me Section Eight housing, and I want a butler! So what if I have a record!"

And then, from the edge of the stage, Maye saw something approaching Pinky Tuscadero. It was white, thin, and the portion that was closest to the contestant had a curved end, while Merlin held the other end steadily. He marched out onto the stage focused and in control, wrapped the white hook around the scarecrow's waist, and pulled her right off the stage as Rick Titball filmed the whole thing from his attack perch.

"Scratch my butt! Scratch my butt!" Pinky screamed as she was dragged away.

"Bring back the little girl with the potty mouth!" an audience member called.

"How did she get in here?" Merlin demanded from the wiry pageant coordinator as he handed Pinky Tuscadero over to the security guard backstage as Rick the Dick Titball captured it all with his camera.

After a brief investigation, it was uncovered that Pinky Tuscaredo wasn't a contestant at all; she had never filled out an application, and she certainly hadn't paid her thirty-five dollars. She was just your average, run-of-the–mill street person of dubious mental cognizance who wandered backstage after following the scent of the lighting guy, who had just returned from Hopkins with a meatball sub.

ψ   ψ   ψ

The audience was already getting a little testy when Lord Karl and Little George took the stage. When Lord Karl announced that Little George was a mime as well as a puppet, it didn't diffuse the situation any, since everyone knows that there's only one thing less welcome on a stage than a mime, and that's a clown, because everyone knows that clowns eat people.

But when Lord Karl announced that Little George was a mime, even Maye had to admit that her curiosity was piqued.

Little George's first feat was to walk against the wind, but since it was relatively impossible to position the puppet at a forty-five-degree angle due to a well-known phenomenon called gravity, the puppet simply looked like he was marching in place.

This was all despite the desperate whisperings of Lord Karl as Maye heard him urging the papier-mâché-and-string doll quietly to "Try harder! Feel the wind! You aren't feeling the wind!"

Next, Lord Karl and Little George tackled the "glass wall" routine with slightly more success, but that merely entailed Lord Karl running across the stage with the puppet and then suddenly stopping.

"That was good, George, that was good," Maye could hear Lord Karl compliment the puppet. "I could tell you really felt that one."

Little George then, and quite affectionately, looked up at Lord Karl and then softly patted him on the leg.

When the team attempted to embark on "pulling the rope," the portion of the act truly built on faith, since Little George had no thumbs, the puppet merely moved its arms alternately up and down slightly at its midsection. To give Little George credit, it did look like he was pulling on something, but perversely, it did not appear to anyone that it was a rope but something much, much more private.

"Get off my stage, you skanky doll!" Merlin declared as he swooped in with the hook and scooped them both away, although Lord Karl, in one last desperate measure to showcase Little George's talents, proclaimed gleefully, "Look! He's a puppet! He's miming puppetry!"

A thin stream of scattered applause trickled through the audience as Merlin dragged his prey out of the spotlight.

From her corner backstage, Maye shook her head and looked at her talent partner. "I'm not friggin' clapping for the puppet," she told Mickey. "Yes, I know you can fight the wind better than that. You can kick that puppet's ass in the glass-wall event, too."

ψ   ψ   ψ

When Frankette glided onstage in a hail of red sequins, including the ones that studded every inch of his wheelchair, he was a glory to behold with human eyes. Dressed in a lovely shimmering crimson dress that shot off sparks of light as he moved across the stage under the command of his mother and to the blaring song "You Spin Me Right Round," he was the most darling paraplegic transvestite the town had ever seen as he shook his flirty feather boa at them.

Frankette beamed broadly at the audience as his mother rolled him to one side of the stage, then, as quick as a fox, the contestant began flipping what looked like bowling pins in the air. Quickly, Mother Frankette took to the charge and bolted across the stage as her son caught one, she spun around in a circle, he caught another, and she spun again as he secured his third pin.

The audience responded with polite applause, but when Frankette pulled out a trio of glistening, shiny Chinese throwing stars, the townsfolk not only gasped, but several of those in the front row frantically pushed their way back deeper into the crowd to avoid having one lodge in their skull or sever their spine. Again, he tossed them across the stage as his mother took off after them, and in mere seconds, one, two, three, he had all of the pointy blades secured between his showgirl-red-painted fingernails.

The audience was slightly more impressed.

Ramping it up a notch, Frankette suddenly produced three wickerlike balls that he kissed with an open and blazing Zippo lighter, instantly igniting them, as if they had been soaking in gas. In amazingly quick succession, he lit all three balls and had them in the air just in time for his mother to take off pushing the chair like Wilma Rudolph in order to reach the balls so that Frankette could whip each one with his scarlet boa, snuffing out the ball of flame before it hit the ground.

The audience went wild.

"Oh, shit," Maye said aloud to Mickey. "Why couldn't we have followed the puppet?"

Additionally, Maye wasn't sure just how Frankette planned on topping Chinese throwing stars and slapping the hell out of balls of fire with a feather boa, and she was a little afraid to find out. That fear turned to ice-cold reality as Mother Frankette brought what looked like a basket onstage and, one by one, delivered the next trick onto Frankette's glimmering, claret-colored lap. Over the pounding music, Maye couldn't hear a thing, but she caught a glimpse of something striped and thought she saw an eye.

It can't be true, it can't, Maye cried to herself as she tried not to reveal her panic to Mickey. He can't do this right before I go on! He's performing *an urban legend*? Juggling fire and lethal weapons weren't enough? For his talent segment, that sequined asshole is going to juggle kittens?

But it was true, and as Frankette gently tossed the first kitten up into the air, the audience was taken aback. Then the second and third went up, the first one was caught, then tossed again, as were the second and third, and when it became clear that the kitties weren't being hurt and really weren't objecting at all due to Frankette's velvet touch and intensive training, the people of

Spaulding began to clap well before Frankette's assistants had finished their final round. When they all landed and were safe and sound on the contestant's sparkly lap, the crowd exploded into applause that to Maye's ears sounded much more like automatic gunfire.

She was an idiot not to have let Ruby come. Right now, she needed her more than ever.

Frankette, his mother, and all of the kitties waved to the audience as they made their way offstage to continuous, thundering, and loving applause.

ϒ   ϒ   ϒ

It was Maye's turn.

She wanted to run. Her mouth had suddenly gone dry, her nerves were sizzling as if she had stuck a part of herself into a light socket, and she felt very, very cold.

She wanted nothing more than to run, run all the way offstage, run all the way home, run all the way up to her bedroom and into her bed, where she would be content to stay friendless forever.

But it wasn't just about Maye anymore, she realized; she wasn't the only one who had worked for this. Mickey deserved a chance out there, not just to prove to the mailman that he'd been wrong about him, but because Mickey was exceptional. And most of all, of course, she owed it to Ruby, who had just wanted to be left alone and instead opened up a little bit of her life to let this happen.

Now out on the darkened stage with moments to go, Maye thought she made a wise decision to position Mickey with his back to the judges so that Balthazar Leopold, Letter Carrier of the Gods, would not be able to make eye contact and torment him. She put Mickey in a sit position, told him to stay as he had countless times before in training.

The silence before the music started was torture for Maye; it was here, it was happening, she was standing up there in front of the whole town. Then, as the first notes sounded and the lights went up, Maye gave the signal to "tinkle," and she heard something from the audience, a low, quiet murmur. The murmur of chuckling.

This is good, Maye thought to herself as Mickey got the beginnings of a laugh, making Maye feel quite a bit more at ease.

" 'We are young,' " Maye said quietly, just as she had rehearsed. " 'Heartache to heartache, we stand.' "

She glanced over at the people in the front row, and some of them were smiling.

She continued speaking with the beginning lyrics, and when she finished, she spun and pointed at Mickey, who delightfully answered on cue, "Woo woo woo woo woo woo woo woo woooooooo!"

Maye bit into the song with all of her teeth, belting it out as if she was in eighth grade, had braces, was wearing her leg warmers with scrunchy boots and a pink sweatshirt with the collar cut off, and was standing in front of her bedroom mirror with a hairbrush for a microphone. She scrunched her fist up and shook it in the air when she wailed, "We are strong!" She slunk up the stage and back, snapping her fingers and being the best Pat Benatar she could be. She had watched that fuzzy bootleg video so many times she dreamed about it. She knew it backward and forward, where her cues were, where she needed to be onstage at what points in the song. To be truthful, Maye wasn't a great singer, she wasn't really even a good singer, but the range of the song wasn't all that difficult—nothing like rockin' the audience with an F6, Mariah Carey–force hurricane.

Maye's whole performance was basically karaoke with a costume and a dog, and anyone could have done it; all that was needed was enough courage to go out and make an ass out of oneself in front of neighbors and friends. Maye didn't have any friends, so that wasn't an issue; her neighbors were in various stages of glaucoma or cataract surgeries, so that solved that problem; and her husband's co-workers had already seen her in a state it usually took women her weight and height a half bottle of tequila to get to—freaking out and sweaty in an advanced stage of undress. With all of the work she and Ruby had put into the act, she figured that if Charlie ever lost his job, she could take her gig to a casino on the rez and become Pat Benatar in smoky rooms with Gambling Anonymous flunkies, if Pat wasn't doing that already. When the music quieted before the first verse, she stood still, looked off to the left dramatically, and nodded just enough to show that she, indeed, was strong.

Because she *was*.

When the verse started, she catwalked over to Mickey slowly, singing him the song as she flipped up her rag skirt with each step, just to be flashy. Once she got to him, she slipped him a treat from her secret pocket and gave him the hand signal for "stay," which he did, as he howled along, the best background singer ever.

Maye turned around and walked back toward center stage, where she was about to jump, kick-ass style, right into the chorus.

"We are young!" Maye announced, and that was when she noticed that the drumbeat sounded oddly loud, louder than it should have been, and as the chorus progressed, it got louder and louder. From where she was, she couldn't see Merlin, and no one else seemed to notice. Maye kept moving, trying to ignore the aberration in the sound system. She kept her groove in flow, and to her surprise, when she looked into the audience, there was Patty, her Realtor, in the front row, smiling widely and clapping along. Maye broke her Benatar Mystique for a moment because she couldn't help but smile.

The drumbeat was getting progressively louder, but when Maye saw Patty, she realized why. The lady next to Patty was clapping. So was the woman behind her. And the lady next to that lady. And not only were they clapping, they were singing along. A woman in the front row in a tank top who had made a bad decision when she bypassed the option of a bra that day stood up and started dancing as she, too, sang along, her head bent over, her gray hair flopping as she shook her head from side to side.

" 'We are strong! No one can tell us we're wrong!' " Maye sang as she launched her first series of war shimmies. Ruby was right. The crowd went nuts, even sent out a couple of catcalls. Maye shook and snapped as she belted out the rest of the chorus along with most of the audience.

People were singing along and clapping their hands, and more dancers had gathered up front. Maye could see people dancing all over the place. The crowd felt charged, the air electric, and suddenly Maye understood what Ruby meant about coming alive in front of an audience, because it was happening, and it was happening to her.

She shimmied over to Mickey, slipped him another liver treat, and gave him the hand signal to follow her. Like the pro he was, he did, stopped when he needed to, and backed up as Maye war-shimmied. Then, as they had practiced, they repeated the whole sequence again, except this time as Mickey came toward Maye he smiled, showing his gold tooth, as she pretended to push the little dog pimp away and he rolled over and played dead.

To Maye, the applause sounded like a roar, most of all because she had never expected it. She had imagined going through their routine from beginning to end as the audience watched and hopefully didn't throw their organic produce at her (which was unlikely, since organic tomatoes were $4.99 a pound at the farmers' market), and with any luck, someone might clap at the end. But she'd never, ever imagined she'd be leading a sing-along with clapping and *dancers*.

Maye was elated. She was beyond elated, she was ecstatic. In addition, she was having fun. It really was like an eighth-grade dream come true, or like an episode of *Fame*!

Oh my God, Maye realized as she rounded the corner of the song and headed for the final chorus— love really *is* a battlefield!

And then, quickly, she saw something flash out of the corner of her right eye and turned her head just in time to see Mickey, in his leisure suit, shoot from his playing-dead position and head for Balthazar Leopold. In two bounds, he was there.

"Mickey!" Maye yelled over and above the music. "STOP! STOP NOW!"

And Mickey, to his credit and being the well-trained dog that he was, did stop. He halted a millisecond after he had leaped up onto the judges' table and was staring eye to eye with the Letter Carrier of the Year, his gold tooth flashing.

The audience collectively gasped; the clapping stopped. Silence, except for the recorded remainder of "Love Is a Battlefield," swept the town square as all eyes were on Mickey to see what would happen next.

"Mickey, down!" Maye called firmly. "Come!"

The dog turned, looked at Maye, jumped down, and came directly to her side.

"Good boy," Maye said, and reached into her secret pocket for a treat.

She was never, for one moment, afraid of what Mickey might do; he would never have gone after the crotchety bastard, but with the Letter Carrier of the Year's penchant for drama, Maye was concerned about what hubbub he was going to instigate. He'd already sent Mickey to dog rehab once; Maye would not put it past him to take even further measures this time.

And apparently, there must have been some additional letter carriers in the audience with a flair for the dramatic, because ominous sounds began drifting onto the stage.

"Booo! Boooooo!" Maye heard from all the way in the back. "What kind of talent is attacking the mailman? Anyone can do that!"

Maye looked at Mickey, who sat patiently by her side, panting from his energetic spurt.

"Peace, man!" she heard another voice yell out. "Leave the mail dude alone!"

"You're not going to win by mauling the judge!" a lady's voice yelled. "I told my husband that was a pit bull!"

"He's *not* a pit bull," Maye replied. "He's an Australian shepherd!"

"Those are attack dogs!" someone from the left called out.

"No they're *not*," Maye responded. "They herd sheep!"

"Peace and love!" another voice pronounced. "Make the dog hug the mailman!"

"You taught your dog to do that! Shame on you!" called yet another. "I liked you until then!"

"Boo! Boooo!" came again from the back.

Maye glanced at Balthazar Leopold, who was looking suspiciously guilty on the other side of the table. And Mickey, for the first time that night, did a bad-dog thing.

In a moment of miraculously awful timing, Mickey barked at the mailman, which just encouraged more members of the audience to register their vast and extreme displeasure.

"That's not like my dog," Maye said as she looked determinedly at the letter carrier as the last bars of "Love Is a Battlefield" faded away with a whistle. "He doesn't bark unless there's something to bark at."

Leopold stalled for a moment, not saying anything but moving his mouth in several false starts.

"Why is my dog barking?" Maye prompted as she ripped a long shredded rag from her skirt and tied it to Mickey's collar as a make-do leash in case they had to run for it.

Finally, the mailman stretched out his fingers, amid gathering protests from the crowd.

"He might be barking at this," he said, exposing a big fat dog cookie right in the center of his palm. "I guess I still had one in my pocket."

Maye's brow furrowed and she could feel her face getting hot, her Rowena fist beginning to curl back up in her hand.

"Do you mean to tell me that you always carry those in your pocket?" she demanded angrily. "*That's* why he jumped on you? Do you know I sent Mickey to reform school with felon dogs because of you? Felon dogs with fresh blood on their faces? When all the while you had cookies in your pocket?"

"Cookies don't give him the right to attack me!" Balthazar Leopold creaked.

"This dog was never going to attack you," she replied angrily. "He just wanted the delicious snack you were taunting him with!"

Leopold shrugged a small apology, but it was nothing the crowd was ever going to see. The comments from the audience kept coming, boos kept rolling in, in conjunction with calls for harmony, peace, love, understanding, and requests for the name of a good restaurant where a vegan could get some decent protein.

"Hey!" Maye heard someone shout from the audience. "Hey! I know her! Isn't that the raccoon lady? That's the sympathizer of the killer raccoon that ate that lady's face! I saw her on TV!"

"BOOO! BOOO!" the calls came before Maye could even protest or defend herself. "BOO THE RACCOON LOVER! Booo her!"

"She's nothing less than a killer herself!" a voice rang out.

"She is a killer! She infiltrated Vegging Out and then ate a cow!" a familiar voice declared, and as Maye looked out into the audience, she saw the gray, scraggly, wispy head of Vegging Out Bob.

More than one person gasped.

"She hates bathing!" another voice added. "We tried to give her a bath, but instead she ate all of my Triscuits and then ran away! She owes me a box of Triscuits! She's a bath hater. *Bath hater!*"

"She wouldn't let us put glitter on her face, either, remember?" said someone with a small head in a bike helmet.

"Bring Little George back!" someone demanded.

"There'th nothing wrong with a couple of glatheth of wine on an empty thtomach and talking about periodth!" someone slurred loudly. "Why do you hate periodths? What did they ever do to you?"

"The Grand Duchess Anastasia went to dog school with that pimp!" someone else cried. "And the raccoon lover made fun of a pregnant dog-school dropout!"

"She's a swinger!" another voice shrieked. "She did a strip-tease at a faculty party and we all saw her bra! It had a hole in it!"

Stay calm, Maye told herself as her face flushed hot. This is bad, but you've experienced worse. At least you're not in middle school onstage with your robe swinging open and your bike shorts exposed. Be brave. Stand strong. Your triangle is not show-ing, and if it was, you have shaved. Hopefully this will end before morning or a huge white hook will come to drag you offstage *any moment now.*

Suddenly, a flash of bright light in the front row caught Maye's attention, and as she shielded her eyes from the glare, she saw Miss Teeny Royalty Universe, who, although she had her Dolly Parton wig back on, was still wearing her mechanic's jumpsuit with a terrific stain on the front of it. But next to the littlest con-testant, who should she see counting one, two, three, and then screaming "Action!" to no one but himself, with his camera pointed directly at the lead story on the evening news, Maye and Mickey, but Rick Titball.

"Boo! Boo! Hiss! Boo!" the audience continued to shout.

But from the back of the boiling crowd, ripples were beginning to form. A path was being made, indistinguishable from the regular movement of a large assembly of people, but it was happening nonetheless. Slowly and patiently, it came forward as people moved aside, some people flinched, and others jumped away. It came closer, and closer, leaving tiny little holes in its wake, a little red glow in an otherwise dark shadowy sea of people. It was Rick Titball's light that illuminated the area enough to cause Maye to see it, moving quietly and stealthily through the hordes of people, unnoticed and almost invisible.

No one would have seen it unless they were paying attention.

It was Death.

Maye gasped slightly, pulling Mickey closer to her. She had seen it before, once, at the library, when she seemed to be the only one who saw a dark, cloaked, faceless figure walking among them.

There was no indication from any of the hundreds of people in the square that anyone but Maye saw the image of the Great Taker. She stared at the faceless hood, unable to take her eyes away, unable to move them in case she needed to be prepared for something, in case she needed to be ready. If this was indeed her time, she was ready for her boat trip to the hopefully least gross circle of hell.

Another voice, craggy, raspy, shrill, and mean, roared out from the darkness, accompanied by a gnarled, wrinkly skeleton hand holding up a smoldering cigarette.

"You want something to yell about?" it demanded, cracking the night air and immediately hushing all other voices. "I'll give you something to yell about!"

Death reached up its other withered and worn hand and pulled back the heavy, dark hood that had been protecting its face in darkness to reveal a small, shrunken hellcat named Ruby Spicer, now missing both eyebrows.

The crowd sucked in one giant breath, then collapsed into random rumblings and incoherent, ghostly whispers.

"Quiet!" she demanded shrilly, then lunged toward the newsman. "Shut up or I'll burn Titball!"

"Burn him! Burn him!" someone called out. "He's an asshole!"

"Keep your dirty handth off him!" the slurring voice returned. "He'th the man I love!"

"Shit," Ruby said, looking around for a moment until she found and seized her prey. "Shut up or I'll burn the Tiny Miss!"

"RUBY!" Maye called quickly. "She's got pee all over her!"

"Echhhh," the old woman cringed, pushing the pee girl away. "ALL RIGHT, THEN, SHUT UP ANYWAY!" she screamed, which was a demand null and void, since a hush had smothered the crowd as soon as the mention of pee popped up.

"Do you know why that girl and her dog wanted to be the Sewer Pipe Queen?" Ruby bellowed as she pointed her cigarette at Maye and Mickey. "To make friends. All she wanted to do was to make some nice friends. Look at you! Look at all of you! Who would want to be friends with the lot of you? Screaming at a girl because her dog wanted a treat! Booing and hissing because she doesn't like glitter! Well, it does look stupid on your face! What kind of people are you, huh? You're the same nasty people that ran another girl out of town years ago because of what you heard rather than what you knew, aren't you? You gotta be. You're doing the same thing all over again with your booing and catcalls! What a sorry bunch you are. Boo! Boo at you! Hiss! Hiss at you! That's what I think!"

Ruby stuck out her tongue and shook her head, hissing like a cat, her fingers reared like claws. Then she turned and looked up at Maye.

"Any of you would be lucky to have a friend like her!" she continued. "A friend that would keep your secrets . . . and catch a butt that's about to burn a third-degree hole through your chest. That's what I call a friend. Yes, sir, that's a friend, all right. So you leave this girl alone. I don't wanna hear another boo or word outta any of you about her! You oughtta be ashamed of yourselves!"

Ruby moved closer to the stage and stretched out her warped, buckled hand. Maye knelt down to reach her, and took her hand in her own.

"We're friends," Maye said as she nodded.

"We are friends," the old woman said as she smiled.

Maye wrapped her hand tighter around Ruby's.

"Isn't that sweet?" Maye heard a calculating cackle erupt behind her. "The two biggest disgraces this town has ever seen are best friends. The stripper and the firebug. What a pretty picture! What's the matter, Ruby? Was there a building you forgot to torch the last time you were in town?"

Maye's first instinct was to land that punch she had so desperately felt emerge from within her, but Ruby gripped her hand tighter, keeping her where she was. She looked back at Ruby, who was holding her own steady, hawklike glare at Rowena.

"Look at her," Ruby retorted. "Standing up there, looking down on us like she was somebody!"

Johnny Guitar, Maye recognized with a grin.

"Do you see *me* holed up on an old, barren farm hiding with nothing but all of my secrets?" Rowena shot back.

"Time hasn't been as kind to you as you think it has," Ruby continued. "Yes, I can see the makeup now, along the lines that weren't there before. . . . There'll be more and more, and one day your face will begin to decay and you'll have nothing left to make a man growl."

"Ooooo, that was good," Maye whispered.

"First line was mine," Ruby whispered back. "The rest is Burt Lancaster, *Separate Tables,* although Rowena's days of growling men look like they've been over for some time now."

"But if you wanna talk about secrets, I have a few," Ruby said aloud. "Secrets of yours, though." And quickly, Ruby let Maye's hand go as hers disappeared into the robe, and when it resurfaced, it held a red bundle enclosed in plastic wrap.

Rowena just stared, not saying a word.

"I've had it wrapped up just the way the Captain did when it got 'lost' as evidence, and I found it after he died," the old woman continued. "It mighta been my scarf, but I never had a chance to wear it before you borrowed it. And I have the A&E and Court TV channels, Rowena. I watch a lot of crime stories. A lot of them. Whaddya think some DNA testing will show on this should I hand it over to my nephew?"

"That was fifty years ago," Rowena scoffed, not flinching. "There's nothing left on there! You're not as smart as you think."

"They do DNA testing on the remains of Civil War soldiers," Ruby scoffed. "Don't you watch TV, you idiot? Or are you too busy writing anonymous letters to the editor?"

"Everyone knows you're a crazy drunk," Rowena added. "No one would believe such a preposterous allegation. I'm a pillar of the community."

"You're a pillar of salt," the old woman sizzled. "It won't be long until you're nobody, Wendy. Unless you count the somebody that really did light those fires years ago. You're the one who left this town in cinders and ash, not me. Not me. You lit up the sewer-pipe factory, City Hall, the movie theater, all of it. It was you. You and your jealousy."

"That's ridiculous," Rowena hissed. "No one will ever believe you. I had nothing to do with any of that!"

Then, suddenly, with the agility of a geriatric cat, Rowena

lunged for the scarf in Ruby's hand, but Maye was quicker and plucked it away before Rowena's claw could even graze it.

Maye stood up and looked Rowena right in the eyes. "Sometimes you don't need a cookie for my dog to go for you," she said firmly. "Sometimes all it takes is a command."

"You didn't win, Wendy!" Ruby called out. "You didn't win."

"Really, now?" Rowena countered. "Is that really what you think? Because I have the mansion. I have Minty. I have the nice clothes, and I have the fresh flowers. I have the respect of this entire town. What exactly is it that you have, Ruby? A hovel for a house and a nephew that drops off toilet paper once a week. It's hardly a contest."

"Ya think so, huh? *Then point to a friend,*" Ruby told her. "Point to one friend."

Maye smiled and looked at Ruby, who had a smile beginning to stretch across her face.

"You did good, Girl, you did good," Ruby said, looking at Maye. "Almost as good as the splits."

Mickey whined slightly, backing away a few steps.

And that was all. That was all the warning they had before Ruby's soft smile shifted into a look of surprise, and with a shot of blue flame and a blinding, brilliant flash that smelled of a fart, she was gone. Ruby Spicer, once magnificent and beautiful, was now nothing but cinders and ash herself, being carried by a soft breeze away from the crowd and hopefully toward something white and bright and forever where there would be an endless supply of free cigarettes and an open bar just waiting for her.

"Ruby!" Maye called, looking frantically at the spot where the old woman had been. *"Ruby!"*

The crowd was amazed, in awe, believing the disappearance to be an unannounced magic trick in Maye's act. Some of the audience even began to clap.

"Ruby!" Maye began to cry frantically, not knowing what to

do except scour the crowd for a wrinkled crone in a reaper outfit. There was none. The old woman was gone without a trace. She had vanished. Evaporated.

Then Maye heard a scream from behind her. She turned to look, hoping to see Ruby, or something that made sense, anything that could explain what had happened or where she had gone, but what she saw running toward her wasn't the old woman at all. It was a scarecrow with a jangly staff, scrambling across the stage, then leaping off it and into the crowd like a raccoon with distemper, shrieking furiously, "FIRE! IT'S ON FIRE! IT'S ALL ON FIRE! THE STAGE IS ON FIRE!"

There was no moment of hesitation; the crowd moved like quicksilver away from the stage, and with screaming and running all around her, Maye stood up and saw the black, inky, billowing smoke begin to stack up in the sky behind the stage. There was no time to think. She picked up her dog with both arms, held him tight to her, and jumped off. As she ran, with adrenaline pumping like hospital-grade drugs through her veins at an astonishing rate, she didn't even feel the welts and burn that her inner thighs were creating as her lycra body shaper and her nude-colored tights melted together as one control-top garment with friction, as if they were always intended to be that way.

And, with the other residents of Spaulding, including those who had booed her, she sat on the steps of City Hall across the street and watched as the town square burned to the ground before the wails of a fire engine were even audible.

16

Ash and Bone

Even after most of the people had cleared the area, Maye and Mickey sat on the steps of City Hall, watching the last charred beams of the stage smolder. It was on those steps that Charlie found her, staring at the smoking, heaped mound like she was in a trance. He touched her shoulder, urged her to get up and come home, but she wouldn't budge. Maye shook her head without looking at her husband. She was searching for Ruby, she said; she could be wearing a robe or she could be in a tracksuit, and she had to look, she had to keep looking. She had to be somewhere. She had simply vanished into thin air, and Maye needed to find her.

She tried to explain what had happened, but how can you possibly describe with any measure of rationale that a little old woman who was dressed up like death and burning people in the audience with her cigarette, POOF! suddenly disappeared before your eyes like a rabbit in a top hat, leaving only a puff of ash and bone and a lingering odor of sulfur behind? How can it possibly make sense that someone you knew disappeared as if sucked into a black hole? Who would remotely believe you unless they saw it for themselves? How do you expound that your little, wrinkled elderly friend suddenly combusted in front of hundreds of people, who applauded like she was David Blaine climbing out of a water tomb after a week? Certainly her blood-alcohol level ran an average of ninety proof and some part of her was always ablaze, making her not only a living Molotov cocktail, but the most obvious answer was also the most unbelievable.

Take Mickey home, Maye told Charlie. He's hungry, tired. It's been a long day.

Give him a special bone. Give him whatever he wants. He was a good boy.

Maye handed Charlie the makeshift rag leash and at the bottom of the steps saw John Smith, standing there with both hands on his hips, on duty. As Charlie climbed down, John climbed up, and they exchanged nods as they passed.

"Can you make sure she gets home okay, John?" Charlie asked.

John nodded again. He took two more steps and sat next to Maye.

"You all right?"

It took her some time to answer, and then she barely shrugged.

"People thought it was a magic trick," she explained. "They clapped. But I am not understanding. Where is she? What could have happened to her? Please tell me she knew magic. Please tell me she's back at the house falling asleep in her dirty slippers with a cigarette in her hand in that recliner watching Susan Hayward almost set her baby on fire."

John paused and he took a deep breath. He didn't know what to say. He wasn't sure what happened, but he had seen it while writing out parking tickets along Broadway and wasn't able to run more than four steps before the crowd turned and surged toward him.

"I can't explain it, Maye," he said, rubbing his eyes. "I'm as confused as you are. I only saw it from across the square, after I heard her yelling and hissing."

"There wasn't a trace of her left," Maye said, feeling a tear break free and run down the side of her nose. "She didn't make a sound. And then I—I couldn't find her. Just some wisps of ash. She was just gone."

"I'm sorry, Maye," John said, patting Maye's knee.

"I'm sorry, too, John," she replied as she wiped her eyes, sniffled, and took a deep, deep breath. "I know she meant a lot to you."

John nodded, his mouth pursed tightly. For a while, the two of them sat side by side on the steps, not saying anything but each understanding what the other wanted to say. They looked at the firefighters poking at the ruins, hosing down small eruptions of flame and trying to figure out what happened in the last seconds before Ruby went missing.

"They're going to think she set this fire, too," he finally told her. "It will be a couple of days before the investigation is fully over, but it looks like a deliberate fire, probably another lit cigarette, just like all the others. They'll have to send evidence to the lab, but so far, it's too much of a coincidence, Maye. The thinking will be that she comes back into Spaulding again and another town landmark goes up. Case closed."

"If you're sending stuff to the lab," Maye said, pulling a bundle from her pocket, still with the evidence number marked on it, "send this, too. Ruby didn't set this fire or any of the others. It's the truth. I was holding her hand, her fingers were yellow, like a sinew yellow. The first knuckles on her pointer and middle fingers were like mummy yellow. I've seen a yellow finger like that before, the fingers of a heavy smoker, someone who's smoked for decades. And I've seen it on Rowena Spaulding, who created quite a scene with Ruby before the fire spread."

Maye handed him the red scarf, wrapped in plastic.

"Where did you get this?" he asked, puzzled.

"She had it, Ruby had it. She pulled it out, Rowena went for it, I got it. It's the scarf that your father found, I'm guessing. Ruby said she never wore it before Rowena borrowed it and then planted it to implicate her. Check Rowena's purse. You'll find cigarettes, too. Whatever brand you're looking for, you'll find in there. But I'm betting whatever butts you have won't match Viceroys."

"Statute of limitations expired forty-five years ago for those fires," John said, tucking the scarf into his pocket. "Even if we had DNA or photographic evidence it was her or a confession, we couldn't prosecute her for any of that stuff."

"Why can't they just leave Ruby alone," Maye said angrily. "She was in the audience the whole time. I saw her. Titball's got it all on tape, her taking the pee girl hostage for a second and her fighting with the audience."

"Considering the speed of acceleration, it looks like that fire was set right about the time you started your song," John explained. "That's three, maybe four minutes. They'll estimate Ruby could have walked from backstage to the back of the audience in that time—it's only a couple of hundred yards."

"And ample time to walk from the backstage to onstage," she added.

"Listen," he said frankly. "I don't want to believe that Ruby did it either, but we don't have any proof that she didn't. What do I have to rule her out? Unless you can give me something that's feasible evidence Rowena did it, they're going to go after Ruby like a pack of wolves, I'm just telling you. If she's the scapegoat, then I want her name cleared more than anybody, believe me."

Looking at the wreckage of the town square, Maye shook her head.

"I can't," she said simply, shrugging. "I don't have it. I have nothing to give you. Rowena's going to get away with this one just like the other ones. And Ruby will, once again, take the blame."

"You know, Maye, I'm afraid you're right," John said simply. He stood up, then extended his hand to Maye, and she took it.

17

Why, Mrs. Spaulding!
How Nice to See You!

Maye looked out the window of the café to the florist across the street, trying to decide, if she was so inclined, which bouquet of the dozens of delightful ones that lined the sidewalk in buckets she would pick to take home after her tea. She saw peonies and tulips, some roses and even irises.

Spring had hit Spaulding sideways, spilling flowers onto the street from front yards and planters and forcing every tree to bloom and create canopied webs of foliage over every street. Crocuses and daffodils, finally free from the stiff, frigid ground of winter, ruptured out of any spot with soil, from raised beds to sidewalk cracks to traffic medians. In downtown Spaulding, two blocks away from her house, every light pole bore the weight of a blooming basket overflowing with pansies, petunias, and Queen Anne's lace. The sun was bright and pale yellow; smooth, light breezes crept in, and in the morning a minuscule bubble of dew crowned every pointy blade of emerald-colored grass.

Maye decided she loved spring.

She had also decided on a daily routine, and that entailed getting up early every morning and heading down to the café where
she would have her morning tea with honey, a blueberry muffin
or a basil roll with a pat of butter, and read the freshly printed
paper.

That morning marked the beginning of the second week of
her routine. She had slipped on her loafers and a light sweater
and headed out, arriving at the café and asking for a table for
one. And every day, she'd look at the flowers lined up across the
street and decide which ones she was going to take home. Looking through the window, she decided on a bouquet of pink,
white, and lavender ruffled irises, since those seemed to be the
most vibrant and alive representation of spring.

"Maye, how's that tea holding up?" the waitress sang as she
swished by.

"Oh, I'm great, thanks," she replied as she looked up at
the waitress, then turned her attention back to the paper.

The clanky, tinny bell from the door rattled as it opened and
a middle-aged man with snowy white hair and a flashy smile
stepped inside.

"Hey, Maye," he said, tipping the brim of his Sierra Club
baseball hat to her. "How're you doing this morning?"

"Oh, I'm fine, Mr. Keene, and yourself?" she replied with a
smile.

"Couldn't be better, couldn't be better," he said, laughing, as
he took a seat at the counter. "I'm planning on stirring up some
trouble today. There's a protest against field burning, and I've got
the bullhorn! Don't tell Mrs. Keene!"

"My lips are sealed," Maye said with a wink.

The woman from the table behind her turned around and put
her hand on Maye's shoulder. "Is that a new sweater, Maye?" she
asked, her lipstick far too perfect for that hour of the morning.

"It is, thank you for noticing," Maye answered. "It's my morning, afternoon, and night sweater."

"It's lovely on you, dear," she said, giving Maye a pat before she turned back around to her Belgian waffle. "It shows off your boobies nicely."

After she finished up with the city section, Maye took it back to the shared-newspaper stand up near the counter. She shuffled through the various sections until she found arts and entertainment and was just about to pull it out of the stack when the cook came out of the kitchen with a dish towel slapped over his shoulder.

"The batch of cranberry orange muffins I promised you yesterday are thirty seconds away from coming out of the oven," he told her, pointing a finger gun at her. "You game?"

"Oh, you bet," she replied. "I couldn't sleep last night just thinking about them!"

She tried to pull the A&E section out of the stack to go back to her table, but it was stuck and wouldn't budge. She went to give it another, more forceful tug, but this time it came effortlessly.

"I'm sorry!" a faceless voice on the other side of the rack exclaimed. "I didn't know you were trying to get that section, too!"

"Ooops." Maye laughed as she craned her neck around the rack to apologize to the person on the other side.

It was a young woman, about Maye's age, with dark, perfectly messy cropped hair, pink cheeks, and bright, friendly eyes. She wore a white, slightly wrinkled linen shirt and a cotton knee-length skirt with daisies on it. Around her neck was a chalcedony pendant on a silver chain.

"Why, Mrs. Spaulding!" Maye blurted out joyously. "How nice to see you!"

The woman looked puzzled. "No, no, no," she said with a hesitant laugh. "I used to work for her, but—"

"I'm sorry, I know that," Maye said, a little embarrassed. "We met once before, in the fall, right when school started, at a faculty party."

Not Mrs. Spaulding nodded. "I remember, you were from Arizona," she said with a smile.

Maye nodded back. "You studied architecture and art history," she said, extending her hand. "I'm Maye."

"Oh, I know who you are," the young woman said with a laugh, shaking Maye's hand. "You were on the front page of the paper and on the news every night for weeks for solving the town square mystery."

"All of that is dying down now, thank God," Maye replied. "My fifteen minutes seemed to get stuck in a time warp. I just kept waiting for it to end."

"Well, it will probably kick back up when the trial starts, don't you think?" the woman queried.

Maye shook her head. "Nah, it won't be focused on me," she answered, "I doubt I'll even be called as a witness."

"I'm so sorry about your friend," the young woman said. "She seemed like quite a character. Did you ever find out what really happened?"

"Not really," Maye said, trying to be stoic. "You know, her nephew and I got a copy of Rick Titball's tape, and the only thing it showed is what we actually saw. She was there one minute and then she was gone. I don't think there will ever be a very good explanation for any of us about what happened. I just know that I miss her, every day. There will never be another Ruby. But it was when we were scouring that tape that we caught a split-second glimpse of Rowena backstage, pouring accelerant on the canvas curtain and using a cigarette to light it. Old habits die hard, I guess. Wouldn't you know, Rick Titball broke the biggest story of his life and had absolutely no idea he did it. But I'm sorry if you lost your job because of Rowena's stay in county jail."

"Oh no," the woman told her. "I had quit long before then. She was . . . difficult. Impossible. Insulting. And that was usually even before I got there in the mornings. Besides, I was just in between things around that time. A curator's position at the university art museum opened up, and I'm over there now. I'm pretty happy. Have you seen Dean Spaulding lately? He was such a nice man. I could never really pair those two, you know?"

"I always thought the same thing. I guess that's why I just assumed you were Mrs. Spaulding." Maye laughed. "I've seen him a few times. He arranged a beautiful memorial service for Ruby up at the house; it was incredible. Flowers, there were so many flowers, more flowers than this town has ever seen, and that's saying something. It was held in one of the rose gardens off the terrace. It was very pretty. The service was lovely, right after he refused to bail Rowena out of jail. And he has donated all of the necessary funds for the statue of Ruby in the new town square. I think they decided to go with an image of her being crowned, which I think is appropriate, since it's now Ruby Spicer Square."

"I read they had revoked Rowena's crown and had reinstated Ruby as Sewer Pipe Queen for that year," the woman said. "For Rowena, that's akin to a beheading. You know, I think you should have won the title yourself. I couldn't have belted out that song better if I had a mirror and a hairbrush microphone! I even clapped along and yelled out when you had the dance-off with your dog."

"You know," Maye said, laughing and shaking her head, "no one had a chance against a transvestite in sequins, his mom, balls of fire, and flying kittens. I don't even know why I bothered to go on. But, Mickey did get first runner-up, not that I'm hoping for a horrible kitten-juggling accident or anything."

"And where is the Sewer Pipe Queen first runner-up?" the woman asked. "I can't believe you'd leave His Royal Highness at home!"

"Oh, you've got to be kidding." Maye laughed again. "We have a new addition to the family, you know. He's very busy playing with his new brother, Puppy. The two of them have a grand time together. In fact, they had a doggie slumber party last night out at Ruby's farm with all the other dogs. Her nephew, John— he was the one who arrested Rowena—decided to retire from the force early and try to get the farm back up and running, although if you ever need a plumber, he's the best one in town. And he knows the cleanliness of every restaurant kitchen in Spaulding. This place got an A plus from him."

"I will keep that in mind," the young woman said, smiling. "By the way, I'm Erika."

"It's really nice to finally meet you, Erika." Maye smiled back. "You know, I have a booth over here by the window. Would you care to join me?"

"Thank you, but I can't." Erika shook her head. "I have a meeting at the museum in fifteen minutes. I just needed to stop in for some joe and a muffin."

"Yeah, I need to get to work, too," Maye realized, looking at the clock on the wall above the chalkboard menu. "I think it would look better if the city-beat reporter was on time for her second day at the newspaper."

"Would you like to have lunch sometime?" Erika asked, fishing a business card out of her purse and handing it to Maye.

Maye smiled. "You know," she said. "I really would."

Acknowledgments

A mighty big thanks to: Bruce Tracy, who insanely insisted that I could do this; Jenny Bent, who forced me to; David Dunton, who kept reading it as I kept writing it; C. E. Upton, who listened every night to what happened in Spaulding that day, no matter how weird it got; Grace Dunstan (Idiot Girl of the Year, 2006), who so graciously gave me the title; and, ultimately, Patty Keene, who drove me to the purple and green house where I found the story of Maye and Ruby.

I'd also like to thank every one of the IGs on our little board that I have come to know, admire, respect, and sometimes get a little drunk with. I love our vacations! All of you have come together to form our circle that is wide, diverse, wonderful, and hysterical at the same time and very dear to me. Thank you as well to my family, Kartz Ucci, Beth Pearson, Adam Korn, Brian McLendon, Jamie Schroeder, Jeff Abbott, Amelia Zalcman, Kate Blum, Meg Halverson, Bill Hummel, Heather Megyesi, Nancy Ragghianti, Heather English, Allison Johnson, Scott Long, and the people of Eugene, who came through every damn time when I was stumped and needed a chunk of inspiration.

Muchos gracias, mi amigos.

(P.S. Will somebody PLEASE send me a green mixed burro from Ritos?)

LAURIE

About the Author

LAURIE NOTARO is the author of five collections of humorous essays. She recently moved to Eugene, Oregon, a town that bears no resemblance whatsoever to the fictional town of Spaulding, Washington. Her new neighbors are not in this book. Incredibly, she has one friend.

Visit Laurie's website at www.idiotgirls.com